# The Cock and Anchor by Joseph Sheridan Le Fanu

Joseph Thomas Sheridan Le Fanu was born on August 28th, 1814, at 45 Lower Dominick Street, Dublin, into a literary family with Huguenot, Irish and English roots

The children were tutored but, according to his brother William, the tutor taught them little if anything. Le Fanu was eager to learn and used his father's library to educate himself about the world. He was a creative child and by fifteen had taken to writing poetry.

Accepted into Trinity College, Dublin to study law he also benefited from the system used in Ireland that he did not have to live in Dublin to attend lectures, but could study at home and take examinations at the university as and when necessary.

This enabled him to also write and by 1838 Le Fanu's first story The Ghost and the Bonesetter was published in the Dublin University Magazine. Many of the short stories he wrote at the time were to form the basis for his future novels. Indeed, throughout his career Le Fanu would constantly revise, cannabilise, embellish and re-publish his earlier works to use in his later efforts.

Between 1838 and 1840 Le Fanu had written and published twelve stories which purported to be the literary remains of an 18th-century Catholic priest called Father Purcell. Set mostly in Ireland they include classic stories of gothic horror, with grim, shadowed castles, as well as supernatural visitations from beyond the grave, together with madness and suicide. One of the themes running through them is a sad nostalgia for the dispossessed Catholic aristocracy of Ireland, whose ruined castles stand in mute salute and testament to this history.

On 18 December 1844 Le Fanu married Susanna Bennett, the daughter of a leading Dublin barrister. The union would produce four children. Le Fanu was now stretching his talents across the length of a novel and his first was The Cock and Anchor published in 1845.

A succession of works followed and his reputation grew as well as his income. Unfortunately, a decade after his marriage it became an increasing source of difficulty. Susanna was prone to suffer from a range of neurotic symptoms including great anxiety after the deaths of several close relatives, including her father two years before.

In April 1858 she suffered an "hysterical attack" and died in circumstances that are still unclear. The anguish, profound guilt as well as overwhelming loss were channeled into Le Fanu's work. Working only by the light of two candles he would write through the night and burnish his reputation as a major figure of 19th Century supernaturalism. His work challenged the focus on the external source of horror and instead he wrote about it from the perspective of the inward psychological potential to strike fear in the hearts of men.

A series of books now came forth: Wylder's Hand (1864), Guy Deverell (1865), The Tenants of Malory (1867), The Green Tea (1869), The Haunted Baronet (1870), Mr. Justice Harbottle (1872), The Room in the Dragon Volant (1872) and In a Glass Darkly. (1872).

But his life was drawing to a close. Joseph Thomas Sheridan Le Fanu died in Merrion Square in his native Dublin on February 7th, 1873, at the age of 58.

# Index of Contents

CHAPTER I.

THE "COCK AND ANCHOR"—TWO HORSEMEN—AND A SUPPER BY THE INN FIRE.

Some time within the first ten years of the last century, there stood in the fair city of Dublin, and in one of those sinuous and narrow streets which lay in the immediate vicinity of the Castle, a goodly and capacious hostelry, snug and sound, and withal carrying in its aspect something staid and aristocratic, and perhaps in nowise the less comfortable that it was rated, in point of fashion, somewhat obsolete. Its structure was quaint and antique; so much so, that had its counterpart presented itself within the precincts of "the Borough," it might fairly have passed itself off for the genuine old Tabard of Geoffry Chaucer.

The front of the building, facing the street, rested upon a row of massive wooden blocks, set endwise, at intervals of some six or eight feet, and running parallel at about the same distance, to the wall of the lower story of the house, thus forming a kind of rude cloister or open corridor, running the whole length of the building.

The spaces between these rude pillars were, by a light frame-work of timber, converted into a succession of arches; and by an application of the same ornamental process, the ceiling of this extended porch was made to carry a clumsy but not unpicturesque imitation of groining. Upon this open-work of timber, as we have already said, rested the second story of the building; protruding beyond which again, and supported upon beams whose projecting ends were carved into the semblance of heads hideous as the fantastic monsters of heraldry, arose the third story, presenting a series of tall and fancifully-shaped gables, decorated, like the rest of the building, with an abundance of grotesque timber-work. A wide passage, opening under the corridor which we have described, gave admission into the inn-yard, surrounded partly by the building itself, and partly by the stables and other offices connected with it. Viewed from a little distance, the old fabric presented by no means an unsightly or ungraceful aspect: on the contrary, its very irregularities and antiquity, however in reality objectionable, gave to it an air of comfort and almost of dignity to which many of its more pretending and modern competitors might in vain have aspired. Whether it was, that from the first the substantial fabric had asserted a conscious superiority over all the minor tenements which surrounded it, or that they in modest deference had gradually conceded to it the prominence which it deserved—whether, in short, it had always stood foremost, or that the street had slightly altered its course and gradually receded, leaving it behind, an immemorial and immovable landmark by which to measure the encroachments of ages—certain it is, that at the time we speak of, the sturdy hostelry stood many feet in advance of the line of houses which flanked it on either side, narrowing the street with a most aristocratic indifference to the comforts of the pedestrian public, thus forced to shift for life and limb, as best they might, among the vehicles and horses which then thronged the city streets—no doubt, too, often by the very difficulties which it presented, entrapping the over-cautious passenger, who preferred entering the harbour which its hospitable and capacious doorway offered, to encountering all the perils involved in doubling the point.

Such as we have attempted to describe it, the old building stood more than a century since; and when the level sunbeams at eventide glinted brightly on its thousand miniature window panes, and upon the broad hanging panel, which bore, in the brightest hues and richest gilding, the portraiture of a Cock and Anchor; and when the warm, discoloured glow of sunset touched the time-worn front of the old building with a rich and cheery blush, even the most fastidious would have allowed that the object was no unpleasing one.

A dark autumnal night had closed over the old city of Dublin, and the wind was blustering in hoarse gusts through the crowded chimney-stacks—careening desolately through the dim streets, and occasionally whirling some loose tile or fragment of plaster from the house tops. The streets were silent and deserted, except when occasionally traversed by some great man's carriage, thundering and clattering along the broken pavement, and by its passing glare and rattle making the succeeding darkness and silence but the more dreary. None stirred abroad who could avoid it; and with the exception of such rare interruptions as we have mentioned, the storm and darkness held undisputed possession of the city. Upon this ungenial night, and somewhat past the hour of ten, a well-mounted traveller rode into the narrow and sheltered yard of the "Cock and Anchor;" and having bestowed upon the groom who took the bridle of his steed such minute and anxious directions as betokened a kind and knightly tenderness for the comforts of his good beast, he forthwith entered the public room of the inn—a large and comfortable chamber, having at the far end a huge hearth overspanned by a broad and lofty mantelpiece of stone, and now sending forth a warm and ruddy glow, which penetrated in genial streams to every recess and corner of the room, tinging the dark wainscoting of the walls, glinting red and brightly upon the burnished tankards and flagons with which the cupboard was laden, and playing cheerily over the massive beams which traversed the ceiling. Groups of men, variously occupied and variously composed, embracing all the usual company of a well frequented city tavern—from the staid and sober man of business, who smokes his pipe in peace, to the loud disputatious, half-tipsy town idler, who calls for more flagons than he can well reckon, and then quarrels with mine host about the shot—were disposed, some singly, others in social clusters, in cosy and luxurious ease at the stout oak tables which occupied the expansive chamber. Among these the stranger passed leisurely to a vacant table in the neighbourhood of the good fire, and seating himself thereat, doffed his hat and cloak, thereby exhibiting a finely proportioned and graceful figure, and a face of singular nobleness and beauty. He might have seen some thirty summers—perhaps less—but his dark and expressive features bore a character of resolution and melancholy which seemed to tell of more griefs and perils overpast than men so young in the world can generally count.

The new-comer, having thrown his hat and gloves upon the table at which he had placed himself, stretched his stalwart limbs toward the fire in the full enjoyment of its genial influence, and advancing the heels of his huge jack boots nearly to the bars, he seemed for a time wholly lost in the comfortable contemplation of the red embers which flickered, glowed, and shifted before his eyes. From his quiet reverie he was soon recalled by mine host in person, who, with all courtesy, desired to know "whether his honour wished supper and a bed?" Both questions were promptly answered in the affirmative: and before many minutes the young horseman was deep in the discussion of a glorious pasty, flanked by a flagon of claret, such as he had seldom tasted before. He had scarcely concluded his meal, when another traveller, cloaked, booted, and spurred, and carrying under his arm a pair of long horse-pistols, and a heavy whip, entered the apartment, walked straight up to the fire-place, and having obtained permission of the cavalier already established there to take share of his table, he deposited thereon the formidable weapons which he carried, cast his hat, gloves, and cloak upon the floor, and threw himself luxuriously into a capacious leather-bottomed chair which confronted the cheery fire.

"A bleak night, sir, and a dark, for a ride of twenty miles," observed the stranger, addressing the younger guest.

"I can the more readily agree with you, sir," replied the latter, "seeing that I myself have ridden nigh forty, and am but just arrived."

"Whew! that beats me hollow," cried the other, with a kind of self-congratulatory shrug. "You see, sir, we never know how to thank our stars for the luck we have until we come to learn what luck we might have had. I rode from Wicklow—pray, sir, if it be not too bold a question, what line did you travel?"

"The Cork road."

"Ha! that's an ugly line they say to travel by night. You met with no interruption?"

"Troth, but I did, sir," replied the young man, "and none of the pleasantest either. I was stopped, and put in no small peril, too."

"How! stopped—stopped on the highway! By the mass, you outdo me in every point! Would you, sir, please to favour me, if 'twere not too much trouble, with the facts of the adventure—the particulars?"

"Faith, sir," rejoined the young man, "as far as my knowledge serves me, you are welcome to them all. When I was still about twelve miles from this, I was joined from a by-road by a well mounted, and (as far as I could discern) a respectable-looking traveller, who told me he rode for Dublin, and asked to join company by the way. I assented; and we jogged on pleasantly enough for some two or three miles. It was very dark—"

"As pitch," ejaculated the stranger, parenthetically.

"And what little scope of vision I might have had," continued the younger traveller, "was well nigh altogether obstructed by the constant flapping of my cloak, blown by the storm over my face and eyes. I suddenly became conscious that we had been joined by a third horseman, who, in total silence, rode at my other side."

"How and when did he come up with you?"

"I can't say," replied the narrator—"nor did his presence give me the smallest uneasiness. He who had joined me first, all at once called out that his stirrup strap was broken, and halloo'd to me to rein in until he should repair the accident. This I had hardly done, when some fellow, whom I had not seen, sprang from behind upon my horse, and clasped my arms so tightly to my body, that so far from making use of them, I could hardly breathe. The scoundrel who had dismounted caught my horse by the head and held him firmly, while my hitherto silent companion clapped a pistol to my ear."

"The devil!" exclaimed the elder man, "that was checkmate with a vengeance."

"Why, in truth, so it turned out," rejoined his companion; "though I confess my first impulse was to balk the gentlemen of the road at any hazard; and with this view I plied my spurs rowel deep, but the rascal who held the bridle was too old a hand to be shaken off by a plunge or two. He swung with his whole weight to the bit, and literally brought poor Rowley's nose within an inch of the road. Finding that resistance was utterly vain, and not caring to squander what little brains I have upon so paltry an adventure, I acknowledged the jurisdiction of the gentleman's pistol, and replied to his questions."

"You proved your sound sense by so doing," observed the other. "But what was their purpose?"

"As far as I could gather," replied the younger man, "they were upon the look-out for some particular person, I cannot say whom; for, either satisfied by my answers, or having otherwise discovered their mistake, they released me without taking anything from me but my sword, which, however, I regret much, for it was my father's; and having blown the priming from my pistols, they wished me the best of good luck, and so we parted, without the smallest desire on my part to renew the intimacy. And now, sir, you know just as much of the matter as I do myself."

"And a very serious matter it is, too," observed the stranger, with an emphatic nod. "Landlord! a pint of mulled claret—and spice it as I taught you—d'ye mind? A very grave matter—do you think you could possibly identify those men?"

"Identify them! how the devil could I?—it was dark as pitch—a cat could not have seen them."

"But was there no mark—no peculiarity discernible, even in the dense obscurity—nothing about any of them, such as you might know again?"

"Nothing—the very outline was indistinct. I could merely pee that they were shaped like men."

"Truly, truly, that is much to be lamented," said the elder gentleman; "though fifty to one," he added, devoutly, "they'll hang one day or another—let that console us. Meantime, here comes the claret."

So saying, the new-comer rose from his seat, coolly removed his black matted peruke from his shorn head, and replaced it by a dark velvet cap, which he drew from some mysterious nook in his breeches pocket; then, hanging the wig upon the back of his chair, he wheeled the seat round to the table, and for the first time offered to his companion an opportunity of looking him fairly in the face. If he were a believer in the influence of first impressions, he had certainly acted wisely in deferring the exhibition until the acquaintance had made some progress, for his countenance was, in sober truth, anything but attractive—a pair of grizzled brows overshadowed eyes of quick and piercing black, rather small, and unusually restless and vivid—the mouth was wide, and the jaw so much underhung as to amount almost to a deformity, giving to the lower part of the face a character of resolute ferocity which was not at all softened by the keen fiery glance of his eye; a massive projecting forehead, marked over the brow with a deep scar, and furrowed by years and thought, added not a little to the stern and commanding expression of the face. The complexion was swarthy; and altogether the countenance was one of that sinister and unpleasant kind which the imagination associates with scenes of cruelty and terror, and which might appropriately take a prominent place in the foreground of a feverish dream. The young traveller had seen too many ugly sights, in the course of a roving life of danger and adventure, to remember for a moment the impression which his new companion's visage was calculated to produce. They chatted together freely; and the elder (who, by the way, exhibited no very strong Irish peculiarities of accent or idiom, any more than did the other) when he bid his companion good-night, left him under the impression that, however forbidding his aspect might be, his physical disadvantages were more than counterbalanced by the shrewd, quick sagacity, correct judgment, and wide range of experience of which he appeared possessed.

CHAPTER II.

A BED IN THE "COCK AND ANCHOR"—A LANTERN AND AN UGLY VISITOR BY THE BEDSIDE.

Leaving the public room to such as chose to push their revels beyond the modesty of midnight, our young friend betook himself to his chamber; where, snugly deposited in one of the snuggest beds which the "Cock and Anchor" afforded, with the ample tapestry curtains drawn from post to post, while the rude wind buffeted the casements and moaned through the antique chimney-tops, he was soon locked in the deep, dreamless slumber of fatigue.

How long this sweet oblivion may have lasted it was not easy to say; some hours, however, had no doubt intervened, when the sleeper was startled from his repose by a noise at his chamber door. The latch was raised, and someone bearing a shaded light entered the room and cautiously closed the door again. In the belief that the intruder was some guest or domestic of the inn who either mistook the room or was not aware of its occupation, the young man coughed once or twice slightly in token of his presence, and observing that his signal had not the desired effect, he inquired rather sharply,—

"Who is there?"

The only answer returned was a long "Hist!" and forthwith the steps of the unseasonable visitor were directed to the bedside. The person thus disturbed had hardly time to raise himself half upright when the curtains at one side were drawn apart, and by the imperfect light which forced its way through the horn enclosure of a lantern, he beheld the bronzed and sinister features of his fireside companion of the previous evening. The stranger was arrayed for the road, with his cloak and cocked hat on. Both parties, the visited and the visitor, for a time remained silent and in the same fixed attitude.

"Pray, sir," at length inquired the person thus abruptly intruded upon, "to what special good fortune do I owe this most unlooked-for visit?"

The elder man made no reply; but deliberately planted the large dingy lantern which he carried upon the bed in which the young man lay.

"You have tarried somewhat too long over the wine-cup," continued he, not a little provoked at the coolness of the intruder. "This, sir, is not your chamber; seek it elsewhere. I am in no mood to bandy jests. You will consult your own ease as well as mine by quitting this room with all dispatch."

"Young gentleman," replied the elder man in a low, firm tone, "I have used short ceremony in disturbing you thus. To judge from your face you are no less frank than hardy. You will not require apologies when you have heard me. When I last night sate with you I observed about you a token long since familiar to me as the light—you wear it on your finger—it is a diamond ring. That ring belonged to a dear friend of mine—an old comrade and a tried friend in a hundred griefs and perils: the owner was Richard O'Connor. I have not heard from him for ten years or more. Can you say how he fares?"

"The brave soldier and good man you have named was my father," replied the young man, mournfully.

"Was!" repeated the stranger. "Is he then no more—is he dead?"

"Even so," replied the young man, sadly.

"I knew it—I felt it. When I saw that jewel last night something smote at my heart and told me, that the hand that wore it once was cold. Ah, me! it was a friendly and a brave hand. Through all the wars of King James" (and so saying he touched his hat) "we were together, companions in arms and bosom friends. He was a comely man and a strong; no hardship tired him, no difficulty dismayed him; and the merriest fellow he was that ever trod on Irish ground. Poor O'Connor! in exile; away, far away from the country he loved so well; among foreigners too. Well, well, wheresoever they have laid thee, there moulders not a truer nor a braver heart in the fields of all the world!"

He paused, sighed deeply, and then continued,—

"Sorely, sorely are thine old comrades put to it, day by day, and night by night, for comfort and for safety—sorely vexed and pillaged. Nevertheless—over-ridden, and despised, and scattered as we are, mercenaries and beggars abroad, and landless at home—still something whispers in my ear that there will come at last a retribution, and such a one as will make this perjured, corrupt, and robbing ascendency a warning and a wonder to all after times. Is it a common thing, think you, that all the gentlemen, all the chivalry of a whole country—the natural leaders and protectors of the people—should be stripped of their birthright, ay, even of the poor privilege of seeing in this their native country, strangers possessing the inheritances which are in all right their own; cast abroad upon the world; soldiers of fortune, selling their blood for a bare subsistence; many of them dying of want; and all because for honour and conscience sake they refused to break the oath which bound them to a ruined prince? Is it a slight thing, think you, to visit with pains and penalties such as these, men guilty of no crimes beyond those of fidelity and honour?"

The stranger said this with an intensity of passion, to which the low tone in which he spoke but gave an additional impressiveness. After a short pause he again spoke,—

"Young gentleman," said he, "you may have heard your father—whom the saints receive!—speak, when talking over old recollections, of one Captain O'Hanlon, who shared with him the most eventful scenes of a perilous time. He may, I say, have spoken of such a one."

"He has spoken of him," replied the young man; "often, and kindly too."

"I am that man," continued the stranger; "your father's old friend and comrade; and right glad am I, seeing that I can never hope to meet him more on this side the grave, to renew, after a kind, a friendship which I much prized, now in the person of his son. Give me your hand, young gentleman: I pledge you mine in the spirit of a tried and faithful friendship. I inquire not what has brought you to this unhappy country; I am sure it can be nothing which lies not within the eye of honour, so I ask not concerning it; but on the contrary, I will tell you of myself what may surprise you—what will, at least, show that I am ready to trust you freely. You were stopped to-night upon the Southern road, some ten miles from this. It was I who stopped you!"

O'Connor made a sudden but involuntary movement of menace; but without regarding it, O'Hanlon continued,—

"You are astonished, perhaps shocked—you look so; but mind you, there is some difference between stopping men on the highway, and robbing them when you have stopped them. I took you for one who we were informed would pass that way, and about the same hour—one who carried letters from a pretended friend—one whom I have long suspected, a half-faced, cold-hearted friend—carried letters, I say, from such a one to the Castle here; to that malignant, perjured reprobate and apostate, the so-called Lord Wharton—as meet an ornament for a gibbet as ever yet made a feast for the ravens. I was mistaken: here is your sword; and may you long wear it as well as he from whom it was inherited." Here he raised the weapon, the blade of which he held in his hand, and the young man saw it and the hilt flash and glitter in the dusky light. "And take the advice of an old soldier, young friend," continued O'Hanlon, "and when you are next, which I hope may not be for many a long day, overpowered by odds and at their mercy, do not by fruitless violence tempt them to disable you by a simpler and less pleasant process than that of merely taking your sword and unpriming your pistols. Many a good man has thrown away his life by such boyish foolery. Upon the table by your bed you will in the morning find your rapier, and God grant that it and you may long prove fortunate companions!" He was turning to go, but recollecting himself, he added, "One word before I go. I am known here as Mr. Dwyer—remember the name, Dwyer—I am generally to be heard of in this place. Should you at any time during your stay in this city require the assistance of a friend who has a cheerful willingness to serve you, and who is not perhaps altogether destitute of power, you have only to leave a billet in the hand of the keeper of this inn, and if I be above ground it will reach me—of course address it under the name I have last mentioned—and so, young gentleman, fare you well." So saying, he grasped the hand of his new friend, shook it warmly, and then, turning upon his heel, strode swiftly to the door, and so departed, leaving O'Connor with so much abruptness as not to allow him time to utter a question or remark on what had passed.

The excitement of the interview speedily passed away, the fatigues of the preceding day were persuasively seconded by the soothing sound of the now abated wind and by the utter darkness of the chamber, and the young man was soon deep in the forgetfulness of sleep once more. When the broad, red light of the morning sun broke cheerily into his room, streaming through the chinks of the old shutters, and penetrating through the voluminous folds of the vast curtains of rich, faded damask which surmounted the huge hearse-like bed in which he lay, so as to make its inmate aware that the hour of repose was past and that of action come, O'Connor remembered the circumstances of the interview which had been so strangely intruded upon him but as a dream; nor was it until he saw the sword which he had believed irrecoverably lost lying safely upon the table, that he felt assured that the visit and its purport were not the creation of his slumbering fancy. In reply to his questions when he descended, he was informed by mine host of the "Cock and Anchor," that Mr. Dwyer had left the inn-yard upon his stout hack, a good hour before daybreak.


CHAPTER III.

THE LITTLE MAN IN BLUE AND SILVER.

Among the loungers who loitered at the door of the "Cock and Anchor," as the day wore on, there appeared a personage whom it behoves us to describe. This was a small man, with a very red face and little grey eyes—he wore a cloth coat of sky blue, with here and there a piece of silver lace laid upon it without much regard to symmetry; for the scissors had evidently displaced far the greater part of the original decorations, whose primitive distribution might be traced by the greater freshness of the otherwise faded cloth which they had covered, as well as by some stray threads, which stood like stubbles here and there to mark the ravages of the sickle. One hand was buried in the deep flap pocket of a waistcoat of the same hue and material, and bearing also, in like manner, the evidences of a very decided retrenchment in the article of silver lace. These symptoms of economy, however, in no degree abated the evident admiration with which the wearer every now and then stole a glance on what remained of its pristine splendours—a glance which descended not ungraciously upon a leg in whose fascinations its owner reposed an implicit faith. His right hand held a tobacco-pipe, which, although its contents were not ignited, he carried with a luxurious nonchalance ever and anon to the corner of his mouth, where it afforded him sundry imaginary puffs—a cheap and fanciful luxury, in which my Irish readers need not be told their humbler countrymen, for lack of better, are wont to indulge. He leaned against one of the stout wooden pillars on which the front of the building was reared, and interlarded his economical pantomime of pipe-smoking with familiar and easy conversation with certain of the outdoor servants of the inn—a familiarity which argued not any sense of superiority proportionate to the pretension of his attire.

"And so," said the little man, turning with an aristocratic ease towards a stout fellow in a jerkin, with bluff visage and folded arms, who stood beside him, and addressing him in a most melodious brogue—"and so, for sartain, you have but five single gintlemen in the house—mind, I say single gintlemen—for, divil carry me if ever I take up with a family again—it doesn't answer—it don't shoot me—I was never made for a family, nor a family for me—I can't stand their b——y regularity; and—" with a sigh of profound sentiment, and lowering his voice, he added—"and, the maid-sarvants—no, devil a taste—they don't answer—they don't shoot. My disposition, Tom, is tindher—tindher to imbecility—I never see a petticoat but it flutters my heart—the short and the long of it is, I'm always falling in love—and sometimes the passion is not retaliated by the object, and more times it is—but, in both cases, I'm aiqually the victim—for my intintions is always honourable, and of course nothin' comes of it. My life was fairly frettin' away in a dhrame of passion among the housemaids—I felt myself witherin' away like a flower in autumn—I was losing my relish for everything, from bacon and table-dhrink upwards—dangers were thickening round me—I had but one way to execrate myself—I gave notice—I departed, and here I am."

Having wound up the sentence, the speaker leaned forward and spat passionately on the ground—a pause ensued, which was at length broken by the same speaker.

"Only two out of the five," said he, reflectively, "only two unprovided with sarvants."

"And neither of 'em," rejoined Tom, a blunt English groom, "very likely to want one. The one is a lawyer, with a hack as lean as himself, and more holes, I warrant, than half-pence in his breeches pocket. He's out a-looking for lodgings, I take it."

"He's not exactly what I want," rejoined the little man. "What's th'other like?"

"A gentleman, every inch, or I'm no judge," replied the groom. "He came last night, and as likely a bit of horseflesh under him as ever my two hands wisped down. He chucked me a crown-piece this morning, as if it had been no more nor a cockle shell—he did."

"By gorra, he'll do!" exclaimed the little man energetically. "It's a bargain—I'm his man."

"Ay, but you mayn't answer, brother; he mayn't take you," observed Tom.

"Wait a bit—jist wait a bit, till he sees me," replied he of the blue coat.

"Ay, wait a bit," persevered the groom, coolly—"wait a bit, and when he does see you, it strikes me wery possible he mayn't like your cut."

"Not like my cut!" exclaimed the little man, as soon as he had recovered breath; for the bare supposition of such an occurrence involved in his opinion so utter and astounding a contradiction of all the laws by which human antipathies and affections are supposed to be regulated, that he felt for a moment as if his whole previous existence had been a dream and an illusion. "Not like my cut!"

"No," rejoined the groom, with perfect imperturbability.

The little man deigned no other reply than that conveyed in a glance of the most inexpressible contempt, which, having wandered over the person and accoutrements of the unconscious Tom, at length settled upon his own lower extremities, where it gradually softened into a gaze of melancholy complacency, while he muttered, with a pitying smile, "Not like my cut—not like it!" and then, turning majestically towards the groom, he observed, with laconic dignity,—

"I humbly consave the gintleman has an eye in his head."

This rebuke had hardly been administered when the subject of their conference in person passed from the inn into the street.

"There he goes," observed Tom.

"And here I go after him," added the candidate for a place; and in a moment he was following O'Connor with rapid steps through the narrow streets of the town, southward. It occurred to him, as he hurried after his intended master, that it might not be amiss to defer his interview until they were out of the streets, and in some more quiet place; nor in all probability would he have disturbed himself at all to follow the young gentleman, were it not that even in the transient glimpse which he had had of the person and features of O'Connor, the little man thought, and by no means incorrectly, that he recognized the form of one whom he had often seen before.

"That's Mr. O'Connor, as sure as my name's Larry Toole," muttered the little man, half out of breath with his exertions—"an' it's himself'll be proud to get me. I wondher what he's afther now. I'll soon see, at any rate."

Thus communing within himself, Larry alternately walked and trotted to keep the chase in view. He might very easily have come up with the object of his pursuit, for on reaching St. Patrick's Cathedral, O'Connor paused, and for some minutes contemplated the old building. Larry, however, did not care to commence his intended negotiation in the street; he purposed giving him rope enough, having, in truth, no peculiar object in following him at that precise moment, beyond the gratification of an idle curiosity; he therefore hung back until O'Connor was again in motion, when he once more renewed his pursuit.

O'Connor had soon passed the smoky precincts of the town, and was now walking at a slackened pace among the green fields and the trees, all clothed in the rich melancholy hues of early autumn. The evening sun was already throwing its mellow tint on all the landscape, and the lengthening shadows told how far the day was spent. In the transition from the bustle of a town to the lonely quiet of the country at eventide, and especially at that season of the year when decay begins to sadden the beauties of nature, there is something at once soothing and unutterably melancholy. Leaving behind the glare, and dust, and hubbub of the town, who has not felt in his inmost heart the still appeal of nature? The saddened beauty of sear autumn, enhanced by the rich and subdued light of gorgeous sunset—the filmy mist—the stretching shadows—the serene quiet, broken only by rural sounds, more soothing even than silence—all these, contrasted with the sounds and sights of the close, restless city, speak tenderly and solemnly to the heart of man of the beauty of creation, of the goodness of God, and, along with these, of the mournful condition of all nature—change, decay, and death. Such thoughts and feelings, stealing in succession upon the heart, touch, one by one, the springs of all our sublimest sympathies, and fill the mind with the beautiful sense of brotherhood, under God, with all nature. Under the not unpleasing influence of such suggestions, O'Connor slackened his pace to a slow irregular walk, which sorely tried the patience of honest Larry Toole.

"After all," exclaimed that worthy, "it's nothin' more nor less than an evening walk he's takin', God bless the mark! What business have I followin' him? unless—see—sure enough he's takin' the short cut to the manor. By gorra, this is worth mindin'—I must not folly him, however—I don't want to meet the family—so here I'll plant myself until sich times as he's comin' back again."

So saying, Larry Toole clambered to the top of the grassy embankment which fenced the road, and seating himself between a pair of aged hawthorn-trees, he watched young O'Connor as he followed the wanderings of a wild bridle-road until he was at length fairly hidden from view by the intervening trees and brushwood.

## CHAPTER IV

The path which O'Connor followed was one of those quiet and pleasant by-roads which, in defiance of what are called improvements, are still to be discovered throughout Ireland here and there, in some unsuspected region, winding their green and sequestered ways through many a varied scene of rural beauty; and, unless when explored by some chance fisherman or tourist, unknown to all except the poor peasant to whose simple conveniences they minister.

Low and uneven embankments, overgrown by a thousand kinds of weeds and wild flowers and brushwood, marked the boundaries of this rustic pathway, but in so friendly a sort, and with so little jealousy or exclusion, that they seemed designed rather to lend a soft and sheltered resting-place to the tired traveller than to check the wayward excursions of the idle rambler into the merry fields and woodlands through which it wound. On either side the tall, hoary trees, like time-worn pillars, reared their grey, moss-grown trunks and arching branches, now but thinly clothed with the discoloured foliage of autumn, and casting their long shadows in the evening sun far over the sloping and unequal sward. The scene, the hour, and the loneliness of the place, would of themselves have been enough to induce a pensive train of thought; but, beyond the silence and seclusion, and the falling of the leaves in their eternal farewell, and all the other touching signs of nature's beautiful decay, there were deep in O'Connor's breast recollections and passions with which the scene before him was more nearly associated, than with the ordinary suggestions of fantastic melancholy.

At some distance from this road, and half hidden among the trees, there stood an old and extensive building, chiefly of deep red brick, presenting many and varied fronts and quaint gables, antique-fashioned casements, and whole groups of fantastic chimneys, sending up their thin curl of smoke into the still air, and glinting tall and red in the declining sun; while the dusky hue of the old bricks was every here and there concealed under rich mantles of dark, luxuriant ivy, which, in some parts of the structure, had not only mounted to the summits of the wall, but clambered, in rich profusion, over the steep roof, and even to the very chimney tops. This antique building—rambling, massive, and picturesque in no ordinary degree—might well have attracted the observation of the passer-by, as it presented in succession, through the irregular vistas of the rich old timber, now one front, now another, alternately hidden and revealed as the point of observation was removed. But the eyes of O'Connor sought this ancient mansion, and dwelt upon its ever-varying aspects, as he pursued his way, with an interest more deep and absorbing than that of mere curiosity or admiration; and as he slowly followed the grass-grown road, a thousand emotions and remembrances came crowding upon his mind, impetuous, passionate, and wild, but all tinged with a melancholy which even the strong and sanguine heart of early manhood could not overcome. As the path proceeded, it became more closely sheltered by the wild bushes and trees, and its windings grew more wayward and frequent, when on a sudden, from behind a screen of old thorns which lay a little in advance, a noble dog, of the true old Irish wolf breed, came bounding towards him, with every token of joy and welcome.

"Rover, Rover—down, boy, down," said the stranger, as the huge animal, in his boisterous greeting, leaped upon him again and again, flinging his massive paws upon his shoulders, and thrusting his cold nose into his bosom—"down, Rover, down."

The first transport of welcome past, the noble dog waited to receive from his old friend some marks of recognition in return, and then, swinging his long tail from side to side, away he sprang, as if to carry the joyful tidings to the companion of his evening ramble.

O'Connor knew that some of those whom he should not have chosen to meet just then or there were probably within a stone's throw of the spot where he now stood, and for a moment he was strongly tempted to turn, and, if so it might be, unobserved to retrace his steps. The close screen of wild trees which overshadowed the road would have rendered this design easy of achievement; but while he was upon the point of turning to depart, a few notes of some wild and simple Irish melody, carelessly lilted by a voice of silvery sweetness, floated to his ear. Every cadence and vibration of that voice was to him enchantment—he could not choose but pause. The sweet sounds were interrupted by a rustling among the withered leaves which strewed the ground. Again the fine old dog made his appearance, dashing joyously along the path towards him, and following in his wake, with slow and gentle steps, came a light and graceful female form. On her shoulders rested a short mantle of scarlet cloth; the hood was thrown partially backward, so as to leave the rich dark ringlets to float freely in the light breeze of evening; the faintest flush imaginable tinged the clear paleness of her cheek, giving to her exquisitely beautiful features a lustre, whose richness did not, however, subdue their habitual and tender melancholy. The moment the full dark eyes of the girl encountered O'Connor, the song died away upon her lips—the colour fled from her cheeks, and as instantaneously the sudden paleness was succeeded by a blush of such depth and brilliancy as threw far into shade even the brightest imagery of poetic fancy.

"Edmond!" she exclaimed, in a tone so faint and low as scarcely to reach his ear, and which yet thrilled to his very heart.

"Yes, Mary—it is, indeed, Edmond O'Connor," answered he, passionately and mournfully—"come, after long years of separation, over many a mile of sea and land—unlooked-for, and, mayhap, unwished-for—come once more to see you, and, in seeing you, to be happy, were it but for a moment—come to tell you that he loves you fondly, passionately as ever—come to ask you, dear, dear Mary, if you, too, are unchanged?"

As he thus spoke, standing by her side, O'Connor gazed on the sad, sweet face of her he loved so well, and held that little hand, which he would have given worlds to call his own. The beautiful girl was too artless to disguise her agitation. She would have spoken, but the effort was vain—the tears gathered in her dark eyes, and fell faster and faster, till at length the fruitless struggle ceased, and she wept long and bitterly.

"Oh! Edmond," said she, at length, raising her eyes sorrowfully and fondly to O'Connor's face—"what has called you hither? We two should hardly have met now or thus."

"Dear Mary," answered he, with melancholy fervour, "since last I held this loved hand, years have passed away—three long years and more—in which we two have never met—in which you scarce have even heard of me. Mary, three years bring many changes—changes irreparable. Time—which has, if it were possible, made you more beautiful even than when I saw you last—may yet have altered earlier feelings, and turned your heart from me. Were it so, Mary, I would not seek to blame you. I am not so vain—your rank—your great attractions—your surpassing beauty, must have won many admirers—drawn many suitors round you; and I—I, among all these, may well have been forgotten—I, whose best merit is but in loving you beyond my life. I will not, then—I will not, Mary, ask if you love me still: but coming thus unbidden and unlooked-for, am I forgiven—am I welcome, Mary?"

The artless girl looked up in his face with such a beautiful smile of trust and love as told more in one brief moment than language could in volumes.

"Yes, Mary," said O'Connor, reading that smile aright, with swelling heart and proud devotion; "yes, Mary. I am remembered—you are still my own—my own: true, faithful, unchanged, in spite of years of time and leagues of separation; in spite of all!—my true-hearted, my adored, my own!"

He spoke; and in the fulness of their hearts they were both for a while silent, each gazing on the other in the rapt tenderness of long-tried love—in the deep, guileless joy of this chance meeting.

"Hear me," he whispered, lower almost than the murmur of the breeze through the arching boughs above them, as if fearful that even a breath would trouble the still enchantment that held them spell-bound: "hear me, for I have much to tell. The years that have passed since I spoke to you before have brought to me their store of good and ill, of sorrow and of hope. I have many things to tell you, Mary; much that gives me hope—the cheeriest hope—even that of overcoming Sir Richard's opposition! Ay, Mary, reasonable hope; and why? Because I am no longer poor: an old friend of my father's, Mr. Audley, has taken me by the hand, adopted me, made me his heir—the heir to riches and possessions which even your father will allow to be considerable—which he well may think enough to engage his prudence in favour of our union. In this hope, dearest, I am here. I daily expect the arrival of my generous friend and benefactor; and with him I will go to your father and urge my suit once more, and with God's blessing at last prevail—but hark! some one comes."

Even while he spoke, the lovers were startled by the sound of voices in gay colloquy, approaching along the quiet by-road on which they stood.

"Leave me, Edmond, leave me," said the beautiful girl, with earnest entreaty; "they must not see you with me now."

"Farewell then, dearest, since it must be so," replied O'Connor, as he pressed her hand closely in his own; "but meet me to-morrow evening—meet me by the old gate in the beech-tree walk, at the hour when you used to walk there. Nay, refuse me not, Mary. Farewell, farewell till then!" and so saying, before she had time to frame an answer, he turned from her, and was quickly lost among the trees and underwood which skirted the pathway.

In the speakers who approached, the young lady at once recognized her brother, Henry Ashwoode, and Emily Copland, her pretty cousin. The young man was handsome alike in face and figure, slightly made, and bearing in his carriage that indescribable air of aristocratic birth and pretension which sits not ungracefully upon a handsome person; his countenance, too, bore a striking resemblance to that of his sister, and, allowing for the difference of sex, resembled it as nearly as any countenance which had never expressed a passion but such as had its aim and origin alike in self, could do. He was dressed in the extreme of the prevailing fashion; and altogether his outward man was in all respects such as to justify his acknowledged pretensions to be considered one of the prettiest men in the then gay city of Dublin. The young lady who accompanied him was, in all points except in that of years, as unlike her cousin, Mary Ashwoode, as one pretty girl could well be to another. She was very fair; had a quick, clear eye, which carried in its glance something more than mere mirth or vivacity; an animated face, with, however, something of a bold, and at times even of a haughty expression. Laughing and chatting in light, careless gaiety, the youthful pair approached the spot where Mary Ashwoode stood.

"So, so, fair sister," cried the young man, gaily, "alone and musing, and doubtless melancholy. Shall we venture to approach her, Emily?"

Women have keener eyes in small matters than men; and Miss Copland at a glance perceived her fair cousin's flushed cheek and embarrassed manner.

"Angels and ministers of grace defend us!" cried she; "the girl has certainly seen a ghost or a dragoon officer."

"Neither, I assure you, cousin," replied Miss Ashwoode, with an effort; "my evening's ramble has not extended beyond this spot; and as yet I've seen no monster more alarming than my brother's new periwig."

The young man bowed.

"Nay, nay," cried Miss Copland, "but I must hear it. There certainly is some awful mystery at the bottom of all these conscious looks; but apropos of awful mysteries," continued she, turning to young Ashwoode, half in pity for Mary's increasing embarrassment; "where is Major O'Leary? What has become of your amusing old uncle?"

"That's more than I can tell," replied the young man; "I wash my hands of the scapegrace. I know nothing of him. I saw him for a moment in town this morning, and he promised, with a round dozen of oaths, to be out to dine with us to-day. Thus much you know, and thus much I know; for the rest, having sins enough of my own to carry, as I said before, I wash my hands of him and his."

"Well, now remember, Henry," continued she, "I make it a point with you to bring him out here to-morrow. In sober seriousness I can't get on without him. It is a melancholy and a terrible truth, but still one which I feel it my duty to speak boldly, that Major O'Leary is the only gallant and susceptible man in the family."

"Monstrous assertion?" exclaimed the young man; "why, not to mention myself, the acknowledged pink and perfection of everything that is irresistible, have you not the perfect command of my worthy cousin, Arthur Blake?"

"Now don't put me in a passion, Henry," exclaimed the girl. "How dare you mention that wretch—that irreclaimable, unredeemed fox-hunter. He never talks, nor thinks, nor dreams of anything but dogs and badgers, foxes and other vermin. I verily believe he never yet was seen off a horse's back, except sometimes in a stable—he is an absolute Irish centaur! And then his odious attempts at finery—his elaborate, perverse vulgarity—the perpetual pinching and mincing of his words! An off-hand, shameless brogue I can endure—a brogue that revels and riots, and defies the world like your uncle O'Leary's, I can respect and even admire—but a brogue in a strait waistcoat——"

"Well, well," rejoined the young man, laughing, "though you may not find any sprout of the family tree, excepting Major O'Leary, worthy to contribute to your laudable requirements; yet surely you have a very fair catalogue of young and able-bodied gentlemen among our neighbours. What say you to young Lloyd—he lives within a stone's throw. He is a most proper, pious, and punctual young gentleman; and would make, I doubt not, a most devout and exemplary 'Cavalier servente.'"

"Worse and worse," cried the young lady despondingly; "the most domestic, stupid, affectionate, invulnerable wretch. He never flirts out of his own family, and then, for charity I believe, with the oldest and ugliest. He is the very person for whose special case the rubric provided that no man shall marry his grandmother."

"My fair cousin," replied the young man, laughing, "I see you are hard to please. Meanwhile, sweet ladies both, let me remind you that the sun has just set; we must make our way homeward—at least I must. By the way, can I do anything in town for you this evening, beyond a tender message to my reverend uncle?"

"Dear me," exclaimed Miss Copland, "you have not passed an evening at home this age. What can you want, morning, noon, and night in that smoky, dirty town?"

"Why, the fact is," replied the young man, "business must be done; I positively must attend two routs to-night."

"Whose routs—what are they?" inquired the young lady.

"One is Mrs. Tresham's, the other Lady Stukely's."

"I guessed that ugly old kinswoman of mine was at the bottom of it," exclaimed the young lady with great vivacity. "Lady Stukely—that pompous, old, frightful goose!—she has laid herself out to seduce you, Harry; but don't let that dismay you, for ten to one if you fall, she'll make an honest man of you in the end and marry you. Only think, Mary, what a sister you shall have," and the young lady laughed heartily, and then added, "There are some excellent, worthy, abominable people, who seem made expressly to put one in a passion—perpetual appeals to one's virtuous indignation. Now do, Henry, for goodness sake, if a matrimonial catastrophe must come, choose at least some nymph with less rouge and wrinkles than poor dear Lady Stukely."

"Kind cousin, thyself shalt choose for me," answered the young man; "but pray, suffer me to be at large for a year or two more. I would fain live and breathe a little, before I go down into the matrimonial pit and be no more seen. But let us mend our pace, the evening turns chill."

Thus chatting carelessly, they moved towards the large brick building which we have already described, embowered among the trees; where arrived, the young man forthwith applied himself to prepare for a night of dissipation, and the young ladies to get through a dull evening as best they might.

The two fair cousins sate in a large, old-fashioned drawing-room; the walls were covered with elaborately-wrought tapestry representing, in a manner sufficiently grim and alarming, certain scenes from Ovid's Metamorphoses; a cheerful fire blazed in the capacious hearth; and the cumbrous mantelpiece was covered with those grotesque and monstrous china figures, misnamed ornaments, which were then beginning to find favour in the eyes of fashion. Abundance of richly carved furniture was disposed variously throughout the room. The young ladies sate by a small table on which lay some books and materials for work, placed near the fire. They occupied each one of those huge, high-backed, and well-stuffed chairs in which it is a mystery how our ancestors could sit and remain awake. Both were silently occupied with their own busy reflections; and it was not until the rapid clank of the horse's hoofs upon the pavement underneath the windows, as young Ashwoode started upon his night ride to the city, rose sharp and clear, that Miss Copland, waking from her reverie, exclaimed,—

"Well, sweet coz, were ever so woebegone and desolate a pair of damsels. The only available male creature in the establishment, with the exception of Sir Richard, who has actually gone to bed, has fairly turned his back upon us."

"Dear Emily," replied her cousin, "pray be serious. I wish to tell you what has passed this evening. You observed my confusion and agitation when you and Henry overtook me."

"Why, to be sure I did," replied the young lady; "and now, like an honest coz, you are going to tell me all about it." She drew her chair nearer as she spoke. "Come, my dear, tell me everything—what was your discovery? Come, now, there's a good girl, do confess." So saying she threw one arm round her cousin's neck and laid the other in her lap, looking curiously into her face the while.

"Oh! Emily, I have seen him!" exclaimed Miss Ashwoode, with an effort.

"Seen him!—seen whom?—old Nick, if I may judge from your looks. Whom have you seen, dear?" eagerly inquired Miss Copland.

"I have seen Edmond O'Connor," answered she.

"Edmond O'Connor!" repeated the girl in unfeigned surprise, "why, I thought he was in France, eating frogs and dancing cotillons. What has brought him here?—why, he'll be taken for a spy and executed on the spot. But seriously, can you conceive anything more rash and ill-judged than his coming over just now?"

"It is indeed, I greatly fear, very rash," replied the young lady; "he is resolved to speak with my father once more."

"And your father in such a precious ill-humour just at this precise moment," exclaimed Miss Copland. "I never was so much afraid of Sir Richard as I have been for the last two days; he has been a perfect bruin—begging your pardon, my dear girl—but even you must admit, let filial piety and all the cardinal virtues say what they will, that whenever Sir Richard is recovering from a fit of the gout he is nothing short of a perfect monster. I wager my diamond cross to a thimble, that he breaks the poor young man's head the moment he comes within reach of him. But jesting apart, I fear, my dear cousin, that my uncle is in no mood just now to listen to heroics."

A sharp knocking upon the floor immediately above the chamber in which the young ladies sate, interrupted the conference at this juncture.

"There is my father's signal—he wants me," exclaimed Miss Ashwoode, and rising as she spoke, without more ado she ran to render the required attendance.

"Strange girl," exclaimed Miss Copland, as her cousin's step was heard ascending the stairs, "strange girl!—she is the veriest simpleton I ever yet encountered. All this fuss to marry a fellow who is, in plain words, little better than a beggarman—a good-looking beggarman, to be sure, but still a beggar. Oh, Mary, simple Mary! I am very much tempted to despise you—there is certainly something wrong about you! I hate to see people without ambition enough even to wish to keep their own natural position. The girl is full of nonsense; but what's that to me? she'll unlearn it all one day; but I'm much afraid, simple cousin, a little too late."

Having thus soliloquized, she called her maid, and retired for the night to her chamber.

## CHAPTER V.

### OF O'CONNOR'S MOONLIGHT WALK TO THE "COCK AND ANCHOR," AND WHAT BEFELL HIM BY THE WAY.

As soon as O'Connor had made some little way from the scene of his sudden and agitating interview with Miss Ashwoode, he slackened his pace, and with slow steps began to retrace his way toward the city. So listless and interrupted was his progress, that the sun had descended, and twilight was fast melting into darkness before he reached that point in the road at which diverged the sequestered path which he had followed. As he approached the spot, he observed a small man, with a pipe in his mouth, and his person arranged in an attitude of ease and graceful negligence, admirably calculated to exhibit the symmetry and perfection of his bodily proportions. This man had planted himself in the middle of the road, so as completely to command the pass, and, as our reader need scarcely be informed, was no other than Larry Toole—the important personage to whom we have already introduced him.

As O'Connor approached, Larry advanced, with a slow and dignified motion, to receive him: and removing his pipe from his mouth with a nonchalant air, he compressed the lighted contents of the bowl with his finger, and then deposited the utensil in his coat pocket, at the same time, executing, in a very becoming manner, his most courtly bow. Somewhat surprised, and by no means pleasantly, at an interruption of so unlooked-for a kind, O'Connor observed, impatiently, "I have neither time nor temper, friend, to suffer delay or listen to foolery;" and observing that Larry was preparing to follow him, he added curtly, "I desire no company, sirrah, and choose to be alone."

"An' it's exactly because you wish to be alone, and likes solitude," observed the little man, "that you and me will shoot, being formed by the bountiful hand iv nature, barrin' a few small exceptions,"—here he glanced complacently at his right leg, which was a little in advance of its companion—"as similiar as two eggs."

Being in no mood to tolerate, far less to encourage this annoying intrusion, O'Connor pursued his way at a quickened pace, and in obstinate silence, and in a little time exhibited a total and very mortifying forgetfulness of Mr. Toole's bodily proximity. That gentleman, however, was not so easily to be shaken off—he perseveringly followed, keeping a pace or two behind.

"It's parfectly unconthrovertible," pursued that worthy, with considerable solemnity and emphasis, "and at laste as plain as the nose on your face, that you haven't the smallest taste of a conciption who it is you're spakin' too, Mr. O'Connor."

"And pray who may you be, friend?" inquired he, somewhat surprised at being thus addressed by name.

"Who else would I be, your honour," rejoined the persevering applicant—"who else could I be, if you had but a glimmer iv light to contemplate my forrum and fatures, but Laurence Toole—called by the men for the most part Misthur Toole, and (he added in a softened tone) by the girls most commonly designated Larry."

"Ha—Larry—Larry Toole!" exclaimed O'Connor, half reconciled to an intrusion up to that moment so ill endured. "Well, Larry, tell me briefly how are the family at the manor, yonder?"

"Why, plase your honour," rejoined Larry, promptly, "the ould masthur, that's Sir Richard, is much oftener gouty than good-humoured, and more's the pity. I b'lieve he's breaking down very fast, and small blame to him, for he lived hard, like a rale honourable gentleman. An' then, the young masthur, that's Masthur Henry—but you didn't know him so well—he's getting on at the divil's rate—scatt'ring guineas like small shot. They say he plays away a power of money; and he and the masthur himself has often hard words enough between them about the way things is goin' on; but he ates and dhrinks well, an' the health he gets is as good as he wants for his purposes."

"Well—but your young mistress," suggested O'Connor—"you have not told me yet how Miss Ashwoode has been ever since. How have her health and spirits been—has she been well?"

"Mixed middlin', like belly bacon," replied Mr. Toole, with an air of profound sympathy—"shilly-shally, sir—off an' on, like an April day—sometimes atin' her victuals, sometimes lavin' them—no sartainty. I think the ould masthur's gout and crossness, and the young one's vagaries, is frettin' her; and it's sorry I am to see it. An' there's Miss Emily—that's Miss Copland—a rale jovial slip iv a young lady. I think you've seen her once or twice up at the manor; but now, since her father, the ould General, died, she is stayin' for good with the family. She's a fine lady, and" (drawing close to O'Connor, and speaking with very significant emphasis) "she has ten thousand pounds of her own—do you mind me, ten thousand—it's a good fortune—is not it, sir?"

He paused for a moment, and receiving no answer, which he interpreted as a sign that the announcement was operating as it ought, he added with a confidential wink—

"I thought I might as well put you up to it, you know, for no one knows where a blessin' may light."

"Larry," said O'Connor, after a considerable silence, somewhat abruptly and suddenly recollecting the presence of that little person—"if you have aught to say to me, speak it quickly. What may your business be?"

"Why, sir," replied he, "the long and short of it is, I left Sir Richard more than a week since. Not that I was turned away—no, Mr. O'Connor," continued Mr. Toole, with edifying majesty, "no sich thing at all in the wide world. My resignation, sir, was the fruit of my own solemn convictions—for the five years I was with the family, I had no comfort, or aise, or pace. I may as well spake plain to you, sir, for you, like myself, is young"—Mr. Toole was certainly at the wrong side of fifty—"you can aisily understand me, sir, when I say that I'm the victim iv romance, bad cess to it—romance, sir; my buzzam, sir, was always open to tindher impressions—impressions, sir, that came into it as natural as pigs into a pittaty garden. I could not shut them out—the short and the long iv it is, I was always fallin' in love, since I was the size iv a quart pot—eternally fallin' in love." Mr. Toole sighed, and then resumed. "I done my best to smother my emotions, but passion, sir, young and ardent passion, is impossible to be suppressed: you might as well be trying to keep strong beer in starred bottles durin' the pariod iv the dog days. But I never knew rightly what love was all out, in rale, terrible perfection, antil Mistress Betsy came to live in the family. I'll not attempt to describe her—it's enough to say she fixed my affections, and done for myself. She is own maid to the young mistress. I need not expectorate upon the progress iv my courtship—it's quite enough to observe, that for a considherable time my path was strewed with flowers, antil a young chap—an English bliggard, one Peter Clout—an' it's many's the clout he got, the Lord be thanked for that same!—a lump iv a chap ten times as ugly as the divil, and without more shapes about him than a pound of cruds—an impittant, ignorant, presumptuous, bothered, bosthoon—antil this gentleman—this Misthur Peter Clout, made his b——y appearance; then all at once the divil's delight began. Betsy—the lovely Betsy Carey—the lovely, the vartious, the beautiful, and the exalted—began to play thricks. I know she was in love with me—over head and ears, as bad as myself—but woman is a mystarious agent, an' bangs Banagher. Long as I've been larnin', I never could larn why it is they take delight in tormentin' the tindher-hearted."

This reflection was uttered in a tone of tender woe, and the speaker paused for some symptom of assent from his auditor. It is, however, hardly necessary to say that he paused in vain. O'Connor had enough to occupy his mind; and so far from listening to his companion's narrative, he was scarcely conscious that Mr. Toole, in bodily presence, was walking beside him. That "tindher-hearted" individual accordingly resumed the thread of his discourse.

"But, at any rate, she laid herself out to make me jealous of Peter Clout; and, with the blessin' iv the divil, she succeeded complately. Things were going on this way—she lettin' on to be mighty fond iv Peter, an' me gettin' angrier an' angrier, and Mr. Clout more an' more impittent every day, antill I seen there was no use in purtendin'; so one mornin' when we were both of us—myself and Mr. Peter Clout—clainin' up the things in the pantry, I thought I might as well have a bit iv discourse with him—when I seen, do ye mind, there was no use in mortifyin' the chap with contempt, for I did not spake to him, good, bad, or indifferent, for more than a fortnight, an' he was so ignorant and unmannerly he never noticed the differ. When I seen there was no use in keepin' him at a distance, says I to him one day in the pantry—'Mr. Clout,' says I, 'your conduct in regard iv some persons in this house,' says I, 'is iv a description that may be shuitable to the English spalpeens,' says I, 'but is about as like the conduct of a gintleman,' says I, 'as blackin' is to plate powder.' So he turns round, an' he looks at me as if I was a Pollyphamius. 'Mind your work,' says I, 'young man,' an' don't be lookin' at me as if I was a hathian godess,' says I. 'It's Mr. Toole that's speakin' to you, an' you betther mind what he says. The long an' the short iv it is, I don't like you to be hugger-muggering with a sartain delicate famale in this establishment; an' if I catch you talkin' any more to Misthress Betsy Carey, I give you fair notice, it's at your own apparel. Beware of me—for as sure as you don't behave to my likin', you might as well be in the one panthry with a hyania,' says I, an' it was thrue for me, an' it was the same way with my father before me, an' all the Tooles up to the time of Noah's ark. In pace I'm a turtle-dove all out; but once I'm riz, I'm a rale tarin' vulture.'"

Here Mr. Toole paused to call up a look, and after a grim shake of the head, he resumed.

"Things went on aisy enough for a day or two, antill I happened to walk into the sarvants' hall, an' who should I see but Mr. Clout sittin' on the same stool with Misthriss Betsy, an' his arm round her waist—so when I see that, before any iv them could come between us, with the fair madness I made one jump at him, an' we both had one another by the windpipe before you'd have time to bless yourself. Well, round an' round we went, rowlin' with our heads and backs agin the walls, an' divil a spot of us but was black an' blue, antill we kem to the chimney; an' sure enough when we did, down we rowled both together, glory be to God! into the fire, an' upset a kittle iv wather on top iv us; an' with that there was sich a screechin' among the women, an' maybe a small taste from ourselves, that the masthur kem in, an' if he didn't lay on us with his walkin' stick it's no matter; but, at any rate, as soon as we recovered from the scaldin' an' the bruises. I retired, an' the English chap was turned away; an' that's the whole story, an' I tuk my oath that I'll never go into sarvice in a family again. I can't make any hand of women—they're made for desthroyin' all sorts iv pace iv mind—they're etarnally triflin' with the most sarious and sacred emotions. I'll never sarve any but single gentlemen from this out, if I was to be sacrificed for it—never a bit, by the hokey!"

So saying, Mr. Toole, having, in the course of his harangue, reproduced his pipe from his pocket, with a view to flourish it in emphatic accompaniment with the cadences of his voice, smote the bowl of it upon the edge of his cocked hat, which he held in his hand, with so much passion, that the head of the pipe flew across the road, and was for ever lost among the docks and nettles. One glance he deigned to the stump which remained in his hand, and then, with an air of romantic recklessness which laughs at all sacrifices, he flung it disdainfully from him, clapped his cocked hat upon his head with a vehemence which brought it nearly to the bridge of his nose, and, planting his hands in his breeches pockets, he glanced at the stars with a scowl which, if they take any note of things terrestrial, must have filled them with alarm.

Suddenly recollecting himself, Mr. Toole perceived that his intended master, having walked on, had left him considerably behind; he therefore put himself into an easy amble, which speedily brought him up with the chase.

"Mr. O'Connor, plase your honour," he exclaimed, "sure it's not possible it's goin' to lave me behind you are, an' me so proud iv your company; an', moreover, after axin' you for a situation—that is, always supposin' you want the services iv a rale dashin' young fellow, that's up to everything, an' willing to sarve you in any incapacity. An' by gorra, sir," continued he, pathetically, "it's next door to a charity to take me, for I've but one crown in the wide world left, an' I must change it to-night; an' once I change money, the shillin's makes off with themselves like a hat full of sparrows into the elements, the Lord knows where."

With a desolate recklessness, he chucked the crown-piece into the air, caught it in his palm, and walked silently on.

"Well, well," said O'Connor, "if you choose to make so uncertain an engagement as for the term of my stay in Dublin, you are welcome to be my servant for so long."

"It's a bargain," shouted Mr. Toole—"a bargain, plase your honour, done and done on both sides. I'm your man—hurra!"

They had already entered the suburbs, and before many minutes were involved in the dark and narrow streets, threading their way, as best they might, toward the genial harbourage of the "Cock and Anchor."

## CHAPTER VI

Short as had been O'Connor's sojourn, it nevertheless had been sufficiently long to satisfy mine host of the "Cock and Anchor," an acute observer in such particulars, that whatever his object might have been in avoiding the more fashionably frequented inns of the city, economy at least had no share in his motive. O'Connor, therefore, had hardly entered the public room of the inn, when a servant respectfully informed him that a private chamber was prepared for his reception, if he desired to occupy it. The proposition suited well with his temper at the minute, and with all alacrity he followed the waiter, who bowed him upstairs and through a dingy passage into a room whose claims, if not to elegance, at least to comfort, could hardly have been equalled, certainly not excelled, by the more luxurious pretensions of most modern hotels.

It was a large, capacious chamber, nearly square, wainscoted with dark shining wood, and decorated with certain dingy old pictures, which might have been, for anything to the contrary, appearing in so uncertain a light, chefs d'oeuvre of the mighty masters of the olden time: at all events, they looked as warm and comfortable as if they were. The hearth was broad, deep, and high enough to stable a Kerry pony, and was surmounted by a massive stone mantelpiece, rudely but richly carved—abundance of old furniture—tables, at which the saintly Cromwell might have smoked and boozed, and chairs old enough to have supported Sir Walter Raleigh himself, were disposed about the room with a profuseness which argued no niggard hospitality. A pair of wax-lights burned cheerily upon a table beside the bright crackling fire which blazed in the huge cavity of the hearth; and O'Connor threw himself into one of those cumbrons, tall-backed, and well-stuffed chairs, which are in themselves more potent invitations to the sweet illusive visitings from the world of fancy and of dreams than all the drugs or weeds of eastern climes. Thus suffering all his material nature to rest in absolute repose, he loosed at once the reins of imagination and memory, and yielded up his mind luxuriously to their mingled realities and illusions.

He may have been, perhaps, for two or three hours employed thus listlessly in chewing the cud of sweet and bitter fancy, when his meditations were interrupted by a brisk step upon the passage leading to the apartment in which he sate, instantly succeeded by as brisk a knocking at the chamber door itself.

"Is this Mr. O'Connor's chamber?" inquired a voice of peculiar richness, intonated not unpleasingly with a certain melodious modification of the brogue, bespeaking a sort of passionate devil-may-carishness which they say in the good old times wrought grievous havoc among womankind. The summons was promptly answered by an invitation to enter; and forthwith the door opened, and a comely man stepped into the room. The stranger might have seen some fifty or sixty summers, or even more; for his was one of those joyous, good-humoured, rubicund visages, upon which time vainly tries to write a wrinkle. His frame was robust and upright, his stature tall, and there was in his carriage something not exactly a swagger (for with all his oddities, the stranger was evidently a gentleman), but a certain rollicking carelessness, which irresistibly conveyed the character of a reckless, head-long good-humour and daring, to which nothing could come amiss. In the hale and jolly features, which many would have pronounced handsome, were written, in characters which none could mistake, the prevailing qualities of the man—a gay and sparkling eye, in which lived the very soul of convivial jollity, harmonized right pleasantly with a smile, no less of archness than bonhomie, and in the brow there was a certain indescribable cock, which looked half pugnacious and half comic. On the whole, the stranger, to judge by his outward man, was precisely the person to take his share in a spree, be the same in joke or earnest—to tell a good story—finish a good bottle—share his last guinea with you—or blow your brains out, as the occasion might require. He was arrayed in a full suit of regimentals, and taken for all in all, one need hardly have desired a better sample of the dashing, light-hearted, daredevil Irish soldier of more than a century since.

"Ah! Major O'Leary," cried O'Connor, starting from his seat, and grasping the soldier's hand, "I am truly glad to see you; you are the very man of all others I most require at this moment. I was just about to have a fit of the blue devils."

"Blue devils!" exclaimed the major; "don't talk to a youngster like me of any such infernal beings; but tell me how you are, every inch of you, and what brings you here?"

"I never was better; and as to my business," replied O'Connor, "it is too long and too dull a story to tell you just now; but in the meantime, let us have a glass of Burgundy; mine host of the 'Cock and Anchor' boasts a very peculiar cellar." So saying, O'Connor proceeded to issue the requisite order.

"That does he, by my soul!" replied the major, with alacrity; "and for that express reason I invariably make it a point to renew my friendly intimacy with its contents whenever I visit the metropolis. But I can't stay more than five minutes, so proceed to operations with all dispatch."

"And why all this hurry?" inquired O'Connor. "Where need you go at this hour?"

"Faith, I don't precisely know myself," rejoined the soldier; "but I've a strong impression that my evil genius has contrived a scheme to inveigle me into a cock-pit not a hundred miles away."

"I'm sorry for it, with all my heart, Major," replied O'Connor, "since it robs me of your company."

"Nay, you must positively come along with me," resumed the major; "I sip my Burgundy on these express conditions. Don't leave me at these years without a mentor. I rely upon your prudence and experience; if you turn me loose upon the town to-night, without a moral guide, upon my conscience, you have a great deal to answer for. I may be fleeced in a hell, or milled in a row; and if I fall in with female society, by the powers of celibacy! I can't answer for the consequences."

"Sooth to say, Major," rejoined O'Connor, "I'm in no mood for mirth."

"Come, come! never look so glum," insisted his visitor. "Remember I have arrived at years of indiscretion, and must be looked after. Man's life, my dear fellow, naturally divides itself into three great stages; the first is that in which the youthful disciple is carefully instructing his mind, and preparing his moral faculties, in silence, for all sorts of villainy—this is the season of youth and innocence; the second is that in which he practises all kinds of rascality—and this is the flower of manhood, or the prime of life; the third and last is that in which he strives to make his soul—and this is the period of dotage. Now, you see, my dear O'Connor, I have unfortunately arrived at the prime of life, while you are still in the enjoyment of youth and innocence; I am practising what you are plotting. You are, unfortunately for yourself, a degree more sober than I; you can therefore take care that I sin with due discretion—permit me to rob or murder, without being robbed or murdered in return."

Here the major filled and quaffed another glass, and then continued,—

"In short, I am—to speak in all solemnity and sobriety—so drunk, that it's a miracle how I mounted these rascally stairs without breaking my neck. I have no distinct recollection of the passage, except that I kissed some old hunks instead of the chamber-maid, and pulled his nose in revenge. I solemnly declare I can neither walk nor think without assistance; my heels and head are inclined to change places, and I can't tell the moment the body politic may be capsized. I have no respect in the world for my intellectual or physical endowments at this particular crisis; my sight is so infernally acute that I see all surrounding objects considerably augmented in number; my legs have asserted their independence, and perform 'Sir Roger de Coverley,' altogether unsolicited; and my memory and other small mental faculties have retired for the night. Under those melancholy circumstances, my dear fellow, you surely won't refuse me the consolation of your guidance."

"Had not you better, my dear Major," said O'Connor, "remain with me quietly here for the night, out of the reach of sharks and sharpers, male and female? You shall have claret or Burgundy, which you please—enough to fill a skin!"

"I can't hold more than a bottle additional," replied the major, regretfully, "if I can even do that; so you see I'm bereft of domestic resources, and must look abroad for occupation. The fact is, I expect to meet one or two fellows whom I want to see, at the place I've named; so if you can come along with me, and keep me from falling into the gutters, or any other indiscretion by the way, upon my conscience, you will confer a serious obligation on me."

O'Connor plainly perceived that although the major's statement had been somewhat overcharged, yet that his admissions were not altogether fanciful; there were in the gallant gentleman's face certain symptoms of recent conviviality which were not to be mistaken—a perceptible roll of the eye, and a slight screwing of the lips, which peculiarities, along with the faintest possible approximation to a hiccough, and a gentle see-saw vibration of his stalwart person, were indications highly corroborative of the general veracity of his confessions. Seeing that, in good earnest, the major was not precisely in a condition to be trusted with the management of anything pertaining to himself or others, O'Connor at once resolved to see him, if possible, safely through his excursion, if after the discussion of the wine which was now before them, he should persevere in his fancy for a night ramble. They therefore sate down together in harmonious fellowship, to discuss the flasks which stood upon the board.

O'Connor was about to fill his guest's glass for the tenth or twelfth time, when the major suddenly ejaculated,—

"Halt! ground arms! I can no more. Why, you hardened young reprobate, it's not to make me drunk you're trying? I must keep senses enough to behave like a Christian at the cock-fight; and, upon my soul! I've very little rationality to spare at this minute. Put on your hat, and come without delay, before I'm fairly extinguished."

O'Connor accordingly donned his hat and cloak, and yielding the major the double support of his arm on the one side, and of the banisters on the other, he conducted him safely down the stairs, and with wonderful steadiness, all things considered, they entered the street, whence, under the major's direction, they pursued their way. After a silence of a few minutes, that military functionary exclaimed, with much gravity,—

"I'm a great social philosopher, a great observer, and one who looks quite through the deeds of men. My dear boy, believe me, this country is in the process of a great moral reformation; hospitality—which I take to be the first, and the last, and the only one of all the virtues of a bishop which is fit for the practice of a gentleman—hospitality, my dear O'Connor, is rapidly approaching to a climax in this country. I remember, when I was a little boy, a gentleman might pay a visit of a week or so to another in the country, and be all the time nothing more than tipsy—tipsy merely. However, matters gradually improved, and that stage which philosophers technically term simple drunkenness, became the standard of hospitality. This passed away, and the sense of the country, in its silent but irresistible operation, has substituted blind drunkenness; and in the prophetic spirit of sublime philosophy, I foresee the arrival of that time when no man can escape the fangs of hospitality upon any conditions short of brain fever or delirium tremens."

As the major delivered this philosophic discourse, he led O'Connor through several obscure streets and narrow lanes, till at length he paused in one of the very narrowest and darkest before a dingy brick house, whose lower windows were secured with heavy bars of iron. The door, which was so incrusted with dirt and dust that the original paint was hardly anywhere discernible, stood ajar, and within burned a feeble and ominous light, so faint and murky, that it seemed fearful of disclosing the deeds and forms which itself was forced to behold. Into this dim and suspicious-looking place the major walked, closely followed by O'Connor. In the hall he was encountered by a huge savage-looking fellow, who raised his squalid form lazily from a bench which rested against the wall at the further end, and in a low, gruff voice, like the incipient growl of a roused watch-dog, inquired what they wanted there.

"Why, Mr. Creigan, don't you know Major O'Leary?" inquired that gentleman. "I and a friend have business here."

The man muttered something in the way of apology, and opening the dingy lantern in which burned the wretched tallow candle which half lighted the place, he snuffed it with his finger and thumb, and while so doing, desired the major to proceed. Accordingly, with the precision of one who was familiar with every turn of the place, the gallant officer led O'Connor through several rooms, lighted in the same dim and shabby way, into a corridor leading directly to the rearward of the house, and connecting it with some other detached building. As they threaded this long passage, the major turned towards O'Connor, who followed him, and whispered,—

"Did you mark that ill-looking fellow in the hall? Poor Creigan!—a gentleman!—would you think it?—a gentleman by birth, and with a snug property, too—four hundred good pounds a year, and more—all gone, like last year's snow, chiefly here in backing mains of his own! poor dog! I remember him one of the best dressed men on town, and now he's fain to pick up a few shillings by the week in the place where he lost his thousands; this is the state of man!"

As he spoke thus, they had reached the end of the passage. The major opened the door which terminated the corridor, and thus displayed a scene which, though commonplace enough in its ingredients, was, nevertheless, in its coup d'oeil, sufficiently striking. In the centre of a capacious and ill-finished chamber stood a circular platform, with a high ledge running round it. This arena, some fourteen feet in diameter, was surrounded by circular benches, which rose one outside the other, in parallel tiers, to the wall. Upon these seats were crowded some hundreds of men—a strange mixture;

gentlemen of birth and honour sate side by side with notorious swindlers; noblemen with coalheavers; simpletons with sharks; the unkempt, greasy locks of squalid destitution mingled in the curls of the patrician periwig; aristocratic lace and embroidery were rubbed by the dusty shoulders of draymen and potboys;—all these gross and glaring contrarieties reconciled and bound together by one hellish sympathy. All sate locked in breathless suspense, every countenance fixed in the hard lines of intense, excited anxiety and vigilance; all leaned forward to gaze upon the combat whose crisis was on the point of being determined. Those who occupied the back seats had started up, and pressing forward, almost crushed those in front of them to death. Every aperture in this living pile was occupied by some eager, haggard, or ruffian face; and, spite of all the pushing, and crowding, and bustling, all were silent, as if the powers of voice and utterance were unknown among them.

The effect of this scene, so suddenly presented—the crowd of ill-looking and anxious faces, the startling glare of light, and the unexpected rush of hot air from the place—all so confounded him, that O'Connor did not for some moments direct his attention to the object upon which the gaze of the fascinated multitude was concentrated; when he did so he beheld a spectacle, abstractedly, very disproportioned in interest to the passionate anxiety of which it was the subject. Two game cocks, duly trimmed, and having the long and formidable steel weapons with which the humane ingenuity of "the fancy" supplies the natural spur of the poor biped, occupied the centre of the circular stage which we have described; one of the birds lay upon his back, beneath the other, which had actually sent his spurs through and through his opponent's neck. In this posture the wounded animal lay, with his beak open, and the blood trickling copiously through it upon the board. The victorious bird crowed loud and clear, and a buzz began to spread through the spectators, as if the battle were already determined, and suspense at an end. The "law" had just expired, and the gentlemen whose business it was to handle the birds were preparing to withdraw them.

"Twenty to one on the grey cock," exclaimed a large, ill-looking fellow, who sat close to the pit, clutching his arms in his brawny hands, as if actually hugging himself with glee, while he gazed with an exulting grin upon the combat, whose issue seemed now beyond the reach of chance. The challenge was, of course, unaccepted.

"Fifty to one!" exclaimed the same person, still more ecstatically. "One hundred to one—two hundred to one!"

"I'll give you one guinea to two hundred," exclaimed perhaps the coolest gambler in that select assembly, young Henry Ashwoode, who sat also near the front.

"Done, Mr. Ashwoode—done with you; it's a bet, sir," said the same ill-looking fellow.

"Done, sir," replied Ashwoode.

Again the conqueror crowed the shrill note of victory, and all seemed over, when, on a sudden, by one of those strange vicissitudes of which the annals of the cock-pit afford so many examples, the dying bird—it may be roused by the vaunting challenge of his antagonist—with one convulsive spasm, struck both his spurs through and through the head of his opponent, who dropped dead upon the table, while the wounded bird, springing to his legs, flapped his wings, as if victory had never hovered, and then as momentarily fell lifeless on the board, by this last heroic feat winning a main on which many thousands of pounds depended. A silence for a moment ensued, and then there followed the loud exulting cheers of some, and the hoarse, bitter blasphemies of others, clamorous expostulation, hoarse laughter, curses, congratulations, and invectives—all mingled with the noise occasioned by those who came in or went out, the shuffling and pounding of feet, in one torrentuous and stunning volume of sound.

Young Ashwoode having secured and settled all his bets, shouldered his way through the crowd, and with some difficulty, reached the door at which Major O'Leary and O'Connor were standing.

"How do you do, uncle? Were you in the room when I took the two hundred to one?" inquired the young man.

"By my conscience, I was, Hal, and wish you joy with all my heart. It was a sporting bet on both sides, and as game a fight as the world ever saw."

"I must be off," continued the young man. "I promised to look in at Lady Stukely's to-night; but before I go, you must know they are all affronted with you at the manor. The girls are positively outrageous, and desired me to command your presence to-morrow on pain of excommunication."

"Give my tender regards to them both," replied the major, "and assure them that I will be proud to obey them. But don't you know my friend O'Connor," he added, in a lower tone, "you are old acquaintances, I believe?"

"Unless my memory deceives me, I have had the honour of meeting Mr. O'Connor before," said the young man, with a cold bow, which was returned by O'Connor with more than equal hauteur. "Recollect, uncle, no excuses," added young Ashwoode, as he retreated from the chamber—"you have promised to give to-morrow to the girls. Adieu."

"There goes as finished a specimen of a mad-cap, rake-helly young devil as ever carried the name of Ashwoode or the blood of the O'Leary's," observed the uncle; "but come, we must look to the sport."

So saying, the major, exerting his formidable strength, and accompanying his turbulent progress with a large distribution of apologetic and complimentary speeches of the most high-flown kind, shoved and jostled his way to a vacant place near the front of the benches, and, seating himself there, began to give and take bets to a large amount upon the next main. Tired of the noise, and nearly stifled with the heat of the place, O'Connor, seeing that the major was resolved to act independently of him, thought that he might as well consult his own convenience as stay there to be stunned and suffocated without any prospect of expediting the major's retreat; he therefore turned about and retraced his steps through the passage which we have mentioned. The grateful coolness of the air, and the lassitude induced by the scene in which he had taken a part, though no very prominent one, induced him to pause in the first room to which the passage, as we have said, gave access; and happening to espy a bench in one of the recesses of the windows, he threw himself upon it, thoroughly to receive the visitings of the cool, hovering air. As he lay listless and silently upon this rude couch, he was suddenly disturbed by a sound of someone treading the yard beneath. A figure sprang across toward the window; and almost instantaneously Larry Toole—for the moonlight clearly revealed the features of the intruder—was presented at the aperture, and with an energetic spring, accompanied by a no less energetic, devotional ejaculation, that worthy vaulted into the chamber, agitated, excited, and apparently at his wits' end.

CHAPTER VII.

A liberal and unsolicited attention to the affairs of other people, was one among the many amiable
peculiarities of Mr. Laurence Toole: he had hardly, therefore, seen the major and O'Connor fairly beyond
the threshold of the "Cock and Anchor," when he donned his cocked hat and followed their steps,
allowing, however, an interval sufficiently long to secure himself against detection. Larry Toole well
knew the purposes to which the squalid mansion which we have described was dedicated, and having
listened for a few moments at the door, to allow his master and his companion time to reach the inner
sanctuary of vice and brutality, whither it was the will of Major O'Leary to lead his reluctant friend, this
faithful squire entered at the half-open door, and began to traverse the passage which we have before
mentioned. He was not, however, permitted long to do so undisturbed. The grim sentinel of these
unhallowed regions on a sudden upreared his towering proportions, heaving his huge shoulders with a
very unpleasant appearance of preparation for an effort, and with two or three formidable strides,
brought himself up with the presumptuous intruder.

"What do you want here—eh! you d——d scarecrow?" exclaimed the porter, in a tone which made the
very walls to vibrate.

Larry was too much astounded to reply—he therefore remained mute and motionless.

"See, my good cove," observed the gaunt porter, in the same impressive accents of admonition—"make
yourself scarce, d'ye mind; and if you want to see the pit, go round—we don't let potboys and
pickpockets in at this side—cut and run, or I'll have to give you a lift."

Larry was no poltroon; but another glance at the colossal frame of the porter quelled effectually
whatever pugnacious movements might have agitated his soul; and the little man, having deigned one
look of infinite contempt, which told his antagonist, as plainly as any look could do, that he owed his
personal safety solely and exclusively to the sublime and unmerited pity of Mr. Laurence Toole, that
dignified individual turned on his heel, and withdrew somewhat precipitately through the door which he
had just entered.

The porter grinned, rolled his quid luxuriously till it made the grand tour of his mouth, shrugged his
square shoulders, and burst into a harsh chuckle. Such triumphs as the one he had just enjoyed, were
the only sweet drops which mingled in the bitter cup of his savage existence. Meanwhile, our romantic
friend, traversing one or two dark lanes, made his way easily enough to the more public entrance of this
temple of fortune. The door which our friend Larry now approached lay at the termination of a long and
narrow lane, enclosed on each side with dead walls of brick—at the far end towered the dark outline of
the building, and over the arched doorway burned a faint and dingy light, without strength enough to
illuminate even the bricks against which it hung, and serving only in nights of extraordinary darkness as
a dim, solitary star, by which the adventurous night rambler might shape his course. The moon,
however, was now shining broad and clear into the broken lane, revealing every inequality and pile of
rubbish upon its surface, and throwing one side of the enclosure into black, impenetrable shadow.
Without premeditation or choice, it happened that our friend Larry was walking at the dark side of the
lane, and shrouded in the deep obscurity he advanced leisurely toward the doorway. As he proceeded,
his attention was arrested by a figure which presented itself at the entrance of the building,
accompanied by two others, as it appeared, about to pass forth into the lane through which he himself

was moving. They were engaged in animated debate as they approached—the conversation was conducted in low and earnest tones—their gestures were passionate and sudden—their progress interrupted by many halts—and the party evinced certain sinister indications of uneasy vigilance and caution, which impressed our friend with a dark suspicion of mischief, which was strengthened by his recognition of two of the persons composing the little group. His curiosity was irresistibly piqued, and he instinctively paused, lest the sound of his advancing steps should disturb the conference, and more than half in the undefined hope that he might catch the substance of their conversation before his presence should be detected. In this object he was perfectly successful.

In the form which first offered itself, he instantly detected the well-known proportions and features of young Ashwoode's groom, who had attended his master into town; and in company with this fellow stood a person whom Larry had just as little difficulty in recognizing as a ruffian who had twice escaped the gallows by the critical interposition of fortune—once by a flaw in the indictment, and again through lack of sufficient evidence in law—each time having stood his trial on a charge of murder. It was not very wonderful, then, that this startling companionship between his old fellow-servant and Will Harris (or, as he was popularly termed, "Brimstone Bill") should have piqued the curiosity of so inquisitive a person as Larry Toole.

In company with these worthies was a third, wrapped in a heavy riding-coat, and who now and then slightly took part in the conversation. They all talked in low, earnest whispers, casting many a stealthy glance backward as they advanced through the dim avenue toward our curious friend.

As the party approached, Larry ensconced himself in the recess formed by the projection of two dilapidated brick piers, between which hung a crazy door, and in whose front there stood a mound of rubbish some three feet in height. In such a position he not unreasonably thought himself perfectly secure.

"Why, what the devil ails you now, you cursed cowardly ninny," whispered Brimstone Bill, through his set teeth—"what can happen you, win or lose?—turn up black, or turn up red, is it not all one to you, you mouth, you? Your carcase is safe and sound—then what do you funk for now? Rouse yourself, you damned idiot, or I'll drive a brace of lead pellets through your brains—rouse yourself!"

Thus speaking, he shook the groom roughly by the collar.

"Stop, Bill—hands off," muttered the man, sulkily—"I'm not funking—you know I'm not; but I don't want to see him finished—I don't want to see him murdered when there's no occasion for it—there's no great harm in that; we want his ribben, not his blood; there's no profit in taking his life."

"Booby! listen to me," replied the ruffian, in the same tone of intense impatience. "What do I want with his life any more than you do? Nothing. Do not I wish to do the thing genteelly as much as you? He shall not lose a drop of blood, nor his skin have a scratch, if he knows how to behave and be a good boy. Bah! we need but show him the lead towels, and the job's done. Look you, I and Jack will sit in the private room of the 'Bleeding Horse.' Old Tony's a trump, and asks no questions; so, as you pass, give the window a skelp of the whip, and we'll be out in the snapping of a flint. Leave the rest to us. You have your instructions, you kedger, so act up to them, and the devil himself can't spoil our sport."

"You may look out for us, then," said the servant, "in less than two hours. He never stays late at Lady Stukely's, and he must be home before two o'clock."

"Do not forget to grease the hammers," suggested the fellow in the heavy coat.

"He doesn't carry pistols to-night," replied the attendant.

"So much the better—all my luck," exclaimed Brimstone—"I would not swap luck with the chancellor."

"The devil's children, they say," observed the gentleman in the large coat, "have the devil's luck."

These were the last words Larry Toole could distinguish as the party moved onward. He ventured, however, although with grievous tremors, to peep out of his berth to ascertain the movements of the party. They all stopped at a distance of some twenty or thirty yards from the spot where he crouched, and for a time appeared again absorbed in earnest debate. On a sudden, however, the fellow in the riding-coat, having frequently looked suspiciously up the lane in which they stood, stooped down, and, picking up a large stone, hurled it with his whole force in the direction of the embrasure in which Larry was lurking. The missile struck the projecting pier within a yard of that gentleman's head, with so much force that the stone burst into fragments and descended in a shower of splinters about his ears. This astounding salute was instantly followed by an occurrence still more formidable—for the ruffian, not satisfied with the test already applied, strode up in person to the doorway in which Larry had placed himself. It was well for that person that he was sheltered in front by the mass of rubbish which we have mentioned: at the foot of this he lay coiled, not daring even to breathe; every moment expecting to feel the cold point of the villain's sword poking against his ribs, and half inclined to start upon his feet and shout for help, although conscious that to do so would scarcely leave him a chance for his life. The suspicions of the wretch were, fortunately for Larry, ill-directed. He planted one foot upon the heap of loose materials which, along with the deep shadow, constituted poor Mr. Toole's only safeguard; and while the stones which his weight dislodged rolled over that prostrate person, he pushed open the door and gazed into the yard, lest any inquisitive ear or eye might have witnessed more than was consistent with the safety of the confederates of Brimstone Bill. The fellow was satisfied, and returned whistling, with affected carelessness, towards his comrades.

More dead than alive, Larry remained mute and motionless for many minutes, not daring to peep forth from his hiding-place; when at length he mustered courage to do so, he saw the two robbers still together, and again shrunk back into his retreat. Luckily for the poor wight, the fellow who had looked into the yard left the door unclosed, which, after a little time perceiving, Larry glided stealthily in on all fours, and in a twinkling sprang into the window at which his master lay, as we have already recorded.

CHAPTER VIII.

THE WARNING—SHOWING HOW LARRY TOOLE FARED—WHOM HE SAW AND WHAT HE SAID—AND HOW MUCH GOOD AND HOW LITTLE HE DID—AND MOREOVER RELATING HOW SOMEBODY WAS LAID IN THE MIRE—AND HOW HENRY ASHWOODE PUT HIS FOOT IN THE STIRRUP.

Flurried and frightened as Larry was, his agitation was not strong enough to overcome in him the national, instinctive abhorrence of the character of an informer. To the close interrogatories of his master, he returned but vague and evasive answers. A few dark hints he threw out as to the cause of his alarm, but preserved an impenetrable silence respecting alike its particular nature and the persons of whose participation in the scheme he was satisfied.

In language incoherent and nearly unintelligible from excitement, he implored O'Connor to allow him to absent himself for about one hour, promising the most important results, in case his request was complied with, and vowing upon his return to tell him everything about the matter from beginning to end.

Seeing the agonized earnestness of the man, though wholly uninformed of the cause of his uneasiness, which Larry constantly refused to divulge, O'Connor granted him the permission which he desired, and both left the building together. O'Connor pursued his way to the "Cock and Anchor," where, restored to his chamber and to solitude, he abandoned himself once more to the current of his wayward thoughts.

Our friend Larry, however, was no sooner disengaged from his master, than he began, at his utmost speed, to thread the narrow and complicated lanes and streets which lay between the haunt of profligacy which we have just described, and the eastern extremity of the city. After an interrupted run of nearly half an hour through pitchy dark and narrow streets, he emerged into Stephen's Green; at the eastern side of which, among other buildings of lesser note, there then stood, and perhaps (with a new face, and some slight external changes) still stands, a large and handsome mansion. Toward this building, conspicuous in the distance by the red glare of dozens of links and torches which flared and flashed outside, and by the gay light streaming from its many windows, Larry made his way. Too eager and hurried to pass along the sides of the square by the common road, he clambered over the broken wall which surrounded it, plunged through the broad trench, and ran among the deep grass and rank weeds, now heavy with the dews of night; over the broad area he pursued his way, startling the quiet cattle from their midnight slumbers, and hastening rather than abating his speed, as he drew near to the termination of his hurried mission. As he approached, the long dark train of carriages, every here and there lighted by some flaming link still unextinguished, and surrounded by crowds of idle footmen, sufficiently indicated the scene of Lady Stukely's hospitalities. In a moment Larry had again crossed the fences which enclosed the square, and passing the broad road among the carriages, chairs, and lackeys, he sprang up the steps of the house, and thundered lustily at the hall-door. It was opened by a gruff and corpulent porter with a red face and majestic demeanour, who, having learned from Larry that he had an important message for Mr. Henry Ashwoode, desired him, in as few words as possible, to step into the hall. The official then swung the massive door to, rolled himself into his well-cushioned throne, and having scanned Larry's proportions for a minute or two with one eye, which he kept half open for such purposes, he ejaculated—

"Mr. Finley, I say, Mr. Finley, here's one with a message upwards." Having thus delivered himself, he shut down his open eye, screwed his eyebrows, and became absorbed in abstruse meditation. Meanwhile, Mr. Finley, in person arrayed in a rich livery, advanced languidly toward Larry Toole, throwing into his face a dreamy and supercilious expression, while with one hand he faintly fanned himself with a white pocket handkerchief.

"Your most obedient servant to command," drawled the footman, as he advanced. "What can I do, my good soul, to obleege you?"

"I only want to see the young master—that's young Mr. Ashwoode," replied Larry, "for one minute, and that's all."

The footman gazed upon him for a moment with a languid smile, and observed in the same sleepy tone, "Absolutely impossible—amposseeble, as they say at the Pallais Royal."

"But, blur an' agers," exclaimed Larry, "it's a matther iv life an' death, robbery an' murdher."

"Bloody murder!" echoed the man in a sweet, low voice, and with a stare of fashionable abstraction.

"Well, tear an' 'oun's," cried Larry, almost beside himself with impatience, "if you won't bring him down to me, will you even as much as carry him a message?"

"To say the truth, and upon my honour," replied the man, "I can't engage to climb up stairs just now, they are so devilish fatiguing. Don't you find them so?"

The question was thrown out in that vacant, inattentive way which seems to dispense with an answer.

"By my soul!" rejoined Larry, almost crying with vexation, "it's a hard case. Do you mane to tell me, you'll neither bring him down to me nor carry him up a message?"

"You have, my excellent fellow," replied the footman, placidly, "precisely conveyed my meaning."

"By the hokey!" cried Larry, "you're fairly breaking my heart. In the divil's name, can you as much as let me stop here till he's comin' down?"

"Absolutely impossible," replied the footman, in the same dulcet and deliberate tone. "It is indeed amposseeble, as the Parisians have it. You must be aware, my good old soul, that you're in a positive pickle. You are, pardon me, my excellent friend, very dirty and very disgusting. You must therefore go out in a few moments into the fresh air." At any other moment, such a speech would have infallibly provoked Mr. Toole's righteous and most rigorous vengeance; but he was now too completely absorbed in the mission which he had undertaken to suffer personal considerations to have a place in his bosom.

"Will you, then," he ejaculated desperately, "will you as much as give him a message yourself, when he's comin' down?"

"What message?" drawled the lackey.

"Tell him, for the love of God, to take the old road home, by the seven sallies," replied Larry. "Will you give him that message, if it isn't too long?"

"I have a wretched memory for messages," observed the footman, as he leisurely opened the door—"a perfect sieve: but should he catch my eye as he passes, I'll endeavour, upon my honour; good night—adieu!"

As he thus spoke, Larry had reached the threshold of the door, which observing, the polished footman, with a nonchalant and easy air, slammed the hall-door, thereby administering upon Larry's back, shoulders, and elbows, such a bang as to cause Mr. Toole to descend the flight of steps at a pace much more marvellous to the spectators than agreeable to himself. Muttering a bitter curse upon his exquisite acquaintance, Larry took his stand among the expectants in the street; there resolved to wait and watch for young Ashwoode, and to give him the warning which so nearly concerned his safety.

Meanwhile, Lady Stukely's drawing-rooms were crowded by the gay, the fashionable, and the frivolous, of all ages. Young Ashwoode stood behind his wealthy hostess's chair, while she played quadrille, scarce knowing whether she won or lost, for Henry Ashwoode had never been so fascinating before. Lady Stukely was a delicate, die-away lady, not very far from sixty; the natural blush upon her nose outblazoned the rouge upon her cheeks; several very long teeth—"ivory and ebon alternately"—peeped roguishly from beneath her upper lip, which her ladyship had a playful trick of screwing down, to conceal them—a trick which made her ladyship's smile rather a surprising than an attractive exhibition. It is but justice, however, to admit that she had a pair of very tolerable eyes, with which she executed the most masterly evolutions. For the rest, there having existed a very considerable disparity in years between herself and her dear deceased, Sir Charles Stukely, who had expired at the mature age of ninety, more than a year before, she conceived herself still a very young, artless, and interesting girl; and under this happy hallucination she was more than half inclined to return in good earnest the disinterested affection of Henry Ashwoode.

There, too, was old Lord Aspenly, who had, but two days before, solicited and received Sir Richard Ashwoode's permission to pay his court to his beautiful daughter, Mary. There, jerking and shrugging and grimacing, he hobbled through the rooms, all wrinkles and rappee; bandying compliments and repartees, flirting and fooling, and beyond measure enchanted with himself, while every interval in frivolity and noise was filled up with images of his approaching nuptials and intended bride, while she, poor girl, happily unconscious of all their plans, was spared, for that night, the pangs and struggles which were hereafter but too severely to try her heart.

'Twere needless to enumerate noble peers, whose very titles are now unknown—poets, who alas! were mortal—men of promise, who performed nothing—clever young men, who grew into stupid old ones—and millionaires, whose money perished with them; we shall not, therefore, weary the reader by describing Lady Stukely's guests; let it suffice to mention that Henry Ashwoode left the rooms with young Pigwiggynne, of Bolton's regiment of dragoons, and one of Lord Wharton's aides-de-camp. This circumstance is here recorded because it had an effect in producing the occurrences which we have to relate by-and-by; for young Pigwiggynne having partaken somewhat freely of Lady Stukely's wines, and being unusually exhilarated, came forth from the hall-door to assist Ashwoode in procuring a chair, which he did with a good deal more noise and blasphemy than was strictly necessary. Our friend Larry Toole, who had patiently waited the egress of his quondam young master, no sooner beheld him than he hastened to accost him, but Pigwiggynne being, as we have said, in high spirits and unusual good humour, cut short poor Larry's address by jocularly knocking him on the head with a heavy walking-cane—a pleasantry which laid that person senseless upon the pavement. The humorist passed on with an exhilarating crow, after the manner of a cock; and had not a matter-of-fact chairman drawn Mr. Toole from among the coach-wheels where the joke had happened to lay him, we might have been saved the trouble of recording the subsequent history of that very active member of society. Meanwhile, young Ashwoode was conveyed in a chair to a neighbouring fashionable hotel, where, having changed his suit, and again equipped himself for the road, he mounted his horse, and followed by his treacherous groom, set out at a brisk pace upon his hazardous, and as it turned out, eventful night-ride toward the manor of Morley Court.

CHAPTER IX.

At the time in which the events that we have undertaken to record took place, there stood at the southern extremity of the city, near the point at which Camden Street now terminates, a small, old-fashioned building, something between an ale-house and an inn. It occupied the roadside by no means unpicturesquely; one gable jutted into the road, with a projecting window, which stood out from the building like a glass box held together by a massive frame of wood; and commanded by this projecting gable, and a few yards in retreat, but facing the road, was the inn door, over which hung a painted panel, representing a white horse, out of whose neck there spouted a crimson cascade, and underneath, in large letters, the traveller was informed that this was the genuine old "Bleeding Horse." Old enough, in all conscience, it appeared to be, for the tiled roof, except where the ivy clustered over it, was crowded with weeds of many kinds, and the boughs of the huge trees which embowered it had cracked and shattered one of the cumbrous chimney-stacks, and in many places it was evident that but for the timely interposition of the saw and the axe, the giant limbs of the old timber would, in the gradual increase of years, have forced their way through the roof and the masonry itself—a tendency sufficiently indicated by sundry indentures and rude repairs in those parts of the building most exposed to such casualties. Upon the night in which the events that are recorded in the immediately preceding chapters occurred, two horsemen rode up to this inn, and leisurely entering the stable yard, dismounted, and gave their horses in charge to a ragged boy who acted as hostler, directing him with a few very impressive figures of rhetoric, on no account to loosen girth or bridle, or to suffer the beasts to stir one yard from the spot where they stood. This matter settled, they entered the house. Both were muffled; the one—a large, shambling fellow—wore a capacious riding-coat; the other—a small, wiry man—was wrapped in a cloak; both wore their hats pressed down over their brows, and had drawn their mufflers up, so as to conceal the lower part of the face. The lesser of the two men, leaving his companion in the passage, opened a door, within which were a few fellows drowsily toping, and one or two asleep. In a chair by the fire sat Tony Bligh, the proprietor of the "Bleeding Horse," a middle-aged man, rather corpulent, as pale as tallow, and with a sly, ugly squint. The little man in the cloak merely introduced his head and shoulders, and beckoned with his thumb. The signal, though scarcely observed by one other of the occupants of the room, was instantly and in silence obeyed by the landlord, who, casting one uneasy glance round, glided across the floor, and was in the passage almost as soon as the gentleman in the cloak.

"Here, Tony, boy," whispered the man, as the innkeeper approached, "fetch us a pint of Hollands, a couple of pipes, and a glim; but first turn the key in this door here, and come yourself, do ye mind?"

Tony squeezed the speaker's arm in token of acquiescence, and turning a key gently in the lock, he noiselessly opened the door which Brimstone Bill had indicated, and the two cavaliers strode into the dark and vacant chamber. Brimstone walked to the window, pushed open the casement, and leaned out. The beautiful moon was shining above the old and tufted trees which lined the quiet road; he looked up and down the shaded avenue, but nothing was moving upon it, save the varying shadows as the night wind swung the branches to and fro. He listened, but no sound reached his ears, excepting the rustling and moaning of the boughs, through which the breeze was fitfully soughing.

Scarcely had he drawn back again into the room, when Tony returned with the refreshments which the gentleman had ordered, and with a dark lantern enclosing a lighted candle.

"Right, old cove," said Bill. "I see you hav'n't forgot the trick of the trade. Who are your pals inside?"

"Three of them sleep here to-night," replied Tony. "They're all quiet coves enough, such as doesn't hear nor see any more than they ought."

The two fellows filled a pipe each, and lighted them at the lantern.

"What mischief are you after now, Bill?" inquired the host, with a peculiar leer.

"Why should I be after any mischief," replied Brimstone jocularly, "any more than a sucking dove, eh? Do I look like mischief to-night, old tickle-pitcher—do I?"

He accompanied the question with a peculiar grin, which mine host answered by a prolonged wink of no less peculiar significance.

"Well, Tony boy," rejoined Bill, "maybe I am and maybe I ain't—that's the way: but mind, you did not see a stim of me, nor of him, to-night (glancing at his comrade), nor ever, for that matter. But you did see two ill-looking fellows not a bit like us; and I have a notion that these two chaps will manage to get into a sort of shindy before an hour's over, and then mizzle at once; and if all goes well, your hand shall be crossed with gold to-night."

"Bill, Bill," said the landlord, with a smile of exquisite relish, and drawing his hand coaxingly over the man's forehead, so as to smooth the curls of his periwig nearly into his eyes, "you're just the same old dodger—you are the devil's own bird—you have not cast a feather."

It is hard to say how long this tender scene might have continued, had not the other ruffian knocked his knuckles sharply on the table, and cried—

"Hist! brother—chise it—enough fooling—I hear a horse-shoe on the road."

All held their breath, and remained motionless for a time. The fellow was, however, mistaken. Bill again advanced to the window, and gazed intently through the long vista of trees.

"There's not a bat stirring," said he, returning to the table, and filling out successively two glasses of spirits, he emptied them both. "Meanwhile, Tony," continued he, "get back to your company. Some of the fellows may be poking their noses into this place. If you don't hear from me, at all events you'll hear of me before an hour. Hop the twig, boy, and keep all hard in for a bit—skip."

With a roguish grin and a shake of the fist, honest Tony, not caring to dispute the commands of his friend, of whose temper he happened to know something, stealthily withdrew from the room, where we, too, shall for a time leave these worthy gentlemen of the road vigilantly awaiting the approach of their victim.

Larry Toole had no sooner recovered his senses—which was in less than a minute—than he at once betook himself to the "Cock and Anchor," resolved, as the last resource, to inform O'Connor of the fact that an attack was meditated. Accordingly, he hastened with very little ceremony into the presence of his master, told him that young Ashwoode was to be waylaid upon the road, near the "Bleeding Horse," and implored him, without the loss of a moment, to ride in that direction, with a view, if indeed it might not already be too late, to intercept his passage, and forewarn him of the danger which awaited him.

Without waiting to ask one useless question, O'Connor, before five minutes were passed, was mounted on his trusty horse, and riding at a hard pace through the dark streets towards the point of danger.

Meanwhile, young Ashwoode, followed by his mounted attendant, proceeded at a brisk trot in the direction of the manor; his brain filled with a thousand busy thoughts and schemes, among which, not the least important, were sundry floating calculations as to the probable and possible amount of Lady Stukely's jointure, as well as some conjectures respecting the maximum duration of her ladyship's life. Involved in these pleasing ruminations, sometimes crossed by no less agreeable recollections, in which the triumphs of vanity and the successes of the gaming-table had their share, he had now reached that shadowy and silent part of the road at which stood the little inn, embowered in the great old trees, and peeping forth with a sort of humble and friendly aspect, but ill-according with the dangerous designs it served to shelter.

Here the servant, falling somewhat further behind, brought his horse close under the projecting window of the inn as he passed, and with a sharp cut of his whip gave the concerted signal. Before sixty seconds had elapsed, two well-mounted cavaliers were riding at a hard gallop in their wake. At this headlong pace, the foremost of the two horsemen had passed Ashwoode by some dozen yards, when, checking his horse so suddenly as to throw him back upon his haunches, he wheeled him round, and plunging the spurs deep into his flanks, with two headlong springs, he dashed him madly upon the young man's steed, hurling the beast and his rider to the earth. Tremendous as was the fall, young Ashwoode, remarkable alike for personal courage and activity, was in a moment upon his feet, with his sword drawn, ready to receive the assault of the ruffian.

"Let go your skiver—drop it, you greenhorn," cried the fellow, hoarsely, as he wheeled round his plunging horse, and drew a pistol from the holster, "or, by the eternal —, I'll blow your head into dust!"

Young Ashwoode attempted to seize the reins of the fellow's horse, and made a desperate pass at the rider.

"Take it, then," cried the fellow, thrusting the muzzle of the pistol into Ashwoode's face and drawing the trigger. Fortunately for Ashwoode, the pistol missed fire, and almost at the same moment the rapid clang of a horse's hoofs, accompanied by the loud shout of menace, broke startlingly upon his ear. Happy was this interruption for Henry Ashwoode, for, stunned and dizzy from the shock, he at that moment tottered, and in the next was prostrate upon the ground. "Blowed, by —!" cried the villain, furiously, as the unwelcome sounds reached his ears, and dashing the spurs into his horse, he rode at a furious gallop down the road towards the country. This scene occupied scarce six seconds in the acting. Brimstone Bill, who had but a moment before come up to the succour of his comrade, also heard the rapid approach of the galloping hoofs upon the road; he knew that before he could count fifty seconds the new comer would have arrived. A few moments, however, he thought he could spare—important moments they turned out to be to one of the party. Bill kept his eye steadily fixed upon the point some three or four hundred yards distant at which he knew the horseman whose approach was announced must first appear.

In that brief moment, the cool-headed villain had rapidly calculated the danger of the groom's committing his accomplices through want of coolness and presence of mind, should he himself, as was not unlikely, become suspected. The groom's pistols were still loaded, and he had taken no part in the conflict. Brimstone Bill fixed a stern glance upon his companion while all these and other thoughts flashed like lightning across his brain.

"Darby," said he, hurriedly, to the man who sat half-stupefied in the saddle close beside him, "blaze off the lead towels—crack them off, I say."

Bill impatiently leaned forward, and himself drew the pistols from the groom's saddle-bow; he fired one of them in the air—he cocked the other. "This dolt will play the devil with us all," thought he, looking with a peculiar expression at the bewildered servant. With one hand he grasped him by the collar to steady his aim, and with the other, suddenly thrusting the pistol to his ear, and drawing the trigger, he blew the wretched man's head into fragments like a potsherd; and wheeling his horse's head about, he followed his comrade pell-mell, beating the sparks in showers from the stony road at every plunge.

All this occurred in fewer moments than it has taken us lines to describe it; and before our friend Brimstone Bill had secured the odds which his safety required, O'Connor was thundering at a furious gallop within less than a hundred yards of him. Bill saw that his pursuer was better mounted than he—to escape, therefore, by a fair race was out of the question. His resolution was quickly taken. By a sudden and powerful effort he reined in his horse at a single pull, and, with one rearing wheel, brought him round upon his antagonist; at the same time, drawing one of the large pistols from the saddle-bow, he rested it deliberately upon his bridle-arm, and fired at his pursuer, now within twenty yards of him. The ball passed so close to O'Connor's head that his ear rang shrilly with the sound of it for hours after. They had now closed; the highwayman drew his second pistol from the holster, and each fired at the same instant. O'Connor's shot was well directed—it struck his opponent in the bridle-arm, a little below the shoulder, shattering the bone to splinters. With a hoarse shriek of agony, the fellow, scarce knowing what he did, forced the spurs into his horse's sides; and the animal reared, wheeled, and bore its rider at a reckless speed in the direction which his companion had followed.

It was well for him that the shot, which at the same moment he had discharged, had not been altogether misdirected. O'Connor, indeed, escaped unscathed, but the ball struck his horse between the eyes, and piercing the brain, the poor beast reared upright and fell dead upon the road. Extricating himself from the saddle, O'Connor returned to the spot where young Ashwoode and the servant still lay. Stunned and dizzy with the fall which he had had, the excitement of actual conflict was no sooner over, than Ashwoode sank back into a state of insensibility. In this condition O'Connor found him, pale as death, and apparently lifeless. Raising him against the grassy bank at the roadside, and having cast some water from a pool close by into his face, he saw him speedily recover.

"Mr. O'Connor," said Ashwoode, as soon as he was sufficiently restored, "you have saved my life—how can I thank you?"

"Spare your thanks, sir," replied O'Connor, haughtily; "for any man I would have done as much—for anyone bearing your name I would do much more. Are you hurt, sir?"

"O'Connor, I have done you much injustice," said the young man, betrayed for the moment into something like genuine feeling. "You must forget and forgive it—I know your feelings respecting others of my family—henceforward I will be your friend—do not refuse my hand."

"Henry Ashwoode," replied O'Connor, "I take your hand—gladly forgetting all past causes of resentment—but I want no vows of friendship, which to-morrow you may regret. Act with regard to me henceforward as if this night had not been—for I tell you truly again, that I would have done as much for the meanest peasant breathing as I have done to-night for you; and once more I pray you tell me, are you much hurt?"

"Nothing, nothing," replied Ashwoode—"merely a fall such as I have had a thousand times after the hounds. It has made my head swim confoundedly; but I'll soon be steady. What, in the meantime, has become of honest Darby? If I mistake not, I see his horse browsing there by the roadside."

A few steps showed them what seemed a bundle of clothes lying heaped upon the road; they approached it—it was the body of the servant.

"Get up, Darby—get up, man," cried Ashwoode, at the same time pressing the prostrate figure with his boot. It had been lying with the back uppermost, and in a half-kneeling attitude; it now, however, rolled round, and disclosed, in the bright moonlight, the hideous aspect of the murdered man—the head a mere mass of ragged flesh and bone, shapeless and blackened, and hollow as a shell. Horror-struck at the sight, they turned in silence away, and having secured the two horses, they both mounted and rode together back to the little inn, where, having procured assistance, the body of the wretched servant was deposited. Young Ashwoode and O'Connor then parted, each on his respective way.

## CHAPTER X.

THE MASTER OF MORLEY COURT AND THE LITTLE GENTLEMAN IN BOTTLE-GREEN—THE BARONET'S DAUGHTER—AND THE TWO CONSPIRATORS.

Encounters such as those described in the last chapter were, it is needless to say, much more common a hundred and thirty years ago than they are now. In fact, it was unsafe alike in town and country to stir abroad after dark in any district affording wealth and aristocracy sufficient to tempt the enterprise of professional gentlemen. If London and its environs, with all their protective advantages, were, nevertheless, so infested with desperadoes as to render its very streets and most frequented ways perilous to pass through during the hours of night, it is hardly to be wondered at that Dublin, the capital of a rebellious and semi-barbarous country—haunted by hungry adventurers, who had lost everything in the revolutionary wars—with a most notoriously ineffective police, and a rash and dissolute aristocracy, with a great deal more money and a great deal less caution than usually fall to the lot of our gentry of the present day—should have been pre-eminently the scene of midnight violence and adventure. The continued frequency of such occurrences had habituated men to think very lightly of them; and the feeble condition of the civil executive almost uniformly secured the impunity of the criminal. We shall not, therefore, weary the reader by inviting his attention to the formal investigation which was forthwith instituted; it is enough for all purposes to record that, like most other investigations of the kind at that period, it ended in—just nothing.

Instead, then, of attending inquests and reading depositions, we must here request the gentle reader to accompany us for a brief space into the dressing-room of Sir Richard Ashwoode, where, upon the morning following the events which in our last we have detailed, the aristocratic invalid lay extended upon a well-cushioned sofa, arrayed in a flowered silk dressing-gown, lined with crimson, and with a velvet cap upon his head. He was apparently considerably beyond sixty—a slightly and rather an elegantly made man, with thin, anxious features, and a sallow complexion: his head rested upon his hand, and his eyes wandered with an air of discontented abstraction over the fair landscape which his window commanded. Before him was placed a small table, with all the appliances of an elegant breakfast; and two or three books and pamphlets were laid within reach of his hand. A little way from him sate his beautiful child, Mary Ashwoode, paler than usual, though not less lovely—for the past night had been to her one of fevered excitement, griefs, and fears. There she sate, with her work before her, and while her small hands plied their appointed task, her soft, dark eyes wandered often with sweet looks of affection toward the reclining form of that old haughty and selfish man, her father.

The silence had continued long, for the old man's temper might not, perhaps, have brooked an interruption of his ruminations, although, if the sour and spited expression of his face might be trusted, his thoughts were not the most pleasant in the world. The train of reflection, whatever it might have been, was interrupted by the entrance of a servant, bearing in his hand a note, with which he approached Sir Richard, but with that air of nervous caution with which one might be supposed to present a sandwich to a tiger.

"Why the devil, sirrah, do you pound the floor so!" cried Sir Richard, turning shortly upon the man as he advanced, and speaking in sharp and bitter accents. "What's that you've got?—a note?—take it back, you blockhead—I'll not touch it—it's some rascally scrap of dunning paper—get out of my sight, sirrah."

"An it please you, sir," replied the man, deferentially, "it comes from Lord Aspenly."

"Eh! oh! ah!" exclaimed Sir Richard, raising himself upon the sofa, and extending his hand with alacrity. "Here, give it to me; so you may go, sir—but stay, does a messenger wait?—ask particularly from me how his lordship does, do you mind? and let the man have refreshment; go, sirrah, go—begone!"

Sir Richard then took the note, broke the seal, and read the contents through, evidently with considerable satisfaction. Having completed the perusal of the note twice over, with a smile of unusual gratification, tinctured, perhaps, with the faintest possible admixture of ridicule, Sir Richard turned toward his daughter with more real cheerfulness than she had seen him exhibit for years before.

"Mary, my good child," said he, "this note announces the arrival here, on to-morrow, of my old, or rather, my most particular friend, Lord Aspenly; he will pass some days with us—days which we must all endeavour to make as agreeable to him as possible. You look—you do look extremely well and pretty to-day; come here and kiss me, child."

Overjoyed at this unwonted manifestation of affection, the girl cast her work away, and with a beating heart and light step, she ran to her father's side, threw her arms about his neck, and kissed him again and again, in happy unconsciousness of all that was passing in the mind of him she so fondly caressed.

The door again opened, and the same servant once more presented himself.

"What do you come to plague me about now?" inquired the master, sharply; recovering, in an instant, his usual peevish manner—"What's this you've got?—what is it?"

"A card, sir," replied the man, at the same time advancing the salver on which it lay within reach of the languid hand of his master.

"Mr. Audley—Mr. Audley," repeated Sir Richard, as he read the card; "I never heard of the man before, in the course of my life; I know nothing about him—nothing—and care as little. Pray what is he pestering about?—what does he want here?"

"He requests permission to see you, sir," replied the man.

"Tell him, with my compliments, to go to hell!" rejoined the invalid;—"Or, stay," he added, after a moment's pause—"what does he look like?—is he well or ill-dressed?—old or young?"

"A middle-aged man, sir; rather well-dressed," answered the servant.

"He did not mention his business?" asked Sir Richard.

"No, sir," replied the man; "but he said that it was very important, and that you would be glad to see him."

"Show him up, then," said Sir Richard, decisively.

The servant accordingly bowed and departed.

"A stranger!—a gentleman!—and come to me upon important and pleasant business," muttered the baronet, musingly—"important and pleasant!—Can my old, cross-grained brother-in-law have made a favourable disposition of his property, and—and—died!—that were, indeed, news worth hearing; too much luck to happen me, though—no, no, it can't be—it can't be."

Nevertheless, he thought it might be; and thus believing, he awaited the entrance of his visitor with extreme impatience. This suspense, however, was not of long duration; the door opened, and the servant announced Mr. Audley—a dapper little gentleman, in grave habiliments of bottle-green cloth; in person somewhat short and stout; and in countenance rather snub-featured and rubicund, but bearing an expression in which good-humour was largely blended with self-importance. This little person strutted briskly into the room.

"Hem!—Sir Richard Ashwoode, I presume?" exclaimed the visitor, with a profound bow, which threatened to roll his little person up like an armadillo.

Sir Richard returned the salute by a slight nod and a gracious wave of the hand.

"You will excuse my not rising to receive you, Mr. Audley," said the baronet, "when I inform you that I am tied here by the gout; pray, sir, take a chair. Mary, remove your work to the room underneath, and lay the ebony wand within my reach; I will tap upon the floor when I want you."

The girl accordingly glided from the room.

"We are now alone, sir," continued Sir Richard, after a short pause. "I fear, sir—I know not why—that your business has relation to my brother; is he—is he ill?"

"Faith, sir," replied the little man bluntly, "I never heard of the gentleman before in my life."

"I breathe again, sir; you have relieved me extremely," said the baronet, swallowing his disappointment with a ghastly smile; "and now, sir, that you have thus considerately and expeditiously dispelled what were, thank heaven! my groundless alarms, may I ask you to what accident I am indebted for the singular good fortune of making your acquaintance—in short, sir, I would fain learn the object of your visit."

"That you shall, sir—that you shall, in a trice," replied the little gentleman in green. "I'm a plain man, my dear Sir Richard, and love to come to the point at once—ahem! The story, to be sure, is a long one, but don't be afraid, I'll abridge it—I'll abridge it." He drew his watch from his fob, and laying it upon the table before him, he continued—"It now wants, my dear sir, precisely seven minutes of eleven, by London time; I shall limit myself to half-an-hour."

"I fear, Mr. Audley, you should find me a very unsatisfactory listener to a narrative of half-an-hour's length," observed Sir Richard, drily; "in fact, I am not in a condition to make any such exertion; if you will obligingly condense what you have to say into a few minutes, you will confer a favour upon me, and lighten your own task considerably." Sir Richard then indignantly took a pinch of snuff, and muttered, almost audibly—"A vulgar, audacious, old boor."

"Well, then, we must try—we must try, my dear sir," replied the little gentleman, wiping his face with his handkerchief, by way of preparation—"I'll just sum up the leading points, and leave particulars for a more favourable opportunity; in fact, I'll hold over all details to our next merry meeting—our next tête-à-tête—when I hope we shall meet upon a pleasanter footing—your gouty toes, you know—d'ye take me? Ha! ha! excuse the joke—ha! ha! ha!"

Sir Richard elevated his eyebrows, and looked upon the little gentleman with a gaze of stern and petrifying severity during this burst of merriment.

"Well, my dear sir," continued Mr. Audley, again wiping his face, "to proceed to business. You have learned my name from my card, but beyond my name you know nothing about me."

"Nothing whatever, sir," replied Sir Richard, with profound emphasis.

"Just so; well, then, you shall," rejoined the little gentleman. "I have been a long time settled in France—I brought over every penny I had in the world there—in short, sir, something more than twelve thousand pounds. Well, sir, what did I do with it? There's the question. Your gay young fellows would have thrown it away at the gaming table, or squandered it on gold lace and velvets—or again, your prudent, plodding fellow would have lived quietly on the interest and left the principal to vegetate; but what did I do? Why, sir, not caring for idleness or show, I threw some of it into the wine trade, and with the rest I kept hammering at the funds, winning twice for every once I lost. In fact, sir, I prospered—the money rolled in, sir, and in due course I became rich, sir—rich—warm, as the phrase goes."

"Very warm, indeed, sir," replied Sir Richard, observing that his visitor again wiped his face—"but allow me to ask, beyond the general interest which I may be presumed to feel in the prosperity of the whole human race, how on earth does all this concern me?"

"Ay, ay, there's the question," replied the stranger, looking unutterably knowing—"that's the puzzle. But all in good time; you shall hear it in a twinkling. Now, being well to do in the world, you may ask me, why do not I look out for a wife? I answer you simply, that having escaped matrimony hitherto, I have no wish to be taken in the noose at these years; and now, before I go further, what do you take my age to be—how old do I look?"

The little man squared himself, cocked his head on one side, and looked inquisitively at Sir Richard from the corner of his eye. The patience of the baronet was nigh giving way outright.

"Sir," replied he, in no very gracious tones, "you may be the 'Wandering Jew,' for anything I either know or see to the contrary."

"Ha! good," rejoined the little man, with imperturbable good humour, "I see, Sir Richard, you are a wag—the Wandering Jew—ha, ha! no—not that quite. The fact is, sir, I am in my sixty-seventh year—you would not have thought that—eh?"

Sir Richard made no reply whatever.

"You'll acknowledge, sir, that that is not exactly the age at which to talk of hearts and darts, and gay gold rings," continued the communicative gentleman in the bottle-green. "I know very well that no young woman, of her own free choice, could take a liking to me."

"Quite impossible," with desperate emphasis, rejoined Sir Richard, upon whose ear the sentence grated unpleasantly; for Lord Aspenly's letter (in which "hearts and darts" were profusely noticed) lay before him on the table; "but once more, sir, may I implore of you to tell me the drift of all this?"

"The drift of it—to be sure I will—in due time," replied Mr. Audley. "You see, then, sir, that having no family of my own, and not having any intention of taking a wife, I have resolved to leave my money to a fine young fellow, the son of an old friend; his name is O'Connor—Edmond O'Connor—a fine, handsome, young dog, and worthy to fill any place in all the world—a high-spirited, good-hearted, dashing young rascal—you know something of him, Sir Richard?"

The baronet nodded a supercilious assent; his attention was now really enlisted.

"Well, Sir Richard," continued the visitor, "I have wormed out of him—for I have a knack of my own of getting at people's secrets, no matter how close they keep them, d'ye see—that he is over head and ears in love with your daughter—I believe the young lady who just left the room on my arrival; and indeed, if such is the case, I commend the young scoundrel's taste; the lady is truly worthy of all admiration—and—"

"Pray, sir, proceed as briefly as may be to the object of your conversation with me," interrupted Sir Richard, drily.

"Well, then, to return—I understand, sir," continued Audley, "that you, suspecting something of the kind, and believing the young fellow to be penniless, very naturally, and, indeed, I may say, very prudently, and very sensibly, opposed yourself to the thing from the commencement, and obliged the sly young dog to discontinue his visits;—well, sir, matters stood so, until I—cunning little I—step in, and change the whole posture of affairs—and how? Marry, thus, I come hither and ask your daughter's hand for him, upon these terms following—that I undertake to convey to him, at once, lands to the value of one thousand pounds a year, and that at my death I will leave him, with the exception of a few small legacies, sole heir to all I have; and on his wedding-day give him and his lady their choice of either of two chateaux, the worst of them a worthy residence for a nobleman."

"Are these chateaux in Spain?" inquired Sir Richard, sneeringly.

"No, no, sir," replied the little man, with perfect guilelessness; "both in Flanders."

"Well, sir," said Sir Richard Ashwoode, raising himself almost to a sitting posture, and preluding his observations with two unusually large pinches of snuff, "I have heard you very patiently throughout a statement, all of which was fatiguing, and much of which was positively disagreeable to me: and I trust that what I have now to say will render it wholly unnecessary for you and me ever again to converse upon the same topic. Of Mr. O'Connor, whom, in spite of this strange repetition of an already rejected application, I believe to be a spirited young man, I shall say nothing more than that, from the bottom of my heart I wish him every success of every kind, so long as he confines his aspirations to what is suitable to his own position in society; and, consequently, conducive to his own comfort and respectability. With respect to his very flattering vicarious proposal, I must assure you that I do not suspect Miss Ashwoode of any inclination to descend from the station to which her birth and fortune entitle her; and if I did suspect it, I should feel it to be my imperative duty to resist, by every means in my power, the indulgence of any such wayward caprice; but lest, after what I have said, any doubt should rest upon your mind as to the value of these obstacles, it may not be amiss to add that my daughter, Miss Ashwoode, is actually promised in marriage to a gentleman of exalted rank and great fortune, and who is, in all respects, an unexceptionable connection. I have the honour, sir, to wish you good-morning."

"The devil!" exclaimed the little gentleman, as soon as his utter amazement allowed him to take breath. A long pause ensued, during which he twice inflated his cheeks to their utmost tension, and puffed the air forth with a prolonged whistle of desolate wonder. Recollecting himself, however, he hastily arose, wished Sir Richard good-day, and walked down stairs, and out of the house, all the way muttering, "God bless my body and soul—a thousand pounds a year—the devil—can it be?—body o' me—refuse a thousand a year—what the deuce is he looking for?"—and such other ejaculations; stamping all the while emphatically upon every stair as he descended, to give vent to his indignation, as well as impressiveness to his remarks.

Something like a smile for a moment lit up the withered features of the old baronet; he leaned back luxuriously upon his sofa, and while he listened with delighted attention to the stormy descent of his visitor, he administered to its proper receptacle, with prolonged relish, two several pinches of rappee.

"So, so," murmured he, complacently, "I suspect I have seen the last of honest Mr. Audley—a little surprised and a little angry he does appear to be—dear me!—he stamps fearfully—what a very strange creature it is."

Having made this reflection, Sir Richard continued to listen pleasantly until the sounds were lost in the distance; he then rang a small hand-bell which lay upon the table, and a servant entered.

"Tell Mistress Mary," said the baronet, "that I shall not want her just now, and desire Mr. Henry to come hither instantly—begone, sirrah."

The servant disappeared, and in a few moments young Ashwoode, looking unusually pale and haggard, and dressed in a morning suit, entered the chamber. Having saluted his father with the formality which the usages of the time prescribed, and having surveyed himself for a moment at the large mirror which stood in the room, and having adjusted thereat the tie of his lace cravat, he inquired,—

"Pray, sir, who was that piece of 'too, too solid flesh' that passed me scarce a minute since upon the stairs, pounding all the way with the emphasis of a battering ram? As far as I could judge, the thing had just been discharged from your room."

"You have happened, for once in your life, to talk with relation to the subject to which I would call your attention," said Sir Richard. "The person whom you describe with your wonted facetiousness, has just been talking with me; his name is Audley; I never saw him till this morning, and he came coolly to make proposals, in young O'Connor's name, for your sister's hand, promising to settle some scurvy chateaux, heaven knows where, upon the happy pair."

"Well, sir, and what followed?" asked the young man.

"Why simply, sir," replied his father, "that I gave him the answer which sent him stamping down stairs, as you saw him. I laughed in his face, and desired him to go about his business."

"Very good, indeed, sir," observed young Ashwoode.

"There is no occasion for commentary, sir," continued Sir Richard. "Attend to what I have to say: a nobleman of large fortune has requested my permission to make his suit to your sister—that I have, of course, granted; he will arrive here to-morrow, to make a stay of some days. I am resolved the thing shall be concluded. I ought to mention that the nobleman in question is Lord Aspenly."

The young man looked for a moment or two the very impersonation of astonishment, and then, burst into an uncontrollable fit of laughter.

"Either be silent, sir, or this moment quit the room," said Sir Richard, in a tone which few would have liked to disobey—"how dare you—you—you insolent, dependent coxcomb—how dare you, sir, treat me with this audacious disrespect?"

The young man hastened to avert the storm, whose violence he had more than once bitterly felt, by a timely submission.

"I assure you, sir, nothing was further from my intention than to offend you," said he—"I am fully alive—as a man of the world, I could not be otherwise—to the immense advantages of the connection; but Lord Aspenly I have known so long, and always looked upon as a confirmed old bachelor, that on hearing his name thus suddenly, something of incongruity, and—and—and I don't exactly know what—struck me so very forcibly, that I involuntarily and very thoughtlessly began to laugh. I assure you, sir, I regret it very much, if it has offended you."

"You are a weak fool, sir, I am afraid," replied his father, shortly: "but that conviction has not come upon me by surprise; you can, however, be of some use in this matter, and I am determined you shall be. Now, sir, mark me: I suspect that this young fellow—this O'Connor, is not so indifferent to Mary as he should be to a daughter of mine, and it is more than possible that he may endeavour to maintain his interest in her affections, imaginary or real, by writing letters, sending messages, and such manoeuvring. Now, you must call upon the young man, wherever he is to be found, and either procure from him a distinct pledge to the effect that he will think no more of her (the young fellow has a sense of honour, and I would rely upon his promise), or else you must have him out—in short, make him fight you—you attend, sir—if you get hurt, we can easily make the country too hot to hold him; and if, on the other hand, you poke him through the body, there's an end of the whole difficulty. This step, sir, you must take—you understand me—I am very much in earnest."

This was delivered with a cold deliberateness, which young Ashwoode well understood, when his father used it to imply a fixity of purpose, such as brooked no question, and halted at no obstacle.

"Sir," replied Henry Ashwoode, after an embarrassed pause of a few minutes, "you are not aware of one particular connected with last night's affray—you have heard that poor Darby, who rode with me, was actually brained, and that I escaped a like fate by the interposition of one who, at his own personal risk, saved my life—that one was the very Edmond O'Connor of whom we speak."

"What you allude to," observed Sir Richard, with very edifying coolness, "is, no doubt, very shocking and very horrible. I regret the destruction of the man, although I neither saw nor knew much about him; and for your eminently providential escape, I trust I am fully as thankful as I ought to be; and now, granting all you have said to be perfectly accurate—which I take it to be—what conclusion do you wish me to draw from it?"

"Why, sir, without pretending to any very extraordinary proclivity to gratitude," replied the young man—"for O'Connor told me plainly that he did not expect any—I must consider what the world will say, if I return what it will be pleased to regard as an obligation, by challenging the person who conferred it."

"Good, sir—good," said the baronet, calmly: and gazing upon the ceiling with elevated eyebrows and a bitter smile, he added, reflectively, "he's afraid—afraid—afraid—ay, afraid—afraid."

"You wrong me very much, sir," rejoined young Ashwoode, "if you imagine that fear has anything to do with my reluctance to act as you would have me; and no less do you wrong me, if you think I would allow any school-boy sentimentalism to stand in the way of my family's interests. My real objection to the thing is this—first, that I cannot see any satisfactory answer to the question, What will the world say of my conduct, in case I force a duel upon him the day after he has saved my life?—and again, I think it inevitably damages any young woman in the matrimonial market, to have low duels fought about her."

Sir Richard screwed his eyebrows reflectively, and remained silent.

"But at the same time, sir," continued his son, "I see as clearly as you could wish me to do, the importance, under present circumstances—or rather the absolute necessity—of putting a stop to O'Connor's suit; and, in short, to all communication between him and my sister, and I will undertake to do this effectually."

"And how, sir, pray?" inquired the baronet.

"I shall, as a matter of course, wait upon the young man," replied Henry Ashwoode—"his services of last night demand that I should do so. I will explain to him, in a friendly way, the hopelessness of his suit. I should not hesitate either to throw a little colouring of my own over the matter. If I can induce O'Connor once to regard me as his friend—and after all, it is but the part of a friend to put a stop to this foolish affair—I will stake my existence that the matter shall be broken off for ever and a day. If, however, the young fellow turn out foolish and pig-headed, I can easily pick a quarrel with him upon some other subject, and get him out of the way as you propose; but without mixing up my sister's name in the dispute, or giving occasion for gossip. However, I half suspect that it will require neither crafty stratagem nor shrewd blows to bring this absurd business to an end. I daresay the parties are beginning to tire heartily of waiting, and perhaps a little even of one another; and, for my part, I really do not know that the girl ever cared for him, or gave him the smallest encouragement."

"But I know that she did," replied Sir Richard. "Carey has shown me letters from her to him, and from him to her, not six months since. Carey is a very useful woman, and may do us important service. I did not choose to mention that I had seen these letters; but I sounded Mary somewhat sternly, and left her with a caution which I think must have produced a salutary effect—in short, I told her plainly, that if I had reason to suspect any correspondence or understanding between her and O'Connor, I should not scruple to resort to the sternest and most rigorous interposition of parental authority, to put an end to it peremptorily. I confess, however, that I have misgivings about this. I regard it as a very serious obstacle—one, however, which, so sure as I live, I will entirely annihilate."

There was a pause for a little while, and Sir Richard continued,—

"There is a good deal of sense in what you have suggested. We will talk it over and arrange operations systematically this evening. I presume you intend calling upon the fellow to-day; it might not be amiss if you had him to dine with you once or twice in town: you must get up a kind of confidential acquaintance with him, a thing which you can easily terminate, as soon as its object is answered. He is, I believe, what they call a frank, honest sort of fellow, and is, of course, very easily led; and—and, in short—made a fool of: as for the girl, I think I know something of the sex, and very few of them are so romantic as not to understand the value of a title and ten thousand a year! Depend upon it, in spite of all her sighs, and vapours, and romance, the girl will be dazzled so effectually before three weeks, as to be blind to every other object in the world; but if not, and should she dare to oppose my wishes, I'll make her cross-grained folly more terrible to her than she dreams of—but she knows me too well—she dares not."

Both parties remained silent and abstracted for a time, and then Sir Richard, turning sharply to his son, exclaimed, with his usual tart manner,—

"And now, sir, I must admit that I am a good deal tired of your very agreeable company. Go about your business, if you please, and be in this room this evening at half-past six o'clock. You had better not forget to be punctual; and, for the present, get out of my sight."

With this very affectionate leave-taking, Sir Richard put an end to the family consultation, and the young man, relieved of the presence of the only person on earth whom he really feared, gladly closed the door behind him.


CHAPTER XI.

THE OLD BEECH-TREE WALK AND THE IVY-GROWN GATEWAY—THE TRYSTE AND TUE CRUTCH-HANDLED CANE.

In the snug old "Cock and Anchor," the morning after the exciting scenes in which O'Connor had taken so active a part, that gentleman was pacing the floor of his sitting-room in no small agitation. On the result of that interview, which he had resolved no longer to postpone, depended his happiness for years—it might be for life. Again and again he applied himself to the task of arranging clearly and concisely, and withal adroitly and with tact, the substance of what he had to say to Sir Richard Ashwoode. But, spite of all, his mind would wander to the pleasant hours he had passed with Mary Ashwoode in the quiet green wood and by the dark well's side, and through the moss-grown rocks, and by the chiming current of the wayward brook, long before the cold and worldly had suspected and repulsed that love which he knew could never die but when his heart had ceased to beat for ever. Again would he, banishing with a stoical effort these unbidden visions of memory, seek to accomplish the important task which he had proposed to himself; but still all in vain. There was she once more—there was the pale, pensive, lovely face—there the long, dark, silken tresses—there the deep, beautiful eyes—and there the smile—the artless, melancholy, enchanting smile.

"It boots not trying," exclaimed O'Connor. "I cannot collect my thoughts; and yet what use in conning over the order and the words of what, after all, will be judged merely by its meaning? Perhaps it is better that I should yield myself wholly up to the impulse of the moment, and so speak but the more directly and the more boldly. No; even in such a cause I will not accommodate myself to his cramp and crooked habits of thought and feeling. If I let him know all, it matters little how he learns it."

As O'Connor finished this sentence, his meditations were dispelled by certain sounds, which issued from the passage leading to his room.

"A young man," exclaimed a voice, interrupted by a good deal of puffing and blowing, probably caused by the steep ascent, "and a good-looking, eh?—(puff)—dark eyes, eh?—(puff, puff)—black hair and straight nose, eh?—(puff, puff)—long-limbed, tall, eh?—(puff)."

The answers to these interrogatories, whatever they may have been, were, where O'Connor stood, wholly inaudible; but the cross-examination was accompanied throughout by a stout, firm, stumping tread upon the old floor, which, along with the increasing clearness with which the noise made its way to O'Connor's door, sufficiently indicated that the speaker was approaching. The accents were familiar to him. He ran to his door, opened it; and in an instant Hugh Audley, Esquire, very hot and very much out of breath, pitched himself, with a good deal of precision, shoulders foremost, against the pit of the young man's stomach, and, embracing him a little above the hips, hugged him for some time in silence, swaying him to and fro with extraordinary energy, as if preparatory to tripping him up, and taking him off his feet altogether—then giving him a shove straight from him, and holding him at arm's length, he looked with brimful eyes, and a countenance beaming with delight, full in O'Connor's face.

"Confound the dog, how well he looks," exclaimed the old gentleman, vehemently—"devilish well, curse him!" and he gave O'Connor a shove with his knuckles, and succeeded in staggering himself—"never saw you look better in my life, nor anyone else for that matter; and how is every inch of you, and what have you been doing with yourself? Come, you young dog, account for yourself."

O'Connor had now, for the first time, an opportunity of bidding the kind old gentleman welcome, which he did to the full as cordially, if not so boisterously.

"Let me sit down and rest myself: I must take breath for a minute," exclaimed the old gentleman. "Give me a chair, you undutiful rascal. What a devil of a staircase that is, to be sure. Well, and what do you intend doing with yourself to-day?"

"To say the truth," said the young man, while a swarthier glow crossed his dark features. "I was just about to start for Morley Court, to see Sir Richard Ashwoode."

"About his daughter, I take it?" inquired the old gentleman.

"Just so, sir," replied the younger man.

"Then you may spare yourself the pains," rejoined the old gentleman, briskly. "You are better at home. You have been forestalled."

"What—how, sir? What do you mean?" asked O'Connor, in great perplexity and alarm.

"Just what I say, my boy. You have been forestalled."

"By whom, sir?"

"By me."

"By you?"

"Ay."

The old gentleman screwed his brows and pursed up his mouth until it became a Gordian involution of knots and wrinkles, threw a fierce and determined expression into his eyes, and wagged his head slightly from side to side—looking altogether very like a "Cromwell guiltless of his country's blood." At length he said,—

"I'm an old fellow, and ought to know something by this time—think I do, for that matter; and I say deliberately—cut the whole concern and blow them all."

Having thus delivered himself, the old gentleman resumed his sternest expression of countenance, and continued in silence to wag his head from time to time with an air of infinite defiance, leaving his young companion, if possible, more perplexed and bewildered than ever.

"And have you, then, seen Sir Richard Ashwoode?" inquired O'Connor.

"Have I seen him?" rejoined the old gentleman. "To be sure I have. The moment the boat touched the quay, and I fairly felt terra firma, I drove to the 'Fox in Breeches,' and donned a handsome suit"—(here the gentleman glanced cursorily at his bottle-green habiliments)—"I ordered a hack-coach—got safely to Morley Court—saw Sir Richard, laid up with the gout, looking just like an old, dried-up, cross-grained monkey. There was, of course, a long explanation, and all that sort of thing—a good deal of tact and diplomacy on my side, doubling about, neat fencing, and circumbendibus; but all would not do—an infernal smash. Sir Richard was all but downright uncivil—would not hear of it—said plump and plain he would never consent. The fact is, he's a sour, hard, insolent old scoundrel, and a bitter pill; and I congratulate you heartily on having escaped all connection with him and his. Don't look so down in the mouth about the matter; there's as good fish in the sea as ever was caught; and if the young woman is half such a shrew as her father is a tartar, you have had an escape to be thankful for the longest day you live."

We shall not attempt to describe the feelings with which O'Connor received this somewhat eccentric communication. He folded his arms upon the table, and for many minutes leaned his head upon them, without motion, and without uttering one word. At length he said,—

"After all, I ought to have expected this. Sir Richard is a bigoted man in his own faith—an ambitious and a worldly man, too. It was folly, mere folly, knowing all this, to look for any other answer from him. He may indeed delay our union for a little, but he cannot bar it—he shall not bar it. I could more easily doubt myself than Mary's constancy; and if she be but firm and true—and she is all loyalty and all truth—the world cannot part us two. Our separation cannot outlast his life; nor shall it last so long. I will overcome her scruples, combat all her doubts, satisfy her reason. She will consent—she will be mine—my own—through life and until death. No hand shall sunder us for ever,"—he turned to the old man, and grasped his hand—"My dear, kind, true friend, how can I ever thank you for all your generous acts of kindness. I cannot."

"Never mind, never mind, my dear boy," said the old gentleman, blubbering in spite of himself—"never mind—what a d——d old fool I am, to be sure. Come, come, you, shall take a turn with me towards the country, and get an appetite for dinner. You'll be as well as ever in half an hour. When all's done, you stand no worse than you did yesterday; and if the girl's a good girl, as I make no doubt she is, why, you are sure of her constancy—and the devil himself shall not part you. Confound me if I don't run away with the girl for you myself if you make a pother about the matter. Come along, you dog—come along, I say."

"Nay, sir," replied O'Connor, "forgive me. I am keenly pained. I am agitated—confounded at the suddenness of this—this dreadful blow. I will go alone, pardon me, my kind and dear friend, I must go alone. I may chance to see the lady. I am sure she will not fail me—she will meet me. Oh! heart and brain, be still—be steady—I need your best counsels now. Farewell, sir—for a little time, farewell."

"Well, be it so—since so it must be," said Mr. Audley, who did not care to combat a resolution, announced with all the wild energy of despairing passion, "by all means, my dear boy, alone it shall be, though I scarce think you would be the worse of a staid old fellow's company in your ramble—but no matter, boys will be boys while the world goes round."

The conclusion of this sentence was a soliloquy, for O'Connor had already descended to the inn yard, where he procured a horse, and was soon, with troubled mind and swelling heart, making rapid way toward Morley Court. It was now the afternoon—the sun had made nearly half his downward course—the air was soft and fresh, and the birds sang sweetly in the dark nooks and bowers of the tall trees: it seemed almost as if summer had turned like a departing beauty, with one last look of loveliness to gladden the scene which she was regretfully leaving. So sweet and still the air—so full and mellow the thrilling chorus of merry birds among the rustling leaves, flitting from bough to bough in the clear and lofty shadow—so cloudless the golden flood of sunlight. Such was the day—so gladsome the sounds—so serene the aspect of all nature—as O'Connor, dismounting under the shadow of a tall, straggling hawthorn hedge, and knotting the bridle in one of its twisted branches, crossed a low stile, and thus entered the grounds of Morley Court. He threaded a winding path which led through a neglected wood of thorn and oak, and found himself after a few minutes in the spot he sought. The old beech walk had been once the main avenue to the house. Huge beech-trees flung their mighty boughs high in air across its long perspective—and bright as was the day, the long lane lay in shadow deep and solemn as that of some old Gothic aisle. Down this dim vista did O'Connor pace with hurried steps toward the spot where, about midway in its length, there stood the half-ruined piers and low walls of what had once been a gateway.

"Can it be that she shrinks from this meeting?" thought O'Connor, as his eye in vain sought the wished-for form of Mary Ashwoode, "will she disappoint me?—surely she who has walked with me so many lonely hours in guileless trust need not have feared to meet me here. It was not generous to deny me this boon—to her so easy—to me so rich—yet perchance she judges wisely. What boots it that I should see her? Why see again that matchless beauty—that touching smile—those eyes that looked so fondly on me? Why see her more—since mayhap we shall never meet again? She means it kindly. Her nature is all nobleness—all generosity; and yet—and yet to see her no more—to hear her voice no more—have we—have we then parted at last for ever? But no—by heavens—'tis she—Mary!"

It was indeed Mary Ashwoode, blushing and beautiful as ever. In an instant O'Connor stood by her side.

"My own—my true-hearted Mary."

"Oh! Edmond," said she, after a brief silence, "I fear I have done wrong—have I?—in meeting you thus. I ought not—indeed I know I ought not to have come."

"Nay, Mary, do not speak thus. Dear Mary, have we not been companions in many a pleasant ramble: in those times—the times, Mary, that will never come again? Why, then, should you deny me a few minutes' mournful converse, where in other days we two have passed so many pleasant hours?"

There was in the tone in which he spoke something so unutterably melancholy—and in the recollections which his few simple words called crowding to her mind, something at once so touching, so dearly cherished, and so bitterly regretted—that the tears gathered in her full dark eyes, and fell one by one fast and unheeded.

"You do not grieve, then, Mary," said he, "that you have come here—that we have met once more: do you, Mary?"

"No, no, Edmond—no, indeed," answered she, sobbing. "God knows I do not, Edmond—no, no."

"Well, Mary," said he, "I am happy in the belief that you feel toward me just as you used to do—as happy as one so wretched can hope to be."

"Edmond, your words affright me," said she, fixing her eyes full upon him with imploring earnestness: "you look sadder—paler than you did yesterday; something has happened since then. What—what is it, Edmond? tell me—ah, tell me!"

"Yes, Mary, much has happened," answered he, taking her hand between both of his, and meeting her gaze with a look of passionate sorrow and tenderness—"yes, Mary, without my knowledge, the friend of whom I told you had arrived, and this morning saw your father, told him all, and was repulsed with sternness—almost with insult. Sir Richard has resolved that it shall never be; there is no more hope of bending him—none—none—none."

While O'Connor spoke, the colour in Mary's cheeks came and fled in turn with quick alternations, in answer to every throb and flutter of the poor heart within.

"See him—speak to him—yourself, Edmond, yourself. Oh! do not despair—see him—speak to him," she almost whispered, for agitation had well-nigh deprived her of voice—"see him, Edmond—yourself—for God's sake, dear Edmond—yourself—yourself"—and she grasped his arm in her tiny hand, and gazed in his pale face with such a look of agonized entreaty as cut him to the very heart.

"Yes, Mary, if it seems good to you, I will speak to him myself," said O'Connor, with deep melancholy. "I will, Mary, though my own heart—my reason—tells me it is all—all utterly in vain; but, Mary," continued he, suddenly changing his tone to one of more alacrity, "if he should still reject me—if he shall forbid our ever meeting more—if he shall declare himself unalterably resolved against our union—Mary, in such a case, would you, too, tell me to see you no more—would you, too, tell me to depart without hope, and never come again? or would you, Mary—could you—dare you—dear, dear Mary, for once—once only—disobey your stern and haughty father—dare you trust yourself with me—fly with me to France, and be at last, and after all, my own—my bride?"

"No, Edmond," said she, solemnly and sadly, while her eyes again filled with tears; and though she trembled like the leaf on the tree, yet he knew by the sound of her sad voice that her purpose could not alter—"that can never be—never, Edmond—no—no."

"Then, Mary, can it be," he answered, with an accent so desolate that despair itself seemed breathing in its tone—"can it be, after all—all we have passed and proved—all our love and constancy, and all our bright hopes, so long and fondly cherished—cherished in the midst of grief and difficulty—when we had no other stay but hope alone—are we, after all—at last, to part for ever?—is it, indeed, Mary, all—all over?"

As the two lovers stood thus in deep and melancholy converse by the ivy-grown and ruined gateway, beneath the airy shadow of the old beech-trees, they were recalled to other thoughts by the hurried patter of footsteps, and the rustling of the branches among the underwood which skirted the avenue. As fortune willed it, however, the intruder was no other than the honest dog, Rover, Mary's companion in many a silent and melancholy ramble; he came sniffing and bounding with boisterous greeting to hail his young mistress and her companion. The interruption, harmless as it was, startled Mary Ashwoode.

"Were my father to find us here, Edmond," said she, "it were fatal to all our hopes. You know his temper well. Let us then part here. Follow the by-path leading to the house. Go and see him—speak with him for my sake—for my sake, Edmond—and so—and so—farewell."

"And farewell, Mary, since it must be," said O'Connor, with a bitter struggle. "Farewell, but only for a time—only for a little time, Mary; and whatever befalls, remember—remember me. Farewell, Mary."

As he thus spoke, he raised her hand to his lips, and kissed it for the first time, it might be for the last, in his life. For a moment he stood, and gazed with sad devotion upon the loved face. Then, with an effort, he turned abruptly away, and strode rapidly in the direction she had indicated; and when he turned to look again, she was gone.

O'Connor followed the narrow path, which, diverging a little from the broad grass lane, led with many a wayward turn among the tall trees toward the house. As he thus pursued his way, a few moments of reflection satisfied him of the desperate nature of the enterprise which he had undertaken. But if lovers are often upon unreal grounds desponding, it is likewise true that they are sometimes sanguine when others would despair; and, spite of all his misgivings—of all the irresistible conclusions of stern reason—hope still beckoned him on. Thus agitated, he pursued his way, until, on turning an abrupt angle, he beheld, scarcely more than a dozen paces in advance, and moving slowly toward him in the shadowy pathway, a figure, at sight of which, thus suddenly presented, he recoiled, and stood for a moment fixed as a statue. He had encountered the object of his search. The form was that of Sir Richard Ashwoode himself, who, wrapped in his scarlet roquelaure, and leaning upon the shoulder of his Italian valet, while he limped forward slowly and painfully, appeared full before him.

"So, so, so, so," repeated the baronet, at first with unaffected astonishment, which speedily, however, deepened into intense but constrained anger—his dark, prominent eyes peering fiercely upon the young man, while, stooping forward, and clutching his crutch-handled cane hard in his lean fingers, he limped first one and then another step nearer.

"Mr. O'Connor! or my eyes deceive me."

"Yes, Sir Richard," replied O'Connor, with a haughty bow, and advancing a little toward him in turn. "I am that Edmond O'Connor whom you once knew well, and whom it would seem you still know. I ought, doubtless—"

"Nay, sir, no flowers of rhetoric, if you please," interrupted Sir Richard, bitterly—"no fustian speeches—to the point—to the point, sir. If you have ought to say to me, deliver it in six words. Your business, sir. Be brief."

"I will not indeed waste words, Sir Richard Ashwoode," replied O'Connor, firmly. "There is but one subject on which I would seek a conference with you, and that subject you well may guess."

"I do guess it," retorted Sir Richard. "You would renew an absurd proposal—one opened three years since, and repeated this morning by the old booby, your elected spokesman. To that proposal I have ever given one answer—no. I have not changed my mind, nor ever shall. Am I understood, sir? And least of all should I think of changing my purpose now," continued he, more pointedly, as a suspicion crossed his mind—"now, sir, that you have forfeited by your own act whatever regard you once seemed to me to merit. You did not seek me here, sir. I'm not to be fooled, sir. You did not seek me—don't assert it. I understand your purpose. You came here clandestinely to tamper like a schemer with my child. Yes, sir, a schemer!" repeated Sir Richard, with bitter emphasis, while his sharp sallow features grew sharper and more sallow still; and he struck the point of his cane at every emphatic word deep into the sod—"a mean, interested, cowardly schemer. How dare you steal into my place, you thrice-rejected, dishonourable, spiritless adventurer?"

The blood rushed to O'Connor's brow as the old man uttered this insulting invective. The fiery impulse which under other circumstances would have been uncontrollable, was, however, speedily, though with difficulty, mastered; and O'Connor replied bitterly,—

"You are an old man, Sir Richard, and her father—you are safe, sir. How much of chivalry or courage is shown in heaping insult upon one who will not retort upon you, judge for yourself. After what has passed, I feel that I were, indeed, the vile thing you have described, if I were again to subject myself to your unprovoked insolence: be assured, I shall never place foot of mine within your boundaries again: relieve yourself, sir, of all fears upon that score; and for your language, you know you can appreciate the respect that makes me leave you thus unanswered and unpunished."

So saying, he turned, and with long and rapid strides retraced his steps, his heart swelling with a thousand struggling emotions. Scarce knowing what he did, O'Connor rode rapidly to the "Cock and Anchor," and too much stunned and confounded by the scenes in which he had just borne a part to exchange a word with Mr. Audley, whom he found still established in his chamber, he threw himself dejectedly into a chair, and sank into gloomy and obstinate abstraction. The good-natured old gentleman did not care to interrupt his young friend's ruminations, and hours might have passed away and found them still undisturbed, were it not that the door was suddenly thrown open, and the waiter announced Mr. Ashwoode. There was a spell in the name which instantly recalled O'Connor to the scene before him. Had a viper sprung up at his feet, he could not have recoiled with a stronger antipathy. With a mixture of feelings scarcely tolerable, he awaited his arrival, and after a moment or two of suspense, Henry Ashwoode entered the room.

Mr. Audley, having heard the name, scowled fearfully from the centre of the room upon the young gentleman as he entered, stuffed his hands half-way to the elbows in his breeches pockets, and turning briskly upon his heel, marched emphatically to the window, and gazed out into the inn yard with remarkable perseverance. The obvious coldness with which he was received did not embarrass young Ashwoode in the least. With perfect ease and a graceful frankness of demeanour, he advanced to O'Connor, and after a greeting of extraordinary warmth, inquired how he had gotten home, and whether he had suffered since any inconvenience from the fall which he had. He then went on to renew his protestations of gratitude for O'Connor's services, with so much ardour and apparent heartiness, that spite of his prejudices, the old man was moved in his favour; and when Ashwoode expressed in a low voice to O'Connor his wish to be introduced to his friend, honest Mr. Audley felt his heart quite softened, and instead of merely bowing to him, absolutely shook him by the hand. The young man then, spite of O'Connor's evident reluctance, proceeded to relate to his new acquaintance the details of the adventures of the preceding night, in doing which, he took occasion to dwell, in the most glowing terms, upon his obligations to O'Connor. After sitting with them for nearly half an hour, young Ashwoode took his leave in the most affectionate manner possible, and withdrew.

"Well, that is a good-looking young fellow, and a warm-hearted," exclaimed the old gentleman, as soon as the visitor had disappeared—"what a pity he should be cursed with such a confounded old father."


CHAPTER XII.

THE APPOINTED HOUR—THE SCHEMERS AND THE PLOT.

"And here comes my dear brother," exclaimed Mary Ashwoode, joyously, as she ran to welcome the young man, now entering her father's room, in which, for more than an hour previously, she had been sitting. Throwing her arm round his neck, and looking sweetly in his face, she continued—"You will stay with us this evening, dear Harry—do, for my sake—you won't refuse—it is so long since we have had you;" and though she spoke with a gay look and a gladsome voice, a sense of real solitariness called a tear to her dark eye.

"No, Mary—not this evening," said the young man coldly; "I must be in town again to-night, and before I go must have some conversation upon business with my father, so that I may not see you again till morning."

"But, dear Henry," said she, still clinging affectionately to his arm, "you have been in such danger, and I knew nothing of it until after you went out this morning: are you quite well, Henry?—you were not hurt—were you?"

"No, no—nothing—nothing—I never was better," said he, impatiently.

"Well, brother—dear brother," she continued imploringly, "come early home to-night—do not be upon the road late—won't you promise?"

"There, there, there," said he rudely, "run away—take your work, or your book, or whatever it may be, down stairs; your father wants to speak with me alone," and so saying, he turned pettishly from her.

His habitual coldness and carelessness of manner had never before seemed so ungracious. The poor girl felt her heart swell within her, as though it would burst. She had never felt so keenly that in all this world there lived but one being upon whose love she might rely, and he separated, it might be for ever, from her: she gathered up her work, and ran quickly from the room, to hide the tears which she could not restrain.

Young Ashwoode was to the full as worldly and as unprincipled a man as was his father; and whatever reluctance he may have felt as to adopting Sir Richard's plans respecting O'Connor, the reader would grievously wrong him in attributing his unwillingness to any visitings of gratitude, or, indeed, to any other feeling than that which he had himself avowed. A few hours' reflection had satisfied the young man of the transcendent importance of securing Lord Aspenly; and by a corresponding induction he had arrived at the conclusion to which his father had already come—namely, that it was imperatively necessary by all means to put an end effectually to his sister's correspondence with O'Connor. To effect this object both were equally resolved; and with respect to the means to be employed both were equally unscrupulous. With Henry Ashwoode courage was constitutional, and art habitual. If, therefore, either duplicity or daring could ensure success, he felt that he must triumph; and, at all events, he was sufficiently impressed with the importance of the object, to resolve to leave nothing untried for its achievement.

"You are punctual, sir," said Sir Richard, glancing at his richly-chased watch; "sit down; I have considered your suggestions of this morning, and I am inclined to adopt them; it is most probable that Mary, like the rest of her sex, will be taken by the splendour of the proposal—fascinated—in short, as I said this morning—dazzled. Now, whether she be or not—observe me, it shall be our object to make O'Connor believe that she is so. You will have his ear, and through her maid, Carey, I can manage their correspondence; not a letter from either can reach the other, without first meeting my eye. I am very certain that the young fellow will lose no time in writing to her some more of those passionate epistles, of which, as I told you, I have seen a sample. I shall take care to have their letters re-written for the future, before they come to hand; and it shall go hard, or between us we shall manage to give each a very moderate opinion of the other's constancy; thus the affair will—or rather must—die a natural death—after all, the most effectual kind of mortality in such cases."

"I called to-day upon the fellow," said the young man. "I made him out, and without approaching the point of nearest interest, I have, nevertheless, opened operations successfully—so far as a most auspicious re-commencement of our acquaintance may be so accounted."

"And, stranger still to say," rejoined the baronet, "I also encountered him to-day; but only for some dozen seconds."

"How!—saw O'Connor!" exclaimed young Ashwoode.

"Yes, sir, O'Connor—Edmond O'Connor," repeated Sir Richard. "He was coolly walking up to the house to see me, as it would seem; and I do believe the fellow speaks truth—he did see me, and that is all. I fancy he will scarcely come here again uninvited; he said so pretty plainly, and I believe the fellow has spirit enough to feel an affront."

"He did not see Mary?" inquired Henry.

"I did not ask him, and don't choose to ask her; I don't mean to allude to the subject in her presence," replied Sir Richard, quickly. "I think—indeed I know—I can mar their plans better by appearing never once to apprehend anything from O'Connor's pretensions. I have reasons, too, for not wishing to deal harshly with Mary at present; we must have no scenes, if possible. Were I to appear suspicious and uneasy, it would put them on their guard. And now, upon the other point, did you speak to Craven about the possibility of raising ten thousand pounds on the Glenvarlogh property?"

"He says it can be done very easily, if Mary joins you," replied the young man; "but I have been thinking that if you ask her to sign any deed, it might as well be one assigning over her interest absolutely to you. Aspenly does not want a penny with her—in fact, from what fell from him to-day, when I met him in town, I'm inclined to think he believes that she has not a penny in the world; so she may as well make it over to you, and then we can turn it all into money when and how we please. I desired Craven to work night and day at the deeds, and have them over by ten o'clock to-morrow morning."

"You did quite rightly," rejoined the old gentleman. "I hardly expect any opposition from the girl—at least no more than I can easily frighten her out of. Should she prove sulky, however, I do not well know where to turn: as to asking my brother Oliver, I might as well, or better, ask a Jew broker; he hates me and mine with his whole heart; and to say the truth, there is not much love lost between us. No, no, there's nothing to be looked for in that quarter. I daresay we'll manage one way or another—lead or drive to get Mary to sign the deed, and if so, the ship rights again. Craven comes, you say, at ten to-morrow?"

"He engaged to be here at that hour with the deeds," repeated the young man.

"Well," said his father, yawning, "you have nothing more to say, nor I neither—oblige me by withdrawing." So parted these congenial relations.

The past day had been an agitating one to Mary Ashwoode. Still suspense was to be her doom, and the same alternations of hope and of despair were again to rob her pillow of repose; yet even thus, happy was she in comparison with what she must have been, had she but known the schemes of which she was the unconscious subject. At this juncture we shall leave the actors in this true tale, and conclude the chapter with the close of day.

## CHAPTER XIII

THE INTERVIEW—THE PARCHMENT—AND THE NOBLEMAN'S COACH.

Sir Richard Ashwoode had never in the whole course of his life denied himself the indulgence of any passion or of any whim. From his childhood upward he had never considered the feelings or comforts of any living being but himself alone. As he advanced in life, this selfishness had improved to a degree of hardness and coldness so intense, that if ever he had felt a kindly impulse at any moment in his existence, the very remembrance of it had entirely faded from his mind: so that generosity, compassion, and natural affection were to him not only unknown, but incredible. To him mankind seemed all either fools, or such as he himself was. Without one particle of principle of any kind, he had uniformly maintained in the world the character of an honourable man. The ordinary rules of honesty and morality he regarded as so many conventional sentiments, to which every gentleman subscribed, as a matter of course, in public, but which in private he had an unquestionable right to dispense with at his own convenience. He was imperious, fiery, and unforgiving to the uttermost; but when he conceived it advantageous to do so, he could practise as well as any man the convenient art of masking malignity, hatred, and inveteracy behind the pleasantest of all pleasant smiles. Capable of any secret meanness for the sake of the smallest advantage to be gained by it, he was yet full of fierce and overbearing pride; and although this world was all in all to him, yet there never breathed a man who could on the slightest provocation risk his life in mortal combat with more alacrity and absolute sang froid than Sir Richard Ashwoode. In his habits he was unboundedly luxurious—in his expenditure prodigal to recklessness. His own and his son's extravagance, which he had indulged from a kind of pride, was now, however, beginning to make itself sorely felt in formidable and rapidly accumulating pecuniary embarrassments. These had served to embitter and exasperate a temper which at the best had never been a very sweet one, and of whose ordinary pitch the reader may form an estimate, when he hears that in the short glimpses which he has had of Sir Richard, the baronet happened to be, owing to the circumstances with which we have acquainted him, in extraordinarily good humour.

Sir Richard had not married young; and when he did marry it was to pay his debts. The lady of his choice was beautiful, accomplished, and an heiress; and, won by his agreeability, and by his well-assumed devotedness and passion, she yielded to the pressure of his suit. They were married, and she gave birth successively to a son and a daughter. Sir Richard's temper, as we have hinted, was not very placid, nor his habits very domestic; nevertheless, the world thought the match (putting his money difficulties out of the question) a very suitable and a very desirable one, and took it for granted that the gay baronet and his lady were just as happy as a fashionable man and wife ought to be—and perhaps they were so; but, for all that, it happened that at the end of some four years the young wife died of a broken heart. Some strange scenes, it is said, followed between Sir Richard and the brother of the deceased lady, Oliver French. It is believed that this gentleman suspected the cause of Lady Ashwoode's death—at all events he had ascertained that she had not been kindly used, and after one or two interviews with the baronet, in which bitter words were exchanged, the matter ended in a fierce and bloodily contested duel, in which the baronet received three desperate wounds. His recovery was long doubtful; but life burns strongly in some breasts; and, contrary to the desponding predictions of his surgeons, the valuable life of Sir Richard Ashwoode was prolonged to his family and friends.

Since then, Sir Richard had by different agencies sought to bring about a reconciliation with his brother-in-law, but without the smallest success. Oliver French was a bachelor, and a very wealthy one. Moreover, he had it in his power to dispose of his lands and money just as he pleased. These circumstances had strongly impressed Sir Richard with a conviction that quarrels among relations are not only unseemly, but un-Christian. He was never in a more forgiving and forgetting mood. He was willing even to make concessions—anything that could be reasonably asked of him, and even more, he was ready to do—but all in vain. Oliver was obdurate. He knew his man well. He saw and appreciated the baronet's motives, and hated and despised him ten thousand times more than ever.

Repulsed in his first attempt, Sir Richard resolved to give his adversary time to cool a little; and accordingly, after a lapse of twelve or fourteen years, his son Henry being then a handsome lad, he wrote to his brother-in-law a very long and touching epistle, in which he proposed to send his son down to Ardgillagh, the place where the alienated relative resided, with a portrait of his deceased lady, which, of course, with no object less sacred, and to no relative less near and respected, could he have induced himself to part. This, too, was a total failure. Oliver French, Esquire, wrote back a very succinct epistle, but one very full of unpleasant meaning. He said that the portrait would be odious to him, inasmuch as it would be necessarily associated in his mind with a marriage which had killed his sister, and with persons whom he abhorred—that therefore he would not allow it into his house. He stated, that to the motives which prompted his attention he was wide awake—that he was, however, perfectly determined that no person bearing the name or the blood of Sir Richard Ashwoode should ever have one penny of his; adding, that the baronet could leave his son, Mr. Henry Ashwoode, quite enough for a gentleman to live upon respectably; and that, at all events, in his father's virtues the young gentleman would inherit a legacy such as would insure him universal respect, and a general welcome wherever he might happen to go, excepting only one locality, called Ardgillagh.

With the failure of this last attempt, of course, disappeared every hope of success with the rich old bachelor; and the forgiving baronet was forced to content himself, in the absence of all more substantial rewards, with the consciousness of having done what was, under all the circumstances, the most Christian thing he could have done, as well as played the most knowing game, though unsuccessful, which he could have played.

Sir Richard Ashwoode limped downstairs to receive his intended son-in-law, Lord Aspenly, on the day following the events which we have detailed in our last and the preceding chapters. That nobleman had intimated his intention to be with Sir Richard about noon. It was now little more than ten, and the baronet was, nevertheless, restless and fidgety. The room he occupied was a large parlour, commanding a view of the approach to the house. Again and again he consulted his watch, and as often hobbled over, as well as he could, to the window, where he gazed in evident discontent down the long, straight avenue, with its double row of fine old giant lime-trees.

"Nearly half-past ten," muttered Sir Richard, to himself, for at his desire he had been left absolutely alone—"ay, fully half-past, and the fellow not come yet. No less than, two notes since eight this morning, both of them with gratuitous mendacity renewing the appointment for ten o'clock; and ten o'clock comes and goes, and half-an-hour more along with it, and still no sign of Mr. Craven. If I had fixed ten o'clock to pay his accursed, unconscionable bill of costs, he'd have been prowling about the grounds from sunrise, and pounced upon me before the last stroke of the clock had sounded."

While thus the baronet was engaged in muttering his discontent, and venting secret imprecations on the whole race of attorneys, a vehicle rolled up to the hall-door. The bell pealed, and the knocker thundered, and in a moment a servant entered, and announced Mr. Craven—a square-built man of low stature, wearing his own long, grizzled hair instead of a wig—having a florid complexion, hooked nose, beetle brows, and long-cut, Jewish, black eyes, set close under the bridge of his nose—who stepped with a velvet tread into the room. An unvarying smile sate upon his thin lips, and about his whole air and manner there was a certain indescribable sanctimoniousness, which was rather enhanced by the puritanical plainness of his attire.

"Sir Richard, I beg pardon—rather late, I fear," said he, in a dulcet, insinuating tone—"hard work, nevertheless, I do assure you—ninety-seven skins—splendidly engrossed—quite a treat—five of my young men up all night—I have got one of them outside to witness it along with me. Some reading in the thing, I promise you; but I hope—I do hope, I am not very late?"

"Not at all—not at all, my dear Mr. Craven," said Sir Richard, with his most engaging smile; for, as we have hinted, "dear Mr. Craven" had not made the science of conveyancing peculiarly cheap in practice to the baronet, who accordingly owed him more costs than it would have been quite convenient to pay upon a short notice—"I'll just, with your assistance, glance through these parchments, though to do so be but a matter of form. Pray take a chair beside me—there. Now then to business."

Accordingly to business they went. Practice, they say, makes perfect, and the baronet had had, unfortunately for himself, a great deal of it in such matters during the course of his life. He knew how to read a deed as well as the most experienced counsel at the Irish bar, and was able consequently to detect with wonderfully little rummaging and fumbling in the ninety-seven skins of closely written verbiage, the seven lines of sense which they enveloped. Little more than half-an-hour had therefore satisfied Sir Richard that the mass of parchment before him, after reciting with very considerable accuracy the deeds and process by which the lands of Glenvarlogh were settled upon his daughter, went on to state that for and in consideration of the sum of five shillings, good and lawful money, she, being past the age of twenty-one, in every possible phrase and by every word which tautology could accumulate, handed over the said lands, absolutely to her father, Sir Richard Ashwoode, Bart., of Morley Court, in the county of Dublin, to have, and to hold, and to make ducks and drakes of, to the end of time, constantly affirming at the end of every sentence that she was led to do all this for and in consideration of the sum of five shillings, good and lawful money. As soon as Sir Richard had seen all this, which was, as we have said, in little more than half-an-hour, he pulled the bell, and courteously informing Mr. Craven, the immortal author of the interesting document which he had just perused, that he would find chocolate and other refreshments in the library, and intimating that he would perhaps disturb him in about ten minutes, he consigned that gentleman to the guidance of the servant, whom he also directed to summon Miss Ashwoode to his presence.

"Her signing this deed," thought he, as he awaited her arrival, "will make her absolutely dependent upon me—it will make rebellion, resistance, murmuring, impossible; she then must do as I would have her, or—Ah? my dear child," exclaimed the baronet, as his daughter entered the room, addressing her in the sweetest imaginable voice, and instantaneously dismissing the sinister menace which had sat upon his countenance, and clothing it instead as suddenly with an absolute radiance of affection, "come here and kiss me and sit down by my side—are you well to-day? you look pale—you smile—well, well! it cannot be anything very bad. You shall run out just now with Emily. But first, I must talk with you for a little, and, strange enough, on business too." The old gentleman paused for an instant to arrange the order of his address, and then continued. "Mary, I will tell you frankly more of my affairs than I have told to almost any person breathing. In my early days, and indeed after my marriage, I was far, far too careless in money matters. I involved myself considerably, and owing to various circumstances, tiresome now to dwell upon, I have never been able to extricate myself from these difficulties. Henry too, your brother, is fearfully prodigal—fearfully; and has within the last three or four years enormously aggravated my embarrassments, and of course multiplied my anxieties most grievously, most distractingly. I feel that my spirits are gone, my health declining, and, worse than all, my temper, yes—my temper soured. You do not know, you cannot know, how bitterly I feel, with what intense pain, and sorrow, and contrition, and—and remorse, I reflect upon those bursts of ill-temper, of acrimony, of passion, to which, spite of every resistance, I am becoming every day more and more prone." Here the baronet paused to call up a look of compunctious anguish, an effort in which he was considerably assisted by an acute twinge in his great toe.

"Yes," he continued, when the pain had subsided, "I am now growing old, I am breaking very fast, sinking, I feel it—I cannot be very long a trouble to anybody—embarrassments are closing around me on all sides—I have not the means of extricating myself—despondency, despair have come upon me, and with them loss of spirits, loss of health, of strength, of everything which makes life a blessing; and, all these privations rendered more horrible, more agonizing, by the reflection that my ill-humour, my peevish temper, are continually taxing the patience, wounding the feelings, perhaps alienating the affections of those who are nearest and dearest to me."

Here the baronet became very much affected; but, lest his agitation should be seen, he turned his head away, while he grasped his daughter's hand convulsively: the poor girl covered his with kisses. He had wrung her very heart.

"There is one course," continued he, "by adopting which I might extricate myself from all my difficulties"—here he raised his eyes with a haggard expression, and glared wildly along the cornice—"but I confess I have great hesitation in leaving you."

He wrung her hand very hard, and groaned slightly.

"Father, dear father," said she, "do not speak thus—do not—you frighten me."

"I was wrong, my dear child, to tell you of struggles of which none but myself ought to have known anything," said the baronet, gloomily. "One person indeed has the power to assist, I may say, to save me."

"And who is that person, father?" asked the girl.

"Yourself," replied Sir Richard, emphatically.

"How?—I!" said she, turning very pale, for a dreadful suspicion crossed her mind—"how can I help you, father?"

The old gentleman explained briefly; and the girl, relieved of her worst fears, started joyously from her seat, clapped her hands together with gladness, and, throwing her arms about her father's neck, exclaimed,—

"And is that all?—oh, father; why did you defer telling me so long? you ought to have known how delighted I would have been to do anything for you; indeed you ought; tell them to get the papers ready immediately."

"They are ready, my dear," said Sir Richard, recovering his self-possession wonderfully, and ringing the bell with a good deal of hurry—for he fully acknowledged the wisdom of the old proverb, which inculcates the expediency of striking while the iron's hot—"your brother had them prepared yesterday, I believe. Inform Mr. Craven," he continued, addressing the servant, "that I would be very glad to see him now, and say he may as well bring in the young gentleman who has accompanied him."

Mr. Craven accordingly appeared, and the "young gentleman," who had but one eye, and a very seedy coat, entered along with him. The latter personage bustled about a good deal, slapped the deeds very emphatically down on the table, and rumpled the parchments sonorously, looked about for pen and ink, set a chair before the document, and then held one side of the parchment, while Mr. Craven screwed his knuckles down upon the other, and the parties forthwith signed; whereupon Mr. Craven and the one-eyed young gentleman both sat down, and began to sign away with a great deal of scratching and flourishing on the places allotted for witnesses; after all which, Mr. Craven, raising himself with a smile, told Miss Ashwoode, facetiously, that the Chancellor could not have done so much for the deed as she had done; and the one-eyed young gentleman held his nose contemplatively between his finger and thumb, and reviewed the signatures with his solitary optic.

Miss Ashwoode then withdrew, and Mr. Craven and the "young gentleman" made their bows. Sir Richard beckoned to Mr. Craven, and he glided back and closed the door, having commanded the "young gentleman" to see if the coach was ready.

"You see, Mr. Craven," said Sir Richard, who, spite of all his philosophy, felt a little ashamed even that the attorney should have seen the transaction which had just been completed—"you see, sir, I may as well tell you candidly: my daughter, who has just signed this deed, is about immediately to be married to Lord Aspenly; he kindly offered to lend me some fifteen thousand pounds, or thereabouts, and I converted this offer (which I, of course, accepted), into the assignment, from his bride, that is to be, of this little property, giving, of course, to his lordship my personal security for the debt which I consider as owed to him: this arrangement his lordship preferred as the most convenient possible. I thought it right, in strict confidence, of course, to explain the real state of the case to you, as at first sight the thing looks selfish, and I do not wish to stand worse in my friends' books than I actually deserve to do." This was spoken with Sir Richard's most engaging smile, and Mr. Craven smiled in return, most artlessly—at the same time he mentally ejaculated, "damned sly!" "You'll bring this security, my dear Mr. Craven," continued the baronet, "into the market with all dispatch—do you think you can manage twenty thousand upon it?"

"I fear not more than fourteen, or perhaps, sixteen, with an effort. I do not think Glenvarlogh would carry much more—I fear not; but rely upon me, Sir Richard; I'll do everything that can be done—at all events, I'll lose no time about it, depend upon it—I may as well take this deed along with me—I have the rest; and title is very—very satisfactory—good-morning, Sir Richard," and the man of parchments withdrew, leaving Sir Richard in a more benevolent mood than he had experienced for many a long day.

The attorney had not been many seconds gone, when a second vehicle thundered up to the door, and a perfect storm of knocking and ringing announced the arrival of Lord Aspenly himself.

CHAPTER XIV.

ABOUT A CERTAIN GARDEN AND A DAMSEL—AND ALSO CONCERNING A LETTER AND A RED LEATHERN BOX.

Several days passed smoothly away—Lord Aspenly was a perfect paragon of politeness; but although his manner invariably assumed a peculiar tenderness whenever he approached Miss Ashwoode, yet that young lady remained in happy ignorance of his real intentions. She saw before her a grotesque old fop, who might without any extraordinary parental precocity have very easily been her grandfather, and in his airs and graces, his rappee and his rouge (for his lordship condescended to borrow a few attractions from art), and in the thousand-and-one et ceteras of foppery which were accumulated, with great exactitude and precision, on and about his little person, she beheld nothing more than so many indications of obstinate and inveterate celibacy, and, of course, interpreted the exquisite attentions which were meant to enchain her young heart, merely as so much of that formal target practice in love's archery, in which gallant single gentlemen of seventy, or thereabout, will sometimes indulge themselves. Emily Copland, however, at a glance, saw and understood the nature of Lord Aspenly's attentions, and she saw just as clearly the intended parts and the real position of the other actors in this somewhat ill-assorted drama, and thereupon she took counsel with herself, like a wise damsel, and arrived at the conclusion, that with some little management she might, very possibly, play her own cards to advantage among them.

We must here, however, glance for a few minutes at some of the subordinate agents in our narrative, whose interposition, nevertheless, deeply, as well as permanently, affected the destinies of more important personages.

It was the habit of the beautiful Mistress Betsy Carey, every morning, weather permitting, to enjoy a ramble in the grounds of Morley Court; and as chance (of course it was chance) would have it, this early ramble invariably led her through several quiet fields, and over a stile, into a prettily-situated, but neglected flower-garden, which was now, however, undergoing a thorough reform, according to the Dutch taste, under the presiding inspiration of Tobias Potts. Now Tobias Potts was a widower, having been in the course of his life twice disencumbered. The last Mrs. Potts had disappeared some five winters since, and Tobias was now well stricken in years; he possessed the eyes of an owl, and the complexion of a turkey-cock, and was, moreover, extremely hard of hearing, and, withal, a man of few words; he was, however, hale, upright, and burly—perfectly sound in wind and limb, and free from vice and children—had a snug domicile, consisting of two rooms and a loft, enjoyed a comfortable salary, and had, it was confidently rumoured, put by a good round sum of money somewhere or other. It therefore struck Mrs. Carey very forcibly, that to be Mrs. Potts was a position worth attaining; and accordingly, without incurring any suspicion—for the young women generally regarded Potts with awe, and the young men with contempt—she began, according to the expressive phrase in such case made and provided, to set her cap at Tobias.

In this, his usual haunt, she discovered the object of her search, busily employed in superintending the construction of a terrace walk, and issuing his orders with the brevity, decision, and clearness of a consummate gardener.

"Good-morning, Mr. Potts," said the charming Betsy. Mr. Potts did not hear. "Good-morning, Mr. Potts," repeated the damsel, raising her voice to a scream.

Tobias touched his hat with a gruff acknowledgment.

"Well, but how beautiful you are doing it," shouted the handmaid again, gazing rapturously upon the red earthen rampart, in which none but the eye of an artist could have detected the rudiments of a terrace, "it's wonderful neat, all must allow, and indeed it puzzles my head to think how you can think of it all; it is now, raly elegant, so it is."

Tobias did not reply, and the maiden continued, with a sentimental air, and still hallooing at the top of her voice—

"Well, of all the trades that is—and big and little, there's a plenty of them—there's none I'd choose, if I was a man, before the trade of a gardener."

"No, you would not, I'm sure," was the laconic reply.

"Oh, but I declare and purtest I would though," bawled the young woman; "for gardeners, old or young, is always so good-humoured, and pleasant, and fresh-like. Oh, dear, but I would like to be a gardener."

"Not an old one, howsomever," growled Mr. Potts.

"Yes, but I would though, I declare and purtest to goodness gracious," persisted the nymph; "I'd rather of the two perfer to be an old gardener" (this was a bold stroke of oratory; but Potts did not hear it); "I'd rather be an old gardener," she screamed a second time; "I'd rather be an old gardener of the two, so I would."

"That's more than I would," replied Potts, very abruptly, and with an air of uncommon asperity, for he silently cherished a lingering belief in his own juvenility, and not the less obstinately that it was fast becoming desperate—a peculiarity of which, unfortunately, until that moment the damsel had never been apprised. This, therefore, was a turn which a good deal disconcerted the young woman, especially as she thought she detected a satirical leer upon the countenance of a young man in crazy inexpressibles, who was trundling a wheelbarrow in the immediate vicinity; she accordingly exclaimed not loud enough for Tobias, but quite loud enough for the young man in the infirm breeches to hear,—

"What an old fool. I purtest it's meat and drink to me to tease him—so it is;" and with a forced giggle she tripped lightly away to retrace her steps towards the house.

As she approached the stile we have mentioned, she thought she distinguished what appeared to be the inarticulate murmurings of some subterranean voice almost beneath her feet. A good deal startled at so prodigious a phenomenon, she stopped short, and immediately heard the following brief apostrophe delivered in a rich brogue:—

"Aiqually beautiful and engaging—vartuous Betsy Carey—listen to the voice of tindher emotion."

The party addressed looked with some alarm in all directions for any visible intimation of the speaker's presence, but in vain. At length, from among an unusually thick and luxuriant tuft of docks and other weeds, which grew at the edge of a ditch close by, she beheld something red emerging, which in a few moments she clearly perceived to be the classical countenance of Larry Toole.

"The Lord purtect us all, Mr. Toole. Why in the world do you frighten people this way?" ejaculated the nymph, rather shrilly.

"Whist! most evangelical iv women," exclaimed Larry in a low key, and looking round suspiciously—"whisht! or we are ruined."

"La! Mr. Laurence, what are you after?" rejoined the damsel, with a good deal of asperity. "I'll have you to know I'm not used to talk with a man that's squat in a ditch, and his head in a dock plant. That's not the way for to come up to an honest woman, sir—no more it is."

"I'd live ten years in a ditch, and die in a dock plant," replied Larry with enthusiasm, "for one sight iv you."

"And is that what brought you here?" replied she, with a toss of her head. "I purtest some people's quite overbearing, so they are, and knows no bounds."

"Stop a minute, most beautiful bayin'—for one instant minute pay attintion," exclaimed Mr. Toole, eagerly, for he perceived that she had commenced her retreat. "Tare an' owns! divine crature, it's not goin' you are?"

"I have no notions, good or bad, Mr. Toole," replied the young lady, with great volubility and dignity, "and no idaya in the wide world for to be standing here prating, and talking, and losing my time with such as you—if my business is neglected, it is not on your back the blame will light. I have my work, and my duty, and my business to mind, and if I do not mind them, no one else will do it for me; and I am astonished and surprised beyant telling, so I am, at the impittence of some people, thinking that the likes of me has nothing else to be doing but listening to them discoorsing in a dirty ditch, and more particular when their conduct has been sich as some people's that is old enough at any rate to know better."

The fair handmaiden had now resumed her retreat; so that Larry, having raised himself from his lowly hiding-place, was obliged to follow for some twenty yards before he again came up with her.

"Wait one half second—stop a bit, for the Lord's sake," exclaimed he, with most earnest energy.

"Well, wonst for all, Mr. Laurence," exclaimed Mistress Carey severely, "what is your business with me?"

"Jist this," rejoined Larry, with a mysterious wink, and lowering his voice—"a letter to the young mistress from"—here he glanced jealously round, and then bringing himself close beside her, he whispered in her ear—"from Mr. O'Connor—whisht—not a word—into her own hand, mind."

The young woman took the letter, read the superscription, and forthwith placed it in her bosom, and rearranged her kerchief.

"Never fear—never fear," said she, "Miss Mary shall have it in half an hour. And how," added she, maliciously, "is Mr. O'Connor? He is a lovely gentleman, is not he?"

"He's uncommonly well in health, the Lord be praised," replied Mr. Toole, with very unaccountable severity.

"Well, for my part," continued the girl, "I never seen the man yet to put beside him—unless, indeed, the young master may be. He's a very pretty young man—and so shocking agreeable."

Mr. Toole nodded a pettish assent, coughed, muttered something to himself, and then inquired when he should come for an answer.

"I'll have an answer to-morrow morning—maybe this evening," pursued she; "but do not be coming so close up to the house. Who knows who might be on our backs in an instant here? I'll walk down whenever I get it to the two mulberries at the old gate; and I'll go there either in the morning at this hour, or else a little before supper-time in the evening."

Mr. Toole, having gazed rapturously at the object of his tenderest aspirations during the delivery of this address, was at its termination so far transported by his feelings, as absolutely to make a kind of indistinct and flurried attempt to kiss her.

"Well, I purtest, this is overbearing," exclaimed the virgin; and at the same time bestowing Mr. Toole a sound box on the ear, she tripped lightly toward the house, leaving her admirer a prey to what are usually termed conflicting emotions.

When Sir Richard returned to his dressing-room at about noon, to prepare for dinner, he had hardly walked to the toilet, and rung for his Italian servant, when a knock was heard at his chamber door, and, in obedience to his summons, Mistress Carey entered.

"Well, Carey," inquired the baronet, as soon as she had appeared, "do you bring me any news?"

The lady's-maid closed the door carefully.

"News?" she repeated. "Indeed, but I do, Sir Richard—and bad news, I'm afeard, sir. Mr. O'Connor has written a great long letter to my mistress, if you please, sir."

"Have you gotten it?" inquired the baronet, quickly.

"Yes, sir," rejoined she, "safe and sound here in my breast, Sir Richard."

"Your young mistress has not opened it—or read it?" inquired he.

"Oh, dear! Sir Richard, it is after all you said to me only the other day," rejoined she, in virtuous horror. "I hope I know my place better than to be fetching and carrying notes and letters, and all soarts, unnonst to my master. Don't I know, sir, very well how that you're the best judge what's fitting and what isn't for the sight of your own precious child? and wouldn't I be very unnatural, and very hardened and ungrateful, if I was to be making secrets in the family, and if any ill-will or misfortunes was to come out of it? I purtest I never—never would forgive myself—never—no more I ought—never."

Here Mistress Carey absolutely wept.

"Give me the letter," said Sir Richard, drily.

The damsel handed it to him; and he, having glanced at the seal and the address, deposited the document safely in a small leathern box which stood upon his toilet, and having locked it safely therein, he turned to the maid, and patting her on the cheek with a smile, he remarked,—

"Be a good girl, Carey, and you shall find you have consulted your interest best."

Here Mistress Carey was about to do justice to her own disinterestedness in a very strong protestation, but the baronet checked her with an impatient wave of the hand, and continued,—

"Say not on any account one word to any person touching this letter, until you have your directions from me. Stay—this will buy you a ribbon. Good-bye—be a good girl."

So saying, the baronet placed a guinea in the girl's hand, which, with a courtesy, having transferred to her pocket, she withdrew rather hurriedly, for she heard the valet in the next room.

CHAPTER XV.

THE TRAITOR.

Upon the day following, O'Connor had not yet received any answer to his letter. He was, however, not a little surprised instead to receive a second visit from young Ashwoode.

"I am very glad, my dear O'Connor," said the young man as he entered, "to have found you alone. I have been wishing very much for this opportunity, and was half afraid as I came upstairs that I should again have been disappointed. The fact is, I wish much to speak to you upon a subject of great difficulty and delicacy—one in which, however, I naturally feel so strong an interest, that I may speak to you upon it, and freely, too, without impertinence. I allude to your attachment to my sister. Do not imagine, my dear O'Connor, that I am going to lecture you on prudence and all that; and above all, my dear fellow, do not think I want to tax your confidence more deeply than you are willing I should; I know quite enough for all I would suggest; I know the plain fact that you love my sister—I have long known it, and this is enough."

"Well, sir, what follows?" said O'Connor, dejectedly.

"Do not call me sir—call me friend—fellow—fool—anything you please but that," replied Ashwoode, kindly; and after a brief pause, he continued: "I need not, and cannot disguise it from you, that I was much opposed to this, and vexed extremely at the girl's encouragement of what I considered a most imprudent suit. I have, however, learned to think differently—very differently. After all my littlenesses and pettishness, for which you must have, if not abhorred, at least despised me from your very heart—after all this, I say, your noble conduct in risking your own life to save my worthless blood is what I never can enough admire, and honour, and thank." Here he grasped O'Connor's hand, and shook it warmly. "After this, I tell you, O'Connor, that were there offered to me, on my sister's behoof, on the one side the most brilliant alliance in wealth and rank that ever ambition dreamed of, and upon the other side this hand of yours, I would, so heaven is my witness, forego every allurement of titles, rank, and riches, and give my sister to you. I have come here, O'Connor, frankly to offer you my aid and advice—to prove to you my sincerity, and, if possible, to realize your wishes."

O'Connor could hardly believe his senses. Here was the man who, scarcely six days since, he felt assured, would more readily have suffered him to thrust him through the body than consent to his marriage with Mary Ashwoode, now not merely consenting to it, but offering cordially and spontaneously all the assistance in his power towards effecting that very object. Had he heard him aright? One look at his expressive face—the kindly pressure of his hand—everything assured him that he had justly comprehended all that Ashwoode had spoken, and a glow of hope, warmer than had visited him for years, cheered his heart.

"In the meantime," continued Ashwoode, "I must tell you exactly how matters stand at Morley Court. The Earl of Aspenly, of whom you may have heard, is paying his addresses to my sister."

"The Earl of Aspenly," echoed O'Connor, slightly colouring. "I had not heard of this before—she did not name him."

"Yet she has known it a good while," returned Ashwoode, with well-affected surprise—"a month, I believe, or more. He's now at Morley Court, and means to make some stay—are you sure she never mentioned him?"

"Titled, and, of course, rich," said O'Connor, scarce hearing the question. "Why should I have heard of this by chance, and from another—why this reserve—this silence?"

"Nay, nay," replied Henry, "you must not run away with the matter thus. Mary may have forgotten it, or—or not liked to tell you—not cared to give you needless uneasiness."

"I wish she had—I wish she had—I am—I am, indeed, Ashwoode, very, very unhappy," said O'Connor, with extreme dejection. "Forgive me—forgive my folly, since folly it seems—I fear I weary you."

"Well, well, since it seems you have not heard of it," rejoined Henry, carelessly throwing himself back in his chair, "you may as well learn it now—not that there is any real cause of alarm in the matter, as I shall presently show you, but simply that you may understand the position of the enemy. Lord Aspenly, then, is at present at Morley Court, where he is received as Mary's lover—observe me, only as her lover—not yet, and I trust never as her accepted lover."

"Go on—pray go on," said O'Connor, with suppressed but agonized anxiety.

"Now, though my father is very hot about the match," resumed his visitor, "it may appear strange enough to you that I never was. There are a few—a very few—advantages in the matter, of course, viewing it merely in its worldly aspect. But Lord Aspenly's property is a good deal embarrassed, and he is of violently Whig politics and connections, the very thing most hated by my old Tory uncle, Oliver French, whom my father has been anxious to cultivate; besides, the disparity in years is so very great that it is ridiculous—I might almost say indecent—and this even in point of family standing, and indeed of reputation, putting aside every better consideration, is objectionable. I have urged all these things upon my father, and perhaps we should not find any insurmountable obstacle there; but the fact is, there is another difficulty, one of which until this morning I never dreamed—the most whimsical difficulty imaginable." Here the young man raised his eyebrows, and laughed faintly, while he looked upon the floor, and O'Connor, with increasing earnestness, implored him to proceed. "It appears so very absurd and perverse an obstacle," continued Ashwoode, with a very quizzical expression, "that one does not exactly know how to encounter it—to say the truth, I think that the girl is a little—perhaps the least imaginable degree—taken—dazzled—caught by the notion of being a countess; it's very natural, you know, but then I would have expected better from her."

"By heavens, it is impossible!" exclaimed O'Connor, starting to his feet; "I cannot believe it; you must, indeed, my dear Ashwoode, you must have been deceived."

"Well, then," rejoined the young man, "I have lost my skill in reading young ladies' minds—that's all; but even though I should be right—and never believe me if I am not right—it does not follow that the giddy whim won't pass away just as suddenly as it came; her most lasting impressions—with, I should hope, one exception—were never very enduring. I have been talking to her for nearly half an hour this morning—laughing with her about Lord Aspenly's suit, and building castles in the air about what she will and what she won't do when she's a countess. But, by the way, how did you let her know that you intend returning to France at the end of this month, only, as she told me, however, for a few weeks? She mentioned it yesterday incidentally. Well, it is a comfort that I hear your secrets, though you won't entrust them to me. But do not, my dear fellow—do not look so very black—you very much overrate the firmness of women's minds, and greatly indeed exaggerate that of my sister's character if you believe that this vexatious whim which has entered her giddy pate will remain there longer than a week. The simple fact is that the excitement and bustle of all this has produced an unusual flow of high spirits, which will, of course, subside with the novelty of the occasion. Pshaw! why so cast down?—there is nothing in the matter to surprise one—the caprice of women knows do rule. I tell you I would almost stake my reputation as a prophet, that when this giddy excitement passes away, her feelings will return to their old channel." O'Connor still paced the room in silence. "Meanwhile," continued the young man, "if anything occur to you—if I can be useful to you in any way, command me absolutely, and till you see me next, take heart of grace." He grasped O'Connor's hand—it was cold as clay; and bidding him farewell, once more took his departure.

"Well," thought he, as he threw his leg across his high-bred gelding at the inn door, "I have shot the first shaft home."

And so he had, for the heart at which it was directed, unfenced by suspicion, lay open to his traitorous practices. O'Connor's letter, an urgent and a touching one, was still unanswered; it never for a moment crossed his mind that it had not reached the hand for which it was intended. The maid who had faithfully delivered all the letters which had passed between them had herself received it; and young Ashwoode had but the moment before mentioned, from his sister's lips, the subject on which it was written—his meditated departure for France. This, too, it appeared, she had spoken of in the midst of gay and light-hearted trilling, and projects of approaching magnificence and dissipation with his rich and noble rival. Twice since the delivery of that letter had his servant seen Miss Ashwoode's maid; and in the communicative colloquy which had ensued she had told—no doubt according to well-planned instructions—how gay and unusually merry her mistress was, and how she passed whole hours at her toilet, and the rest of her time in the companionship of Lord Aspenly—so that between his lordship's society, and her own preparations for it, she had scarcely allowed herself time to read the letter in question, much less to answer it.

All these things served to fill O'Connor's mind with vague but agonizing doubts—doubts which he vainly strove to combat; fears which had not their birth in an alarmed imagination, but which, alas! were but too surely approved by reason. The notion of a systematic plot, embracing so many agents, and conducted with such deep and hellish hypocrisy, with the sole purpose of destroying affections the most beautiful, and of alienating hearts the truest, was a thought so monstrous and unnatural that it never for a second flashed upon his mind; still his heart struggled strongly against despair. Spite of all that looked gloomy in what he saw—spite of the boding suggestions of his worst fears, he would not believe her false to him—that she who had so long and so well loved and trusted him—she whose gentle heart he knew unchanged and unchilled by years, and distance, and misfortunes—that she should, after all, have fallen away from him, and given up that heart, which once was his, to vanity and the hollow glitter of the world—this he could hardly bring himself to believe, yet what was he to think? alas! what?

CHAPTER XVI.

SHOWING SIGNOR PARUCCI ALONE WITH THE WIG-BLOCKS—THE BARONET'S HAND-BELL AND THE ITALIAN'S TASK.

Morley Court was a queer old building—very large and very irregular. The main part of the dwelling, and what appeared to be the original nucleus, upon which after-additions had grown like fantastic incrustations, was built of deep-red brick, with many recesses and projections and gables, and tall and grotesquely-shaped chimneys, and having broad, jutting, heavily-sashed windows, such as belonged to Henry the Eighth's time, to which period the origin of the building was, with sufficient probability, referred. The great avenue, which extended in a direct line to more than the long half of an Irish mile, led through double rows of splendid old lime-trees, some thirty paces apart, and arching in a vast and shadowy groining overhead, to the front of the building. To the rearward extended the rambling additions which necessity or caprice had from time to time suggested, as the place, in the lapse of years, passed into the hands of different masters. One of these excrescences, a quaint little prominence, with a fanciful gable and chimney of its own, jutted pleasantly out upon the green sward, courting the friendly shelter of the wild and graceful trees, and from its casement commanding through the parting boughs no views but those of quiet fields, distant woodlands, and the far-off blue hills. This portion of the building contained in the upper story one small room, to the full as oddly shaped as the outer casing of fantastic masonry in which it was inclosed—the door opened upon a back staircase which led from the lower apartments to Sir Richard's dressing-room; and partly owing to this convenient arrangement, and partly perhaps to the comfort and seclusion of the chamber itself, it had been long appropriated to the exclusive occupation of Signor Jacopo Parucci, Sir Richard's valet and confidential servant. This man was, as his name would imply, an Italian. Sir Richard had picked him up, some thirty years before the period at which we have dated our story, in Naples, where it was said the baronet had received from him very important instructions in the inner mysteries of that golden science which converts chance into certainty—a science in which Sir Richard was said to have become a masterly proficient; and indeed so loudly had fame begun to bruit his excellence therein, that he found it at last necessary, or at least highly advisable, to forego the fascinations of the gaming-table, and to bid to the worship of fortune an eternal farewell, just at the moment when the fickle goddess promised with golden profusion to reward his devotion.

Whatever his reason was, Sir Richard had been to this man a good master; he had, it was said, and not without reason, enriched him; and, moreover, it was a strange fact, that in all his capricious and savage moods, from whose consequences not only his servants but his own children had no exemption, he had never once treated this person otherwise than with the most marked civility. What the man's services had actually been, and to what secret influence he owed the close and confidential terms upon which he unquestionably stood with Sir Richard, these things were mysteries, and, of course, furnished inexhaustible matter of scandalous speculation among the baronet's dependents and most intimate friends.

The room of which we speak was Parucci's snuggery. It contained in a recess behind the door that gentleman's bed—a plain, low, uncurtained couch; and variously disposed about the apartment an abundance of furniture of much better kind; the recess of the window was filled by a kind of squat press, which was constructed in the lower part, and which contained, as certain adventurous chambermaids averred, having peeped into its dim recesses when some precious opportunity presented itself, among other shadowy shapes, the forms of certain flasks and bottles with long necks, and several tall glasses of different dimensions. Two or three tables of various sizes of dark shining wood, with legs after the fashion of the nether limbs of hippogriffs and fauns, seemed about to walk from their places, and to stamp and claw at random about the floor. A large, old press of polished oak, with spiral pillars of the same flanking it in front, contained the more precious articles of Signor Parucci's wardrobe. Close beside it, in a small recess, stood a set of shelves, on which were piled various matters, literary and otherwise, among which perhaps none were disturbed twice in the year, with the exception of six or eight packs of cards, with which, for old associations' sake, Signor Jacopo used to amuse himself now and again in his solitary hours.

On one of the tables stood two blocks supporting each a flowing black peruke, which it was almost the only duty of the tenant of this interesting sanctuary to tend, and trim, and curl. Upon the dusky tapestry were pinned several coloured prints, somewhat dimmed by time, but evidently of very equivocal morality. A birding-piece and a fragment of a fishing-rod covered with dust, neither of which Signor Parucci had ever touched for the last twenty years, were suspended over the mantelpiece; and upon the side of the recess, and fully lighted by the window, in attestation of his gentler and more refined pursuits, hung a dingy old guitar apparently still in use, for the strings, though a good deal cobbled and knotted, were perfect in number. A huge, high-backed, well-stuffed chair, in which a man might lie as snugly as a kernel in its shell, was placed at the window, and in it reclined the presiding genius of the place himself, with his legs elevated so as to rest upon the broad window-sill, formed by the roof of the mysterious press which we have already mentioned. The Italian was a little man, very slight, with long hair, a good deal grizzled, flowing upon his shoulders; he had a sallow complexion and thin hooked nose, piercing black eyes, lean cheeks, and sharp chin—and altogether a lank, attenuated, and somewhat intellectual cast of face, with, however, a certain expression of malice and cunning about the leer of his eye, as well as in the character of his thin and colourless lip, which made him by no means a very pleasant object to look upon.

"Fine weather—almost Italy," said the little man, lazily pushing open the casement with his foot. "I am surprise, good, dear, sweet Sir Richard, his bell is stop so long quiet. Why is it not go ding, ding, dingeri, dingeri, ding-a-ding, ding, as usual. Damnation! what do I care he ring de bell and I leesten. We are not always young, and I must be allow to be a leetle deaf when he is allow to be a leetle gouty. Gode blace my body, how hot is de sun. Come down here, leer of Apollo—come to my arm, meestress of my heart—Orpheus' leer, come queekly." This was addressed to the ancient instrument of music which we have already mentioned, and the invitation was accompanied by an appropriate elevation of his two little legs, which he raised until he gently closed his feet upon the sides of the "leer of Apollo," which, with a good deal of dexterity, he unhung from its peg, and conveyed within reach of his hand. He cast a look of fond admiration at its dingy and time-dried face, and forthwith, his heels still resting upon the window-sill, he was soon thrumming a tinkling symphony, none of the most harmonious, and then, with uncommon zeal, he began, to his own accompaniment, to sing some ditty of Italian love. While engaged in this refined and touching employment, he espied, with unutterable indignation, a young urchin, who, attracted by the sounds of his amorous minstrelsy, and with a view to torment the performer, who was an extremely unpopular personage, had stationed himself at a little distance before the casement, and accompanied the vocal performance of the Italian with the most hideous grimaces, and the most absurd and insulting gesticulations.

Signor Parucci would have given a good round sum to have had the engaging boy by the ears; but this he knew was out of the question; he therefore (for he was a philosopher) played and sung on without evincing the smallest consciousness of what was going forward. His plans of vengeance were, however, speedily devised and no less quickly executed. There lay upon the window-sill a fragment of biscuit, which in the course of an ecstatic flourish the little man kicked carelessly over. The bait had hardly touched the ground beneath the casement when Jacopo, continuing to play and sing the while, and apparently unconscious of anything but his own music, to his infinite delight beheld the boy first abate his exertions, and finally put an end to his affronting pantomime altogether, and begin to manoeuvre in the direction of the treacherous windfall. The youth gradually approached it, and just at the moment when it was within his grasp, Signor Parucci, with another careless touch of his foot, sent over a large bow-pot well stored with clay, which stood upon the window-block. The descent of this ponderous missile was followed by a most heart-stirring acclamation from below; and good Mr. Parucci, clambering along the window-sill, and gazing downward, was regaled by the spectacle of the gesticulating youth stamping about the grass among what appeared to be the fragments of a hundred flower-pots, writhing and bellowing in transports of indignation and bodily torment.

"Povero ragazzo—Carissimo figlio," exclaimed the valet, looking out with an expression of infinite sweetness, "my dear child and charming boy, how 'av you broke my flower-pote, and when 'av you come here. Ah! per Bacco, I think I 'av see you before. Ah! yees, you are that sweetest leetel boy that was leestening at my music—so charming just now. How much clay is on your back! a cielo! amiable child, you might 'av keel yourself. Sacro numine, what an escape! Say your prayer, and thank heaven you are safe, my beautiful, sweetest, leetel boy. God blace you. Now rone away very fast, for fear you pool the other two flower-potes on your back, sweetest child. Gode bless you, amiable boy—they are very large and very heavy."

The youth took the hint, and having had quite enough of Mr. Parucci's music for the evening, withdrew under the combined influences of fury and lumbago. The little man threw himself back in his chair, and hugged his shins in sheer delight, grinning and chattering like a delirious monkey, and rolling himself about, and laughing with the most exquisite relish. At length, after this had gone on for some time, with the air of a man who has had enough of trifling, and must now apply himself to matters of graver importance, he arose, hung up his guitar, sent his chair, which was upon casters, rolling to the far end of the room, and proceeded to arrange the curls of one of the two magnificent perukes, on which it was his privilege to operate. After having applied himself with uncommon attention to this labour of taste for some time in silence, he retired a few paces to contemplate the effect of his performance—whereupon he fell into a musing mood, and began after his fashion to soliloquize with a good deal of energy and volubility in that dialect which had become more easy to him than his mother tongue.

"Corpo di Bacco! what thing is life! who would believe thirty years ago I should be here now in a barbaroose island to curl the wig of an old gouty blackguard—but what matter. I am a philosopher—damnation—it is very well as it is—per Bacco! I can go way when I like. I am reech leetle fellow, and with Sir Richard, good Sir Richard, I do always whatever I may choose. Good Sir Richard," he continued, addressing the block on which hung the object of his tasteful labours, as if it had been the baronet in person—"good Sir Richard, why are you so kind to me, when you are so cross as the old devil in hell with all the rest of the world?—why, why, why? Shall I say to you the reason, good, kind Sir Richard? Well, I weel. It is because you dare not—dare not—dare not-da-a-a-are not vaix me. I am, you know, dear Sir Richard, a poor, leetle foreigner, who is depending on your goodness. I 'ave nothing but your great pity and good charity—oh, no! I am nothing at all; but still you dare not vaix me—you moste not be angry—note at all—but very quiet—you moste not go in a passion—oh! never—weeth me—even if I was to make game of you, and to insult you, and to pool your nose."

Here the Italian seized, with the tongs which he had in his hand, upon that prominence in the wooden block which corresponded in position with the nose, which at other times the peruke overshadowed, and with a grin of infinite glee pinched and twisted the iron instrument until the requirements of his dramatic fancy were satisfied, when he delivered two or three sharp knocks on the smooth face of the block, and resumed his address.

"No, no—you moste not be angry, fore it would be great misfortune—oh, it would—if you and I should quarrel together; but tell me now, old truffatore—tell me, I say, am I not very quiet, good-nature, merciful, peetying faylow? Ah, yees—very, very—Madre di Dio—very moche; and dear, good Sir Richard, shall I tell you why I am so very good-nature? It is because I love you joste as moche as you love me—it is because, most charitable patron, it is my convenience to go on weeth you quietly and 'av no fighting yet—bote you are going to get money. Oh! so coning you are, you think I know nothing—you think I am asleep—bote I know it—I know it quite well. You think I know nothing about the land you take from Miss Mary. Ah! you are very coning—oh! very; but I 'av hear it all, and I tell you—and I swear per sangue di D——, when you get that money I shall, and will, and moste—mo-ooste 'av a very large, comfortable, beeg handful—do you hear me? Oh, you very coning old rascal; and if you weel not geeve it, oh, my dear Sir Richard, echellent master, I am so moche afaid we will 'av a fight between us—a quarrel—that will spoil our love and friendship, and maybe, helas! horte your reputation—shoking—make the gentlemen spit on you, and avoid you, and call you all the ugly names—oh! shoking."

Here he was interrupted by a loud ringing in Sir Richard's chamber.

"There he is to pool his leetle bell—damnation, what noise. I weel go up joste now—time enough, dear, good, patient Sir Richard—time enough—oh, plainty, plainty."

The little man then leisurely fumbled in his pocket until he brought forth a bunch of keys, from which, having selected one, he applied it to the lock of the little press which we have already mentioned, whence he deliberately produced one of the flasks which we have hinted at, along with a tall glass with a spiral stem, and filling himself a bumper of the liquor therein contained, he coolly sipped it to the bottom, accompanied throughout the performance by the incessant tinkling of Sir Richard's hand-bell.

"Ah, very good, most echellent—thank you, Sir Richard, you 'av give me so moche time and so moche music, I 'av drunk your very good health."

So saying, he locked up the flask and glass again, and taking the block which had just represented Sir Richard in the imaginary colloquy in his hand, he left his own chamber, and ran upstairs to the baronet's dressing-room. He found his master alone.

"Ah, Jacopo," exclaimed the baronet, looking somewhat flushed, but speaking, nevertheless, in a dulcet tone enough, "I have been ringing for nearly ten minutes; but I suppose you did not hear me."

"Joste so as you 'av say," replied the man. "Your signoria is very seldom wrong. I was so charmed with my work I could not hear nothing."

"Parucci," rejoined Sir Richard, after a slight pause, "you know I keep no secrets from you."

"Ah, you flatter me, Signor—you flatter me—indeed you do," said the valet, with ironical humility.

His master well understood the tone in which the fellow spoke, but did not care to notice it.

"The fact is, Jacopo," continued Sir Richard, "you already know so many of my secrets, that I have now no motive in excluding you from any."

"Goode, kind—oh, very kind," ejaculated the valet.

"In short," continued his master, who felt a little uneasy under the praises of his attendant—"in short, to speak plainly, I want your assistance. I know your talents well. You can imitate any handwriting you please to copy with perfect accuracy. You must copy, in the handwriting of this manuscript, the draft of a letter which I will hand you this evening. You require some little time to study the character; so take the letter with you, and be in my room at ten to-night. I will then hand you the draft of what I want written. You understand?"

"Understand! To be sure—most certilly I weel do it," replied the Italian, "so that the great devil himself will not tell the writing of the two, l'un dall' altro, one from the other. Never fear—geeve me the letter. I must learn the writing. I weel be here to-night before you are arrive, and I weel do it very fast, and so like—hote you know how well I can copy. Ah! yees; you know it, Signor. I need not tell."

"No more at present," said the baronet, with a gesture of caution. "Assist me to dress."

The Italian accordingly was soon deep in the mysteries of his elaborate functions, where we shall leave him and his master for the present.

## CHAPTER XVII.

### DUBLIN CASTLE BY NIGHT—THE DRAWING-ROOM—LORD WHARTON AND HIS COURT.

Sir Richard Ashwoode had set his heart upon having Lord Aspenly for his son-in-law; and all things considered, his lordship was, perhaps, according to the standard by which the baronet measured merit, as good a son-in-law as he had any right to hope for. It was true, Lord Aspenly was neither very young nor very beautiful. Spite of all the ingenious arts by which he reinforced his declining graces, it was clear as the light that his lordship was not very far from seventy; and it was just as apparent that it was not to any extraordinary supply of bone, muscle, or flesh that his vitality was attributable. His lordship was a little, spindle-shanked gentleman, with the complexion of a consumptive frog, and features as sharp as edged tools. He condescended to borrow from the artistic talents of his valet the exquisite pencilling of his eyebrows, as well as the fine black line which gave effect to a set of imaginary eyelashes, and depth and brilliancy to a pair of eyes which, although naturally not very singularly effective, had, nevertheless, nearly as much vivacity in them as they had ever had. His smiles were perennial and unceasing, very winning and rather ghastly. He used much gesticulation, and his shrug was absolutely Parisian. To all these perfections he added a wonderful facility in rounding the periods of a compliment, and an inexhaustible affluence of something which passed for conversation. Thus endowed, and having, moreover, the additional recommendation of a handsome income, a peerage, and an unencumbered celibacy, it is hardly wonderful that his lordship was unanimously voted by all prudent and discriminating persons, without exception, the most fascinating man in all Ireland. Sir Richard Ashwoode was not one whit more in earnest in desiring the match than was Lord Aspenly himself. His lordship had for some time begun to suspect that he had nearly sown his wild oats—that it was time for him to reform—that he was ripe for the domestic virtues, and ought to renounce scamp-hood. He therefore, in the laboratory of his secret soul, compounded a virtuous passion, which he resolved to expend upon the first eligible object who might present herself. Mary Ashwoode was the fortunate damsel who first happened to come within the scope and range of his lordship's premeditated love; and he forthwith in a matrimonial paroxysm applied, according to the good old custom, not to the lady herself, but to Sir Richard Ashwoode, and was received with open arms.

The baronet indeed, as the reader is aware, anticipated many difficulties in bringing the match about; for he well knew how deeply his daughter's heart was engaged, and his misgivings were more sombre and frequent than he cared to acknowledge even to himself. He resolved, however, that the thing should be; and he was convinced, that if his lordship only were firm, spite of fate he would effect it. In order then to inspire Lord Aspenly with this desirable firmness, he not unwisely believed that his best course was to exhibit him as much as possible in public places, in the character of the avowed lover of Mary Ashwoode; a position which, when once unequivocally assumed, afforded no creditable retreat, except through the gates of matrimony. It was arranged, therefore, that the young lady, under the protection of Lady Stukely, and accompanied by Lord Aspenly and Henry Ashwoode, should attend the first drawing-room at the Castle, a ceremonial which had been fixed to take place a few days subsequently to the arrival of Lord Aspenly at Morley Court. Those who have seen the Castle of Dublin only as it now stands, have beheld but the creation of the last sixty or seventy years, with the exception only of the wardrobe tower, an old grey cylinder of masonry, very dingy and dirty, which appears to have gone into half mourning for its departed companions, and presents something of the imposing character of an overgrown, mouldy band-box. At the beginning of the last century, however, matters were very different. The trim brick buildings, with their spacious windows and symmetrical regularity of structure, which now complete the quadrangles of the castle, had not yet appeared; but in their stead masses of building, constructed with very little attention to architectural precision, either in their individual formation or in their relative position, stood ranged together, so as to form two irregular and gloomy squares. That portion of the building which was set apart for state occasions and the vice-regal residence, had undergone so many repairs and modifications, that very little if any of it could have been recognized by its original builder. Not so, however, with other portions of the pile: the ponderous old towers, which have since disappeared, with their narrow loop-holes and iron-studded doors looming darkly over the less massive fabrics of the place with stern and gloomy aspect, reminded the passer every moment, that the building whose courts he trod was not merely the theatre of stately ceremonies, but a fortress and a prison.

The viceroyalty of the Earl of Wharton was within a few weeks of its abrupt termination; the approaching discomfiture of the Whigs was not, however, sufficiently clearly revealed, to thin the levees and drawing-rooms of the Whig lord-lieutenant. The castle yards were, therefore, upon the occasion in question, crowded to excess with the gorgeous equipages in which the Irish aristocracy of the time delighted. The night had closed in unusual darkness, and the massive buildings, whose summits were buried in dense and black obscurity, were lighted only by the red reflected glow of crowded flambeaux and links—which, as the respective footmen, who attended the crowding chairs and coaches flourished them according to the approved fashion, scattered their wide showers of sparks into the eddying air, and illumined in a broad and ruddy glare, like that of a bonfire, the gorgeous equipages with which the square was now thronged, and the splendid figures which they successively discharged. There were coaches-and-four—out-riders—running footmen and hanging footmen—crushing and rushing—jostling and swearing—and burly coachmen, with inflamed visages, lashing one another's horses and their own. Lackeys collaring and throttling one another, all "for their master's honour," in the hot and disorderly dispute for precedence, and some even threatening an appeal to the swords—which, according to the barbarous fashion of the day, they carried, to the no small peril of the public and themselves. Others dragging the reins of strangers' horses, and backing them to make way for their own—a proceeding which, of course, involved no small expenditure of blasphemy and vociferation. On the whole, it would not be easy to exaggerate the scene of riot and confusion which, under the very eye of the civil and military executive of the country, was perpetually recurring, and that, too, ostensibly in honour of the supreme head of the Irish Government.

Through all this crash, and clatter, and brawling, and vociferation, the party whom we are bound to follow made their way with some difficulty and considerable delay.

The Earl of Wharton with his countess, surrounded by a brilliant staff, and amid all the pomp and state of vice-regal dignity, received the distinguished courtiers who thronged the castle chambers. At the time of which we write, Lord Wharton was in his seventieth year. Few, however, would have guessed his age at more than sixty, though many might have supposed it under that. He was rather a spare figure, with an erect and dignified bearing, and a countenance which combined vivacity, good-humour, and boldness in an eminent degree. His manners were, to those who did not know how unreal was everything in them that bore the promise of good, singularly engaging, and that in spite of a very strong spice of coarseness, and a very determined addiction to profane swearing. He had, however, in his whole air and address a kind of rollicking, good-humoured familiarity, which was very generally mistaken for the quintessence of candour and good-fellowship, and which consequently rendered him unboundedly popular among those who were not aware of the fact that his complimentary speeches meant just nothing, and were very often followed, the moment the object of them had withdrawn, by the coarsest ridicule, and even by the grossest abuse. For the rest, he was undoubtedly an able statesman, and had clearly discerned and adroitly steered his way through the straits and perils of troublous and eventful times. He was, moreover, a steady and uncompromising Whig, upon whom, throughout a long and active life, the stain of inconsistency had never rested; a thorough partisan, a quick and ready debater, and an unscrupulous and daring political intriguer. In private, however, entirely profligate—a sensualist and an infidel, and in both characters equally without shame.

Through the rooms there wandered a very wild, madcap boy of some ten or eleven years, venting his turbulent spirits in all kinds of mischievous pranks—sometimes planting himself behind Lord Wharton, and mimicking, with ludicrous exaggeration, which the courtly spectators had enough to do to resist, the ceremonious gestures and gracious nods of the viceroy; at other times assuming a staid and manly carriage, and chatting with his elders with the air of perfect equality, and upon subjects which one would have thought immeasurably beyond his years, and this with a sound sense, suavity, and precision which would have done honour to many grey heads in the room. This strange, bold, precocious boy of eleven was Philip, afterwards Duke of Wharton, the wonder and the disgrace of the British peerage.

"Ah! Mr. Morris," exclaimed his excellency, as a middle-aged gentleman, with a fluttered air, a round face, and vacant smile, approached, "I am delighted to see you—by — Almighty I am—give me your hand. I have written across about the matter we wot of: but for these cursed contrary winds, I make no doubt I should have had a letter before now. Is the young gentleman himself here?"

"A—a—not quite, your excellency. That is, not at—all," stammered the gentleman, in mingled delight and alarm. "He is, my lord, a—a—laid up. He—a—it is a sore throat. Your excellency is most gracious."

"Tell him from me," rejoined Wharton, "that he must get well as quickly as may be. We don't know the moment he may be wanted. You understand me?"

"I—a—do indeed," replied Mr. Morris, retiring in graceful confusion.

"A damned impudent booby," whispered Wharton to Addison, who stood beside him, uttering the remark without the change of a single muscle. "He has made some cursed unconscionable request about his son. I'gad, I forget what; but we want his vote on Tuesday; and civility, you know, costs no coin."

Addison smiled faintly, and shook his head.

"May the Lord pardon us all," exclaimed a country clergyman in a rusty gown and ill-dressed wig, with a pale, attenuated, eager face, which told mournful tales of short commons and hard work; he had been for some time an intense and a grieved listener to the lord-lieutenant's conversation, and was now slowly retiring with a companion as humble as himself from the circle which surrounded his excellency, with simple horror impressed upon his pale features—"may the Lord preserve us all, how awful it is to hear one so highly trusted by Him, take His name thus momentarily in vain. Lord Wharton is, I fear me much, an habitual profane swearer."

"Believe me, sir, you are very simple," rejoined a young clergyman who stood close to the position which the speaker now occupied. "His excellency's object in swearing by the different persons of the Trinity is to show that he believes in revealed religion—a fact which else were doubtful; and this being his main object, it is manifestly a secondary consideration to what particular asseveration or promises his excellency happens to tack his oaths."

The lank, pale-faced prebendary looked suddenly and earnestly round upon the person who had accosted him, with an expression of curiosity and wonder, evidently in some doubt as to the spirit in which the observation had been made. He beheld a tall, stalwart man, arrayed in a clerical costume as rich as that of a churchman who has not attained to the rank of a dignitary in his profession could well be, and in all points equipped with the most perfect neatness. In the face he looked in vain for any indication of jocularity. It was a striking countenance—striking for the extreme severity of its expression, and for its stern and handsome outline. The eye which encountered the inquiring glance of the elder man was of the clearest blue, singularly penetrating and commanding—the eyebrow dark and shaggy—the lips full and finely formed, but in their habitual expression bearing a character of haughty and indomitable determination—the complexion of the face was dark; and as the country prebendary gazed upon the countenance, full, as it seemed, of a scornful, stern, merciless energy and decision, something told him, that he looked upon one born to lead and to command the people. All this he took in at a glance: and while he looked, Addison, who had detached himself from the vice-regal coterie, laid his hand upon the shoulder of the stern-featured young clergyman.

"Swift," said he, drawing him aside, "we see you too seldom here. His excellency begins to think and to hope you have reconsidered what I spoke about when last we met. Believe me, you wrong yourself in not rendering what service you can to men who are not ungrateful, and who have the power to reward. You were always a Whig, and a pamphlet were with you but the work of a few days."

"Were I to write a pamphlet," rejoined Swift, "it is odds his excellency would not like it."

"Have you not always been a Whig?" urged Addison.

"Sir, I am not to be taken by nicknames," rejoined Swift. "I know Godolphin, and I know Lord Wharton. I have long distrusted the government of each. I am no courtier, Mr. Secretary. What I suspect I will not seem to trust—what I hate I hate entirely, and renounce openly. I have heard of my Lord Wharton's doing, too. When I refused before to understand your overtures to me to write a pamphlet for his friends, he was pleased to say I refused because he would not make me his chaplain—in saying which he knowingly and malignantly lied; and to this lie he, after his accustomed fashion, tacked a blasphemous oath. He is therefore a perjured liar. I renounce him as heartily as I renounce the devil. I am come here, Mr. Secretary, not to do reverence to Lord Wharton—God forbid!—but to offer my homage to the majesty of England, whose brightness is reflected even in that cracked and battered piece of pinchbeck yonder. Believe me, should his excellency be rash enough to engage me in talk to-night, I shall take care to let him know what opinion I have of him."

"Come, come, you must not be so dogged," rejoined Addison. "You know Lord Wharton's ways. He says a good deal more than he cares to be believed—everybody knows that—and all take his lordship's asseverations with a grain of allowance; besides, you ought to consider that when a man unused to contradiction is crossed by disappointment, he is apt to be choleric, and to forget his discretion. We all know his faults; but even you will not deny his merits."

Thus speaking, he led Swift toward the vice-regal circle, which they had no sooner reached than Wharton, with his most good-humoured smile, advanced to meet the young clergyman, exclaiming,—

"Swift! so it is, by —! I am glad to see you—by — I am."

"I am glad, my lord," replied Swift, gravely, "that you take such frequent occasion to remind this godless company of the presence of the Almighty."

"Well, you know," rejoined Wharton, good-humouredly, "the Scripture saith that the righteous man sweareth to his neighbour."

"And disappointeth him not," rejoined Swift.

"And disappointeth him not," repeated Wharton; "and by —," continued he, with marked earnestness, and drawing the young politician aside as he spoke, "in whatsoever I swear to thee there shall be no disappointment."

He paused, but Swift remained silent. The lord-lieutenant well knew that an English preferment was the nearest object of the young churchman's ambition. He therefore continued,—

"On my soul, we want you in England—this is no stage for you. By — you cannot hope to serve either yourself or your friends in this place."

"Very few thrive here but scoundrels, my lord," rejoined Swift.

"Even so," replied Wharton, with perfect equanimity—"it is a nation of scoundrels—dissent on the one side and popery on the other. The upper order harpies, and the lower a mere prey—and all equally liars, rogues, rebels, slaves, and robbers. By — some fine day the devil will carry off the island bodily. For very safety you must get out of it. By — he'll have it."

"I am not enough in the devil's confidence to speak of his designs with so much authority as your lordship," rejoined Swift; "but I incline to think that under your excellency's administration it will answer his end as well to leave the island where it is."

"Ah! Swift, you are a wag," rejoined the viceroy; "but by — I honour and respect your spirit. I know we shall agree yet—by — I know it. I respect your independence and honesty all the more that they are seldom met with in a presence-chamber. By — I respect and love you more and more every day."

"If your lordship will forego your professions of love, and graciously confine yourself to the backbiting which must follow, you will do for me to the full as much as I either expect or desire," rejoined Swift, with a grave reverence.

"Well, well," rejoined the viceroy, with the most unruffled good-humour, "I see, Swift, you are in no mood to play the courtier just now. Nevertheless, bear in mind what Addison advised you to attempt; and though we part thus for the present, believe me, I love you all the better for your honest humour."

"Farewell, my lord," repeated Swift, abruptly, and with a formal bow he retired among the common throng.

"A hungry, ill-conditioned dog," said Wharton, turning to the person next him, "who, having never a bone to gnaw, whets his teeth on the shins of the company."

Having vented this little criticism, the viceroy resumed once more the formal routine of state hospitality.

"It is time we were going," suggested Mary Ashwoode to Emily Copland. "My lord," she continued, turning to Lord Aspenly, whose attentions had been just as conspicuous and incessant as Sir Richard Ashwoode could have wished them, "Do you know where Lady Stukely is?"

Lord Aspenly professed his ignorance.

"Have you seen her ladyship?" inquired Emily Copland of the gallant Major O'Leary, who stood near her.

"Upon my conscience, I have," rejoined the major. "I'm not considered a poltroon; but I plead guilty to one weakness. I am bothered if I can stand fire when it appears in the nose of a gentlewoman; so as soon as I saw her I beat a retreat, and left my valorous young nephew to stand or fall under the blaze of her artillery. She is at the far end of the room."

The major was easily persuaded to undertake the mission, and a word to young Ashwoode settled the matter. The party accordingly left the rooms, having, however, previously to their doing so, arranged that Major O'Leary should pass the next day at Morley Court, and afterwards accompany them in the evening to the theatre, whither Sir Richard, in pursuance of his plans, had arranged that they should all repair.

## CHAPTER XVIII.

### THE TWO COUSINS—THE NEGLECTED JEWELS AND THE BROKEN SEAL.

It was drawing toward evening when Emily Copland, in high spirits, and richly and becomingly dressed, ran lightly to the door of her cousin's chamber. She knocked, but no answer was returned. She knocked again, but still without any reply. Then opening the door, she entered the room, and beheld her cousin Mary seated at a small work-table, at which it was her wont to read. There she lay motionless—her small head leaned upon her graceful arms, over which flowed all negligently the dark luxuriant hair. An open letter was on the table before her, and two or three rich ornaments lay unheeded on the floor beside her, as if they had fallen from her hand. There was in her attitude such a passionate abandonment of grief, that she seemed the breathing image of despair. Spite of all her levity, the young lady was touched at the sight. She approached her gently, and laying her hand upon her shoulder, she stooped down and kissed her.

"Mary, dear Mary, what grieves you?" she said. "Tell me. It's I, dear—your cousin Emily. There's a good girl—what has happened to vex you?"

Mary raised her head, and looked in her cousin's face. Her eye was wild—she was pale as marble, and in her beautiful face was an expression so utterly woeful and piteous, that Emily was almost moved.

"Oh! I have lost him—for ever and ever I have lost him," said she, despairingly. "Oh! cousin, dear cousin, he is gone from me. God pity me—I am forsaken."

"Nay, cousin, do not say so—be cheerful—it cannot be—there, there," and Emily Copland kissed the poor girl's pale lips.

"Forsaken—forsaken," continued Mary, for she heard not and heeded not the voice of vain consolation. "He has thrown me off for ever—for ever—quite—quite. God pity me, where shall I look for hope?"

"Mary, dear Mary," said her cousin, "you are ill—do not give way thus. Be assured it is not as you think. You must be in error."

"In error! Oh! that I could think so. God knows how gladly I would give my poor life to think so. No, no—it is real—all real. Oh! cousin, he has forsaken me."

"I cannot believe it—I can not," said Emily Copland. "Such folly can hardly exist. I will not believe it. What reason have you for thinking him changed?"

"Read—oh, read it, cousin," replied the girl, motioning toward the letter, which lay open on the table—"read it once, and you will not bid me hope any more. Oh! cousin, dear cousin, there is no more joy for me in this world, turn where I will, do what I may—I am heart-broken."

Emily Copland glanced through the letter, shook her head, and dropped the note again where it had been lying.

"You know, cousin Emily, how I loved him," continued Mary, while for the first time the tears flowed fast—"you know that day after day, among all that happened to grieve me, my heart found rest in his love—in the hope and trust that he would never grow cold; and—and—oh! God pity me—now where is it all? You see—you know his love is gone from me—for evermore—gone from me. Oh! how I used to count the days and hours till the time would come round when I could see him and speak to him—but this has all gone. Hereafter all days are to be the same—morning or evening, summer time or winter—no change of seasons or of hours can bring to me any more hope or gladness, but ever the same—sorrow and desolate loneliness—for oh! cousin, I am very desolate, and hopeless, and heart-broken."

The poor girl threw her arms round her cousin's neck, and sobbed and wept, and wept and sobbed again, as though her heart would break. Long and bitterly she wept upon her cousin's neck in silence, unbroken, except by her sobs. After a time, however, Emily Copland exclaimed,—

"Well, Mary, to say the truth, I never much liked the matter; and as he is a fool, and an ungrateful fool to boot, I am not sorry that he has shown his character as he has done. Believe me, painful as such discoveries are when made thus early, they are incomparably more agonizing when made too late. A little—a very little—time will enable you quite to forget him."

"No, cousin," replied Mary—"no, I never will forget him. He is changed indeed—greatly changed from what he was—bitterly has he disappointed and betrayed me; but I cannot forget him. There shall indeed never more pass word or look between us; he shall be to me as one that is dead, whom I shall hear and see no more; but the memory of what he was—the memory of what I vainly thought him—shall remain with me while my poor heart beats."

"Well, Mary, time will show," said Emily.

"Yes, time will show—time will show," replied she, mournfully; "be the time long or short, it will show."

"You must forget him—you will forget him; a few weeks, and you will thank your stars you found him out so soon."

"Ah, cousin," replied Mary, "you do not know how all my thoughts, and hopes, and recollections—everything I liked to remember, and to look forward to; you cannot know how all that was happy in my life—but what boots it, I will keep my troth with him; I will love no other, and wed with no other; and while this sorrowful life remains I will never—never—forget him."

"I can only say, that were the case my own," rejoined Emily, "I would show the fellow how lightly I held him and his worthless heart, and marry within a month; but every one has her own way of doing things. Remember it is nearly time to start for the theatre; the coach will be at the door in half-an-hour. Surely you will come; it would seem so very strange were you to change your mind thus suddenly; and you may be very sure that, by some means or other, the impudent fellow—about whom, I cannot see why, you care so much—would hear of all your grieving, and pining, and love-sickness. Pah! I'd rather die than please the hollow, worthless creature by letting him think he had caused me a moment's uneasiness; and then, above all, Sir Richard would be so outrageously angry—why, you would never hear the end of it. Come, come, be a good girl. After all, it is only holding up your head, and looking pretty, which you can't help, for an hour or two. You must come to silence gossip abroad, as well as for the sake of peace at home—you must come."

"I would fain stay here at home," said the poor girl; "heart and head are sick: but if you think my father would be angry with me for staying at home, I will go. It is indeed, as you say, a small matter to me where I pass an hour or two; all times, all places—crowds or solitudes—are henceforward indifferent to me. What care I where they bring me! Cousin Emily, I will do whatever you think best."

The poor girl spoke with a voice and look of such utter wretchedness, that even her light-hearted, worldly, selfish cousin was touched with pity.

"Come, then; I will assist you," said she, kissing the pale cheek of the heart-stricken girl. "Come, Mary, cheer up, you must call up your good looks it would never do to be seen thus." And so talking on, she assisted her to dress.

Gaily and richly arrayed in the gorgeous and by no means unbecoming style of the times, and sparkling with brilliant jewels, poor Mary Ashwoode—a changed and stricken creature, scarcely conscious of what was going on around her—took her place in her father's carriage, and was borne rapidly toward the theatre.

The party consisted of the two young ladies, who were respectively under the protection of Lord Aspenly, who sate beside Mary Ashwoode, happily too much pleased with his own voluble frivolity to require anything more from her than her appearing to hear it, and young Ashwoode, who chatted gaily with his pretty cousin.

"What has become of my venerable true-love, Major O'Leary?" inquired Miss Copland.

"He will follow on horseback," replied Ashwoode. "I beheld him, as I passed downstairs, admiring himself before the looking-glass in his new regimentals. He designs tremendous havoc to-night. His coat is a perfect phenomenon—the investment of a year's pay at least—with more gold about it than I thought the country could afford, and scarlet enough to make a whole wardrobe for the lady of Babylon—a coat which, if left to itself, would storm the hearts of nine girls out of ten, and which, even with an officer in it, will enthral half the sex."

"And here comes the coat itself," exclaimed the young lady, as the major rode up to the coach-window—"I'm half in love with it myself already."

"Ladies, your devoted slave: gentlemen, your most obedient," said the major, raising his three-cornered hat. "I hope to see you before half-an-hour, under circumstances more favourable to conversation. Miss Copland, depend upon it, with your permission, I'll pay my homage to you before half-an-hour, the more especially as I have a scandalous story to tell you. Meanwhile, I wish you all a safe journey, and a pleasant one." So saying, the major rode on, at a brisk pace, to the "Cock and Anchor," there intending to put up his horse, and to exchange a few words with young O'Connor.

In the meantime the huge old coach, which contained the rest of the party, jolted and rumbled on, until at length, amid the confusion and clatter of crowded vehicles, restive horses, and vociferous coachmen, with all their accompaniments of swearing and whipping, the clank of scrambling hoofs, the bumping and hustling of carriages, and the desperate rushing of chairmen, bolting this way or that, with their living loads of foppery and fashion—the coach-door was thrown open at the box-entrance of the Theatre Royal, in Smock Alley.

CHAPTER XIX.

THE THEATRE—THE RUFFIAN—THE ASSAULT, AND THE RENCONTRE.

Major O'Leary had hardly dismounted in the quadrangle of the "Cock and Anchor," when O'Connor rode slowly into the inn-yard.

"How are you, my dear fellow?" exclaimed the man of scarlet and gold; "I was just asking where you were. Come down off that beast, I want to have a word in your ear—a bit of news—some fun. Descend, I say, descend."

O'Connor accordingly dismounted.

"Now then—a hearty shake—so. I have great news, and only a minute to tell it. Jack, run like a shot, and get me a chair. Here, Tim, take a napkin and an oyster-knife, and do not leave a bit of mud, or the sign of it, upon my back: take a general survey of the coat and breeches, and a particular review of the wig. And, Jem, do you give my boots a harum-scarum shot of a superficial scrub, and touch up the hat—gently, do you mind—and take care of the lace. So while the fellows are finishing my toilet, I may as well tell you my morsel of news. Do you know who is to be at the playhouse to-night?"

O'Connor expressed his ignorance.

"Well, then, I'll tell you, and make what use you like of it," resumed the major. "Miss Mary Ashwoode! There's for you. Take my advice, get into a decent coat and breeches, and run down to the theatre—it is not five minutes' walk from this; you'll easily find us, and I'll take care to make room for you. Why, you do not seem half pleased: what more can you wish for, unless you expect the girl to put up for the evening at the "Cock and Anchor"? Rouse yourself. If you feel modest, there is nothing like a pint or two of Madeira: don't try brandy—it's the father and mother of all sorts of indiscretions. Now, mind, you have the hint; it is an opportunity you ought to improve. By the powers, if I was in your place—but no matter. You may not have an opportunity of seeing her again these six months; and unless I'm completely mistaken, you are as much in love with the girl as I am with—several that shall be nameless.

Heigho! next after Burgundy, and the cock-pit, and the fox-hounds, and two or three more frailties of the kind, there is nothing in the world I prefer to flirtation, without much minding whether I'm the principal or the second in the affair. But here comes the vehicle."

Accordingly, without waiting to say any more, the major took his seat in the chair, and was borne by the lusty chairmen, at a swinging pace, through the narrow streets, and, without let or accident, safely deposited within the principal entrance of the theatre.

The theatre of Smock Alley (or, as it was then called, Orange Street) was not quite what theatres are nowadays. It was a large building of the kind, as theatres were then rated, and contained three galleries, one above the other, supported by heavy wooden caryatides, and richly gilded and painted. The curtain, instead of rising and falling, opened, according to the old fashion, in the middle, and was drawn sideways apart, disclosing no triumphs of illusive colouring and perspective, but a succession of plain tapestry-covered screens, which, from early habit, the audience accommodatingly accepted for town or country, dry land or sea, or, in short, for any locality whatsoever, according to the manager's good will and pleasure. This docility and good faith on the part of the audience were, perhaps, the more praiseworthy, inasmuch as a very considerable number of the aristocratic spectators actually sate in long lines down either side of the stage—a circumstance involving, by the continuous presence of the same perukes, and the same embroidered waistcoats, the same set of countenances, and the same set of legs, in every variety of clime and situation through which the wayward invention of the playwright hurried his action, a very severe additional tax upon the imaginative faculties of the audience. But perhaps the most striking peculiarities of the place were exhibited in the grim persons of two bonâ fide sentries, in genuine cocked hats and scarlet coats, with their enormous muskets shouldered, and the ball-cartridges dangling in ostentatious rows from their bandoleers, planted at the front, and facing the audience, one at each side of the stage—a vivid evidence of the stern vicissitudes and insecurity of the times. For the rest, the audience of those days, in the brilliant colours, and glittering lace, and profuse ornament, which the gorgeous fashion of the time allowed, presented a spectacle of rich and dazzling magnificence, such as no modern assembly of the kind can even faintly approach.

The major had hardly made his way to the box where his party were seated, when his attention was caught by an object which had for him all but irresistible attractions: this was the buxom person of Mistress Jannet Rumble, a plump, good-looking, young widow of five-and-forty, with a jolly smile, a hearty laugh, and a killing acquaintance with the language of the eyes. These perfections—for of course her jointure, which, by the way, was very considerable, could have had nothing to do with it—were too much for Major O'Leary. He met the widow accidentally, made a few careless inquiries about her finances, and fell over head and ears in love with her upon the shortest possible notice. Our friend had, therefore, hardly caught a glimpse of her, when Miss Copland, beside whom he was seated, observed that he became unusually meditative, and at length, after two or three attempts to enter again into conversation—all resulting in total and incoherent failure, the major made some blundering excuse, took his departure, and in a moment had planted himself beside the fascinating Mistress Rumble—where we shall allow him the protection of a generous concealment, and suffer him to read the lady's eyes, and insinuate his soft nonsense, without intruding for a moment upon the sanctity of lovers' mutual confidences.

Emily Copland having watched and enjoyed the manoeuvres of her military friend till she was fairly tired of the amusement, and having in vain sought to engage Henry Ashwoode, who was unusually moody and absent, in conversation, at length, as a last desperate resource, turned her attention to what was passing upon the stage.

While all this was going forward, young Ashwoode was a good deal disconcerted at observing among the crowd in the pit a personage with whom, in the vicious haunts which he frequented, he had made a sort of ambiguous acquaintance. The man was a bulky, broad-shouldered, ill-looking fellow, with a large, vulgar, red face, and a coarse, sensual mouth, whose blue, swollen lips indicated habitual intemperance, and the nauseous ugliness of which was further enhanced by the loss of two front teeth, probably by some violent agency, as was testified by a deep scar across the mouth; the eyes of the man carried that uncertain expression, half of shame and half of defiance, which belongs to the coward, bully, and ruffian. The blackness of habitually-indulged and ferocious passion was upon his countenance; and the revolting character of the face was the more unequivocally marked by a sort of smile, or rather sneer, which had in it neither intellectuality nor gladness—an odious libel on the human smile, with nothing but brute insolence and scorn, and a sardonic glee in its baleful light—a smile from which every human sympathy recoiled abashed and affrighted. Let not the reader imagine that the man and the character are but the dreams of fiction; the wretch, whose outward seeming we have imperfectly sketched, lived and moved in the scenes where we have fixed our narrative—there grew rich—there rioted in the indulgence of every passion which hell can inspire or to which wealth can pander—there ministered to his insatiate avarice, by the destruction and beggary of thousands of the young and thoughtless—and there at length, in the fulness of his time, died—in the midst of splendour and infamy: with malignant and triumphant perseverance having persisted to his latest hour in the prosecution of his Satanic mission; luring the unwary into the toils of crime and inextricable madness, and thence into the pit of temporal and eternal ruin. This man, Nicholas Blarden, Esquire, was the proprietor of one of those places where fortunes are squandered, time sunk, habits, temper, character, morals, all, corrupted, blasted, destroyed—one of those places which are set apart as the especial temples of avarice, in which, year after year, are for ever recurring the same perennial scenes of mad excess, of calculating, merciless fraud, of bleak, brain-stricken despair—places to which has been assigned, in a spirit of fearful truth, the appellative of "hell."

The man whom we have mentioned, it had never been young Ashwoode's misfortune to meet, except in those scenes where his acquaintance was useful, without being actually discreditable; for it was the fellow's habit, with the instinctive caution which marks such gentlemen, to court public observation as little as possible, and to skulk systematically from the eye of popular scrutiny—seldom embarrassing his aristocratic acquaintances by claiming the privilege of recognition at unseasonable times; and confining himself, for the most part, exclusively to his own coterie. Independently of his unpleasant natural peculiarities there were other circumstances which tended to make him a conspicuous object in the crowd—the fellow was extravagantly over-dressed, and had planted himself in a standing posture upon a bench, and from this elevated position was, with steady effrontery, gazing into the box in which young Ashwoode's party were seated, exchanging whispers and horse-laughs with three or four men who looked scarcely less villainous than himself, and, as soon became apparent, directing his marked and exclusive attention to Miss Ashwoode, who was too deeply absorbed in her own sorrowful reflections to heed what was passing around her. The young man felt his choler mount, as he beheld the insolent conduct of the fellow—he saw, however, that Blarden was evidently not perfectly sober, and hesitated what course he should take. Strongly as he was tempted to spring at once into the pit, and put an end to the impertinence by caning the fellow within an inch of his life, he yet felt that a disreputable conflict of the kind had better be avoided, and could not well be justified except as a last resource; he, therefore, made up his mind to bear it as long as human endurance could.

Whatever hopes he entertained of escaping a collision with this man were, however, destined to be disappointed. Nicky Blarden (as his friends endearingly called him), to the great comfort of that part of the audience in his immediate neighbourhood, at length descended from his elevated stand, but not to conceal himself among the less obtrusive spectators. With an insolent swagger the fellow shouldered his way among the crowd towards the box where the object of his gaze was seated; and, having planted himself directly beneath it, he stared impudently up at young Ashwoode, exclaiming at the same time,—

"I say, Ashwoode, how does the world wag with you?—why ain't you rattling the bones this evening? damn me, you may as well be off, and let me take care of the dimber mot up there?"

"Do you speak to me, sir?" inquired young Ashwoode, turning almost livid with passion, and speaking in that subdued tone, and with that constrained coolness, which precedes some ungovernable outburst of fury.

"Why, — me, how great we've got all at once—I say, you don't know me—Eh! don't you?" exclaimed the fellow, with vulgar scorn, at the same time rather roughly poking Ashwoode's hand with the hilt of his sword.

"I shall show you, sir, when your drunken folly has passed away, by very sore proofs, that I do know you," replied the young man, clutching his cane with such a grip as threatened to force his fingers into it—"be assured, sir, I shall know you, and you me, as long as you have the power to remember."

"Whieu, damn it, don't frighten us," said the fellow, looking round for the approbation of his companions. "I say, damn it, don't frighten the people—come, come, no gammon. I say, Ashwoode, you must introduce me, or present me, or whatever's the word, to your sister up there—I say you must."

"Quit this part of the house this instant, sir, or nothing shall prevent me flogging you until I leave not a whole bone in your body—this warning is the last—profit by it," rejoined Ashwoode, in a low tone of bitter rage.

"Oh, ho! it's there you are—is it?" rejoined the fellow, with a wink at his comrades, "so you're going to beat the people—why, damn it, you're enough to make a horse laugh. I say I want to know your sister, or your miss, or whatever she is, with the black hair up there, and if you won't introduce me, damn it, I must only introduce myself."

So saying, the fellow made a spring and caught the ledge of the front of the box, with the intention of vaulting into the place. Lord Aspenly and the young ladies had arisen in some alarm.

"My lord," said young Ashwoode, "have the goodness to conduct the ladies to the lobby—I will join you in a moment."

This direction was promptly obeyed, and at the same moment the young man caught the fellow, already half into the box, by the neckcloth, dragged his body across the wooden parapet, and while he struggled helplessly to disengage himself—half strangled, and without the power to get either up or down—with his heavy cane, the young gentleman—every nerve, sinew, and muscle being strung to tenfold power by fury—inflicted upon his back and ribs a castigation so prolonged and tremendous, that before it had ended, the scoundrel was perfectly insensible, in which state Henry Ashwoode flung him down again into the pit, amid the obstreperous acclamations of all parts of the house—an uproar of applause in which the spectators in the pit joined with such hearty enthusiasm, that at length, touched with a kindred heroism, they turned upon the associates of the fallen champion, and fairly kicked and cuffed them out of the house.

This feat accomplished, the young gentleman went down the stairs to the street-entrance, and, after considerable delay, succeeded, with the assistance of the footman who had attended him into the house, in finding out their carriage, and having it brought to the door—not judging it expedient that the ladies should return to their places, where they would, of course, be exposed to the gazing curiosity of the multitude. He found the party in the lobby quite recovered from whatever was unpleasant in the excitement of the scene, the more violent part of which they had not witnessed. Lord Aspenly and Emily Copland were laughing over the adventure; and Mary, flashed and agitated, was looking better than she had before upon that night. Taking his cousin under his own protection, and consigning his sister to that of Lord Aspenly, young Ashwoode led the way to the carriage. As they passed slowly along the lobby, the quick eye of Mary Ashwoode discerned a form, at sight of which her heart swelled and throbbed as though it would burst—the colour fled from her cheeks, and she felt for a moment on the point of swooning; the pride of her sex, however, sustained her; the tingling blood again mounted warmly to her cheeks, her eye brightened, and she listened, with more apparent interest than perhaps she ever did before, to Lord Aspenly's remarks—the form was O'Connor's. As she passed him, she returned his salute with a slight and haughty bow, and saw, and felt the stern, cold, proud expression which marked his pale and handsome features. In another moment she was seated in the carriage; the doors were closed, crack went the whip, and clatter go the iron hoofs on the pavement—but before they had traversed a hundred yards on their homeward way, poor Mary Ashwoode sunk back in her place, and fainted away.

CHAPTER XX.

THE LODGING—YOUNG MELANCHOLY AND OLD REMEMBRANCES—AN ADVENTURE AMONG THE YEW HEDGES OF MORLEY COURT.

"There is no more doubt—no more hope"—said O'Connor, as, wrapt in his cloak, he slowly pursued his way homeward—"the worst is true—she is quite estranged from me—how deceived—how utterly blind I have been—yet who could have thought it? Light-hearted, vain, worthless—it is all, all true—my own eyes have seen it. Well, even this must be borne—borne as best it may, and with a manly spirit. I have been, indeed, miserably cheated"—he continued, with bitter vehemence—"and what remains for me? I've been infatuated—a self-flattered fool, and waken thus to find all lost—but grief avails not—there lie before me many paths of honourable toil, and many avenues to honourable death—the ambition of my life is over—henceforth the world has nothing to offer me. I will leave this, the country of my ill-fated birth—leave it for ever, and end my days honourably, and God grant soon, far away from the only one I ever loved—from her who has betrayed me."

Such were the thoughts which darkly and vaguely hurried through O'Connor's mind as he retraced his steps. Before he had arrived, however, at the "Cock and Anchor," whitherward he had mechanically directed his course, he bethought himself, and turned in a different direction towards the house in which his worthy friend, Mr. Audley—having an inveterate prejudice against all inns, which, without exception, he averred to be the especial sanctuaries of damp sheets, bugs, thieves, and rheumatic fevers—had already established himself as a weekly lodger.

"Pooh, pooh! you foolish boy," ejaculated the old bachelor, with considerable energy, in reply to O'Connor's gloomy and passionate language; "nonsense, sir, and folly, and absurdity—you'll give me the vapours if you go on this way—what the devil do you want of foreign service and foreign graves—do you think, booby, it was for that I came over here—tilly vally, tilly vally—I know as well as you, or any other jackanapes, what love is. I tell you, sirrah, I have been in love, and I have been jilted—jilted, sir! and when I was jilted, I thought the jilting itself quite enough, without improving the matter by getting myself buried, dead or alive." Here the little gentleman knocked the table recklessly with his knuckles, buried his hands in his breeches pockets, and rising from his chair, paced the room with an impressive tread. "Had you ever seen Letty Bodkin you might, indeed, have known what love is"—he continued, breathing very hard—"Letty Bodkin jilted me, and I got over it. I did not ask for razors, or cannon balls, or foreign interment, sir; but I vented my indignation like a man of business, in totting up the books, and running up a heavy arrear in the office accounts—yes, sir, I did more good in the way of arithmetic and book-keeping during that three weeks of love-sick agony, than an ordinary man, without the stimulus, would do in a year"—there was another pause here, and he resumed in a softened tone—"but Letty Bodkin was no ordinary woman. Oh! you scoundrel, had you seen her, you'd have been neither to hold nor to bind—there was nothing she could not do—she embroidered a waistcoat for me—heigho! scarlet geraniums and parsley sprigs—and she danced like—like a—a spring board—she'd sail through a minuet like a duck in a pond, and hop and bounce through 'Sir Roger de Coverley' like a hot chestnut on a griddle;—and then she sang—oh, her singing!—I've heard turtle-doves and thrushes, and, in fact, most kind of fowls of all sorts and sizes; but no nightingale ever came up to her in 'The Captain endearing and tall,' and 'The Shepherdess dying for love'—there never lived a man"—continued he, with increasing vehemence—"I don't care when or where, who could have stood, sate, or walked in her company for half-an-hour, without making an old fool of himself—she was just my age, perhaps a year or two more—I wonder whether she is much changed—heigho!"

Having thus delivered himself, Mr. Audley lapsed into meditation, and thence into a faint and rather painful attempt to vocalize his remembrance of "The Captain endearing and tall," engaged in which desperate operation of memory, O'Connor left the old gentleman, and returned to his temporary abode to pass a sleepless night of vain remembrances, regrets, and despair.

On the morning subsequent to the somewhat disorderly scene which we have described as having occurred in the theatre, Mary Ashwoode, as usual, sate silent and melancholy, in the dressing-room of her father, Sir Richard. The baronet was not yet sufficiently recovered to venture downstairs to breakfast, which in those days was a very early meal indeed. After an unusually prolonged silence, the old man, turning suddenly to his daughter, abruptly said, "Mary, you have now had some days to study Lord Aspenly—how do you like him?"

The girl raised her eyes, not a little surprised at the question, and doubtful whether she had heard it aright.

"I say," resumed he, "you ought to have been able by this time to arrive at a fair judgment as to Lord Aspenly's merits—what do you think of him—do you like him?"

"Indeed, father," replied she, "I have observed him very little—he may be a very estimable man, but I have not seen enough of him to form any opinion; and indeed, if I had, my opinion must needs be a matter of the merest indifference to him and everyone else."

"Your opinion upon this point," replied Sir Richard, tartly, "happens not to be a matter of indifference."

A considerable pause again ensued, during which Mary Ashwoode had ample time to reflect upon the very unpleasant doubts which this brief speech, and the tone in which it was uttered, were calculated to inspire.

"Lord Aspenly's manners are very agreeable, very," continued Sir Richard, meditatively—"I may say, indeed, fascinating—very—do you think so?" he added sharply, turning towards his daughter.

This was rather a puzzling question. The girl had never thought about him except as a frivolous old beau; yet it was plain she could not say so without vexing her father; she therefore adopted the simplest expedient under such perplexing circumstances, and preserved an embarrassed silence.

"The fact is," said Sir Richard, raising himself a little, so as to look full in his daughter's face, at the same time speaking slowly and sternly, "the fact is, I had better be explicit on this subject. I am anxious that you should think well of Lord Aspenly; it is, in short, my wish and pleasure that you should like him; you understand me—you had better understand me." This was said with an emphasis not to be mistaken, and another pause ensued. "For the present," continued he, "run down and amuse yourself—and—stay—offer to show his lordship the old terrace garden—do you mind? Now, once more, run away."

So saying, the old gentleman turned coolly from her, and rang his hand-bell vehemently. Scarcely knowing what she did, such was her astonishment at all that had passed, Mary Ashwoode left the room without any very clear notion as to whither she was going, or what to do; nor was her confusion much relieved when, on entering the hall, the first object which encountered her was Lord Aspenly himself, with his triangular hat under his arm, while he adjusted his deep lace ruffles—he had never looked so ugly before. As he stood beneath her while she descended the broad staircase, smiling from ear to ear, and bowing with the most chivalric profundity, his skinny, lemon-coloured face, and cold, glittering little eyes raised toward her—she thought that it was impossible for the human shape so nearly to assume the outward semblance of a squat, emaciated toad.

"Miss Ashwoode, as I live!" exclaimed the noble peer, with his most gracious and fascinating smile. "On what mission of love and mercy does she move? Shall I hope that her first act of pity may be exercised in favour of the most devoted of her slaves? I have been looking in vain for a guide through the intricacies of Sir Richard's yew hedges and leaden statues; may I hope that my presiding angel has sent me one in you?"

Lord Aspenly paused, and grinned wider and wider, but receiving no answer, he resumed,—

"I understand, Miss Ashwoode, that the pleasure-grounds, which surround us, abound in samples of your exquisite taste; as a votary of Flora, may I ask, if the request be not too bold, that you will vouchsafe to lead a bewildered pilgrim to the object of his search? There is—is there not?—shrined in the centre of these rustic labyrinths, a small flower-garden which owes its sweet existence to your creative genius; if it be not too remote, and if you can afford so much leisure, allow me to implore your guidance."

As he thus spoke, with a graceful flourish, the little gentleman extended his hand, and courteously taking hers by the extreme points of the fingers, he led her forward in a manner, as he thought, so engaging as to put resistance out of the question. Mary Ashwoode felt far too little interest in anything but the one ever-present grief which weighed upon her heart, to deny the old fop his trifling request; shrouding her graceful limbs, therefore, in a short cloak, and drawing the hood over her head, she walked forth, with slow steps and an aching heart, among the trim hedges which fenced the old-fashioned pleasure walks.

"Beauty," exclaimed the nobleman, as he walked with an air of romantic gallantry by her side, and glancing as he spoke at the flowers which adorned the border of the path—"beauty is nowhere seen to greater advantage than in spots like this; where nature has amassed whatever is most beautiful in the inanimate creation, only to prove how unutterably more exquisite are the charms of living loveliness: these walks, but this moment to me a wilderness, are now so many paths of magic pleasure—how can I enough thank the kind enchantress to whom I owe the transformation?" Here the little gentleman looked unutterable things, and a silence of some minutes ensued, during which he effected some dozen very wheezy sighs. Emboldened by Miss Ashwoode's silence, which he interpreted as a very unequivocal proof of conscious tenderness, he resolved to put an end to the skirmishing with which he had opened his attack, and to commence the action in downright earnestness. "This place breathes an atmosphere of romance; it is a spot consecrated to the worship of love; it is—it is the shrine of passion, and I—I am a votary—a worshipper."

Miss Ashwoode paused in mingled surprise and displeasure, for his vehemence had become so excessive as, in conjunction with his asthma, to threaten to choke his lordship outright. When Mary Ashwoode stopped short, Lord Aspenly took it for granted that the crisis had arrived, and that the moment for the decisive onset was now come; he therefore ejaculated with a rapturous croak,—

"And you—you are my divinity!" and at the same moment he descended stiffly upon his two knees, caught her hand in his, and began to mumble it with unmistakable devotion.

"My lord—Lord Aspenly!—surely your lordship cannot mean—have done, my lord," exclaimed the astonished girl, withdrawing her hand indignantly from his grasp. "Rise, my lord; you cannot mean otherwise than to mock me by such extravagance. My lord—my lord, you surprise and shock me beyond expression."

"Angel of beauty! most exquisite—most perfect of your sex," gasped his lordship, "I love you—yes, to distraction. Answer me, if you would not have me expire at your feet—ugh—ugh—tell me that I may hope—ugh—that I am not indifferent to you—ugh, ugh, ugh,—that—that you can love me?" Here his lordship was seized with so violent a fit of coughing, that Miss Ashwoode began to fear that he would expire at her feet in downright earnest. During the paroxysm, in which, with one hand pressed upon his side, he supported himself by leaning with the other upon the ground, Mary had ample time to collect her thoughts, so that when at length he had recovered his breath, she addressed him with composure and decision.

"My lord," she said, "I am grateful for your preference of me; although, when I consider the shortness of my acquaintance with you, and how few have been your opportunities of knowing me, I cannot but wonder very much at its vehemence. For me, your lordship cannot feel more than an idle fancy, which will, no doubt, pass away just as lightly as it came; and as for my feelings, I have only to say, that it is wholly impossible for you ever to establish in them any interest of the kind you look for. Indeed, indeed, my lord, I hope I have not given you pain—nothing can be further from my wish than to do so; but it is my duty to tell you plainly and at once my real feelings. I should otherwise but trifle with your kindness, for which, although I cannot return it as you desire, I shall ever be grateful."

Having thus spoken, she turned from her noble suitor, and began to retrace her steps rapidly towards the house.

"Stay, Miss Ashwoode—remain here for a moment—you must hear me!" exclaimed Lord Aspenly, in a tone so altered, that she involuntarily paused, while his lordship, with some difficulty, raised himself again to his feet, and with a flushed and haggard face, in which still lingered the ghastly phantom of his habitual smile, he hobbled to her side. "Miss Ashwoode," he exclaimed, in a tone tremulous with emotions very different from love, "I—I—I am not used to be treated cavalierly—I—I will not brook it: I am not to be trifled with—jilted—madam, jilted, and taken in. You have accepted and encouraged my attentions—attentions which you cannot have mistaken; and now, madam, when I make you an offer—such as your ambition, your most presumptuous ambition, dared not have anticipated—the offer of my hand—and—and a coronet, you coolly tell me you never cared for me. Why, what on earth do you look for or expect?—a foreign prince or potentate, an emperor, ha—ha—he—he—ugh—ugh—ugh! I tell you plainly, Miss Ashwoode, that my feelings must be considered. I have long made my passion known to you; it has been encouraged; and I have obtained Sir Richard's—your father's—sanction and approval. You had better reconsider what you have said. I shall give you an hour; at the end of that time, unless you see the propriety of avowing feelings which, you must pardon me when I say it, your encouragement of my advances has long virtually acknowledged, I must lay the whole case, including all the painful details of my own ill-usage, before Sir Richard Ashwoode, and trust to his powers of persuasion to induce you to act reasonably, and, I will add, honourably."

Here his lordship took several extraordinarily copious pinches of snuff, after which he bowed very low, conjured up an unusually hideous smile, in which spite, fury, and triumph were eagerly mingled, and hobbled away before the astonished girl had time to muster her spirits sufficiently to answer him.

CHAPTER XXI.

WHO APPEARED TO MARY ASHWOODE AS SHE SATE UNDER THE TREES—THE CHAMPION.

With flashing eyes and a swelling heart, struck dumb with unutterable indignation, the beautiful girl stood fixed in the attitude in which his last words had reached her, while the enraged and unmanly old fop hobbled away, with the ease and grace with which a crippled ape might move over a hot griddle. He had disappeared for some minutes before she had recovered herself sufficiently to think or speak.

"If he were by my side," she said, "this noble lord dared not have used me thus. Edmond would have died a thousand deaths first. But oh! God look upon me, for his love is gone from me, and I am now a poor, grieved, desolate creature, with none to help me."

Thus saying, she sate herself down upon the grass bank, beneath the tall and antique trees, and wept with all the bitter and devoted abandonment of hopeless sorrow. From this unrestrained transport of grief she was at length aroused by the pressure of a hand, gently and kindly laid upon her shoulder.

"What vexes you, Mary, my little girl?" inquired Major O'Leary, for he it was that stood by her. "Come, darling, don't fret, but tell your old uncle the whole business, and twenty to one, he has wit enough in his old noddle yet to set matters to rights. So, so, my darling, dry your pretty eyes—wipe the tears away;

why should they wet your young cheeks, my poor little doat, that you always were. It is too early yet for sorrow to come on you. Wouldn't I throw myself between my little pet and all grief and danger? Then trust to me, darling; wipe away the tears, or by — I'll begin to cry myself. Dry your eyes, and see if I can't help you one way or another."

The mellow brogue of the old major had never fallen before with such a tender pathos upon the ear of his beautiful niece, as now that its rich current bore full upon her heart the unlooked-for words of kindness and comfort.

"Were not you always my pet," continued he, with the same tenderness and pity in his tone, "from the time I first took you upon my knee, my poor little Mary? And were not you fond of your old rascally uncle O'Leary? Usedn't I always to take your part, right or wrong; and do you think I'll desert you now? Then tell it all to me—ain't I your poor old uncle, the same as ever? Come, then, dry the tears—there's a darling—wipe them away."

While thus speaking, the warm-hearted old man took her hand, with a touching mixture of gallantry, pity, and affection, and kissed it again and again, with a thousand accompanying expressions of endearment, such as in the days of her childhood he had been wont to lavish upon his little favourite. The poor girl, touched by the kindness of her early friend, whose good-natured sympathy was not to be mistaken, gradually recovered her composure, and yielding to the urgencies of the major, who clearly perceived that something extraordinarily distressing must have occurred to account for her extreme agitation, she at length told him the immediate cause of her grief and excitement. The major listened to the narrative with growing indignation, and when it had ended, he inquired, in a tone, about whose unnatural calmness there was something infinitely more formidable than in the noisiest clamour of fury,—

"Which way, darling, did his lordship go when he left you?"

The girl looked in his face, and saw his deadly purpose there.

"Uncle, my own dear uncle," she cried distractedly, "for God's sake do not follow him—for God's sake—I conjure you, I implore—" She would have cast herself at his feet, but the major caught her in his arms.

"Well, well, my darling." he exclaimed, "I'll not kill him, well as he deserves it—I'll not: you have saved his life. I pledge you my honour, as a gentleman and a soldier, I'll not harm him for what he has said or done this day—are you satisfied?"

"I am, I am! Thank God, thank God!" exclaimed the poor girl, eagerly.

"But, Mary, I must see him," rejoined the major; "he has threatened to set Sir Richard upon you—I must see him; you don't object to that, under the promise I have made? I want to—to reason with him. He shall not get you into trouble with the baronet; for though Richard and I came of the same mother, we are not of the same marriage, nor of the same mould—I would not for a cool hundred that he told his story to your father."

"Indeed, indeed, dear uncle," replied the girl, "I fear me there is little hope of escape or ease for me. My father must know what has passed; he will learn it inevitably, and then it needs no colouring or misrepresentation to call down upon me his heaviest displeasure; his anger I must endure as best I may.

God help me. But neither threats nor violence shall make me retract the answer I have given to Lord Aspenly, nor ever yield consent to marry him—nor any other now."

"Well, well, little Mary," rejoined the major, "I like your spirit. Stand to that, and you'll never be sorry for it. In the meantime, I'll venture to exercise his lordship's conversational powers in a brief conference of a few minutes, and if I find him as reasonable as I expect, you'll have no cause to regret my interposition. Don't look so frightened—haven't I promised, on the honour of a gentleman, that I will not pink him for anything said or done in his conference with you? To send a small sword through a bolster or a bailiff," he continued, meditatively, "is an indifferent action; but to spit such a poisonous, crawling toad as the respectable old gentleman in question, would be nothing short of meritorious—it is an act that 'ud tickle the fancy of every saint in heaven, and, if there's justice on earth, would canonize myself. But never mind, I'll let it alone—the little thing shall escape, since you wish it—Major O'Leary has said it, so let no doubt disturb you. Good-bye, my little darling, dry your eyes, and let me see you, before an hour, as merry as in the merriest days that are gone."

So saying, Major O'Leary patted her cheek, and taking her hand affectionately in both his, he added,—

"Sure I am, that there is more in all this than you care to tell me, my little pet. I am sorely afraid there is something beyond my power to remedy, to change your light-hearted nature so mournfully. What it is, I will not inquire, but remember, darling, whenever you want a friend, you'll find a sure one in me."

Thus having spoken, he turned from her, and strode rapidly down the walk, until the thick, formal hedges concealed his retreating form behind their impenetrable screens of darksome verdure.

Odd as were the manner and style of the major's professions, there was something tender, something of heartiness, in his speech, which assured her that she had indeed found a friend in him—rash, volatile, and violent it might be, but still one on whose truth and energy she might calculate. That there was one being who felt with her and for her, was a discovery which touched her heart and moved her generous spirit, and she now regarded the old major, whose spoiled favourite in childhood she had been, but whom, before, she had never known capable of a serious feeling, with emotions of affection and gratitude, stronger and more ardent than he had ever earned from any other being. Agitated, grieved, and excited, she hurriedly left the scene of this interview, and sought relief for her overcharged feelings in the quiet and seclusion of her chamber.

## CHAPTER XXII.

### THE SPINET.

In no very pleasant frame of mind did Lord Aspenly retrace his steps toward the old house. His lordship had, all his life, been firmly persuaded that the whole female creation had been sighing and pining for the possession of his heart and equipage. He knew that among those with whom his chief experience lay, his fortune and his coronet were considerations not to be resisted; and he as firmly believed, that even without such recommendations, few women, certainly none of any taste or discrimination, could be found with hearts so steeled against the archery of Cupid, as to resist the fascinations of his manner and conversation, supported and directed, as both were, by the tact and experience drawn from a practice of more years than his lordship cared to count, even to himself. He had, however, smiled, danced, and chatted, in impregnable celibacy, through more than half a century of gaiety and frivolity—breaking, as he thought, hearts innumerable, and, at all events, disappointing very many calculations—until, at length, his lordship had arrived at that precise period of existence at which old gentlemen, not unfrequently, become all at once romantic, disinterested, and indiscreet—nobody exactly knows why—unless it be for variety, or to spite an heir presumptive, or else that, as a preliminary to second childhood, nature has ordained a second boyhood too. Certain, however, it is, that Lord Aspenly was seized, on a sudden, with a matrimonial frenzy; and, tired of the hackneyed schemers, in the centre of whose manoeuvres he had stood and smiled so long in contemptuous security, he resolved that his choice should honour some simple, unsophisticated beauty, who had never plotted his matrimony.

Fired with this benevolent resolution, he almost instantly selected Mary Ashwoode as the happy companion of his second childhood, acquainted Sir Richard with his purpose, of course received his consent and blessing, and forthwith opened his entrenchments with the same certainty of success with which the great Duke of Marlborough might have invested a Flanders village. The inexperience of a girl who had mixed, comparatively, so little in gay society, her consequent openness to flattery, and susceptibility of being fascinated by the elegance of his address, and the splendour of his fortune—all these considerations, accompanied by a clear consciousness of his own infinite condescension in thinking of her at all, had completely excluded from all his calculations the very possibility of her doing anything else than jump into his arms the moment he should open them to receive her. The result of the interview which had just taken place, had come upon him with the overwhelming suddenness of a thunderbolt. Rejected!—Lord Aspenly rejected!—a coronet, and a fortune, and a man whom all the male world might envy—each and all rejected!—and by whom?—a chit of a girl, who had no right to look higher than a half-pay captain with a wooden leg, or a fox-hunting boor, with a few inaccessible acres of bog and mountain—the daughter of a spendthrift baronet, who was, as everyone knew, on the high road to ruin. Death and fury! was it to be endured?

The little lover, absorbed in such tranquilizing reflections, arrived at the house, and entered the drawing-room. It was not unoccupied; seated by a spinet, and with a sheet of music-paper in her lap, and a pencil in her hand, was the fair Emily Copland. As he entered, she raised her eyes, started a little, became gracefully confused, and then, with her archest smile, exclaimed,—

"What shall I say, my lord? You have detected me. I have neither defence nor palliation to offer; you have fairly caught me. Here am I engaged in perhaps the most presumptuous task that ever silly maiden undertook—I am wedding your beautiful verses to most unworthy music of my own. After all, there is nothing like a simple ballad. Such exquisite lines as these inspire music of themselves. Would that Henry Purcell had had but a peep at them! To what might they not have prompted such a genius—to what, indeed?"

So sublime was the flight of fancy suggested by this interrogatory, that Miss Copland shook her head slowly in poetic rapture, and gazed fondly for some seconds upon the carpet, apparently unconscious of Lord Aspenly's presence.

"She is a fine creature," half murmured he, with an emphasis upon the identity which implied a contrast not very favourable to Mary—"and—and very pretty—nay, she looks almost beautiful, and so—so lively—so much vivacity. Never was poor poet so much flattered," continued his lordship, approaching, as he spoke, and raising his voice, but not above its most mellifluous pitch; "to have his verses read by such eyes, to have them chanted by such a minstrel, were honour too high for the noblest bards of the noblest days of poetry: for me it is a happiness almost too great; yet, if the request be not a presumptuous one, may I, in all humility, pray that you will favour me with the music to which you have coupled my most undeserving—my most favoured lines?"

The young lady looked modest, glanced coyly at the paper which lay in her lap, looked modest once more, and then arch again, and at length, with rather a fluttered air, she threw her hands over the keys of the instrument, and to a tune, of which we say enough when we state that it was in no way unworthy of the words, she sang, rather better than young ladies usually do, the following exquisite stanzas from his lordship's pen:—

"Tho' Chloe slight me when I woo,
And scorn the love of poor Philander;
The shepherd's heart she scorns is true,
His heart is true, his passion tender.

"But poor Philander sighs in vain,
In vain laments the poor Philander;
Fair Chloe scorns with high disdain,
His love so true and passion tender.

"And here Philander lays him down,
Here will expire the poor Philander;
The victim of fair Chloe's frown,
Of love so true and passion tender.

"Ah, well-a-day! the shepherd's dead;
Ay, dead and gone, the poor Philander;
And Dryads crown with flowers his head,
And Cupid mourns his love so tender."

During this performance, Lord Aspenly, who had now perfectly recovered his equanimity, marked the time with head and hand, standing the while beside the fair performer, and every note she sang found its way through the wide portals of his vanity, directly to his heart.

"Brava! brava! bravissima!" murmured his lordship, from time to time. "Beautiful, beautiful air—most appropriate—most simple; not a note that accords not with the word it carries—beautiful, indeed! A thousand thanks! I have become quite conceited of lines of which heretofore I was half ashamed. I am quite elated—at once overpowered by the characteristic vanity of the poet, and more than recompensed by the reality of his proudest aspiration—that of seeing his verses appreciated by a heart of sensibility, and of hearing them sung by the lips of beauty."

"I am but too happy if I am forgiven," replied Emily Copland, slightly laughing, and with a heightened colour, while the momentary overflow of merriment was followed by a sigh, and her eyes sank pensively upon the ground.

This little by-play was not lost upon Lord Aspenly.

"Poor little thing," he inwardly remarked, "she is in a very bad way—desperate—quite desperate. What a devil of a rascal I am to be sure! Egad! it's almost a pity—she's a decidedly superior person; she has an elegant turn of mind—refinement—taste—egad! she is a fine creature—and so simple. She little knows I see it all; perhaps she hardly knows herself what ails her—poor, poor little thing!"

While these thoughts floated rapidly through his mind, he felt, along with his spite and anger towards Mary Ashwoode, a feeling of contempt, almost of disgust, engendered by her audacious non-appreciation of his merits—an impertinence which appeared the more monstrous by the contrast of Emily Copland's tenderness. She had made it plain enough, by all the artless signs which simple maidens know not how to hide, that his fascinations had done their fatal work upon her heart. He had seen, this for several days, but not with the overwhelming distinctness with which he now beheld it.

"Poor, poor little girl!" said his lordship to himself; "I am very, very sorry, but it cannot be helped; it is no fault of mine. I am really very, very, confoundedly sorry."

In saying so to himself, however, he told himself a lie; for, instead of being grieved, he was pleased beyond measure—a fact which he might have ascertained by a single glance at the reflection of his wreathed smiles in the ponderous mirror which hung forward from the pier between the windows, as if staring down in wondering curiosity upon the progress of the flirtation. Not caring to disturb a train of thought which his vanity told him were but riveting the subtle chains which bound another victim to his conquering chariot-wheels, the Earl of Aspenly turned, with careless ease, to a table, on which lay some specimens of that worsted tapestry-work, in which the fair maidens of a century and a half ago were wont to exercise their taste and skill.

"Your work is very, very beautiful," said he, after a considerable pause, and laying down the canvas, upon whose unfinished worsted task he had been for some time gazing.

"That is my cousin's work," said Emily, not sorry to turn the conversation to a subject upon which, for many reasons, she wished to dwell; "she used to work a great deal with me before she grew romantic—before she fell in love."

"In love!—with whom?" inquired Lord Aspenly, with remarkable quickness.

"Don't you know, my lord?" inquired Emily Copland, in simple wonder. "May be I ought not to have told you—I am sure I ought not. Do not ask me any more. I am the giddiest girl—the most thoughtless!"

"Nay, nay," said Lord Aspenly, "you need not be afraid to trust me—I never tell tales; and now that I know the fact that she is in love, there can be no harm in telling me the less important particulars. On my honour," continued his lordship, with real earnestness, and affected playfulness—"upon my sacred honour! I shall not breathe one syllable of it to mortal—I shall be as secret as the tomb. Who is the happy person in question?"

"Well, my lord, you'll promise not to betray me," replied she. "I know very well I ought not to have said a word about it; but as I have made the blunder, I see no harm in telling you all I know; but you will be secret?"

"On my honour—on my life and soul, I swear!" exclaimed his lordship, with unaffected eagerness.

"Well, then, the happy man is a Mr. Edmond O'Connor," replied she.

"O'Connor—O'Connor—I never saw nor heard of the man before," rejoined the earl, reflectively. "Is he wealthy?"

"Oh! no; a mere beggarman," replied Emily, "and a Papist to boot!"

"Ha, ha, ha—he, he, he! a Papist beggar," exclaimed his lordship, with an hysterical giggle, which was intended for a careless laugh. "Has he any conversation—any manner—any attraction of that kind?"

"Oh! none in the world!—both ignorant, and I think, vulgar," replied Emily. "In short, he is very nearly a stupid boor!"

"Excellent! Ha, ha—he, he, he!—ugh! ugh!—very capital—excellent! excellent!" exclaimed his lordship, although he might have found some difficulty in explaining in what, precisely the peculiar excellence of the announcement consisted. "Is he—is he—a—a—handsome?"

"Decidedly not what I consider handsome!" replied she; "he is a large, coarse-looking fellow, with very broad shoulders—very large—and as they say of oxen, in very great condition—a sort of a prize man!"

"Ha, ha!—ugh! ugh!—he, he, he, he, he!—ugh, ugh, ugh!—de—lightful—quite delightful!" exclaimed the earl, in a tone of intense chagrin, for he was conscious that his own figure was perhaps a little too scraggy, and his legs a leetle too nearly approaching the genus spindle, and being so, there was no trait in the female character which he so inveterately abhorred and despised as their tendency to prefer those figures which exhibited a due proportion of thew and muscle. Under a cloud of rappee, his lordship made a desperate attempt to look perfectly delighted and amused, and effected a retreat to the window, where he again indulged in a titter of unutterable spite and vexation.

"And what says Sir Richard to the advances of this very desirable gentleman?" inquired he, after a little time.

"Sir Richard is, of course, violently against it," replied Emily Copland.

"So I should have supposed," returned the little nobleman, briskly. And turning again to the window, he relapsed into silence, looked out intently for some minutes, took more snuff, and finally, consulting his watch, with a few words of apology, and a gracious smile and a bow, quitted the room.


CHAPTER XXIII.

THE DARK ROOM—CONTAINING PLENTY OF SCARS AND BRUISES AND PLANS OF VENGEANCE.

On the same day a very different scene was passing in another quarter, whither for a few moments we must transport the reader. In a large and aristocratic-looking brick house, situated near the then fashionable suburb of Glasnevin, surrounded by stately trees, and within furnished with the most prodigal splendour, combined with the strictest and most minute attention to comfort and luxury, and in a large and lofty chamber, carefully darkened, screened round by the rich and voluminous folds of the silken curtains, with spider-tables laden with fruits and wines and phials of medicine, crowded around him, and rather buried than supported among a luxurious pile of pillows, lay, in sore bodily torment, with fevered pulse, and heart and brain busy with a thousand projects of revenge, the identical Nicholas Blarden, whose signal misadventure in the theatre, upon the preceding evening, we have already recorded. A decent-looking matron sate in a capacious chair, near the bed, in the capacity of nurse-tender, while her constrained and restless manner, as well as the frightened expression with which, from time to time, she stole a glance at the bloated mass of scars and bruises, of which she had the care, pretty plainly argued the sweet and patient resignation with which her charge endured his sufferings. In the recess of the curtained window sate a little black boy, arrayed according to the prevailing fashion, in a fancy suit, and with a turban on his head, and carrying in his awe-struck countenance, as well as in the immobility of his attitude, a woeful contradiction to the gaiety of his attire.

"Drink—drink—where's that damned hag?—give me drink, I say!" howled the prostrate gambler.

The woman started to her feet, and with a step which fell noiselessly upon the deep-piled carpets which covered the floor, she hastened to supply him.

He had hardly swallowed the draught, when a low knock at the door announced a visitor.

"Come in, can't you?" shouted Blarden.

"How do you feel now, Nicky dear?" inquired a female voice—and a handsome face, with rather a bold expression, and crowned by a small mob-cap, overlaid with a profusion of the richest lace, peeped into the room through the half-open door—"how do you feel?"

"In hell—that's all," shouted he.

"Doctor Mallarde is below, love," added she, without evincing either surprise or emotion of any kind at the concise announcement which the patient had just delivered.

"Let him come up then," was the reply.

"And a Mr. M'Quirk—a messenger from Mr. Chancey."

"Let him come up too. But why the hell did not Chancey come himself?—That will do—pack—be off."

The lady tossed her head, like one having authority, looked half inclined to say something sharp, but thought better of it, and contented herself with shutting the door with more emphasis than Dr. Mallarde would have recommended.

The physician of those days was a solemn personage: he would as readily have appeared without his head, as without his full-bottomed wig; and his ponderous gold-headed cane was a sort of fifth limb, the supposition of whose absence involved a contradiction to the laws of anatomy; his dress was rich and funereal; his step was slow and pompous; his words very long and very few; his look was mysterious; his nod awful; and the shake of his head unfathomable: in short, he was in no respect very much better than a modern charlatan. The science which he professed was then overgrown with absurdities and mystification. The temper of the times was superstitious and credulous, the physician, being wise in his generation, framed his outward man (including his air and language) accordingly, and the populace swallowed his long words and his electuaries with equal faith.

Doctor Mallarde was a doctor-like person, and, in theatrical phraseology, looked the part well. He was tall and stately, saturnine and sallow in aspect, had bushy, grizzled brows, and a severe and prominent dark eye, a thin, hooked nose, and a pair of lips just as thin as it. Along with these advantages he had a habit of pressing the gold head of his professional cane against one corner of his mouth, in a way which produced a sinister and mysterious distortion of that organ; and by exhibiting the medical baton, the outward and visible sign of doctorship, in immediate juxtaposition with the fountain of language, added enormously to the gravity and authority of the words which from time to time proceeded therefrom.

In the presence of such a spectre as this—intimately associated with all that was nauseous and deadly on earth—it is hardly to be wondered at that even Nicholas Blarden felt himself somewhat uneasy and abashed. The physician felt his pulse, gazing the while upon the ceiling, and pressing the gold head of his cane, as usual, to the corner of his mouth; made him put out his tongue, asked him innumerable questions, which we forbear to publish, and ended by forbidding his patient the use of every comfort in which he had hitherto found relief, and by writing a prescription which might have furnished a country dispensary with good things for a twelvemonth. He then took his leave and his fee, with the grisly announcement, that unless the drugs were all swallowed, and the other matters attended to in a spirit of absolute submission, he would not answer for the life of the patient.

"I am damned glad he's gone at last," exclaimed Blarden, with a kind of gasp, as if a weight had been removed from his breast. "Curse me, if I did not feel all the time as if my coffin was in the room. Are you there, M'Quirk?"

"Here I am, Mr. Blarden," rejoined the person addressed, whom we may as well describe, as we shall have more to say about him by-and-by.

Mr. M'Quirk was a small, wiry man, of fifty years and upwards, arrayed in that style which is usually described as "shabby genteel." He was gifted with one of those mean and commonplace countenances which seem expressly made for the effectual concealment of the thoughts and feelings of the possessor—an advantage which he further secured by habitually keeping his eyes as nearly closed as might be, so that, for any indication afforded by them of the movements of the inward man, they might as well have been shut up altogether. The peculiarity, if not the grace, of his appearance, was heightened by a contraction of the muscles at the nape of the neck, which drew his head backward, and produced a corresponding elevation of the chin, which, along with a certain habitual toss of the head, gave to his appearance a kind of caricatured affectation of superciliousness and hauteur, very impressive to behold. Along with the swing of the head, which we have before noticed, there was, whenever he spoke, a sort of careless libration of the whole body, which, together with a certain way of jerking or twitching the right shoulder from time to time, were the only approaches to gesticulation in which he indulged.

"Well, what does your master say?" inquired Blarden—"out with it, can't you."

"Master—master—indeed! Cock him up with master," echoed the man, with lofty disdain.

"Ay! what does he say?" reiterated Blarden, in no very musical tones. "Damn you, are you choking, or moonstruck? Out with it, can't you?"

"Chancey says that you had better think the matter over—and that's his opinion," replied M'Quirk.

"And a fine opinion it is," rejoined Blarden, furiously. "Why, in hell's name, what's the matter with him—the—drivelling idiot? What's law for—what's the courts for? Am I to be trounced and cudgelled in the face of hundreds, and—and half murdered, and nothing for it? I tell you, I'll be beggared before the scoundrel shall escape. If every penny I'm worth in the world can buy it, I'll have justice. Tell that sleepy sot Chancey that I'll make him work. Ho—o—o—oh!" bawled the wretch, as his anguish all returned a hundredfold in the fruitless attempt to raise himself in bed.

"Drink, here—drink—I'm choking! Hock and water. Damn you, don't look so stupid and frightened. I'll not be bamboozled by an old 'pothecary. Quick with it, you fumbling witch."

He finished the draught, and lay silently for a time.

"See—mind me, M'Quirk," he said, after a pause, "tell Chancey to come out himself—tell him to be here before evening, or I'll make him sorry for it, do you mind; I want to give him directions. Tell him to come at once, or I'll make him smoke for it, that's all."

"I understand—all right—very well; and so, as you seem settling for a snooze, I wish you good-evening, Mr. Blarden, and all sorts of pleasure and happiness," rejoined the messenger.

The patient answered by a grin and a stifled howl, and Mr. M'Quirk, having his head within the curtains, which screened him effectually from the observation of the two attendants, and observing that Mr. Blarden's eyes were closely shut in the rigid compression of pain, put out his tongue, and indulged for a few seconds in an exceedingly ugly grimace, after which, repeating his farewell in a tone of respectful sympathy, he took his departure, chuckling inwardly all the way downstairs, for the little gentleman had a playful turn for mischief.

When Gordon Chancey, Esquire, barrister-at-law, in obedience to this summons, arrived at Cherry Hill, for so the residence of the sick voluptuary was called, he found his loving friend and patron, Nicholas Blarden, babbling not of green fields, but of green curtains, theatres, dice-boxes, bright eyes, small-swords, and the shades infernal—in a word, in a high state of delirium. On calling next day, however, he beheld him much recovered; and after an extremely animated discussion, these two well-assorted confederates at length, by their united ingenuity, succeeded in roughly sketching the outlines of a plan of terrific vengeance, in all respects worthy of the diabolical council in which it originated, and of whose progress and development this history very fully treats.

CHAPTER XXIV.

A CRITIC—A CONDITION—AND THE SMALL-SWORDS.

Lord Aspenly walked forth among the trim hedges and secluded walks which surrounded the house, and by alternately taking enormous pinches of rappee, and humming a favourite air or two, he wonderfully assisted his philosophy in recovering his equanimity.

"It matters but little how the affair ends," thought his lordship, "if in matrimony—the girl is, after all, a very fine girl: but if the matter is fairly off, in that case I shall—look very foolish," suggested his conscience faintly, but his lordship dismissed the thought precipitately—"in that case I shall make it a point to marry within a fortnight. I should like to know the girl who would refuse me"—"the only one you ever asked," suggested his conscience again, but with no better result—"I should like to see the girl of sense or discrimination who could refuse me. I shall marry the finest girl in the country, and then I presume very few will be inclined to call me fool."

"Not I for one, my lord," exclaimed a voice close by. Lord Aspenly started, for he was conscious that in his energy he had uttered the concluding words of his proud peroration with audible emphasis, and became instantly aware that the speaker was no other than Major O'Leary.

"Not I for one, my lord," repeated the major, with extreme gravity, "I take it for granted, my lord, that you are no fool."

"I am obliged to you, Major O'Leary, for your good opinion," replied his lordship, drily, with a surprised look and a stiff inclination of his person.

"Nothing to be grateful for in it," replied the major, returning the bow with grave politeness: "if years and discretion increase together, you and I ought to be models of wisdom by this time of day. I'm proud of my years, my lord, and I would be half as proud again if I could count as many as your lordship."

There was something singularly abrupt and uncalled for in all this, which Lord Aspenly did not very well understand; he therefore stopped short, and looked in the major's face; but reading in its staid and formal gravity nothing whatever to furnish a clue to his exact purpose, he made a kind of short bow, and continued his walk in dignified silence. There was something exceedingly disagreeable, he thought, in the manner of his companion—something very near approaching to cool impertinence—which he could not account for upon any other supposition than that the major had been prematurely indulging in the joys of Bacchus. If, however, he thought that by the assumption of the frigid and lofty dignity with which he met the advances of the major, he was likely to relieve himself of his company, he was never more lamentably mistaken. His military companion walked with a careless swagger by his side, exactly regulating his pace by that of the little nobleman, whose meditations he had so cruelly interrupted.

"What on earth is to be done with this brute beast?" muttered his lordship, taking care, however, that the query should not reach the subject of it. "I must get rid of him—I must speak with the girl privately—what the deuce is to be done?"

They walked on a little further in perfect silence. At length his lordship stopped short and exclaimed,—

"My dear major, I am a very dull companion—quite a bore; there are times when the mind—the—the—spirits require solitude—and these walks are the very scene for a lonely ramble. I dare venture to aver that you are courting solitude like myself—your silence betrays you—then pray do not stand on ceremony—that walk leads down toward the river—pray no ceremony."

"Upon my conscience, my lord, I never was less inclined to stand on ceremony than I am at this moment," replied the major; "so give yourself no trouble in the world about me. Nothing would annoy me so much as to have you think I was doing anything but precisely what I liked best myself."

Lord Aspenly bowed, took a violent pinch of snuff, and walked on, the major still keeping by his side. After a long silence his lordship began to lilt his own sweet verses in a careless sort of a way, which was intended to convey to his tormentor that he had totally forgotten his presence:—

"Tho' Chloe slight me when I woo,
And scorn the love of poor Philander;
The shepherd's heart she scorns is true,
His heart is true, his passion tender."

"Passion tender," observed the major—"passion tender—it's a nurse-tender the like of you and me ought to be looking for—passion tender—upon my conscience, a good joke."

Lord Aspenly was strongly tempted to give vent to his feelings; but even at the imminent risk of bursting, he managed to suppress his fury. The major was certainly (however unaccountable and mysterious the fact might be) in a perfectly cut-throat frame of mind, and Lord Aspenly had no desire to present his weasand for the entertainment of his military friend.

"Tender—tender," continued the inexorable major, "allow me, my lord, to suggest the word tough as an improvement—tender, my lord, is a term which does not apply to chickens beyond a certain time of life, and it strikes me as too bold a license of poetry to apply it to a gentleman of such extreme and venerable old age as your lordship; for I take it for granted that Philander is another name for yourself."

As the major uttered this critical remark, Lord Aspenly felt his brain, as it were, fizz with downright fury; the instinct of self-preservation, however, triumphed; he mastered his generous indignation, and resumed his walk in a state of mind nothing short of awful.

"My lord," inquired the major, with tragic abruptness, and with very stern emphasis—"I take the liberty of asking, have you made your soul?"

The precise nature of the major's next proceeding, Lord Aspenly could not exactly predict; of one thing, however, he felt assured, and that was, that the designs of his companion were decidedly of a dangerous character, and as he gazed in mute horror upon the major, confused but terrific ideas of "homicidal monomania," and coroner's inquests floated dimly through his distracted brain.

"My soul?" faltered he, in undisguised trepidation.

"Yes, my lord," repeated the major, with remarkable coolness, "have you made your soul?"

During this conference his lordship's complexion had shifted from its original lemon-colour to a lively orange, and thence faded gradually off into a pea-green; at which hue it remained fixed during the remainder of the interview.

"I protest—you cannot be serious—I am wholly in the dark. Positively, Major O'Leary, this is very unaccountable conduct—you really ought—pray explain."

"Upon my conscience, I will explain," rejoined the major, "although the explanation won't make you much more in love with your present predicament, unless I am very much out. You made my niece, Mary Ashwoode, an offer of marriage to-day; well, she was much obliged to you, but she did not want to marry you, and she told you so civilly. Did you then, like a man and a gentleman, take your answer from her as you ought to have done, quietly and courteously? No, you did not; you went to bully the poor girl, and to insult her; because she politely declined to marry a—a—an ugly bunch of wrinkles, like you; and you threatened to tell Sir Richard—ay, you did—to tell him your pitiful story, you—you—you—but wait awhile. You want to have the poor girl frightened and bullied into marrying you. Where's your spirit or your feeling, my lord? But you don't know what the words mean. If ever you did, you'd sooner have been racked to death, than have terrified and insulted a poor friendless girl, as you thought her. But she's not friendless. I'll teach you she's not. As long as this arm can lift a small-sword, and while the life is in my body, I'll never see any woman maltreated by a scoundrel—a scoundrel, my lord; but I'll bring him to his knees for it, or die in the attempt. And holding these opinions, did you think I'd let you offend my niece? No, sir, I'd be blown to atoms first."

"Major O'Leary," replied his lordship, as soon as he had collected his thoughts and recovered breath to speak, "your conduct is exceedingly violent—very, and, I will add, most hasty and indiscreet. You have entirely misconceived me, you have mistaken the whole affair. You will regret this violence—I protest—I know you will, when you understand the whole matter. At present, knowing the nature of your feelings, I protest, though I might naturally resent your observations, it is not in my nature, in my heart to be angry." This was spoken with a very audible quaver.

"You would, my lord, you would be angry," rejoined the major, "you'd dance with fury this moment, if you dared. You could find it in your heart to go into a passion with a girl; but talking with men is a different sort of thing. Now, my lord, we are both here, with our swords; no place can be more secluded, and, I presume, no two men more willing. Pray draw, my lord, or I'll be apt to spoil your velvet and gold lace."

"Major O'Leary, I will be heard!" exclaimed Lord Aspenly, with an earnestness which the imminent peril of his person inspired—"I must have a word or two with you, before we put this dispute to so deadly an arbitrament."

The major had foreseen and keenly enjoyed the reluctance and the evident tremors of his antagonist. He returned his half-drawn sword to its scabbard with an impatient thrust, and, folding his arms, looked down with supreme contempt upon the little peer.

"Major O'Leary, you have been misinformed—Miss Ashwoode has mistaken me. I assure you, I meant no disrespect—none in the world, I protest. I may have spoken hastily—perhaps I did—but I never intended disrespect—never for a moment."

"Well, my lord, suppose that I admit that you did not mean any disrespect; and suppose that I distinctly assert that I have neither right nor inclination just now to call you to an account for anything you may have said, in your interview this morning, offensive to my niece; I give you leave to suppose it, and, what's more, in supposing it, I solemnly aver, you suppose neither more nor less than the exact truth," said the major.

"Well, then, Major O'Leary," replied Lord Aspenly, "I profess myself wholly at a loss to understand your conduct. I presume, at all events, that nothing further need pass between us about the matter."

"Not so fast, my lord, if you please," rejoined the major; "a great deal more must pass between us before I have done with your lordship; although I cannot punish you for the past, I have a perfect right to restrain you for the future. I have a proposal to make, to which I expect your lordship's assent—a proposal which, under the circumstances, I dare say, you will think, however unpleasant, by no means unreasonable."

"Pray state it," said Lord Aspenly, considerably reassured on finding that the debate was beginning to take a diplomatic turn.

"This is my proposal, then," replied the major: "you shall write a letter to Sir Richard, renouncing all pretensions to his daughter's hand, and taking upon yourself the whole responsibility of the measure, without implicating her directly or indirectly; do you mind: and you shall leave this place, and go wherever you please, before supper-time to-night. These are the conditions on which I will consent to spare you, my lord, and upon no other shall you escape."

"Why, what can you mean, Major O'Leary?" exclaimed the little coxcomb, distractedly. "If I did any such thing, I should be run through by Sir Richard or his rakehelly son; besides, I came here for a wife—my friends know it; I cannot consent to make a fool of myself. How dare you presume to propose such conditions to me?"

The little gentleman as he wound up, had warmed so much, that he placed his hand on the hilt of his sword. Without one word of commentary, the major drew his, and with a nod of invitation, threw himself into an attitude of defence, and resting the point of his weapon upon the ground, awaited the attack of his adversary. Perhaps Lord Aspenly regretted the precipitate valour which had prompted him to place his hand on his sword-hilt, as much as he had ever regretted any act of his whole life; it was, however, too late to recede, and with the hurried manner of one who has made up his mind to a disagreeable thing, and wishes it soon over, he drew his also, and their blades were instantly crossed in mortal opposition.

## CHAPTER XXV.

### THE COMBAT AND ITS ISSUE.

Lord Aspenly made one or two eager passes at his opponent, which were parried with perfect ease and coolness; and before he had well recovered his position from the last of those lunges, a single clanging sweep of the major's sword, taking his adversary's blade from the point to the hilt with irresistible force, sent his lordship's weapon whirring through the air some eight or ten yards away.

"Take your life, my lord," said the major, contemptuously; "I give it to you freely, only wishing the present were more valuable. What do you say now, my lord, to the terms?"

"I say, sir—what do I say?" echoed his lordship, not very coherently. "Major O'Leary, you have disarmed me, sir, and you ask me what I say to your terms. What do I say? Why, sir, I say again what I said before, that I cannot and will not subscribe to them."

Lord Aspenly, having thus delivered himself, looked half astonished and half frightened at his own valour.

"Everyone to his taste—your lordship has an uncommon inclination for slaughter," observed the major coolly, walking to the spot where lay the little gentleman's sword, raising it, and carelessly presenting it to him: "take it, my lord, and use it more cautiously than you have done—defend yourself!"

Little expecting another encounter, yet ashamed to decline it, his lordship, with a trembling hand, grasped the weapon once more, and again their blades were crossed in deadly combat. This time his lordship prudently forbore to risk his safety by an impetuous attack upon an adversary so cool and practised as the major, and of whose skill he had just had so convincing a proof. Major O'Leary, therefore, began the attack; and pressing his opponent with some slight feints and passes, followed him closely as he retreated for some twenty yards, and then, suddenly striking up to the point of his lordship's sword with his own, he seized the little nobleman's right arm at the wrist with a grasp like a vice, and once more held his life at his disposal.

"Take your life for the second and the last time," said the major, having suffered the wretched little gentleman for a brief pause to fully taste the bitterness of death; "mind, my lord, for the last time;" and so saying, he contemptuously flung his lordship from him by the arm which he grasped.

"Now, my lord, before we begin for the last time, listen to me," said the major, with a sternness, which commanded all the attention of the affrighted peer; "I desire that you should fully understand what I propose. I would not like to kill you under a mistake—there is nothing like a clear, mutual understanding during a quarrel. Such an understanding being once established, bloodshed, if it unfortunately occurs, can scarcely, even in the most scrupulous bosom, excite the mildest regret. I wish, my lord, to have nothing whatever to reproach myself with in the catastrophe which you appear to have resolved shall overtake you; and, therefore, I'll state the whole case for your dying consolation in as few words as possible. Don't be in a hurry, my lord, I'll not detain you more than five minutes in this miserable world. Now, my lord, you have two strong, indeed I may call them in every sense fatal, objections to my proposal. The first is, that if you write the letter I propose, you must fight Sir Richard and young Henry Ashwoode. Now, I pledge myself, my soul, and honour, as a Christian, a soldier, and a gentleman, that I will stand between you and them—that I will protect you completely from all responsibility upon that score—and that if anyone is to fight with either of them, it shall not be you. Your second objection is, that having been fool enough to tell the world that you were coming here for a wife, you are ashamed to go away without one. Now, without meaning to be offensive, I never heard anything more idiotic in the whole course of my life. But if it must be so, and that you cannot go away without a wife, why the d——l don't you ask Emily Copland—a fine girl with some thousands of pounds, I believe, and at all events dying for love of you, as I am sure you see yourself? You can't care for one more than the other, and why the deuce need you trouble your head about their gossip, if anyone wonders at the change? And now, my lord, mark me, I have said all that is to be said in the way of commentary or observation upon my proposal, and I must add a word or two about the consequences of finally rejecting it. I have spared your life twice, my lord, within these five minutes. If you refuse the accommodation I have proposed, I will a third time give you an opportunity of disembarrassing yourself of the whole affair by running me through the body—in which, if you fail, so sure as you are this moment alive and breathing before me, you shall, at the end of the next five, be a corpse. So help me God!"

Major O'Leary paused, leaving Lord Aspenly in a state of confusion and horror, scarcely short of distraction.

There was no mistaking the major's manner, and the old beau garçon already felt in imagination the cold steel busy with his intestines.

"But, Major O'Leary," said he, despairingly, "will you engage—can you pledge yourself that no mischief shall follow from my withdrawing as you say? not that I would care to avoid a duel when occasion required; but no one likes to unnecessarily risk himself. Will you indeed prevent all unpleasantness?"

"Did I pledge my soul and honour that I would?" inquired the major sternly.

"Well, I am satisfied. I do agree," replied his lordship. "But is there any occasion for me to remove to-night?"

"Every occasion," replied the major, coolly. "You must come directly with me, and write the letter—and this evening, before supper, you must leave Morley Court. And, above all things, just remember this, let there be no trickery or treachery in this matter. So sure as I see the smallest symptom of anything of the kind, I will bring about such another piece of work as has not been for many a long day. Am I fully understood?"

"Perfectly—perfectly, my dear sir," replied the nobleman. "Clearly understood. And believe me, Major, when I say that nothing but the fact that I myself, for private reasons, am not unwilling to break the matter off, could have induced me to co-operate with you in this business. Believe me, sir, otherwise I should have fought until one or other of us had fallen to rise no more."

"To be sure you would, my lord," rejoined the major, with edifying gravity. "And in the meantime your lordship will much oblige me by walking up to the house. There's pen and paper in Sir Richard's study; and between us we can compose something worthy of the occasion. Now, my lord, if you please."

Thus, side by side, walked the two elderly gentlemen, like the very best friends, towards the old house. And shrewd indeed would have been that observer who could have gathered from the manner of either (whatever their flushed faces and somewhat ruffled exterior might have told), as with formal courtesy they threaded the trim arbours together, that but a few minutes before each had sought the other's life.

CHAPTER XXVI.

THE HELL—GORDON CHANCEY—LUCK—FRENZY AND A RESOLUTION.

The night which followed this day found young Henry Ashwoode, his purse replenished with bank-notes, that day advanced by Craven, to the amount of one thousand pounds, once more engaged in the delirious prosecution of his favourite pursuit—gaming. In the neighbourhood of the theatre, in that narrow street now known as Smock Alley, there stood in those days a kind of coffee-house, rather of the better sort. From the public-room, in which actors, politicians, officers, and occasionally a member of parliament, or madcap Irish peer, chatted, lounged, and sipped their sack or coffee—the initiated, or, in short, any man with a good coat on his back and a few pounds in his pocket, on exchanging a brief whisper with a singularly sleek-looking gentleman, who sate in the prospective of the background, might find his way through a small, baize-covered door in the back of the chamber, and through a lobby or two, and thence upstairs into a suite of rooms, decently hung with gilded leather, and well lighted with a profusion of wax candles, where hazard and cards were played for stakes unlimited, except by the fortunes and the credit of those who gamed. The ceaseless clang of the dice-box and rattle of the dice upon the table, and the clamorous challenging and taking of the odds upon the throwing, accompanied by the ferocious blasphemies of desperate losers, who, with clenched hands and distracted gestures, poured, unheeded, their frantic railings and imprecations, as they, in unpitied agony, withdrew from the fatal table; and now and then the scarcely less hideous interruptions of brutal quarrels, accusations, and recriminations among the excited and half-drunken gamblers, were the sounds which greeted the ear of him who ascended toward this unhallowed scene. The rooms were crowded—the atmosphere hot and stifling, and the company in birth and pretensions, if not in outward attire, to the full as mixed and various as the degrees of fortune, which scattered riches and ruin promiscuously among them. In the midst of all this riotous uproar, several persons sate and played at cards as if (as, perhaps, was really the case), perfectly unconscious of the ceaseless hubbub going on around them. Here you might see in one place the hare-brained young squire, scarcely three months launched upon the road to ruin, snoring in drunken slumber, in his deep-cushioned chair, with his cravat untied, and waistcoat loosened, and his last cup of mulled sack upset upon the table beside him, and streaming upon his velvet breeches and silken hose—while his lightly-won bank notes, stuffed into the loose coat pocket, and peeping temptingly from the aperture, invited the fingers of the first chevalier d'industrie who wished to help himself. In another place you might behold two sharpers fulfilling the conditions of their partnership, by wheedling a half-tipsy simpleton into a quiet game of ombre. And again, elsewhere you might descry some bully captain, whose occupation having ended with the Irish wars, indemnified himself as best he might by such contributions as he could manage to levy from the young and reckless in such haunts as this, busily and energetically engaged in brow-beating a timid greenhorn, who has the presumption to fancy that he has won something from the captain, which the captain has forgotten to pay. In another place you may see, unheeded and unheeding, the wretch who has played and lost his last stake; with white, unmeaning face and idiotic grin, glaring upon the floor, thought and feeling palsied, something worse, and more appalling than a maniac.

The whole character of the assembly bespoke the recklessness and the selfishness of its ingredients. There was, too, among them a certain coarse and revolting disregard and defiance of the etiquettes and conventional decencies of social life. More than half the men were either drunk or tipsy; some had thrown off their coats and others wore their hats; altogether the company had more the appearance of a band of reckless rioters in a public street, than of an assembly of persons professing to be gentlemen, and congregated in a drawing-room.

By the fireplace in the first and by far the largest and most crowded of the three drawing-rooms, there sate a person whose appearance was somewhat remarkable. He was an ill-made fellow, with long, lank, limber legs and arms, and an habitual lazy stoop. His face was sallow; his mouth, heavy and sensual, was continually moistened with the brandy and water which stood beside him upon a small spider-table, placed there for his especial use. His eyes were long-cut, and seldom more than half open, and carrying in their sleepy glitter a singular expression of treachery and brute cunning. He wore his own lank and grizzled hair, instead of a peruke, and sate before the fire with a drowsy inattention to all that was passing in the room; and, except for the occasional twinkle of his eye as it glanced from the corner of his half-closed lids, he might have been believed to have been actually asleep. His attitude was lounging and listless, and all his movements so languid and heavy, that they seemed to be rather those of a somnambulist than of a waking man. His dress had little pretension, and less neatness; it was a suit of threadbare, mulberry-coloured cloth, with steel buttons, and evidently but little acquainted with the clothes-brush. His linen was soiled and crumpled, his shoes ill-cleaned, his beard had enjoyed at least two days' undisturbed growth; and the dingy hue of his face and hands bespoke altogether the extremest negligence and slovenliness of person.

This slovenly and ungainly being, who sate apparently unconscious of the existence of any other earthly thing than the fire on which he gazed, and the grog which from time to time he lazily sipped, was Gordon Chancey, Esquire, of Skycopper Court, Whitefriar Street, in the city of Dublin, barrister-at-law—a gentleman who had never been known to do any professional business, but who managed, nevertheless, to live, and to possess, somehow or other, the command of very considerable sums of money, which he most advantageously invested by discounting, at exorbitant interest, short bills and promissory notes in such places as that in which he now sate—one of his favourite resorts, by the way. At intervals of from five to ten minutes he slowly drew from the vast pocket of his clumsy coat a bulky pocket-book, and sleepily conned over certain memoranda with which its leaves were charged—then having looked into its well-lined receptacles, to satisfy himself that no miracle of legerdemain had abstracted the treasure on which his heart was set, he once more fastened the buckle of the leathern budget, and deposited it again in his pocket. This procedure, and his attentions to the spirits and water, which from time to time he swallowed, succeeded one another with a monotonous regularity altogether undisturbed by the uproarious scene which surrounded him.

As the night wore apace, and fortune played her wildest pranks, many an applicant—some successfully, and some in vain—sought Chancey's succour.

"Come, my fine fellow, tip me a cool hundred," exclaimed a fashionably-dressed young man, flushed with the combined excitement of wine and the dice, and tapping Chancey on the back impatiently with his knuckles—"this moment—will you, and be damned"

"Oh, dear me, dear me, Captain Markham," drawled the barrister in a low, drowsy tone, as he turned sleepily toward the speaker, "have you lost the other hundred so soon? Oh, dear!—oh, dear!"

"Never you mind, old fox. Shell out, if you're going to do it," rejoined the applicant. "What is it to you?"

"Oh, dear me, dear me!" murmured Chancey, as he languidly drew the pocket-book from his pocket. "When shall I make it payable? To-morrow?"

"Damn to-morrow," replied the captain. "I'll sleep all to-morrow. Won't a fortnight do, you harpy?"

"Well, well—sign—sign it here," said the usurer, handing the paper, with a pen, to the young gentleman, and indicating with his finger the spot where the name was to be written.

The roué wrote his name without ever reading the paper; and Chancey carefully deposited it in his book.

"The money—the money—damn you, will you never give it!" exclaimed the young man, actually stamping with impatience, as if every moment's absence from the hazard-table cost him a fortune. "Give—give—give them."

He seized the notes, and without counting, stuffed them into his coat-pocket, and plunged in an instant again among the gamblers who crowded the table.

"Mr. Chancey—Mr. Chancey," said a slight young man, whose whole appearance betokened a far progress in the wasting of a mortal decline. His face was pale as death itself, and glittering with the cold, clammy dew of weakness and excitement. The eye was bright, wild, and glassy; and the features of this attenuated face trembled and worked in the spasms of agonized anxiety and despair—with timid voice, and with the fearful earnestness of one pleading for his life—with knees half bent, and head stretched forward, while his thin fingers were clutched and knotted together in restless feverishness. He still repeated at intervals in low, supplicating accents—"Mr. Chancey—Mr. Chancey—can you spare a moment, sir—Mr. Chancey, good sir—Mr. Chancey."

For many minutes the worthy barrister gazed on apathetically into the fire, as if wholly unconscious that this piteous spectacle was by his side, and all but begging his attention.

"Mr. Chancey, good sir—Mr. Chancey, kind sir—only one moment—one word—Mr. Chancey."

This time the wretched young man advanced one of his trembling hands, and laid it hesitatingly upon Chancey's knee—the seat of mercy, as the ancients thought; but truly here it was otherwise. The hand was repulsed with insolent rudeness; and the wretched suppliant stood trembling in silence before the bill-discounter, who looked upon him with a scowl of brute ferocity, which the timid advances he had made could hardly have warranted.

"Well," growled Chancey, keeping his baleful eyes fixed not very encouragingly upon the poor young man.

"I have been unfortunate, sir—I have lost my last shilling—that is, the last I have about me at present."

"Well," repeated he.

"I might win it all back," continued the suppliant, becoming more voluble as he proceeded. "I might recover it all—it has often happened to me before. Oh, sir, it is possible—certain, if I had but a few pounds to play on."

"Ay, the old story," rejoined Chancey.

"Yes, sir, it is indeed—indeed it is, Mr. Chancey," said the young man, eagerly, catching at this improvement upon his first laconic address as an indication of some tendency to relent, and making, at the same time, a most woeful attempt to look pleasant—"it is, sir—the old story, indeed; but this time it will come out true—indeed it will. Will you do one little note for me—a little one—twenty pounds?"

"No, I won't," drawled Chancey, imitating with coarse buffoonery the intonation of the request—"I won't do a little one for you."

"Well, for ten pounds—for ten only."

"No, nor for ten pence," rejoined Chancey, tranquilly.

"You may keep five out of it for the discount—for friendship—only let me have five—just five," urged the wasted gambler, with an agony of supplication.

"No, I won't; just five," replied the lawyer.

"I'll make it payable to-morrow," urged the suppliant.

"Maybe you'll be dead before that," drawled Chancey, with a sneer; "the life don't look very tough in you."

"Ah! Mr. Chancey, dear sir—good Mr. Chancey," said the young man, "you often told me you'd do me a friendly turn yet. Do not you remember it?—when I was able to lend you money. For God's sake, lend me five pounds now, or anything; I'll give you half my winnings. You'll save me from beggary—ah, sir, for old friendship."

Mr. Gordon Chancey seemed wondrously tickled by this appeal; he gazed sleepily at the fire while he raked the embers with the toe of his shoe, stuffed his hands deep into his breeches pockets, and indulged in a sort of lazy, comfortable laughter, which lasted for several minutes, until at length it subsided, leaving him again apparently unconscious of the presence of his petitioner. Emboldened by the condescension of his quondam friend, the young man made a piteous effort to join in the laughter—an attempt, however, which was speedily interrupted by the hollow cough of consumption. After a pause of a minute or two, during which Chancey seemed to have forgotten his existence, he once more addressed that gentleman,—

"Well, sir—well, Mr. Chancey?"

The barrister turned full upon him with an expression of face not to be mistaken, and in a tone just as unequivocal, he growled,—

"I'm damned if I give you as much as a leaden penny. Be off; there's no begging allowed here—away with you, you blackguard."

Having thus delivered himself, Chancey relapsed into his ordinary dreamy quiet.

Every muscle in the pale, wasted face of the ruined, dying gamester quivered with fruitless agony; he opened his mouth to speak, but could not; he gasped and sobbed, and then, clutching his lank hands over his eyes and forehead as though he would fain have crushed his head to pieces, he uttered one low cry of anguish, more despairing and appalling than the loudest shriek of horror, and passed from the room unnoticed.

"Jeffries, can you lend me fifty or a hundred pounds till to-morrow?" said young Ashwoode, addressing a middle-aged fop who had just reeled in from an adjoining room.

"Cuss me, Ashwoode, if the thing is a possibility," replied he, with a hiccough; "I have just been fairly cleaned out by Snarley and two or three others—not one guinea left—confound them all. I've this moment had to beg a crown to pay my chair and link-boy home; but Chancey is here; I saw him not an hour ago in his old corner."

"So he is, egad—thank you," and Ashwoode was instantly by the monied man's side. "Chancey, I want a hundred and fifty—quickly, man, are you awake?" and so saying, he shook the lawyer roughly by the shoulder.

"Oh, dear! oh, dear!" exclaimed he, in his usual low, sleepy voice, "it's Mr. Ashwoode, it is indeed—dear me, dear me; and can I oblige you, Mr. Ashwoode?"

"Yes; don't I tell you I want a hundred and fifty—or stay, two hundred," said Ashwoode, impatiently. "I'll pay you in a week or less—say to-morrow if you please it."

"Whatever sum you like, Mr. Ashwoode," rejoined he—"whatever sum or whatever date you please; I declare to God I'm uncommonly glad to do it. Oh, dear, but them dice is unruly. Two hundred, you say, and a—a week we'll say, not to be pressing. Well, well, this money has luck in it, maybe. That's a long lane that has no turn—fortune changes sides when it's least expected. Your name here, Mr. Ashwoode."

The name was signed, the notes taken, and Ashwoode once more at the table; but alack-a-day! fortune was for once steady, and frowned with consistent obdurateness upon Henry Ashwoode. Five minutes had hardly passed, when the two hundred pounds had made themselves wings and followed the larger sums which he had already lost. Again he had recourse to Chancey: again he found that gentleman smooth, gracious, and obliging as he could have wished. Still his luck was adverse: as fast as he drew the notes from his pocket, they were caught and whirled away in the eddy of ruin. Once more from the accommodating barrister he drew a larger sum,—still with a like result. So large and frequent were his drafts, that Chancey was obliged to go away and replenish his exhausted treasury; and still again and again, with a terrible monotony of disaster, young Ashwoode continued to lose.

At length the grey, cold light of morning streamed drearily through the chinks of the window-shutters into the hot chamber of destruction and debauchery. The sounds of daily business began to make themselves heard from the streets. The wax lights were flaring in the sockets. The floor strewn with packs of cards, broken glasses, and plates, and fragments of fowls and bread, and a thousand other disgusting indications of recent riot and debauchery which need not to be mentioned. Soiled and jaded, with bloodshot eyes and haggard faces, the gamblers slunk, one by one, in spiritless exhaustion, from the scene of their distracting orgies, to rest the brain and refresh the body as best they might.

With a stunning and indistinct sense of disaster and ruin; a vague, fevered, dreamy remembrance of overwhelming calamity: a stupefying, haunting consciousness that all the clatter, and roaring, and stifling heat, and jostling, and angry words, and smooth, civil speeches of the night past, had been, somehow or other, to him fraught with fearful and tremendous agony, and delirium, and ruin—Ashwoode stalked into the street, and mechanically proceeded to the inn where his horse was stabled.

The ostler saw, by the haggard, vacant stare with which Ashwoode returned his salutation, that something had gone wrong, and, as he held the stirrup for him, he arrived at the conclusion that the young gentleman must have gotten at least a dozen duels upon his hands, to be settled, one and all, before breakfast.

The young man dashed the spurs into the high-mettled horse, and traversing the streets at a perilous speed, without well thinking or knowing whitherward he was proceeding, he found himself at length among the wild lanes and brushwood of the Royal Park, and was recalled to himself by finding his horse rearing and floundering up to his sides in a slough. Having extricated the animal, he dismounted, threw his hat beside him, and, kneeling down, bathed his head and face again and again in the water of a little brook, which ran in many a devious winding through the tangled briars and thorns. The cold, refreshing ablution, assisted by the sharp air of the morning, soon brought him to his recollection.

"The fiend himself must have been by my elbow last night," he muttered, as he stood bare-headed, in wild disorder, by the brook's side. "I've lost before, and lost heavily too, but such a run, such an infernal string of ruinous losses. First, a thousand pounds gone—swallowed up in little more than an hour; and then the devil knows how much more—curse me, if I can remember how much I borrowed. I am over head and ears in Chancey's books. How shall I face my father? and how, in the fiend's name, am I to meet my engagements? Craven will hand me no more of the money. Was I mad or drunk, to go on against such an accursed tide of bad luck?—what fury from hell possessed me? I wish I had thrust my hand between the bars, and burnt it to the elbow, before I took the dice-box last night. What's to be done?"—he paused— "Yes—I must do it—fate, destiny, circumstances drive me to it. I will marry the woman; she can't live very long—it's not likely; and even if she does, what's that to me?—the world is wide enough for us both, and once married, we need not plague one another much with our society. I must see Chancey about those damned bills or notes: curse me, if I even know when they are payable. My brain swims like a sea. Lady Stukely, Lady Stukely, you are a happy woman: it's an ill wind that blows nobody good—I am resolved—my course is taken. First then for Morley Court, and next for the wealthy widow's. I don't half like the thing, but, damn it, what other chance have I? Then away with hesitation, away with thought; fate has ordained it."

So saying, the young man donned his hat, caught the bridle of his well-trained steed, vaulted into the saddle, and was soon far on his way to Morley Court, where strange and startling tidings awaited his arrival.

CHAPTER XXVII.

THE DEPARTURE OF THE PEER—THE BILLET AND THE SHATTERED MIRROR.

Never yet did day pass more disagreeably to mortal man than that whose early events we have recorded did to Lord Aspenly. His vanity and importance had suffered more mortification within the last few hours than he had ever before encountered in all the eight-and-sixty winters of his previous useful existence. And spite of the major's assurances to the contrary, he could not help feeling certain very unpleasant misgivings, as the evening approached, touching the consequences likely to follow to himself from his meditated retreat.

He resolved by the major's advice to leave Morley Court without a formal leave-taking, or, in short, any explanatory interview whatever with Sir Richard. And for the purpose of taking his departure without obstruction or annoyance, he determined that the hour of his setting forth should be that at which the baronet was wont to retire for a time to his dressing-room, previously to appearing at supper. The note which was to announce his departure was written and sealed, and deposited in his waistcoat pocket. He felt that it supplied but a very meagre explanation of so decided a step as he was constrained to take; nevertheless it was the only explanation he had to offer. He well knew that its perusal would be followed by an explosion, and he not unwisely thought it best, under all the circumstances, to withdraw to a reasonable distance before springing the mine.

The evening closed ominously in storm and cloud; the wind was hourly rising, and distant mutterings of thunder bespoke a night of tempest. Lord Aspenly had issued his orders with secrecy, and they were punctually obeyed. At the hour indicated, his own and his servant's horses were at the door. Lord Aspenly was crossing the hall, cloaked, booted, and spurred for the road, when he encountered Emily Copland.

"Dear me, my lord, can it be possible—surely you are not going to leave us to-night?"

"Indeed, it is but too true, fair lady," rejoined his lordship, with a dolorous shrug. "An unlucky contretemps requires my attendance in town; my precipitate flight," he continued, with an attempt at a playful smile, "is accounted for in this note, which perhaps you will kindly deliver to Sir Richard, when next you see him. I trust, Miss Copland, that fortune will often grant me the privilege of meeting you. Be assured it is one which I prize above all others. Adieu."

His lordship gallantly kissed the hand which was extended to receive the note, and then, with his best bow, withdrew.

A few petulant questions, which bespoke his inward acerbity, he addressed to his servant—glanced with a very sour aspect at the lowering sky—clambered stiffly into the saddle, and then, desiring his attendant to follow him, rode down the avenue at a speed which seemed prompted by an instinctive dread of pursuit.

As the wind howled and the thunder rolled and rumbled nearer and nearer, Emily Copland could not but wonder more and more what urgent and peremptory cause could have induced the little peer to adopt this sudden resolution, and to carry it into effect upon such a night of storm. Surely that motive must be a strange and urgent one which would not brook the delay of a few hours, especially during the violence of such weather as the luxurious little nobleman had perhaps never voluntarily encountered in the whole course of his life. Curiosity prompted her to deliver the note which she held in her hand at once; she therefore ran lightly upstairs, and rapidly threading all the intervening lobbies and rambling passages, she knocked at her uncle's door.

"Come in, come in," cried the peevish voice of Sir Richard Ashwoode.

The girl entered the room. The Italian was at the toilet, arranging his master's dressing-case, and the baronet himself in his night-gown and slippers, and with a pamphlet in his hand, reclined listlessly upon a sofa.

"Who is that?—who is it?" inquired he in the same tone, without turning his eyes from the volume which he read.

"Per dina!" exclaimed the Neapolitan—"Mees Emily—she is vary seldom come here. You are wailcome, Mees Emily; weel you seet down?—there is chair. Sir Richard, it is Mees Emily."

"What does the young lady want?" inquired he, drily.

"I have gotten a note for you, uncle," replied she.

"Well, put it down?—put it there on the table, anywhere; I presume it will keep till morning," replied he, without removing his eyes from the pages.

"It is from Lord Aspenly," urged the girl.

"Eh! Lord Aspenly. How—give it to me," said the baronet, raising himself quickly and tossing the pamphlet aside. He broke the seal and read the note. Whatever its contents were, they produced upon the baronet an extraordinary effect; he started from the sofa with clenched hands and frantic gesture.

"Who—where—stop him, after him—he shall answer me—he shall!" cried, or rather shrieked, the baronet in the hoarse, choking scream of fury. "After him all—my sword, my horse. By —, he'll reckon with me this night."

Never did the human form more fearfully embody the passions of hell; he stood before them absolutely transformed. The quivering face was pale as ashes; the livid veins, like blue knotted cordage, protruded upon his forehead; the eye glared and rolled with the light of madness, and as he shook and raved there before them, no dream ever conjured up a spectacle more appalling; he spit upon the letter—he tore it into fragments, and with his gouty feet stamped it into the fire.

There was no extravagance of frenzy which he did not enact. He tossed his arms into the air, and dashed his clenched hands upon the table; he stamped, he stormed, he howled; and as with thick and furious utterance he volleyed forth his incoherent threats, mandates, and curses, the foam hung upon his blackened lips.

"I'll bring him to the dust—to the earth. My very menials shall spurn him. Almighty, that he should dare—trickster—liar—that he should dare to practise upon me this outrageous slight. Ay, ay—ay, ay—laugh, my lord—laugh on; but by the — , this shall bring you to your knees, ay, and to your grave; and you—you," thundered he, turning upon the awe-struck and terrified young lady, "you no doubt had your share in this—ay, you have—you have—yes, I know you—you—you—hollow, lying —, quit my house—out with you—turn her out—drive her out—away with her."

As the horrible figure advanced towards her, the girl by an effort roused herself from the dreadful fascination, and turning from him, fled swiftly downstairs, and fell fainting at the parlour door.

Sir Richard still strode through his chamber with the same frantic evidences of unabated fury; and the Italian—the only remaining spectator of the hideous scene—sate calmly in a chair by the toilet, with his legs crossed, and his countenance composed into a kind of sanctimonious placidity, which, however, spite of all his efforts, betrayed at the corners of the mouth, and in the twinkle of the eye, a certain enjoyment of the spectacle, which was not altogether consistent with the perfect affection which he professed for his master.

"Ay, ay, my lord," continued the baronet, madly, "laugh on—laugh while you may; but by the —, you shall gnash your teeth for this!"

"What coning, old gentleman is mi Lord Aspenly—ah! vary, vary," said the Italian, reflectively.

"You shall, my lord," continued Sir Richard, furiously. "Your disgrace shall be public—exemplary—the insult shall recoil upon, yourself—your punishment shall be memorable-public—tremendous."

"Mi Lord Aspenly and Sir Richard—both so coning," continued the Italian—"yees—yees—set one thief to catch the other."

The Neapolitan had, no doubt, bargained for the indulgence of his pleasant humour, as usual, free of cost; but he was mistaken. With the quickness of light, Sir Richard grasped a massive glass decanter, full of water, and hurled it at the head of his valet. Luckily for that gentleman's brains, it missed its object, and, alighting upon a huge mirror, it dashed it to fragments with a stunning crash. In the extremity of his fury, Sir Richard grasped a heavy metal inkstand, and just as the valet escaped through the private door of his room, hurled it, too, at his head. Two such escapes were quite enough for Signor Parucci on one evening; and not wishing to tempt his luck further, he ran nimbly down the stairs, leaped into his own room, and bolted and double-locked the door; and thence, as the night wore on, he still heard Sir Richard pacing up and down his chamber, and storming and raving in dreadful rivalry with the thunder and hurricane without.

CHAPTER XXVIII.

THE THUNDER-STORM—THE EBONY STICK—THE UNSEEN VISITANT—TERROR.

At length the uproar in Sir Richard's room died away. The hoarse voice in furious soliloquy, and the rapid tread as he paced the floor, were no longer audible. In their stead was heard alone the stormy wind rushing and yelling through the old trees, and at intervals the deep volleying thunder. In the midst of this hubbub the Italian rubbed his hands, tripped lightly up and down his room, placed his ear at the keyhole, and chuckled and rubbed his hands again in a paroxysm of glee—now and again venting his gratification in brief ejaculations of intense delight—the very incarnation of the spirit of mischief.

The sounds in Sir Richard's room had ceased for two hours or more; and the piping wind and the deep-mouthed thunder still roared and rattled. The Neapolitan was too much excited to slumber. He continued, therefore, to pace the floor of his chamber—sometimes gazing through his window upon the black stormy sky and the blue lightning, which leaped in blinding flashes across its darkness, revealing for a moment the ivied walls, and the tossing trees, and the fields and hills, which were as instantaneously again swallowed in the blackness of the tempestuous night; and then turning from the casement, he would plant himself by the door, and listen with eager curiosity for any sound from Sir Richard's room.

As we have said before, several hours had passed, and all had long been silent in the baronet's apartment, when on a sudden Parucci thought he heard the sharp and well-known knocking of his patron's ebony stick upon the floor. He ran and listened at his own door. The sound was repeated with unequivocal and vehement distinctness, and was instantaneously followed by a prolonged and violent peal from his master's hand-bell. The summons was so sustained and vehement, that the Italian at length cautiously withdrew the bolt, unlocked the door, and stole out upon the lobby. So far from abating, the sound grew louder and louder. On tip-toe he scaled the stairs, until he reached to about the midway; and he there paused, for he heard his master's voice exerted in a tone of terrified entreaty,—

"Not now—not now—avaunt—not now. Oh, God!—help," cried the well-known voice.

These words were followed by a crash, as of some heavy body springing from the bed—then a rush upon the floor—then another crash.

The voice was hushed; but in its stead the wild storm made a long and plaintive moan, and the listener's heart turned cold.

"Malora—Corpo di Pluto!" muttered he between his teeth. "What is it? Will he reeng again? Santo gennaro!—there is something wrong."

He paused in fearful curiosity; but the summons was not repeated. Five minutes passed; and yet no sound but the howling and pealing of the storm. Parucci, with a beating heart, ascended the stairs and knocked at the door of his patron's chamber. No answer was returned.

"Sir Richard, Sir Richard," cried the man, "do you want me, Sir Richard?"

Still no answer. He pushed open the door and entered. A candle, wasted to the very socket, stood upon a table beside the huge hearse-like bed, which, for the convenience of the invalid, had been removed from his bed-chamber to his dressing-room. The light was dim, and waved uncertainly in the eddies which found their way through the chinks of the window, so that the lights and shadows flitted ambiguously across the objects in the room. At the end of the bed a table had been upset; and lying near it upon the floor was some-thing—a heap of bed-clothes, or—could it be?—yes, it was Sir Richard Ashwoode.

Parncci approached the prostrate figure: it was lying upon its back, the countenance fixed and livid, the eyes staring and glazed, and the jaw fallen—he was a corpse. The Italian stooped down and took the hand of the dead man—it was already cold; he called him by his name and shook him, but all in vain. There lay the cunning intriguer, the fierce, fiery prodigal, the impetuous, unrelenting tyrant, the unbelieving, reckless man of the world, a ghastly lump of clay.

With strange emotions the Neapolitan gazed upon the lifeless effigy from which the evil tenant had been so suddenly and fearfully called to its eternal and unseen abode.

"Gone—dead—all over—all past," muttered he, slowly, while he pressed his foot upon the dead body, as if to satisfy himself that life was indeed extinct—"quite gone. Canchero! it was ugly death—there was something with him; what was he speaking with?"

Parucci walked to the door leading to the great staircase, but found it bolted as usual.

"Pshaw! there was nothing," said he, looking fearfully round the room as he approached the body again, and repeating the negative as if to reassure himself—"no, no—nothing, nothing."

He gazed again on the awful spectacle in silence for several minutes.

"Corbezzoli, and so it is over," at length he ejaculated—"the game is ended. See, see, the breast is bare, and there the two marks of Aldini's stiletto. Ah! briccone, briccone, what wild faylow were you—panzanera, for a pretty ankle and a pair of black eyes, you would dare the devil. Rotto di collo, his face is moving!—pshaw! it is only the light that wavers. Diamine! the face is terrible. What made him speak? nothing was with him—pshaw! nothing could come to him here—no, no, nothing."

As he thus spoke, the wind swept vehemently upon the windows with a sound as if some great thing had rushed, against them, and was pressing for admission, and the gust blew out the candle; the blast died away in a lengthened wail, and then again came rushing and howling up to the windows, as if the very prince of the powers of the air himself were thundering at the casement; then again the blue dazzling lightning glared into the room and gave place to deeper darkness.

"Pah! that lightning smells like brimstone. Sangue d'un dua, I hear something in the room."

Yielding to his terrors, Parucci stumbled to the door opening upon the great lobby, and with cold and trembling fingers drawing the bolt, sprang to the stairs and shouted for assistance in a tone which speedily assembled half the household in the chamber of death.

## CHAPTER XXIX.

### THE CRONES—THE CORPSE, AND THE SHARPER.

Haggard, exhausted, and in no very pleasant temper, Henry Ashwoode rode up the avenue of Morley Court.

"I shall have a blessed conference with my father," thought he, "when he learns the fate of the thousand pounds I was to have brought him—a pleasant interview, by —. How shall I open it? He'll be no better than a Bedlamite. By —, a pretty hot kettle of fish this—but through it I must flounder as best I may—curse it, what am I afraid of?"

Thus muttering, he leaped from the saddle, leaving the well-trained steed to make his way to the stable, and entered at the half open door. In the hall he encountered a servant, but was too much occupied by his own busy reflections to observe the earnest, awe-struck countenance of the old domestic.

"Mr. Henry—Mr. Henry—stay, sir—stay—one moment," said the man, following and endeavouring to detain him.

Ashwoode, however, without heeding the interruption, hastened by him, and mounted the stairs with long and rapid strides, resolved not unnecessarily to defer the interview which he believed must come sooner or later. He opened Sir Richard's door, and entered the chamber. He looked round the room for the object of his search in vain; but to his unmeasured astonishment, beheld instead three old shrivelled hags seated by the hearth, who all rose upon his entrance, except one, who was warming something in a saucepan upon the fire, and each and all resumed respectively the visages of woe which best became the occasion.

"Eh! How is this? What brings you here, nurse?" exclaimed the young man, in a tone of startled curiosity.

The old lady whom he addressed thought it advisable to weep, and instead of returning any answer, covered her face with her apron, turned away her head, and shook her palsied hand towards him with a gesture which was meant to express the mute anguish of unutterable sorrow.

"What is it?" said Ashwoode. "Are you all tongue-tied? Speak, some of you."

"Oh, musha! musha! the crathur," observed the second witch, with a most lugubrious shake of the head, "but it is he that's to be pitied. Oh, wisha—wisha—wiristhroo!"

"What the devil ails you? Can't you speak out? Where's my father?" repeated the young man, with impatient perplexity.

"With the blessed saints in glory," replied the third hag, giving the saucepan a slight whisk to prevent the contents from burning, "and if ever there was an angel on earth, he was one. Well, well, he has his reward—that's one comfort, sure. The crown of glory, with the holy apostles—it's he's to be envied—up in heaven, though he wint mighty suddint, surely."

This was followed by a kind of semi-dolorous shake of the head, in which the three old women joined.

With a hurried step, young Ashwoode strode to the bedside, drew the curtain, and gazed upon the sharp and fixed features of the corpse, as it leered with unclosed eyes from among the bed-clothes. It would not have been easy to analyze the feelings with which he looked upon this spectacle. A kind of incredulous horror sate upon his compressed features. He touched the hand, which rested stiffly upon the coverlet, as if doubtful that the old man, whom he had so long feared and obeyed, was actually dead. The cold, dull touch that met his was not to be mistaken, and he gazed fixedly with that awful curiosity with which in death the well-known features of a familiar face are looked on. There lay the being whose fierce passions had been to him from his earliest days a source of habitual fear—in childhood, even of terror—henceforth to be no more to him than a thing which had never been. There lay the scheming, busy head, but what availed all its calculations and its cunning now! No more thought or power has it than the cushion on which it stiffly rests. There lies the proud, worldly, unforgiving, violent man, a senseless effigy of cold clay—a grim, impassive monument of the recent presence of the unearthly visitant.

"It's a beautiful corpse, if the eyes were only shut," observed one of the crones, approaching; "a purty corpse as ever was stretched."

"The hands is very handsome entirely," observed another of them, "and so small, like a lady's."

"It's himself was the good master," observed the old nurse, with a slow shake of the head; "the likes of him did not thread in shoe leather. Oh! but my heart's sore for you this day, Misther Harry."

Thus speaking, with a good deal of screwing and puckering, she succeeded in squeezing a tear from one eye, like the last drop from an exhausted lemon, and suffering it to rest upon her cheek, that it might not escape observation, she looked round with a most pity-moving visage upon her companions, and an expression of face which said as plainly as words, "What a faithful, attached, old creature I am, and how well I deserve any little token of regard which Sir Richard's will may have bequeathed me."

"Ah! then, look at him," said the matron of the saucepan, gazing with the most touching commiseration upon Henry Ashwoode, "see how he looks at it. Oh, but it's he that adored him! Oh, the crathur, what will he do this day? Look at him there—he's an orphan now—God help him."

"Be off with yourselves, and leave me here," said Henry (now Sir Henry) Ashwoode, turning sharply upon them. "Send me some one that can speak a word of sense: call Parucci here, and get out of the room every one of you—away!"

With abundance of muttering and grumbling, and many an indignant toss of the head, and many a dignified sniff, the old women hobbled from the room; and Henry Ashwoode had hardly been left alone, when the small private door communicating with Parucci's apartment, opened, and the valet peeped in.

"Come in—come in, Jacopo," said the young man; "come in, and close the door. When did this happen?"

The Neapolitan recounted briefly the events which we have already recorded.

"It was a fit—some sudden seizure," said the young man, glancing at the features of the corpse.

"Yes, vary like, vary like," said Parucci; "he used to complain sometimes that his head was sweeming round, and pains and aches; but there was something more—something more."

"What do you mean?—don't speak riddles," said Ashwoode.

"I mean this, then," replied the Italian; "something came to him—something was in the room when he died."

"How do you know that?" inquired the young man.

"I heard him talking loudly with it," replied he—"talking and praying it to go away from him."

"Why did you not come into the room yourself?" asked Ashwoode.

"So I did, Diamine, so I did," replied he.

"Well, what saw you?"

"Nothing bote Sir Richard, dead—quite dead; and the far door was bolted inside, just so as he always used to do; and when the candle went out, the thing was here again. I heard it myself, as sure as I am leeving man—I heard it—close up with me—by the body."

"Tut, tut, man; speak sense. Do you mean to say that anyone talked with you?" said Ashwoode.

"I mean this, that something was in the chamber with me beside the dead man," replied the valet, doggedly. "I heard it with my own ears. Zucche! I moste 'av been deaf, if I did not hear it. It said 'hish,' and then again, close up to my face, it said it—'hish, hish,' and laughed below its breath. Pah! the place smelt of brimstone."

"In plain terms, then, you believe that the devil was in the room; is that it?" said Ashwoode, with a ghastly smile of contempt.

"Oh! no," replied the servant, with a sneer as ghastly; "it was an angel, of course—an angel from heaven."

"No more of this folly, sirrah," said Ashwoode, sharply. "Your own damned cowardice fills your brain with these fancies. Here, give me the keys, and show me where the papers are laid. I shall first examine the cabinets here, and then in the library. Now open this one; and do you hear, Parucci, not one word of this cock-and-bull story of yours to the servants. Good God! my brain's unsettled. I can scarcely believe my father dead—dead," and again he stood by the bedside, and looked upon the still face of the corpse.

"We must send for Craven at once," said Ashwoode, turning from the bed; "I must confer with him; he knows better than anyone else how all my father's affairs stand. There are some damned bills out, I believe, but we'll soon know."

Having despatched an urgent note to Craven, the insinuating attorney, to whom we have already introduced the reader, Sir Henry Ashwoode proceeded roughly to examine the contents of boxes, escritoires, and cabinets filled with dusty papers, and accompanied and directed in his search by the Italian.

"You never heard him mention a will, did you?" inquired the young man.

The Neapolitan shook his head.

"You did not know of his making one?" he resumed.

"No, no, I cannot remember," said the Italian, reflectively; "but," he added quickly, while a peculiar meaning lit up the piercing eyes which he turned upon the interrogator—"but do you weesh to find one? Maybe I could help you to find one."

"Pshaw! folly; what do you take me for?" retorted Ashwoode, slightly colouring, in spite of his habitual insensibility, for Parucci was too intimate with his principles for him to assume ignorance of his meaning. "Why the devil should I wish to find a will, since I inherit everything without it?"

"Signor," said the little man, after an interval of silence, during which he seemed absorbed in deep reflection, "I have moche to say about what I shall do with myself, and some things to ask from you. I will begin and end it here and now—it is best over at once. I have served Sir Richard there for thirty-four years. I have served him well—vary well. I have taught him great secrets. I have won great abundance of good moneys for him; if he was not reech it is not my fault. I attend him through his sickness; and 'av been his companion for the half of a long life. What else I 'av done for him I need not count up, but most of it you know well. Sir Richard is there—dead and gone—the service is ended, and now I 'av resolved I will go back again to Italy—to Naples—where I was born. You shall never hear of me any more if you will do for me one little thing."

"What is it?—speak out. You want to extort money—is it so?" said Ashwoode, slowly and sternly.

"I want," continued the man, with equal distinctness and deliberateness, "I want one thousand pounds. I do not ask a penny more, and I will not take a penny less; and if you give me that, I will never trouble you more with word of mine—you will never hear or see honest Jacopo Parucci any more."

"Come, come, Jacopo, that were paying a little too dear, even for such a luxury," replied Ashwoode. "A thousand pounds! Ha! ha! A modest request, truly. I half suspect your brain is a little crazed."

"Remember what I have done—all I have done for him." rejoined the Italian, coolly. "And above all, remember what I have not done for him. I could have had him hanged up by the neck—hanged like a dog—but I never did. Oh! no, never—though not a day went by that I might not 'av brought the house full of officers, and have him away to jail and get him hanged. Remember all that, signor, and say is it in conscience too moche?—rotta di collo! It is not half—no, nor quarter so moche as I ought to ask. No, nor as you ought to give, signor, without me to ask at all."

"Parucci, you are either mad or drunk, or take me to be so," said Ashwoode, who could not feel quite comfortable in disputing the claims of the Italian, nor secure in provoking his anger. "But at all events, there is ample time to talk about these matters. We can settle it all more at our ease in a week or so."

"No, no, signor. I will have my answer now," replied the man, doggedly. "Mr. Craven has money now—the money of Miss Mary's land that Sir Richard got from her. But though the money is there now, in a week or leetle more we will not see moche of it, and my pocket weel remain aimpty—corbezzoli! am I a fool?"

"I tell you, Parucci, I will give you no promises now," exclaimed the young man, vehemently. "Why, damn it, the blood is hardly cold in the old man's veins, and you begin to pester me for money. Can't you wait till he's buried?"

"Ay—yees—yees—wait till he's buried—and then wait till the mourning's off—and then wait for something more," said the Neapolitan, with a sneer, "and so wait on till the money's all spent. No, no, signor—corpo di Bacco! I will have it now. I will have my answer now, before Mr. Craven comes—giuro di Dio, I will have my answer."

"Don't talk like a madman, Parucci," replied the young man, angrily. "I have no money here. I will make no promises. And besides, your request is perfectly ridiculous and unconscionable."

"I ask for a thousand pounds," replied the valet. "I must have the promise now, signor, and the money to-day. If you do not promise it here and at once, I will not ask again, and maybe you weel be sorry. I will take one thousand pounds. I want no more, and I accept no less. Signor, your answer."

There was a cool, menacing insolence in the manner of the fellow which stung the pride of the young baronet to the quick.

"Scoundrel," said he, "do you think I am to be bullied by your audacious threats? Do you dream that I am weak enough to suffer a wretch like you to practise his extortions upon me? By —, you'll find to your cost that you have no longer to deal with a master who is in your power. What care I for your utmost? Do your worst, miscreant—I defy you. I warn you only to beware of giving an undue license to your foul, lying tongue—for if I find that you have been spreading your libellous tales abroad, I'll have you pilloried and whipped."

"Well, you 'av given me an answer," replied the Italian coolly. "I weel ask no more; and now, signor, farewell—adieu. I think, perhaps, you will hear of me again. I will not return here any more after I go out; and so, for the last time," he continued, approaching the cold form which lay upon the bed, "farewell to you, Sir Richard Ashwoode. While I am alive I will never see your face again—perhaps, if holy friars tell true, we may meet again. Till then—till then—farewell."

With this strange speech the Neapolitan, having gazed for a brief space, with a strange expression, in which was a dash of something very nearly approaching to sorrow, upon the stern, moveless face before him, and then with an effort, and one long-drawn sigh, having turned away, deliberately withdrew from the room through the small door which led to his own apartment.

"The lazzarone will come to himself in a little," muttered Ashwoode; "he will think twice before he leaves this place—he'll cool—he'll cool."

Thus soliloquizing, the young man locked up the presses and desks which he had opened, bolted the door after the Italian, and hurried from the room; for, somehow or other, he felt uneasy and fearful alone in the chamber with the body.

## CHAPTER XXX.

### SKY-COPPER COURT.

Upon the evening of the same day, the Italian having collected together the few movables which he called his own, and left them ready for removal in the chamber which he had for so long exclusively occupied, might have been seen, emerging from the old manor-house, and with a small parcel in his hand, wending his solitary, moon-lit way across the broad wooded pasture-lands of Morley Court. Without turning to look back upon the familiar scene, which he was now for ever leaving—for all his faculties and feelings, such as they were, had busy occupation in the measures of revenge which he was keenly pursuing, he crossed the little stile which terminated the pathway he was following, and descended upon the public road—shaking from his hat and cloak the heavy drops, which in his progress the close underwood through which he brushed had shed upon him. With a quickened pace, and with a stern, almost a savage countenance, over which from time to time there flitted a still more ominous smile, and muttering between his teeth many a short and vehement apostrophe as he went, he held his way directly toward the city of Dublin; and once within the streets, he was not long in reaching the ancient, and by this time to the reader, familiar mansion, over whose portal swung the glittering sign of the "Cock and Anchor."

"Now, then," thought Parucci, "let us see whether I have not one card left, and that a trump. What, because I wear no sword myself, shall you escape unpunished? Fool—miscreant, I will this night conjure up such an avenger as will appal even you; I will send him with a thousand atrocious wrongs upon his head, frantic into your presence—you had better cope with an actual incarnate demon."

Such were the exulting thoughts which lighted the features of Parucci with a fitful smile of singular grimness as he entered the inn yard, where meeting one of the waiters, he promptly inquired for O'Connor. To his dismay, however, he learnt that that gentleman had quitted the "Cock and Anchor" on the day before, and whither he had gone, none could inform him. As he stood, pondering in bitter disappointment what step was next to be taken, somebody tapped his shoulder smartly from behind. He turned, and beheld the square form and swarthy features of O'Hanlon, whose interview with O'Connor is recorded early in these pages. After a few brief questions and answers, in which, by a reference to the portly proprietor of the "Cock and Anchor," who vouched for the accuracy of his representations, O'Hanlon satisfied the vindictive foreigner that he might safely communicate the subject of his intended communication to him, as to the sure friend of Mr. O'Connor. Both personages, Parucci and O'Hanlon—or, as he was there called, Dwyer—repaired to a private room, where they remained closeted for fully half an hour. That interview had its consequences—consequences of which sooner or later the reader shall fully hear, and which were perhaps somewhat unlike those calculated upon by honest Jacopo.

It is not necessary to detain the reader with a description of the ceremonial which conducted the mortal remains of Sir Henry Ashwoode to the grave. It is enough to say that if pomp and pageantry, lavished upon the fleeting tenement of clay which it has deserted, can delight the departed spirit, that of the deceased baronet was happy. The funeral was an aristocratic procession, well worthy of the rank and pretensions of the distinguished dead, and in numbers and éclat such as to satisfy even the exactions of Irish pride.

Carriages and four were there in abundance, and others of lesser note without number. Outriders, and footmen, and corpulent coachmen filled the court and avenue of the manor, and crowded its hall, where refreshments enough for a garrison were heaped together upon the tables. The funeral feasting and revelry finished, the enormous mob of coaches, horses, and lacqueys began to arrange itself, and assume something like order. The great velvet-covered coffin was carried out upon the shoulders of six footmen, staggering under the leaden load, and was laid in the hearse. The high-born company, dressed in the fantastic trappings of mourning, began to show themselves one by one, or in groups, at the hall-door, and took their places in their respective vehicles; and at length the enormous volume began to uncoil, and gradually passing down the great avenue, and winding along the road, to proceed toward the city, covering from the coffin to the last carriage a space of more than a mile in length.

The body was laid in the aisle of St. Audoen's Church, and a comely monument, recording in eloquent periods the virtues of the deceased, was reared by the piety of his son. The aisle, however, in which it stood, is now a rootless ruin; and this, along with many a more curious relic, has crumbled into dust from its time-worn wall: so that there now remains, except in these idle pages, no record to tell posterity that so important a personage as Sir Richard Ashwoode ever existed at all.

Of all who donned "the customary suit of solemn black" upon the death of Sir Richard Ashwoode, but one human being felt a pang of sorrow. But there was one whose grief was real and poignant—one who mourned for him as though he had been all that was fond and tender—who forgot and forgave all his faults and failings, and remembered only that he had been her father and she his child, and companion, and gentle, patient nurse-tender through many an hour of pain and sickness. Mary wept for his death bitterly for many a day and night; for all that he had ever done or said to give her pain, her noble nature found entire forgiveness, and every look, and smile, and word, and tone that had ever borne the semblance of kindness, were all treasured in her memory, and all called up again in affectionate and sorrowful review. Seldom indeed had the hard nature of Sir Richard evinced even such transient indications of tenderness, and when they did appear they were still more rarely genuine. But Mary felt that an object of her kindly care and companionship was gone—a familiar face for ever hidden—one of the only two who were near to her in the ties of blood, departed to return no more, and with all the deep, strong yearnings of kindred, she wept and mourned after her father.

Emily Copland had left Morley Court and was now residing with her gay relative, Lady Stukely, so that poor Mary was left almost entirely alone, and her brother, Sir Henry, was so immersed in business and papers that she scarcely saw him even for a moment except while he swallowed his hasty meals; and sooth to say, his thoughts were not much oftener with her than his person.

Though, as the reader is no doubt fully aware, Sir Henry's grief for the loss of his parent was by no means of that violent kind which refuses to be comforted, yet he was too chary of the world's opinion, as well as too punctilious an observer of etiquette, to make the cheerfulness of his resignation under this dispensation startlingly apparent by any overt act of levity or indifference. Sir Henry, however, must see Gordon Chancey; he must ascertain how much he owes him, and when it is all payable—facts of which he has, if any, the very dimmest and vaguest possible recollection. Therefore, upon the very day on which the funeral had taken place, as soon as the evening had closed, and darkness succeeded the twilight, the young baronet ordered his trusty servant to bring the horses to the door, and then muffling himself in his cloak, and drawing it about his face, so that even in the reflection of an accidental link he might not by possibility be recognized, he threw himself into the saddle, and telling his servant to follow him, rode rapidly through the dense obscurity towards the town.

When he had reached Whitefriar Street, he checked his pace to a walk, and calling his attendant to his side, directed him to await his return there; then dismounting, he threw him the bridle, and proceeded upon his way. Guided by the hazy starlight and by an occasional gleam from a shop-window or tavern-door, as well as by the dusky glimmer of the wretched street lamps, the young man directed his course for some way along the open street, and then turning to the right into a dark archway which opened from it, he found himself in a small, square court, surrounded by tall, dingy, half-ruinous houses which loomed darkly around, deepening the shadows of the night into impenetrable gloom. From some of these dilapidated tenements issued smothered sounds of quarrelling, indistinctly mingled with the crying of children and the shrill accents of angry females; from others the sounds of discordant singing and riotous carousal; while, as far as the eye could discern, few places could have been conceived with an aspect more dreary, forbidding, and cut-throat, and, in all respects, more depressing and suspicious.

"This is unquestionably the place," exclaimed Ashwoode, as he stepped cautiously over the broken pavement; "there is scarcely another like it in this town or any other; but beshrew me if I remember which is the house."

He entered one of them, the hall-door of which stood half open, and through the chinks of whose parlour-door were issuing faint streams of light and gruff sounds of talking. At one of these doors he knocked sharply with his whip-handle, and instantly the voices were hushed. After a silence of a minute or two, the parties inside resumed their conversation, and Ashwoode more impatiently repeated his summons.

"There is someone knocking—I tould you there was," exclaimed a harsh voice from within. "Open the doore, Corny, and take a squint."

The door opened cautiously; a great head, covered with shaggy elf-locks, was thrust through the aperture, and a singularly ill-looking face, as well as the imperfect light would allow Ashwoode to judge, was advanced towards his. The fellow just opened the door far enough to suffer the ray of the candle to fall upon the countenance of his visitant, and staring suspiciously into his face for some time, while he held the lock of the door in his hand, he asked,—

"Well, neighbour, did you rap at this doore?"

"Yes, I want to be directed to Mr. Chancey's rooms." replied Ashwoode.

"Misthur who?" repeated the man.

"Mr. Chancey—Chancey: he lives in this court, and, unless I am mistaken, in this house, or the next to it," rejoined Ashwoode.

"Chancey: I don't know him," answered the man. "Do you know where Mr. Chancey lives, Garvey?"

"Not I, nor don't care," rejoined the person addressed, with a hoarse growl, and without taking the trouble to turn from the fire, over which he was cowering, with his back toward the door. "Slap the doore to, can't you? and don't keep gostherin' there all night."

"No, he won't slap the doore," exclaimed the shrill voice of a female. "I'll see the gentleman myself. Well, sir," she cried, presenting a tall, raw-boned figure, arrayed in tawdry rags, at the door, and shoving the man with the unkempt locks aside, she eyed Ashwoode with a leer and a grin that were anything but inviting—"well, sir, is there anything I can do for you. The chaps here is not used to quality, an' Pather has a mighty ignorant manner; but they are placible boys, an' manes no offence. Who is it you're lookin' for, sir?"

"Mr. Gordon Chancey: he lives in one of these houses. Can you direct me to him?"

"No, we can't," said the fellow from the fire, in a savage tone. "I tould you before. Won't you take your answer—won't you? Slap that doore, Corny, or I'll get up to him myself."

"Hould your tongue, you gaol bird, won't you?" rejoined the female, in accents of shrill displeasure. "Chancey! is not he the counsellor gentleman; he has a yellow face an' a down look, and never has his hands out of his breeches' pockets?"

"The very man," replied Ashwoode.

"Well, sir, he does live in this court: he has the parlour next doore. The street doore stands open—it's a lodging-house. One doore further on; you can't miss him."

"Thank you, thank you," said Ashwoode. "Good-night." And as the door was closed upon him, he heard the voices of those within raised in hot debate.

He stumbled and groped his way into the hall of the house which the gracious nymph, to whom he had just bidden farewell, indicated, and knocked stoutly at the parlour-door. It was opened by a sluttish girl, with bare feet, and a black eye, which had reached the green and yellow stage of recovery. She had probably been interrupted in the midst of a spirited altercation with the barrister, for ill humour and excitement were unequivocally glowing in her face.

Ashwoode walked in, and found matters as we shall describe them in the next chapter.

CHAPTER XXXI.

THE USURER AND THE OAKEN BOX.

The room which Sir Henry Ashwoode entered was one of squalid disorder. It was a large apartment, originally handsomely wainscoted, but damp and vermin had made woeful havoc in the broad panels, and the ceiling was covered with green and black blotches of mildew. No carpet covered the bare boards, which were strewn with fragments of papers, rags, splinters of an old chest, which had been partially broken up to light the fire, and occasionally a potato-skin, a bone, or an old shoe. The furniture was scant, and no one piece matched the other. Little and bad as it was, its distribution about the room was more comfortless and wretched still. All was dreary disorder, dust, and dirt, and damp, and mildew, and rat-holes.

By a large grate, scarcely half filled with a pile of ashes and a few fragments of smouldering turf, sat Gordon Chancey, the master of this notable establishment; his arm rested upon a dirty deal table, and his fingers played listlessly with a dull and battered pewter goblet, which he had just replenished from a two-quart measure of strong beer which stood upon the table, and whose contents had dabbled that piece of furniture with sundry mimic lakes and rivers. Unrestrained by the ungenerous confinement of a fender, the cinders strayed over the cracked hearthstone, and even wandered to the boards beyond it. Mr. Gordon Chancey was himself, too, rather in deshabille. He had thrown off his shoes, and was in his stockings, which were unfortunately rather imperfect at the extremities. His waistcoat was unbuttoned, and his cravat lay upon the table, swimming in a sea of beer. As Ashwoode entered, with ill-suppressed disgust, this loathly den, the object of his visit languidly turned his head and his sleepy eyes over his shoulder, in the direction of the door, and without making the smallest effort to rise, contented himself with extending his hand along the sloppy table, palm upwards, for Ashwoode to shake, at the same time exclaiming, with a drawl of gentle placidity,—

"Oh, dear—oh, dear me! Mr. Ashwoode, I declare to God I am very glad to see you. Won't you sit down and have some beer? Eliza, bring a cup for my friend, Mr. Ashwoode. Will you take a pipe too? I have some elegant tobacco. Bring my pipe to Mr. Ashwoode, and the little canister that M'Quirk left here last night."

"I am much obliged to you," said Ashwoode, with difficulty swallowing his anger, and speaking with marked hauteur, "my visit, though an unseasonable one, is entirely one of business. I shall not give you the trouble of providing any refreshment for me; in a word, I have neither time nor appetite for it. I want to learn exactly how you and I stand: five minutes will show me the state of the account."

"Oh, dear—oh, dear! and won't you take any beer, then? it's elegant beer, from Mr. M'Gin's there, round the corner."

Ashwoode bit his lips, and remained silent.

"Eliza, bring a chair for my friend, Sir Henry Ashwoode," continued Chancey; "he must be very tired—indeed he must, after his long walk; and here, Eliza, take the key and open the press, and do you see, bring me the little oak box on the second shelf. She's a very good little girl, Mr. Ashwoode, I assure you. Eliza is a very sensible, good little girl. Oh, dear!—oh, dear! but your father's death was very sudden; but old chaps always goes off that way, on short notice. Oh, dear me!—I declare to —, only I had a pain in my—(here he mentioned his lower stomach somewhat abruptly)—I'd have gone to the funeral this morning. There was a great lot of coaches, wasn't there?"

"Pray, Mr. Chancey," said Ashwoode, preserving his temper with an effort, "let us proceed at once to business. I am pressed for time, and I shall be glad, with as little delay as possible, to ascertain—what I suppose there can be no difficulty in learning—the exact state of our account."

"Well, I'm very sorry, so I am, Mr. Ashwoode, that you are in such a hurry—I declare to — I am," observed Chancey, supplying big goblet afresh from the larger measure. "Eliza, have you the box? Well, bring it here, and put it down on the table, like an elegant little girl."

The girl shoved a small oaken chest over to Chancey's elbow; and he forthwith proceeded to unlock it, and to draw forth the identical red leather pocket-book which had received in its pages the records of Ashwoode's disasters upon the evening of their last meeting.

"Here I have them. Captain Markham—no, that is not it," said Chancey, sleepily turning over the leaves; "but this is it, Mr. Ashwoode—ay, here; first, two hundred pounds, promissory note—payable one week after date. Mr. Ashwoode, again, one hundred and fifty—promissory note—one week. Lord Kilblatters—no—ay, here again—Mr. Ashwoode, two hundred—promissory note—one week. Mr. Ashwoode, two hundred and fifty—promissory note—one week. Mr. Ashwoode, one hundred; Mr. Ashwoode, fifty. Oh, dear me! dear me! Mr. Ashwoode, three hundred." And so on, till it appeared that Sir Henry Ashwoode stood indebted to Gordon Chancey, Esq., in the sum of six thousand four hundred and fifty pounds, for which he had passed promissory notes which would all become due in two days' time.

"I suppose," said Ashwoode, "these notes have hardly been negotiated. Eh?"

"Oh, dear me! No—oh, no, Mr. Ashwoode," replied Chancey. "They have not gone out of my desk. I would not put them into the hands of a stranger for any trifling advantage to myself. Oh, dear me! not at all."

"Well, then, I suppose you can renew them for a fortnight or so, or hold them over—eh?" asked Ashwoode.

"I'm sure I can," rejoined Chancey. "The bills belong to the old cripple that lent the money; and he does whatever I bid him. He trusts it all to me. He gives me the trouble, and takes the profit himself. Oh! he does confide in me. I have only to say the word, and it's done. They shall be renewed or held over as often as you wish. Indeed, I can answer for it. Dear me, it would be very hard if I could not."

"Well, then, Mr. Chancey," replied Ashwoode, "I may require it, or I may not. Craven has the promise of a large sum of money, within two or three days—part of the loan he has already gotten. Will you favour me with a call on to-morrow afternoon at Morley Court. I will then have heard definitely from Craven, and can tell you whether I require time or not."

"Very good, sir—very fair, indeed, Mr. Ashwoode. Nothing fairer," rejoined the lawyer. "But don't give yourself any uneasiness. Oh, dear, on no account; for I declare to — I would hold them over as long as you like. Oh, dear me—indeed but I would. Well, then, I'll call out at about four o'clock."

"Very good, Mr. Chancey," replied Ashwoode. "I shall expect you. Meanwhile, good-night." So they separated.

The young baronet reached his ancestral dwelling without adventure of any kind, and Mr. Gordon Chancey poured out the last drops of beer from the inverted can into his pewter cup, and draining it calmly, anon buttoned his waistcoat, shook the wet from his cravat, and tied it on, thrust his feet into his shoes, and flinging his cocked hat carelessly upon his head, walked forth in deep thought into the street, whistling a concerto of his own invention.

## CHAPTER XXXII.

### THE DIABOLIC WHISPER.

Gordon Chancey sauntered in his usual lazy, lounging way, with his hands in his pockets, down the street. After a listless walk of half-an-hour he found himself at the door of a handsome house, in the immediate neighbourhood of the Castle. He knocked, and was admitted by a servant in full livery.

"Is he in the same room?" inquired Chancey.

"Yes, sir," replied the man; and without further parley, the learned counsel proceeded upstairs, and knocked at the drawing-room door, which, without waiting for any answer, he forthwith opened.

Nicholas Blarden—with two ugly black plaisters across his face, his arm in a sling, and his countenance bearing in abundance the livid marks of his late rencounter—stood with his back to the fire-place; a table, blazing with wax-lights, and stored with glittering wine-flasks and other matters, was placed at a little distance before him. As the man of law entered the room, the countenance of the invalid relaxed into an ugly grin of welcome.

"Well, Gordy, boy, how goes the game? Out with your news, old rat-catcher," said Blarden, in high good humour.

"Dear me, dear me! but the night is mighty chill, Mr. Blarden," observed Chancey, filling a glass of wine to the brim, and sipping it uninvited. "News," he continued, letting himself drop into a chair—"news; well, there's not much stirring worth telling you."

"Come, what is it? You're not come here for nothing, old fox," rejoined Blarden, "I know by the — twinkle in the corner of your eye."

"Well, he has been with me, just now," drawled Chancey.

"Ashwoode?"

"Yes."

"Well! what does he want—what does he want, eh?" asked Blarden, with intense excitement.

"He says he'll want time for the notes," replied Chancey.

"God be thanked!" ejaculated Blarden, and followed this ejaculation with a ferocious burst of laughter. "We'll have him, Chancey, boy, if only we know how to play him—by —, we'll have him, as sure as there's heat in hell."

"Well, maybe we will," rejoined Chancey.

"Does he say he can't pay them on the day?" asked Blarden, exultingly.

"No; he says maybe he can't," replied the jackal.

"That's all one," cried Blarden. "What do you think? Do you think he can?"

"I think maybe he can, if we squeeze him," replied Chancey.

"Then don't squeeze him—he must not get out of our books on any terms—we'll lose him if he does," said Nicholas.

"We'll not renew the notes, but hold them over," said Chancey. "He must not feel them till he can't pay them. We'll make them sit light on him till then—give him plenty of line for a while—rope enough and a little patience—and the devil himself can't keep him out of the noose."

"You're right—you are, Gordy, boy," rejoined Blarden. "Let him get through the ready money first—eh?—and then into the stone jug with him—we'll just choose our own time for striking."

"I tell you what it is, if you are just said and led by me, you'll have a quare hold on him before three months are past and gone," said Chancey, lazily—"mind I tell you, you will."

"Well, Gordy, boy, fill again—fill again—here's success to you."

Chancey filled, and quaffed his bumper, with, a matter-of-fact, business-like air.

"And do you mind me, boy," continued Blarden, "spare nothing in this business—bring Ashwoode entirely under my knuckle—and, by —, I'll make it a great job for you."

"Indeed—indeed but I will, Mr. Blarden, if I can," rejoined Chancey; "and I think I can—I think I know a way, so I do, to get a halter round his neck—do you mind?—and leave the rope's end in your hand, to hang him or not, as you like."

"To hang him!" echoed Blarden, like one who hears something too good to be true.

"Yes, to hang him by the neck till he's dead—dead—dead," repeated Chancey, imperturbably.

"How the blazes will you do it?" demanded the wretch, anxiously. "Pish, it's all prate and vapour."

Gordon Chancey stole a suspicious glance round the room from the corner of his eye, and then suffering his gaze to rest sleepily upon the fire once more, he stretched out one of his lank arms, and after a little uncertain groping, succeeding in grasping the collar of his companion's coat, and drawing his head down toward him. Blarden knew Mr. Chancey's way, and without a word, lowered his ear to that gentleman's mouth, who forthwith whispered something into it which produced a marked effect upon Mr. Blarden.

"If you do that," replied he with ferocious exultation, "by —, I'll make your fortune for you at a slap."

And so saving, he struck his hand with heavy emphasis upon the barrister's shoulder, like a man who clenches a bargain.

"Well, Mr. Blarden," replied Chancey, in the same drowsy tone, "as I said before, I declare it's my opinion I can, so it is—I think I can."

"And so do I think you can—by —, I'm sure of it," exclaimed Blarden triumphantly; "but take some more—more wine, won't you? take some more, and stay a bit, can't you?"

Chancey had made his way to the door with his usual drowsy gait; and, passing out without deigning any answer or word of farewell, stumbled lazily downstairs. There was nothing odd, however, in this leave-taking; it was Chancey's way.

"We'll do it, and easily too," muttered Blarden with a grin of exultation. "I never knew him fail—that fellow is worth a mine. Ho! ho! Sir Henry, beware—beware. Egad, you had better keep a bright look-out. It's rather late for green goslings to look to their necks, when the fox claps his nose in the poultry-yard."


CHAPTER XXXIII.

SHOWING HOW SIR HENRY ASHWOODE PLAYED AND PLOTTED—AND OF THE SUDDEN SUMMONS OF GORDON CHANCEY.

Henry Ashwoode was but too anxious to avail himself of the indulgence offered by Gordon Chancey. With the immediate urgency of distress, any thoughts of prudence or retrenchment which may have crossed his mind vanished, and along with the command of new resources came new wants and still more extravagant prodigality. His passion for gaming was now indulged without restraint, and almost without the interruption of a day. For a time his fortune rallied, and sums, whose amount would startle credulity, flowed into his hands, only to be lost and squandered again in dissipation and extravagance, which grew but the wilder and more reckless, in proportion as the sources which supplied them were temporarily increased. At length, after some coquetting, the giddy goddess again deserted him. Night after night brought new and heavier disasters; and with this reverse of fortune came its invariable accompaniment—a wilder and more daring recklessness, and a more unmeasured prodigality in hazarding larger and larger sums; as if the victims of ill luck sought, by this frantic defiance, to bully and browbeat their capricious persecutor into subjection. There was scarcely an available security of any kind which he had not already turned into money, and now he began to feel, in downright earnest, the iron gripe of ruin closing upon him.

He was changed—in spirit and in aspect changed. The unwearied fire of a secret fever preyed upon his heart and brain; an untold horror robbed him of his rest, and haunted him night and day.

"Brother," said Mary Ashwoode, throwing one hand fondly round his neck, and with the other pressing his, as he sate moodily, with compressed lips and haggard face, and eyes fixed upon the floor, in the old parlour of Morley Court—"dear brother, you are greatly changed; you are ill; some great trouble weighs upon your mind. Why will you keep all your cares and griefs from me? I would try to comfort you, whatever your sorrows may be. Then let me know it all, dear brother; why should your griefs be hidden from me? Are there not now but the two of us in the wide world to care for each other?" and as she said this her eyes filled with tears.

"You would know what grieves me?" said Ashwoode, after a short silence, and gazing fixedly in her face, with stern, dilated eyes, and pale features. He remained again silent for a time, and then uttered the emphatic word—"Ruin."

"How, dear brother, what has befallen you?" asked the poor girl, pressing her brother's hand more kindly.

"I say, we are ruined—both of us. I've lost everything. We are little better than beggars," replied he. "There's nothing I can call my own," he resumed, abruptly, after a pause, "but that old place, Incharden. It's worth next to nothing—bog, rocks, brushwood, old stables, and all—absolutely nothing. We are ruined—beggared—that's all."

"Oh! brother, I am glad we have still that dear old place. Oh, let us go down and live there together, among the quiet glens, and the old green woods; for amongst its pleasant shades I have known happier times than shall ever come again for me. I would like to ramble there again in the pleasant summer time, and hear the birds sing, and the sound of the rustling leaves, and the clear winding brook, as I used to hear them long ago. There I could think over many things, that it breaks my heart to think of here; and you and I, brother, would be always together, and we would soon be as happy as either of us can be in this sorrowful world."

She threw her arms around her brother's neck, and while the tears flowed fast and silently, she kissed his pale and wasted cheeks again and again.

"In the meantime," said Ashwoode, starting up abruptly, and looking at his watch, "I must go into town, and see some of these harpies—usurers—that have gotten their fangs in me. It is as well to keep out of jail as long as one can," and, with a very joyless laugh, he strode from the room.

As he rode into town, his thoughts again and again recurred to his old scheme respecting Lady Stukely.

"It is after all my only chance," said he. "I have made my mind up fifty times to it, but somehow or other, damn me, if I could ever bring myself to do it. That woman will live for five-and-twenty years to come, and she would as easily part with the control of her property as with her life. While she lives I must be her dependent—her slave: there is no use in mincing the matter, I shall not have the command of a shilling, but as she pleases; but patience—patience, Henry Ashwoode, sooner or later death will come, and then begins your jubilee."

As these thoughts hurried through his brain, he checked his horse at Lady Betty Stukely's door.

As he traversed the capacious hall, and ascended the handsome staircase—"Well," thought he, "even with her ladyship, this were better than the jail."

In the drawing-room he found Lady Stukely, Emily Copland, and Lord Aspenly. The two latter evidently deep in a very desperate flirtation, and her ladyship meanwhile very considerately employed in trying a piece of music on the spinet.

The entrance of Sir Henry produced a very manifest sensation among the little party. Lady Stukely looked charmingly conscious and fluttered. Emily Copland smiled a gracious welcome, for though she and her handsome cousin perfectly well understood each other, and both well knew that marriage was out of the question, they had each, what is called, a fancy for the other; and Emily, with the unreasonable jealousy of a woman, felt a kind of soreness, secretly and almost unacknowledged to herself, at Sir Henry's marked devotion to Lady Stukely, though, at the same time, no feeling of her own heart, beyond the lightest and the merest vanity, had ever been engaged in favour of Henry Ashwoode. Of the whole party, Lord Aspenly alone was a good deal disconcerted, and no wonder, for he had not the smallest notion upon what kind of terms he and Henry Ashwoode were to meet;—whether that young gentleman would shake hands with him as usual, or proceed to throttle him on the spot. Ashwoode was, however, too completely a man of the world to make any unnecessary fuss about the awkward affair of Morley Court; he therefore met the little nobleman with cold and easy politeness; and, turning from him, was soon engaged in an animated and somewhat tender colloquy with the love-stricken widow, whose last words to him, as at length he arose to take his leave, were,—

"Remember to-morrow evening, Sir Henry, we shall look for you early; and you have promised not to disappoint your cousin Emily—has not he, Emily? I shall positively be affronted with you for a week at least if you are late. I am very absolute, and never forgive an act of rebellion. I'm quite a little sovereign here, and very despotic; so you had better not venture to be naughty."

Here she raised her finger, and shook it in playful menace at her admirer.

Lady Stukely had, however, little reason to doubt his punctuality. If she had but known the true state of the case she would have been aware that in literal matter-of-fact she had become as necessary to Sir Henry Ashwoode as his daily bread.

Accordingly, next evening Sir Henry Ashwoode was one of the gayest of the guests in Lady Stukely's drawing-rooms. His resolution was taken; and he now looked round upon the splendid rooms and all their rich furniture as already his own. Some chatted, some played cards, some danced the courtly minuet, and some hovered about from group to group, without any determinate occupation, and sharing by turns in the frivolities of all. Ashwoode was, of course, devoted exclusively to his fair hostess. She was all smiles, and sighs, and bashful coyness; he all tenderness and fire. In short, he felt that all he wanted at that moment was the opportunity of asking, to ensure his instantaneous acceptance. While thus agreeably employed, the young baronet was interrupted by a footman, who, with a solemn bow, presented a silver salver, on which was placed an exceedingly dirty and crumpled little note. Ashwoode instantly recognized the hand in which the address was written, and snatching the filthy billet from its conspicuous position, he thrust it into his waistcoat pocket.

"A messenger, sir, waits for an answer," murmured the servant.

"Where is he?"

"He waits in the hall, sir."

"Then I shall see him in a moment—tell him so," said Ashwoode; and turning to Lady Stukely, he spoke a few sweet words of gallantry, and with a forced smile, and casting a longing, lingering look behind, he glided from the room.

"So, what can this mean?" muttered he, as he placed himself immediately under a cluster of lights in the lobby, and hastily drew forth the crumpled note. He read as follows:—

"MY DEAR SIR HENRY,—There is bad news—as bad as can be. Wherever you are, and whatever you are doing, come on receipt of these, on the moment, to me. If you don't, you'll be done for to-morrow; so come at once. Bobby M'Quirk will hand you these, and if you follow him, will bring you where I am now. I am desirous to serve you, and if the art of man can do it, to keep you out of this pickle.

"Your obedient, humble servant,

"GORDON CHANCEY."

"N.B.—It is about these infernal notes, so come quickly."

Through this production did Ashwoode glance with no very enviable feelings; and tearing the note into the very smallest possible pieces, he ran downstairs to the hall, where he found the aristocratic Mr. M'Quirk, with his chin as high as ever, marching up and down with a free and easy swagger, and one arm akimbo, and whistling the while an air of martial defiance.

"Did you bring a note to me just now?" inquired Ashwoode.

"I have had that pleasure," replied M'Quirk, with an aristocratic air. "I presume I am addressed by Sir Henry Ashwoode, baronet. I am Mr. M'Quirk—Mr. Robert M'Quirk. Sir Henry, I kiss your hands—proud of the honour of your acquaintance."

"Is Mr. Chancey at his own lodging now?" inquired Ashwoode, without appearing to hear the speeches which M'Quirk thought proper to deliver.

"Why, no," replied the little gentleman. "Our friend Chancey is just now swigging his pot of beer, and smoking his pen'orth of pigtail in the "Old Saint Columbkil," in Ship Street—a comfortable house, Sir Henry, as any in Dublin, and very cheap—cheap as dirt, sir. A Welsh rarebit, one penny; a black pudding, and neat cut of bread, and three leeks, for—how much do you guess?"

"Have the goodness to conduct me to Mr. Chancey, wherever he is," said Ashwoode drily. "I will follow—go on, sir."

"Well, Sir Henry, I'm your man—I'm your man—glad of your company, Sir Henry," exclaimed the insinuating Bobby M'Quirk; and following his voluble conductor in obstinate silence, Sir Henry Ashwoode found himself, after a dark and sloppy walk, for the first, though not for the last time in his life, under the roof tree of the "Old Saint Columbkil."

CHAPTER XXXIV.

THE "OLD ST. COLUMBKIL"—A TÊTE-À-TÊTE IN THE "ROYAL RAM"—THE TEMPTER.

The "Old Saint Columbkil" was a sort of low sporting tavern frequented chiefly by horse-jockeys, cock-fighters, and dog-fanciers; it had its cock-pits, and its badger-baits, and an unpretending little "hell" of its own; and, in short, was deficient in none of the attractions most potent in alluring such company as it was intended to receive.

As Ashwoode, preceded by his agreeable companion, made his way into the low-roofed and irregular chamber, his senses were assailed by the thick fumes of tobacco, the reek of spirits, and the heavy steams of the hot dainties which ministered to the refined palates of the patrons of the "Old Saint Columbkil;" and through the hazy atmosphere, seated at a table by himself, and lighted by a solitary tallow candle with a portentous snuff, and canopied in the clouds of tobacco smoke which he himself emitted, Gordon Chancey was dimly discernible.

"Ah! dear me, dear me. I'm right glad to see you—I declare to —, I am, Mr. Ashwoode," said that eminent barrister, when the young gentleman had reached his side. "Indeed, I was thinking it was maybe too late to see you to-night, and that things would have to go on. Oh, dear me, but it's a regular Providence, so it is. You'd have been up in lavender to-morrow, as sure as eggs is eggs. I'm gladder than a crown piece, upon my soul, I am."

"Don't talk of business here; cannot we have some place to ourselves for five minutes, out of this stifling pig-sty. I can't bear the place; besides, we shall be overheard," urged Ashwoode.

"Well, and that's very true," assented Chancey, gently, "very true, so it is; we'll get a small room above. You'll have to pay an extra sixpenny bit for it though, but what signifies the matter of that? M'Quirk, ask old Pottles if 'Noah's Ark' is empty—either that or the 'Royal Ram'—run, Bobby."

"I have something else to do, Mr. Chancey," replied Mr. M'Quirk, with hauteur.

"Run, Bobby, run, man," repeated Chancey, tranquilly.

"Run yourself," retorted M'Quirk, rebelliously.

Chancey looked at him for a moment to ascertain by his visible aspect whether he had actually uttered the audacious suggestion, and reading in the red face of the little gentleman nothing but the most refractory dispositions, he said with a low, dogged emphasis which experience had long taught Mr. M'Quirk to respect,—

"Are you at your tricks again? Damn you, you blackguard, if you stand prating there another minute, I'll open your head with this pot—be off, you scoundrel."

The learned counsel enforced his eloquence by knocking the pewter pot with an emphatic clang upon the table.

All the aristocratic blood of the M'Quirks mounted to the face of the gentleman thus addressed; he suffered the noble inundation, however, to subside, and after some hesitation, and one long look of unutterable contempt, which Chancey bore with wonderful stoicism, he yielded to prudential considerations, as he had often done before, and proceeded to execute his orders.

The effect was instantaneous—Pottles himself appeared. A short, stout, asthmatic man was Pottles, bearing in his thoughtful countenance an ennobling consciousness that human society would feel it hard to go on without him, and carrying in his hand a soiled napkin, or rather clout, with which he wiped everything that came in his way, his own forehead and nose included.

With pompous step and wheezy respiration did Pottles conduct his honoured guests up the creaking stairs and into the "Royal Ram." He raked the embers in the fire-place, threw on a piece of turf, and planting the candle which he carried upon a table covered with slop and pipe ashes, he wiped the candlestick, and then his own mouth carefully with his dingy napkin, and asked the gentlemen whether they desired anything for supper.

"No, no, we want nothing but to be left to ourselves for ten or fifteen minutes," said Ashwoode, placing a piece of money upon the table. "Take this for the use of the room, and leave us."

The landlord bowed and pocketed the coin, wheezed and bowed again, and then waddled magnificently out of the room. Ashwoode got up and closed the door after him, and then returning, drew his chair opposite to Chancey's, and in a low tone asked,—

"Well, what is all this about?"

"All about them notes, nothing else," replied Chancey, calmly.

"Go on—what of them?" urged Ashwoode.

"Can you pay them all to-morrow morning?" inquired Chancey, tranquilly.

"To-morrow!" exclaimed Ashwoode. "Why, hell and death, man, you promised to hold them over for three months. To-morrow! By —, you must be joking," and as he spoke his face turned pale as ashes.

"I told you all along, Mr. Ashwoode," said Chancey drowsily, "that the money was not my own; I'm nothing more than an agent in the matter, and the notes are in the desk of that old bed-ridden cripple that lent it. Damn him, he's as full of fumes and fancies as old cheese is of maggots. He has taken it into his head that your paper is not safe, and the devil himself won't beat it out of him; and the long and the short of it is, Mr. Ashwoode, he's going to arrest you to-morrow."

In vain Ashwoode strove to hide his agitation—he shook like a man in an ague.

"Good heavens! and is there no way of preventing this? Make him wait for a week—for a day," said Ashwoode.

"Was not I speaking to him ten times to-day—ay, twenty times," replied Chancey, "trying to make him wait even for one day? Why, I'm hoarse talking to him, and I might just as well be speaking to Patrick's tower; so make your mind up to this. As sure as light, you'll be in gaol before to-morrow's past, unless you either settle it early some way or other, or take leg bail for it."

"See, Chancey, I may as well tell you this," said Ashwoode, "before a fortnight, perhaps before a week, I shall have the means of satisfying these damned notes beyond the possibility of failure. Won't he hold them over for so long?"

"I might as well be asking him to cut out his tongue and give it to me as to allow us even a day; he has heard of different accidents that has happened to some of your paper lately—and the long and the short of it is—he won't hear of it, nor hold them over one hour more than he can help. I declare to —, Mr. Ashwoode, I am very sorry for your distress, so I am—but you say you'll have the money in a week?"

"Ay, ay, ay, so I shall, if he don't arrest me," replied Ashwoode; "but if he does, my perdition's sealed; I shall lie in gaol till I rot; but, curse it, can't the idiot see this?—if he waits a week or so he'll get his money—every penny back again—but if he won't have patience, he loses every sixpence to all eternity."

"You might as well be arguing with an iron box as think to change that old chap by talk, when he once gets a thing into his head," rejoined Chancey. Ashwoode walked wildly up and down the dingy, squalid apartment, exhibiting in his aristocratic form and face, and in the rich and elegant suit, flashing even in the dim light of that solitary, unsnuffed candle, with gold lace and jewelled buttons, and with cravat and ruffles fluttering with rich point lace, a strange and startling contrast to the slovenly and deserted scene of low debauchery which surrounded him.

"Chancey," said he, suddenly stopping and grasping the shoulder of the sleepy barrister with a fierceness and energy which made him start—"Chancey, rouse yourself, damn you. Do you hear? Is there no way of averting this awful ruin—is there none?"

As he spoke, Ashwoode held the shoulder of the fellow with a gripe like that of a vice, and stooping over him, glared in his face with the aspect of a maniac.

The lawyer, though by no means of a very excitable temperament, was startled at the horrible expression which encountered his gaze, and sate silently looking into his victim's face with a kind of fascination.

"Well," said Chancey, turning away his head with an effort—"there's but one way I can think of."

"What is it? Do you know anyone that will take my note at a short date? For God's sake, man, speak out at once, or my brain will turn. What is it?" said Ashwoode.

"Why, Mr. Ashwoode, to be plain with you," rejoined Chancey, "I do not know a soul in Dublin that would discount for you to one-fourth of the amount you require—but there is another way."

"In the fiend's name, out with it, then," said Ashwoode, shaking him fiercely by the shoulder.

"Well, then, get Mr. Craven to join you in a bond for the amount," said Chancey, "with a warrant of attorney to confess judgment."

"Craven! Why, he knows as well as you do how I am dipped. He'd just as readily thrust his hand into the fire," replied Ashwoode. "Is that your hopeful scheme?"

"Why, Mr. Craven might not do so well, after all," said Chancey, meditatively, and without appearing to hear what the young baronet said. "Oh! dear, dear, no, he would not do. Old Money-bags knows him—no, no, that would not do."

"Can your damned scheming brain plot no invention to help me? In the devil's name, where are your wits? Chancey, if you get me out of this accursed fix, I'll make a man of you."

"I got a whole lot of bills done for you once by the very same old gentleman," continued Chancey, "and damn heavy bills they were too, but they had Mr. Nicholas Blarden's name across them; would not he lend it again, if you told him how you stand? If you can come by the money in a month or so, you may be sure he'll do it."

"Better and better! Why, Blarden would ask no better fun than to see me ruined, dead, and damned," rejoined Ashwoode, bitterly. "Cudgel your brains for another bright thought."

"Oh! dear me, dear me," said the barrister mildly, "I thought you were the best of friends. Well, well, it's hard to know. But are you sure he don't like you?"

"It's odd if he does," said Ashwoode, "seeing it's scarce a month since I trounced him almost to death in the theatre. Blarden, indeed!"

"Well, Mr. Ashwoode, sit down here for a minute, and I'll say all I have to say; and if you like it, well and good; and if not, there's no harm done, and things must only take their course. Are you quite sure of having the means within a month of taking up the notes?"

"As sure as I am that I see you before me," replied he.

"Well, then, get Mr. Blarden's name along with your own to your joint and several bond—the old chap won't have anything more to do with bills—so, do you mind, your joint and several bond, with warrant of attorney to confess judgment—and I'll stake my life, he'll take it as ready as so much cash, the instant I show it to him," said the lawyer quietly.

"Are you dreaming or drunk? Have not I told you twenty times over that Blarden would cut his throat first?" retorted Ashwoode, passionately.

"Why," said Chancey, fixing his cunning eyes, with a peculiar meaning, upon the young man, and speaking with a lowered voice and marked deliberateness, "perhaps if Mr. Blarden knew that his name was wanted only to satisfy the whim of a fanciful old hunks—if he knew that judgment should never be entered—if he knew that the bond should never go outside a strong iron box, under an old bedridden cripple's bed—if he knew that no questions should be asked as to how he came to write his name at the foot of it—and if he knew that no mortal should ever see it until you paid it long before the day it was due—and if he was quite aware that the whole transaction should be considered so strictly confidential, that even to himself—do you mind—no allusion should be made to it;—don't you think, in such a case, you could, by some means or other, manage to get his—name?"

They continued to gaze fixedly at one another in silence, until, at length, Ashwoode's countenance lighted into a strange, unearthly smile.

"I see what you mean, Chancey—is it so?" said he, in a voice so low, as scarcely to be audible.

"Well, maybe you do," said the barrister, in a tone nearly as low, and returning the young man's smile with one to the full as sinister. Thus they remained without speaking for many minutes.

"There's no danger in it," said Chancey, after a long pause; "I would not take a part in it if there was. You can pay it eleven months before it's due. It's a thing I have known done a hundred times over, without risk; here there can be none. I do all his business myself. I tell you, that for anything that any living mortal but you and me and the old badger himself will ever hear, or see, or know of the matter, the bond might as well be burnt to dust in the back of the fire. I declare to — it's the plain truth I'm telling you—Sir Henry—so it is."

There followed another silence of some minutes. At length Ashwoode said, "I'd rather use any name but Blarden's, if it must be done."

"What does it matter whose name is on it, if there is no one but ourselves to read it?" replied Chancey. "I say Blarden's is the best, because he accepted bills for you before, which were discounted by the same old codger; and again, because the old fellow knows that the money was wanted to satisfy gambling debts, and Blarden would seem a very natural party in a gaming transaction. Blarden's is the name for us. And, for myself, all I ask is fifty pounds for my share in the trouble."

"When must you have the bond?" asked Ashwoode.

"Set about it now," said Chancey; "or stay, your hand shakes too much, and for both our sakes it must be done neatly; so say to-morrow morning, early. I'll see the old gentleman to-night, and have the overdue notes to hand you in the morning. I think that's doing business."

"I would not do it—I'd rather blow my brains out—if there was a single chance of his entering judgment on the bond, or talking of it," said Ashwoode, in great agitation.

"A chance!" said the barrister. "I tell you there's not a possibility. I manage all his money matters, and I'd burn that bond, before it should see the outside of his strong box. Why, d——n! do you think I'd let myself be ruined for fifty pounds? You don't know Gordon Chancey, indeed you don't, Mr. Ashwoode."

"Well, Chancey, I'll see you early to-morrow morning," said Ashwoode; "but are you very—very sure—is there no chance—no possibility of—of mischief?"

"I tell you, Mr. Ashwoode," replied Chancey, "unless I chose to betray myself, you can't come by harm. As I told you before, I'm not such a fool as to ruin myself. Rely on me, Mr. Ashwoode—rely on me. Do you believe what I say?"

Ashwoode walked slowly up to him, and fixing his eyes upon the barrister, with a glance which made Chancey's heart turn chill within him,—

"Yes, Mr. Chancey," he said, "you may be sure I believe you; for if I did not—so help me, God!—you should not quit this room—alive."

He eyed the caitiff for some minutes in silence, and then returning the sword, which he had partially drawn, to its scabbard, he abruptly wished him good-night, and left the room.


CHAPTER XXXV.

OF THE COUSIN AND THE BLACK CABINET—AND OF HENRY ASHWOODE'S DECISIVE INTERVIEW WITH LADY STUKELY.

"Well, then," said Ashwoode, a few days after the occurrences which have just been faithfully recorded, "it behoves me without loss of time to make provision for this infernal bond; until I see it burned to dust, I feel as if I stood in the dock. This sha'n't last long—my stars be thanked, one door of escape lies open to me, and through it I will pass; the sun shall not go down upon my uncertainty. To be sure, I shall be—but curse it, it can't be helped now; and let them laugh, and quiz, and sneer as they please, two-thirds of them would be but too glad to marry Lady Stukely with half her fortune, were she twice as old and twice as ugly—if, indeed, either were possible. Pshaw! the laugh will subside in a week, and in the style in which I shall open, curse me, if half the world won't lie at my feet. Give me but money—money —plenty of money, and though I be a paragon of absurdity and vice, the whole town will vote me a Solomon and a saint; so let's have no more shivering by the brink, but plunge boldly in at once and have it over."

Fortified with these reflections, Sir Henry Ashwoode vaulted lightly into his saddle, and putting his horse into an easy canter, he found himself speedily at Lady Stukely's house in Stephen's Green. His servant held the rein and he dismounted, and, having obtained admission, summoned all his resolution, lightly mounted the stairs, and entered the handsome drawing-room. Lady Stukely was not there, but his cousin, Emily Copland, received him.

"Lady Betty is not visible, then?" inquired he, after a little chat upon indifferent subjects.

"I believe she is out shopping—indeed, you may be very certain she is not at home," replied Emily, with a malicious smile; "her ladyship is always visible to you. Now confess, have you ever had much cruelty or coldness to complain of at dear Lady Stukely's hands?"

Ashwoode laughed, and perhaps for a moment appeared a little disconcerted.

"I do admit, then, as you insist on placing me in the confessional, that I have always found Lady Betty as kind and polite as I could have expected or hoped," rejoined Ashwoode, assuming a grave and particularly proper air; "I were particularly ungrateful if I said otherwise."

"Oh, ho! so her ladyship has actually succeeded in inspiring my platonic cousin with gratitude," continued Emily, in the same tone, "and gratitude we all know is Cupid's best disguise. Alas, and alack-a-day, to what vile uses may we come at last—alas, my poor coz."

"Nay, nay, Emily," replied he, a little piqued, "you need not write my epitaph yet; I don't see exactly why you should pity me so enormously."

"Haven't you confessed that you glow with gratitude to Lady Stukely?" rejoined she.

"Nonsense! I said nothing about glowing; but what if I had?" answered he.

"Then you acknowledge that you do glow! Heaven help him, the man actually glows," ejaculated Emily.

"Pshaw! stuff, nonsense. Emily, don't be a blockhead," said he, impatiently.

"Oh! Harry, Harry, Harry, don't deny it," continued she, shaking her head with intense solemnity, and holding up her fingers in a monitory manner—"you are then actually in love. Oh, Benedick, poor Benedick! would thou hadst chosen some Beatrice not quite so well stricken in years; but what of that?—the beauties of age, if less attractive to the eye of thoughtless folly than those of youth, are unquestionably more durable; time may rob the cheek of its bloom, but I defy him to rob it of its rouge; years—I might say centuries—have no power to blanche a wig or thin its flowing locks; and though the nymph be blind with age, what matters it if the swain be blind with love? I make no doubt you'll be fully as happy together as if she had twice as long to live."

Ashwoode poked the fire and blew his nose violently, but nevertheless answered nothing.

"The brilliant blush of her cheek and the raven blackness of her wig," continued the incorrigible Emily, "in close and striking contrast, will remind you, and I trust usefully, of that rouge et noir which has been your ruin all your days."

Still Ashwoode spoke not.

"The exquisite roundness of her ladyship's figure will remind you that flesh, if not exactly grass, is at least very little better than bran and buckram; and her smile will invariably suggest the great truth, that whenever you do not intend to bite it is better not to show your teeth, especially when they happen to be like her ladyship's; in short, you cannot look at her without feeling that in every particular, if rightly read, she supplied a moral lesson, so that in her presence every unruly passion of man's nature must entirely subside and sink to rest. Yes, she will make you happy—eminently happy; every little attention, every caress, every fond glance she throws at you, will delightfully assure your affectionate spirit, as it wanders in memory back to the days of earliest childhood, that she will be to you all that your beloved grandmother could have been, had she been spared. Oh! Harry, Harry, this will indeed be too much happiness."

Another pause ensued, and Emily approached Sir Henry as he stood sulkily by the mantelpiece, and laying her hand upon his arm, looked archly up into his face, while shaking her head she slowly said,—

"Oh! love, love—oh! Cupid, Cupid, mischievous little boy, what hast thou done with my poor cousin's heart?

"''Twas on a widow's jointure land
The archer, Cupid, took his stand.'"

As she said this, she looked so unutterably mischievous and comical, that in spite of his vexation and all his efforts to the contrary, he burst into a long and hearty fit of laughter.

"Emily," said he, at length, "you are absolutely incorrigible—gravity in your company is entirely out of the question; but listen to me seriously for one moment, if you can. I will tell you plainly how I am circumstanced, and you must promise me in return that you will not quiz me any more about the matter. But first," he added, cautiously, "let us guard against eavesdroppers."

He accordingly walked into the next room, which opened upon that in which they were, and proceeded to close the far door. Before he had reached it, however, that in the other room opened, and Lady Stukely herself entered. The instant she appeared, Emily Copland by a gesture enjoined silence, nodded towards the door of the next room, from which Ashwoode's voice, as he carelessly hummed an air, was audible; she then frowned, nodded, and pointed with vehement repetition toward a dark recess in the wall, made darker and more secure by the flanking projection of a huge, black, varnished cabinet. Lady Stukely looked puzzled, took a step in the direction of the post of concealment indicated by the girl, then looked puzzled, and hesitated again. More impatiently Emily repeated her signal, and her ladyship, without any distinct reason, but with her curiosity all alive, glided behind the protecting cabinet, with all its army of china ornaments, into the recess, and there remained entirely concealed. She had hardly effected this movement, which the deep-piled carpet enabled her to do without noise, when Ashwoode returned, closed the door of communication between the two rooms, and then shut that through which Lady Stukely had just entered, almost brushing against her as he did so, so close was their proximity. These precautions taken, he returned.

"Now," said he, in a low and deliberate tone, "the plain facts of the case are just these. I am dipped over head and ears in debt—debts, too, of the most urgent kind—debts which threaten me with ruin. Now, these must be paid—one way or another they must be met. And to effect this I have but one course— one expedient, and you have guessed it. No man knows better than I what Lady Stukely is. I can see all that is ridiculous and repulsive about her just as clearly as anybody else. She is old enough to be my grandmother, and ugly enough to be the devil's—and, moreover, painted and varnished over like a signboard. She may be a fool—she may be a termagant—she may be what you please—but—but she has money. She has been throwing herself into my arms this twelvemonth or more—and—but what the deuce is that?"

This interrogatory was caused by certain choking sounds which proceeded with fearful suddenness from the place of Lady Stukely's concealment, and which were instantaneously followed by the appearance of her ladyship in bodily presence. She opened her mouth, but gave utterance to nothing but a gasp—drew herself up with such portentous and swelling magnificence, that Ashwoode almost expected to see her expand like the spectre of a magic-lantern until her head touched the ceiling. Forward she came, in her progress sweeping a score of china ornaments from the cabinet, and strewing the whole floor with the crashing fragments of monkeys, monsters, and mandarins, breathless, choking, and almost black with rage, Lady Stukely advanced to Ashwoode, who stood, for the first time in his life, bereft of every vestige of self-possession.

"Painted! varnished!" she screamed hysterically, "ridiculous! repulsive! Oh, heaven and earth! you—you preternatural monster!" With these words she uttered two piercing shrieks, and threw herself in strong hysterics into a chair, holding on her wig distractedly with one hand, for fear of accidents.

"Don't—don't ring the bell," said she, with an abrupt accession of fortitude, observing Emily Copland approach the bell. "Don't, I shall be better presently." And then, with another shriek, she opened afresh.

As the hysterics subsided, Ashwoode began a little to recover his scattered wits, and observing that Lady Stukely had sunk back in extreme languor and exhaustion, with closed eyes, he ventured to approach the shrine of his outraged divinity.

"I feel—indeed I own, Lady Stukely," he said, hesitatingly, "I have much to explain. I ought to explain—yes, I ought. I will, Lady Stukely—and—and I can entirely satisfy—completely dispel—"

He was interrupted here; for Lady Stukely, starting bolt upright in the chair, exclaimed,—

"You wretch! you villain! you perjured, scheming, designing, lying, paltry, stupid, insignificant, outrageous—"

Whether it was that her ladyship wanted words to supply a climax, or that hysterics are usually attended with such results, we cannot pretend to say, but certain it is that at this precise point the languishing, fashionable, die-away Lady Stukely actually spat in the young baronet's face.

Ashwoode changed colour, as he promptly discharged the ridiculous but very necessary task of wiping his face. With difficulty he restrained himself under this provocation, but he did command himself so far as to say nothing. He turned on his heel and walked downstairs, muttering as he went,—

"An old painted devil!"

The cool air, as he passed out, speedily dissipated the confusion and excitement of the scene that had just passed, and all the consequences of his rupture with Lady Stukely rushed upon his mind with overwhelming and maddening force.

"You were right, perfectly right—he is a cheat—a trickster—a villain!" exclaimed Lady Stukely. "Only to think of him! Oh, heaven and earth!" And again she was seized with violent hysterics, in which state she was conducted up to her bedroom by Emily Copland, who had enjoyed the catastrophe with an intensity of relish which none but a female, and a mischievous one to boot, can know.

Loud and repeated were Lady Stukely's thanksgivings for having escaped the snares of the designing young baronet, and warm and multiplied and grateful her acknowledgments to Emily Copland—to whom, however, from that time forth she cherished an intense dislike.


CHAPTER XXXVI.

OF JEWELS, PLATE, HORSES, DOGS, AND FAMILY PICTURES—AND CONCERNING THE APPOINTED HOUR.

In a state little, if at all, short of distraction, Sir Henry Ashwoode threw himself from his horse at Morley Court. That resource which he had calculated upon with absolute certainty had totally failed him; his last stake had been played and lost, and ruin in its most hideous aspect stared him in the face.

Spattered from heel to head with mud—for he had ridden at a reckless speed—with a face pale as that of a corpse, and his dress all disordered, he entered the great old parlour, and scarcely knowing what he did, dashed the door to with violence and bolted it. His brain swam so that the floor seemed to heave and rock like a sea; he cast his laced hat and his splendid peruke (the envy and admiration of half the petit maîtres in Dublin) upon the ground, and stood in the centre of the room, with his hands clutched upon the temples of his bare, shorn head, and his teeth set, the breathing image of despair. From this state he was roused by some one endeavouring to open the door.

"Who's there?" he shouted, springing backward and drawing his sword, as if he expected a troop of constables to burst in.

Whoever the party may have been, the attempt was not repeated.

"What's the matter with me—am I mad?" said Ashwoode, after a terrible pause, and hurling his sword to the far end of the room. "Lie there. I've let the moment pass—I might have done it—cut the Gordian knot, and there an end of all. What brought me here?"

He stared about the room, for the first time conscious where he stood.

"Damn these pictures," he muttered; "they're all alive—everything moves towards me." He flung himself into a chair and clasped his fingers over his eyes. "I can't breathe—the place is suffocating. Oh, God! I shall go mad!" He threw open one of the windows and stood gasping at it as if he stood at the mouth of a furnace.

"Everything is hot and strange and maddening—I can't endure this—brain and heart are bursting—it is HELL."

In a state of excitement which nearly amounted to downright insanity, he stood at the open window. It was long before this extravagant agitation subsided so as to allow room for thought or remembrance. At length he closed the window, and began to pace the room from end to end with long and heavy steps. He stopped by a pier-table, on which stood a china bowl full of flowers, and plunging his hands into it, dashed the water over his head and face.

"Let me think—let me think," said he. "I was not wont to be thus overcome by reverse. Surely I can master as much as will pay that thrice-accursed bond, if I could but collect my thoughts—there must yet be the means of meeting it. Let that be but paid, and then, welcome ruin in any other shape. Let me see. Ay, the furniture; then the pictures—some of them valuable—very valuable; then the horses and the dogs; and then—ay, the plate. Why, to be sure—what have I been dreaming of?—the plate will go half-way to satisfy it; and then—what else? Let me see. The whole thing is six thousand four hundred and fifty pounds—what more? Is there nothing more to meet it? The plate—the furniture—the pictures—ay, idiot that I am, why did I not think of them an hour since?—my sister's jewels—why, it's all settled—how the devil came it that I never thought of them before? It's very well, however, as it is—for if I had, they would have gone long ago. Come, come, I breathe again—I have gotten my neck out of the hemp, at all events. I'll send in for Craven this moment. He likes a bargain, and he shall have one—before to-morrow's sun goes down, that d——d bond shall be ashes. Mary's jewels are valued at two thousand pounds. Well, let him take them at one thousand five hundred; and the pictures, plate, furniture, dogs, and horses for the rest—and he has a bargain. These jewels have saved me—bribed the hangman. What care I how or when I die, if I but avert that. Ten to one I blow my brains out before another month. A short life and a merry one was ever the motto of the Ashwoodes; and as the mirth is pretty well over with me, I begin to think it time to retire. Satis edisti, satis bipisti, satis lusisti, tempus est tibi abire—what am I raving about? There's business to be done now—to it, then—to it like a man—while we are alive let us be alive."

Craven liked his bargain, and engaged that the money should be duly handed at noon next day to Sir Henry Ashwoode, who forthwith bade the worthy attorney good-night, and wrote the following brief note to Gordon Chancey, Esq.:—

"SIR,

"I shall call upon you to-morrow at one of the clock, if the hour suit you, upon particular business, and shall be much obliged by your having a certain security by you, which I shall then be prepared to redeem.

"I remain, sir, your very obedient servant,

"HENRY ASHWOODE."

"So," said Sir Henry, with a half shudder, as he folded and sealed this missive, "I shall, at all events, escape the halter. To-morrow night, spite of wreck and ruin, I shall sleep soundly. God knows, I want rest. Since I wrote that name, and gave that accursed bond out of my hands, my whole existence, waking and sleeping, has been but one abhorred and ghastly nightmare. I would gladly give a limb to have that damned scrap of parchment in my hand this moment; but patience, patience—one night more—one night only—of fevered agony and hideous dreams—one last night—and then—once more I am my own master—my character and safety are again in my own hands—and may I die the death, if ever I risk them again as I have done—one night more—would—would to God it were morning!"

The morning arrived, and at the appointed hour Sir Henry Ashwoode dismounted in Whitefriar Street, and gave the bridle of his horse to the groom who accompanied him.

"Well," thought he, as he entered the dingy, dilapidated square in which Chancey's lodgings were situated, "this matter, at all events, is arranged—I sha'n't hang, though I'm half inclined to allow I deserve to do so for my infernal folly in trying the thing at all; but no matter, it has given me a lesson I sha'n't soon forget. As to the rest, what care I now? Let ruin pounce upon me in any shape but that—luckily I have still enough to keep body and soul together left."

He paused to indulge in ruminations of no very pleasant kind, and then half muttered,—

"I have been a fool—I have walked in a dream. Only to think of a man like me, who has seen something of the world, allowing that damned hag to play him such a trick. Well, I believe it is true, after all, that we cannot have wisdom without paying for it. If my acquisitions bear any proportion to my outlay, I ought to be a Solomon by this time."

The door was opened to his summons by Gordon Chancey himself. When Ashwoode entered, Chancey carefully locked the door on the inside and placed the key in his pocket.

"It's as well, Sir Henry, to be on the safe side," observed Chancey, shuffling towards the table. "Dear me, dear me, there's no such thing as being too careful—is there, Sir Henry?"

"Well, well, well, let's to business," said young Ashwoode, hurriedly, seating himself at the end of a heavy deal table, at which was a chair, and taking from his pocket a large leathern pocket-book. "You have the—the security here?"

"Of course—oh, dear, of course," replied the barrister; "the bond and warrant of attorney—that damned forgery—it is in the next room, very safe—oh, dear me, yes indeed."

It struck Ashwoode that there was something, he could not exactly say what, unusual and sinister in the manner of Mr. Chancey, as well as in his emphasis and language, and he fixed his eye upon him for a moment with a searching glance. The barrister, however, busied himself with tumbling over some papers in a drawer.

"Well, why don't you get it?" asked Ashwoode, impatiently.

"Never mind, never mind," replied Chancey; "do you reckon your money over, and be very sure the bond will come time enough. I don't wonder, though, you're eager to have it fast in your own hands again—but it will come—it will come."

Ashwoode proceeded to open the pocket-book and to turn over the notes.

"They're all right," said he, "they're all right. But, hush!" he added, slightly changing colour—"I hear something stirring in the next room."

"Oh, dear, dear, it's nothing but the cat," rejoined Chancey, with an ugly laugh.

"Your cat treads very heavily," said Ashwoode, suspiciously.

"So it does," rejoined Chancey, "it does tread heavy; it's a very large cat, so it is; it has wonderful great claws; it can see in the dark; it's a great cat; it never missed a rat yet; and I've seen it lure the bird off a branch with the mere power of its eye; it's a great cat—but reckon your money, and I'll go in for the bond."

This strange speech was uttered in a manner at least as strange, and Chancey, without waiting for commentary or interruption, passed into the next room. The step crossed the adjoining chamber, and Ashwoode heard the rustling of papers; it then returned, the door opened, and not Gordon Chancey, but Nicholas Blarden entered the room and confronted Sir Henry Ashwoode. Personal fear in bodily conflict was a thing unknown to the young baronet, but now all courage, all strength forsook him, and he stood gazing in vacant horror upon that, to him, most tremendous apparition, with a face white as ashes, and covered with the starting dews of terror.

With that hideous combination, a smile and a scowl, stamped upon his coarse features, the wretch stood with folded arms, in an attitude of indescribable exultation, gazing with savage, gloating eyes full upon his appalled and terror-stricken victim. Fixed as statues they both remained for several minutes.

"Ho, ho, ho! you look frightened, young man," exclaimed Blarden, with a horse laugh; "you look as if you were going to be hanged—you look as if the hemp were round your neck—you look as if the hangman had you by the collar, you do—ho, ho, ho!"

Ashwoode's bloodless lips moved, but utterance was gone.

"It's hard to get the words out," continued Blarden, with ferocious glee. "I never knew the man yet could do a last dying speech smooth—a sort of choking comes on, eh?—the sight of the minister and the hangman makes a man feel so quare, eh?—and the coffin looks so ugly, and all the crowd; it's confusing somehow, and puts a man out, eh?—ho, ho, ho!"

Ashwoode laid his hand upon his forehead, and gazed on in blank horror.

"Why, you're not such a great man, by half, as you were in the play-house the other evening," continued Blarden; "you don't look so grand, by any manner of means. Some way or other, you look a little sickish or so. I'm afraid you don't like my company—ho, ho, ho!"

Still Sir Henry remained locked in the same stupefied silence.

"Ho, ho! you seem to think your hemp is twisted, and your boards sawed," resumed Blarden; "you seem to think you're in a fix at last—and so do I, by —!" he thundered, "for I have the rope fairly round your weasand, and, by — I'll make you dance upon nothing, at Gallows Hill, before you're a month older. Do you hear that—do you—you swindler? Eh—you gaol-bird, you common forger, you robber, you crows' meat—who holds the winning cards now?"

"Where—where's the bond?" said Ashwoode, scarce audibly.

"Where's your precious bond, you forger, you gibbet-carrion?" shouted Blarden, exultingly. "Where's your forged bond—the bond that will crack your neck for you—where is it, eh? Why, here—here in my breeches pocket—that's where it is. I hope you think it safe enough—eh, you gallows-tassle?"

Yielding to some confused instinctive prompting to recover the fatal instrument, Ashwoode drew his sword, and would have rushed upon his brutal and triumphant persecutor; but Blarden was not unprepared even for this. With the quickness of light, he snatched a pistol from his coat pocket, recoiling, as he did so, a hurried pace or two, and while he turned, coward as he was, pale and livid as death, he levelled it at the young man's breast, and both stood for an instant motionless, in the attitudes of deadly antagonism.

"Put up your sword; I have you there, as well as everywhere else—regularly checkmated, by —!" shouted Blarden, with the ferocity of half-desperate cowardice. "Put up your sword, I say, and don't be a bloody idiot, along with everything else. Don't you see you're done for?—there's not a chance left you. You're in the cage, and there's no need to knock yourself to pieces against the bars—you're done for, I tell you."

With a mute but expressive gesture of despair, Ashwoode grasped his sword by the slender, glittering blade, and broke it across. The fragments dropped from his hands, and he sunk almost lifeless into a chair—a spectacle so ghastly, that Blarden for a moment thought that death was about to rescue his victim.

"Chancey, come out here," exclaimed Blarden; "the fellow has taken the staggers—come out, will you?"

"Oh! dear me, dear me," said Chancey, in his own quiet way, "but he looks very bad."

"Go over and shake him," said Blarden, still holding the pistol in his hand. "What are you afraid of? He can't hurt you—he has broken his bilbo across—the symbol of gentility. By —! he's a good deal down in the mouth."

While they thus debated, Ashwoode rose up, looking more like a corpse endowed with motion than a living man.

"Take me away at once," said he, with a sullen wildness—"take me away to gaol, or where you will—anywhere were better than this place. Take me away; I am ruined—blasted. Make the most of it—your infernal scheme has succeeded—take me to prison."

"Oh, murder! he wants to go to gaol—do you hear him, Chancey?" cried Blarden—"such an elegant, fine gentleman to think of such a thing: only to think of a baronet in gaol—and for forgery, too—and the condemned cell such an ungentlemanly sort of a hole. Why, you'd have to use perfumes to no end, to make the place fit for the reception of your aristocratic visitors—my Lord this, and my Lady that—for, of course, you'll keep none but the best of company—ho, ho, ho! Perhaps the judge that's to try you may turn out to be an old acquaintance, for your luck is surprising—isn't it, Chancey?—and he'll pay you a fine compliment, and express his regret when he's going to pass sentence, eh?—ho, ho, ho! But, after all, I'd advise you, if the condescension is not too much to expect from such a very fine gentleman as you, to consort as much as possible with the turnkey—he's the most useful friend you can make, under your peculiarly delicate circumstances—ho, ho!—eh? It's just possible he mayn't like to associate with you, for some of them fellows are rather stiff, d'ye see, and won't keep company with certain classes of the coves in quod, such as forgers or pickpockets; but if he'll allow it, you'd better get intimate with him—ho, ho, ho!—eh?"

"Take me to the prison, sir," said Ashwoode, sternly—"I suppose you mean to do so. Let your officers remove me at once—you have, no doubt, men for the purpose in the next room. Let them call a coach, and I will go with them—but let it be at once."

"Well, you're not far out there, by —!" replied Blarden. "I have a broad-shouldered acquaintance or two, and a little bit of a warrant—you understand?—in the next apartment. Grimes, Grimes, come in here—you're wanted."

A huge, ill-looking fellow, with his coat buttoned up to his chin, and a short pipe protruding from the corner of his mouth, swaggered into the chamber, with that peculiar gait which seems as if contracted by habitually shouldering and jostling through mobs and all manner of riotous assemblies.

"That's the bird?" said the fellow, interrogatively, and pointing with his pipe carelessly at Ashwoode. "You're my prisoner," he added, gruffly addressing the unfortunate young man, and at the same time planting his ponderous hand heavily upon his shoulder, he in the other exhibited a crumpled warrant.

"Grimes, go call a coach," said Blarden, "and don't be a brace of shakes about it, do you mind."

Grimes departed, and Blarden, after a long pause, suddenly addressing himself to Ashwoode, resumed, in a somewhat altered tone, but with intenser sternness still,—

"Now, I tell you what it is, my young cove, I have a sort of half a notion not to send you to gaol at all, do you hear?"

"Pshaw, pshaw!" said Ashwoode, turning bitterly away.

"I tell you I'm speaking what I mean," rejoined Blarden; "I'll not send you there now at any rate. I want to have a bit of chat with you this evening, and it shall rest with you whether you go there at all or not; I'll give you the choice fairly. We'll meet, then, at Morley Court this evening, at eight o'clock; and for fear of accidents in the meantime, you'll have no objection to our mutual friend, Mr. Chancey, and our common acquaintance, Mr. Grimes, accompanying you home in the coach, and just keeping an eye on you till I come, for fear you might be out walking when I call—you understand me? But here's Grimes. Mr. Grimes, my particular friend Sir Henry Ashwoode has taken an extraordinary remarkable fancy to you, and wishes to know whether you'll do him the favour to take a jaunt with him in a carriage to see his house at Morley Court, and to spend the day with him and Mr. Chancey, for he finds that his health requires him to keep at home, and he has a particular objection to be left alone, even for a minute. Sir Henry, the coach is at the door. You'd better bundle up your bank-notes, they may be useful to you. Chancey, tell Sir Henry's groom, as you pass, that he'll not want his horse any more to-day."

The party went out; Sir Henry, pale as death, and scarcely able to support himself on his limbs, walking between Chancey and the herculean constable. Blarden saw them safely shut up in the vehicle, and giving the coachman his orders, gazed after them as they drove away in the direction of Morley Court, with a flushed face and a bounding heart.

## CHAPTER XXXVIII.

### STRANGE GUESTS AT THE MANOR.

The coach jingled, jolted, and rumbled on, and Ashwoode lay back in the crazy conveyance in a kind of stupefied apathy. The scene which had just closed was, in his mind, a chaos of horrible confusion—a hideous, stunning dream, whose incidents, as they floated through his passive memory, seemed like unreal and terrific exaggerations, into whose reality he wanted energy and power to inquire. Still before him sate a breathing evidence of the truth of all these confused and horrible recollections—the stalwart, ruffianly figure of the constable—with his great red horny hands, and greasy cuffs, and the heavy coat buttoned up to his unshorn chin—and the short, discoloured pipe, protruding from the corner of his mouth—lounging back with half-closed eyes, and the air of a man who had passed the night in wearisome vigils among strife and riot, and who has acquired the compensating power of dividing his faculties at all times pretty nearly between sleep and waking—a kind of sottish, semi-existence—

something between that of a swine and a sloth. Over this figure the eyes of the young man vacantly wandered, and thence to the cheerful fields and trees visible from the window, and back again to the burly constable, until every seam and button in his coat grew familiar to his mind as the oldest tenants of his memory. Beside him, too, sate Chancey—his artful, cowardly betrayer. Yet even against him he could not feel anger; all energy of thought and feeling seemed lost to him; and nothing but a dull ambiguous incredulity and a scared stupor were there in their stead. On—on they rolled and rumbled, among pleasant fields and stately hedge-rows, toward the ancestral dwelling of the miserable prisoner, who sate like a lifeless effigy, yielding passively to every jolt and movement of the carriage.

"I say, Grimes, were you ever out here before?" inquired Mr. Chancey. "We'll soon be in the manor, driving up to Morley Court. It's a fine place, I'm given to understand. I never was here but once before, long as I know Sir Henry; but better late than never. Do you know this place, Mr. Grimes?"

A negative grunt and a short nod relieved Mr. Grimes from the painful necessity of removing his pipe for the purpose of uttering an articulate answer.

"Oh, dear me, dear me," resumed Mr. Chancey, "but I'm uncommon hungry and dry. I wish to God we were safe and sound in Sir Henry's house. Grimes, are you dry?"

Mr. Grimes removed his pipe, and spat upon the coach floor.

"Am I dhry?" said he. "About as dhry as a sprat in a tindher-box, that's all. Is there much more to go?"

Chancey stretched his head out of the coach window.

"I see the old piers of the avenue," said he; "and God knows but it's I that's glad we're near our journey's end. Now we're passing in—we're in the avenue."

Mr. Grimes hereupon uttered a grunt of approbation; and pressing down the ashes of his pipe with his thumb, he deposited that instrument in his waistcoat pocket—whence, at the same time, he drew a small plug of tobacco, which he inserted in his mouth, and rolled it about with his tongue from time to time during the remainder of their progress.

"Sir Henry, we're arrived," said Chancey, admonishing the baronet with his elbow—"we're at the hall-door at Morley Court. Sir Henry—dear me, dear me, he's very abstracted, so he is. I say, Sir Henry, we're at Morley Court."

Ashwoode looked vacantly in Chancey's face, and then upon the stately door of the old house, and suddenly recollecting himself, he said with strange alacrity,—

"Ay, ay—at Morley Court—so we are. Come, then, gentlemen, let us get down."

Accordingly the three companions descended from the conveyance, and entered the ancient dwelling-house together.

"Follow me, gentlemen," said Ashwoode, leading the way to a small, oak-wainscoted parlour. "You shall have refreshments immediately."

He called the servant to the door, and continued addressing himself to Chancey, and his no less refined companion.

"Order what you please, gentlemen—I can't think of these things just now; and, sirrah, do you hear me, bring a large vessel of water—my throat is literally scorched."

"Well, Mr. Chancey, what do you say?" said Grimes. "I'm for a couple of bottles of sack, and a good pitcher of ale, to begin with, in the way of liquor."

"Well, it wouldn't be that bad," said Chancey. "What meat have you on the spit, my good man?"

"I don't exactly know, sir," replied the wondering domestic; "but I'll inquire."

"And see, my good man," continued Chancey, "ask them whether there isn't some cold roast beef in the buttery; and if so, bring it up in a jiffy, for, I declare to G—d I'm uncommon hungry; and let the cook send up a hot joint directly;—and do you mind, my honest man, light a bit of a fire here, for it's rather chill, and put plenty of dry sticks—"

"Give us the ale and the sack this instant minute, do you see," said Mr. Grimes. "You may do the rest after."

"Yes, you may as well," resumed Chancey; "for indeed I'm lost with the drooth myself."

"Cut your stick, saucepan," said Mr. Grimes, authoritatively; and the servant departed in unfeigned astonishment to execute his various commissions.

Ashwoode threw himself into a seat, and in silence endeavoured to collect his thoughts. Faint, sick, and stunned, he nevertheless began gradually to comprehend every particular of his position more and more fully—until at length all the ghastly truth stood revealed to his mind's eye in vivid and glaring distinctness. While Ashwoode was engaged in his agreeable ruminations, Mr. Chancey and Mr. Grimes were busily employed in discussing the substantial fare which his larder had supplied, and pledging one another in copious libations of generous liquor.


CHAPTER XXXIX.

THE BARGAIN, AND THE NEW CONFEDERATES.

At length the evening came—darkness closed over the old place, and as the appointed hour approached, Ashwoode became more and more excited.

"I must," thought he, "keep every faculty intensely on the stretch, to detect, if possible, the nature of their schemes. Blarden and Chancey have unquestionably hatched some other damned plot, though what worse can befall me? I am netted as completely as their worst malice can desire. It is now seven o'clock. Another hour will determine all my doubts. Hark you, sirrah!" continued he, raising his voice, and addressing a servant who had entered the chamber, "I expect a gentleman upon particular business at eight o'clock. On his arrival conduct him directly to this room."

He then relapsed into the same train of gloomy and agitated thought.

Chancey and his burly companion both sat snugly before the fire smoking their pipes in silent enjoyment, while their miserable host paced the room from wall to wall in mental torments indescribable.

At length the weary interval expired, and within a few minutes of the appointed hour, Nicholas Blarden was admitted by the servant, and ushered into the chamber in which Ashwoode expected his arrival.

"Well, Sir Henry," exclaimed Blarden, as he swaggered into the room, "you seem a little flustered still—eh? Hope you found your company pleasant. My friends' society is considered uncommon agreeable."

The visitor here threw himself into a chair, and continued—

"By the holy Saint Paul, as I rode up your cursed old dusky avenue, I began to think the chances were ten to one you had brought your throat and a razor acquainted before this. I have known men do it under your circumstances—of course I mean gentlemen, with fine friends and delicate habits, and who could not stand exposure and all that kind of thing. I say, Mr. Grimes, my sweet fellow, you may leave the room, but keep within call, do ye mind. Mr. Chancey and I want to have a little confidential conversation with my friend, Sir Henry. Bundle out, and the moment you hear me call your name, bolt in again like a shot."

Mr. Grimes, without answering, rose and lounged out of the room.

"Chancey, shut that door," continued Blarden. "Shut it tight, as tight as a drum. There, to your seat again. Now then, Sir Henry, we may as well to business; but first of all, sit down. I have no objection to your sitting. Don't be shy."

Sir Henry Ashwoode did seat himself, and the three members of this secret council drew their chairs around the table, each with very different feelings.

"I take it for granted," said Blarden, planting his elbow upon the table, and supporting his chin upon his hand, while he fixed his baleful eyes upon the young man, "I take it for granted, and as a matter of course, that you have been puzzling your brains all day to come at the reason why I allow you to be sitting in this house, instead of clapping your four bones under lock and key, in another place."

He paused here, as if to allow his exordium to impress itself upon the memory of his auditory, and then resumed,—

"And I take it for granted, moreover, that you are not quite fool enough to imagine that I care one blast if you were strung up by the hangman, and carved by the doctors, to-morrow—eh?"

He paused again.

"Well, then, it's possible you think I have some end of my own to serve, by letting the matter stand over this way. And so I have, by —. You think right, if you never thought right before. I have an object in view, and it lies with you whether it's gained or lost. Do you mind?"

"Go on—go on—go on," repeated Ashwoode, gloomily.

"What a devil of a hurry you're in," observed Blarden, with a scornful chuckle. "But don't tear yourself; you'll have it all time enough. Now I'm going to do great things for you—do you mind me? I'm going, in the first place, to give you your life and your character—such as it is; and, what's more, I'll not let you go to jail for debt neither. I'll not let you be ruined; for Nickey Blarden was never the man to do things by halves. Do you hear all I'm saying?"

"Yes, yes," said Ashwoode, faintly; "but the condition—come to that—the condition."

"Well, I will come to that. I will tell you the terms," rejoined Blarden. "I suppose you need not be told that I am worth a good penny, no matter how much. At any rate I'm rich—that much you do know. Well, perhaps you'll think it odd that I have not taken up a little to live more quiet and orderly; in short, that I have not sown my wild oats, and settled down, and all that, and become what they call an ornament to society—eh? You, perhaps, wonder how it comes I have not taken a rib—why I have not got married—eh? Well, I think myself it is a wonder, especially for such an admirer of the sex as I am, and I think it's a pity besides, and so I've made up my mind to mend the matter, do you see, and to take a wife without loss of time. She must have family, for I want that, and she must have beauty, for I would not marry the queen without it—family and beauty. I don't ask money; I have more of my own than I well know what to do with. Family and beauty is what I require. And I have settled the thing in my own mind, that the very article I want, just the thing to a nicety, is your sister—little, bright-eyed Mary—sporting Molly. I wish to marry her, and her I'll have—and that's the long and the short of the whole business."

"You—you marry my sister," exclaimed Ashwoode, returning the fellow's insolent gaze with a look of indescribable scorn and astonishment.

"Yes—I—I myself—I, Nicholas Blarden, with more gold than a man could count in three lives," shouted Blarden, returning his gaze with a scowl of defiance—"I condescend to marry the sister of a ruined, beggared profligate—a common forger, who has one foot in the dock at this minute. Down upon your marrow-bones, and thank me for my condescension—down, I say."

Overwhelmed with indignation and disgust, Ashwoode could not answer. All his self-command was required to resist his vehement internal impulse to strike the fellow to the ground and trample upon him. This strong emotion, however, had its spring in no generous source. No thought or care for Mary's feelings or fate crossed his mind; but only the sense of insulted pride, for even in the midst of all his misery and abasement, his hereditary pride of birth survived: that this low, this entirely blasted, this branded ruffian should dare to propose to ally himself with the Ashwoodes of Morley Court—a family whose blood was as pure as centuries of aristocratic transmission, and repeated commixture with that of nobility, could make it—a family who stood, in consideration and respect, one of the very highest of the country! Could flesh and blood endure it?

"Make your mind up at once—I have no time to spare; and just remember that the locality of your night's lodging depends upon your decision," said Blarden, coolly, looking at his watch. "If, unfortunately for yourself, you should resolve against the connection, then you must have the goodness to accompany us into town to-night, and the law takes its course quietly with you, and your neck-bone must only reconcile itself to an ugly bit of a twist. If otherwise, you're a made man. Run the matter fairly over in your mind, and see which of us two should desire the thing most. As for me, I tell you plainly, it's a bit of a fancy—no more—and may pass off in a day or two, for I don't pretend to be extraordinarily steady in love affairs, and always had rather a roving eye; and if I should happen to cool, by —, you'll be in a nice hobble. So I think you had best take the ball at the hop—do you mind—and make no mouths at your good fortune."

Blarden paused, and looked at his huge chased-gold watch again, and laid it on the table, as if to measure Ashwoode's deliberation by the minute. Meanwhile the young baronet had ample time to recollect the desperate pressure of his circumstances, which outraged pride had for a moment half obliterated from his mind, and the process of remembrance was in no small degree assisted by the heavy tread of the constable, distinctly audible from the hall.

"Blarden," said Ashwoode, in a voice low and husky with agitation, "she'll never consent—you can't expect it: she'll never marry you."

"I'm not talking of the girl's consent just now," replied Blarden: "I'm asking only for yours in the first place. Am I to understand that you're agreed?"

"Yes," replied Ashwoode, sullenly; "what is there left to me, but to agree?"

"Then leave me alone to gain her consent," retorted Blarden, with a brutal smile. "I have a bit of a winning way with me—a knack of my own—for coming round a girl; and if she don't yield to that, why we must only try another course. When love is wanting, obedience is the next best thing: although we can't charm her, she's no girl if we can't frighten her—eh?"

Ashwoode was silent.

"Now mind, I require your active co-operation," continued Blarden; "there's to be no shamming. I'm no greenhorn, and know a loaded die from a fair one. It's not safe to try hocus pocus with me, and if I don't get the girl, of course you're no brother of mine, and must not expect me to forget the old score that's between us. Do you understand me? Unless you bring this marriage about, you must only take the consequences, and I promise you they'll be of the very ugliest possible description."

"Agreed, agreed; talk no more of it just now," said Ashwoode, vehemently—"we understand one another. Tomorrow we may talk of it again; meanwhile torment me no more!"

"Well, I have said my say," rejoined Blarden, "and have nothing more to do but to inform you, that I intend passing the night here, and, in short, to make a visit of a week or so, for it's right the young lady should have an opportunity of knowing my geography before she marries me; and besides, I have heard a great account of old Sir Richard's cellar. Chancey, do you tell my servant to bring my things up to the room that Sir Henry will point out. Sir Henry, you'll see about my room—have a bit of fire in it—see to it yourself, mind; for do you mind, between ourselves, I think it's on the whole your better course to be uncommonly civil to me. Stir yourselves, gentlemen. And, Chancey, hand Grimes his fee, and let him be off. We'll try a jug of your claret, Sir Henry, and a spatchcock, or some little thing of the kind, and then to our virtuous beds—eh?"

After a carousal protracted to nearly three hours, during which Nickey Blarden treated his two companions to sundry ballads, and other vocal efforts somewhat more boisterous than elegant, and supplying frequent allusion, and not of the most delicate kind, to his contemplated change of condition, that interesting person proceeded somewhat unsteadily upstairs to his bed-chamber. With a suspicion, which even his tipsiness could not overcome, he jealously bolted the door upon the inside, and laid his sword and pistols upon the table by his bed, remembering that it was just possible that his entertainer might conceive an expeditious project for relieving himself of all his troubles, or at least the greater part of them. These pleasant precautions taken, Mr. Blarden undressed himself with all celerity and threw himself into bed.

This gentleman's opinion of mankind was by no means exalted, nor at all complimentary to human nature. Utter, hardened selfishness he believed to be the master-passion of the human race, and any appeal which addressed itself to that, he looked upon as irresistible. In applying this rule to Sir Henry Ashwoode he happened, indeed, to be critically correct, for the young baronet was in very nearly all points fashioned precisely according to honest Nickey's standard of humanity. That gentleman experienced, therefore, no misgivings as to his young friend's preferring at all hazards to remain at Morley Court, rather than quit the country, and enter upon a life of vagabond beggary.

"No, no," thought Blarden, "he'll not take leg bail, just because he can gain nothing earthly by it now; the only thing I can see that could serve him at all—that is, supposing him to be against the match—is to cut my throat; however, I don't think he's wild enough to run that risk, and if he does try it, by —, he'll have the worst of the game."

Thus, after a day of unclouded triumph, did Mr. Blarden compose himself to light and happy slumbers.

## CHAPTER XL

DREAMS—FIRST IMPRESSIONS—THE MAN IN THE PLUM-COLOURED SUIT.

The sun shone cheerily through the casement of the quaint and pretty little chamber which called Mary Ashwoode its mistress. It was a fresh and sunny autumn morning; the last leaves rustled on the boughs, and the thrush and blackbird sang their merry morning lays. Mary sat by the window, looking sadly forth upon the slopes and woods which caught the slanting beams of the ruddy sun.

"I have passed, indeed, a very troubled night—I have been haunted with strange and fearful dreams. I feel very sorrowful and uneasy—indeed, indeed I do, Carey."

"It's only the vapours, my lady," replied the maid; "a glass of orange-flower water and camphor is the sovereignest thing in the world for them."

"Indeed, Carey," continued the young lady, still gazing sadly from the casement, "I know not why it is so—a foolish dream, wild and most extravagant, yet still it will not leave me. I cannot shake off this fear and depression. I will run down stairs and talk with my dear brother—that may cheer me."

She arose, ran lightly down the stairs, and entered the parlour. The first object that met her gaze, standing full before her, was a large and singularly ill-looking man, arrayed in a suit of plum-coloured cloth, richly laced. It was Nicholas Blarden. With a vulgar swagger, half abashed and half impudent, the fellow acknowledged her entrance by retreating a little and making an awkward bow, while a smile and a leer, more calculated to frighten than to attract, lighted his coarse and swollen features. The girl looked at this object with a startled air, she felt that she had seen that sinister face before, but where or when—whether waking or in a dream, she strove in vain to remember.

"I say, Ashwoode, where's your manners?" said Blarden, turning angrily towards the young baronet, who was scarcely less confounded at her sudden entrance than was the girl herself. "What do you stand gaping there for? Don't you see the young lady wants to know who I am?"

Blarden followed this vehement exhortation with a look which at once recalled Ashwoode to his senses.

"Mary," said he, approaching, "this is my particular friend, Mr. Nicholas Blarden. Mr. Blarden, my sister, Miss Mary Ashwoode."

"Your most obedient humble servant, Mistress Mary," said Blarden, with a gallant air. "Wonderful beautiful weather; d—— me, but it's like the middle of summer. I'm just going out to take a bit of a tramp among the bushes and lead goddesses," he added, not feeling, spite of all his effrontery, quite at his ease in the presence of the elegant and high-born girl; and, more confounded and abashed by the simple dignity of her artless nature than he ever remembered to have been before, under any circumstances whatever, he made his exit from the chamber.

"Who is that man?" said the girl, drawing close to her brother's side, and clinging timidly to his arm. "His face is familiar to me—I have seen or dreamed of it before; it has been before me either in some troubled scene or dream. I feel frightened and oppressed when he is near me. Who is he, brother?"

"Pshaw! nonsense, girl," said her brother, in vain attempting to appear unconstrained and at his ease; "he is a very good, honest fellow, not, as you see, the most polished in the world, but in essentials an excellent fellow; you'll easily get over your antipathy—his oddity of manner and appearance is soon forgotten, and in all other points he is an admirable fellow. Pshaw! you have too much sense to hate a man for his face and manner."

"I do not hate him, brother," said Mary, "how could I? The man has never wronged me; but there is something in his eye, in his air and expression, in his whole appearance, sinister and terrible—something which oppresses and terrifies me. I can scarcely move or breathe in his presence. I only hope that I may never meet him so near again."

"Your hope is not likely to be realized, then," replied Ashwoode, abruptly, "he makes a stay here of a week, or perhaps more."

A silence followed, during which he revolved the expediency of hinting at once at the designs of Blarden. As he thus paused, moodily plotting how best to open the subject, the unconscious girl stood beside him, and, looking fondly in his face, she said,—

"Dear brother, you must not be so sad. When all's done, what have we lost but some of the wealth which we can spare? We have still enough, quite enough. You shall live with your poor little sister, and I will take care of you, and read to you, and sing to you whenever you are sad; and we will walk together in the old green woods, and be far happier and merrier than ever we could have been in the midst of cold and heartless luxury and dissipation. Brother, dear brother, when shall we go to Incharden?"

"I can't say; I—I don't know that we shall go there at all," replied he, shortly.

Deep disappointment clouded the poor girl's face for a moment, but as instantly the sweet smile returned, and she laid her hand affectionately upon her brother's shoulder, and looked in his face.

"Well, dear brother, wherever you go, there is my home, and there I will be happy—as happy as being with the only creature that cares for me now can make me."

"Perhaps there are others who care for you—ay—even more than I do," said the young man deliberately, and fixing his eyes upon her searchingly, as he spoke.

"How, brother; what do you mean?" said the poor girl, faintly, and turning pale as death. "Have you seen—have you heard from—" She paused, trembling violently, and Ashwoode resumed,—

"No, no, child; I have neither seen nor heard from anyone whom you know anything of. Why are you so agitated? Pshaw! nonsense."

"I know not how it is, brother; I am depressed, and easily agitated to-day," rejoined she; "perhaps it is that I cannot forget a fearful dream which troubled me last night."

"Tut, tut, child," replied he; "I thought you had other matters to think of."

"And so I have, God knows, dear brother," resumed she—"so I have; but this dream haunted me long, and haunts me still; it was about you. I dreamed that we were walking, lovingly, hand in hand, among the shady walks in this old place; when, on a sudden, a great savage dog—just like the old blood-hound you had shot last summer—came, with open jaws and all its fangs exposed, springing towards us. I threw myself, terrified, into your arms, but you grasped me, with iron strength, and held me forth toward the frightful animal. I saw your face; it was changed and horrible. I struggled—I screamed—and awakened, gasping with afright."

"A silly, unmeaning dream," said Ashwoode, slightly changing colour, and turning from her. "You're not such a child, surely, as to let that trouble you."

"No, indeed, brother," replied she, "I do not suffer it to trouble my mind; but it has fastened somehow upon my imagination, and spite of all I can do, the impression remains— There—there—see that horrible man staring in at us, from behind the evergreens," she added, glancing at a large, tufted laurel, which partially screened the unprepossessing form of Nicholas Blarden, who was intently watching the youthful pair as they conversed. Perhaps conscious that he had been observed, he quitted his lurking-place, and plunged deeper into the thick screen of foliage.

"Dear Henry," said she, turning imploringly toward her brother, "there is something about that man which frightens me; my heart sickens whenever I see him. I feel like some poor bird under the eye of a hawk. I do not feel safe when he is looking at me; there is some evil influence in his gaze—something bad, satanic, in his look and presence; I dread him instinctively. For God's sake, dear, dear brother, do not keep company with him—he will harm you—it cannot lead to good."

"This is mere folly—downright raving," said Ashwoode, vehemently, but with an uneasiness which he could not conceal. "He is my guest, and will remain so for some weeks. I must be civil to him—both of us must."

"Surely, dear brother—after all I have said—you will not ask me to associate with him during his stay, since stay he must," urged Mary.

"We ought not to consult our whims at the expense of civility," retorted the baronet, drily.

"But surely my presence is not required," urged she.

"You cannot tell how that may be," replied Ashwoode, abruptly, and then added, abstractedly, as he walked slowly towards the door: "We often speak, we know not what; we often stand, we know not where—necessity, fate, destiny—whatever is, must be. Let this be our philosophy, Mary."

Wholly at a loss to comprehend this incoherent speech, his sister remained silent for some minutes.

"Well, child, how say you?" exclaimed Ashwoode, turning suddenly round.

"Dear brother," said she, "I would fain not meet that man any more while he remains here. You will not ask me to come down."

"A truce to this folly," exclaimed Ashwoode, with loud and sudden emphasis. "You must—you must, I say, appear at breakfast, at dinner, and at supper. You must see Blarden, and talk with him—he's my friend—you must know him." Then checking himself, he added, in a less vehement tone—"Mary, don't act like a fool—you are none: these silly fancies must not be indulged—remember, he's my friend. There, there, be a good girl—no more folly."

He came over, patted her cheek, and then turned abruptly from her, and left the room. His parting caress, however, was not sufficient to obliterate the painful impression which his momentary violence had left, for in that brief space of angry excitement his countenance had worn the self-same sinister expression which had appalled her in her last night's dream.


CHAPTER XLI.

OF O'CONNOR AND A CERTAIN TRAVELLING ECCLESIASTIC—AND HOW THE DARKNESS OVERTOOK THEM.

It has become necessary, in order to a clear and chronologically arranged exposition of events to return for a little while to our melancholy young friend, Edmond O'Connor, who, with his faithful squire, Larry Toole, following in close attendance upon his progress, was now returning from a last visit to the poor fragment of his patrimony, the wreck of his father's fortunes, and which consisted of a few hundred acres of wild woodland, surrounding a small square tower half gone to decay, and bidding fair to become in a few years a mere roofless ruin. He had seen the few retainers of his family who still remained, and bidden them a last farewell, and was now far in his second day's leisurely journey toward the city of Dublin.

The sun was fast declining among the rich and glowing clouds of an autumnal evening, and pouring its melancholy lustre upon the woods and the old towers of Leixlip, as the young man rode into that ancient town. How different were his present feelings from those with which he had last traversed the quiet little village—then his bright hopes and cheery fancies had tinged every object he looked on with their own warm and happy colouring; but now, alas! how mournful the reverse. With the sweet illusions he had so fondly cherished had vanished all the charm of all he saw; the scene was disenchanted now, and all seemed coloured in the sombre and chastened hues of his own deep melancholy; the river, with all its brawling falls and windings, filled his ear with plaintive harmonies, and all its dancing foam-bells, that chased one another down its broad eddies, glancing in the dim, discoloured light of the evening sun, seemed but so many images of the wayward courses and light illusions of human hope; even the old ivy-mantled towers, as he looked upon their time-worn front, seemed to have suffered a century's decay since last he beheld them; every scene that met his eye, and every sound that floated to his ear on the still air of evening, was alike charged with sadness.

At a slow pace, and with a heart oppressed, he passed the little town, and soon its trees, and humble roofs, and blue curling smoke were left far behind him. He had proceeded more than a mile when the sun descended, and the dusky twilight began to deepen. He spurred his horse, and at a rate more suited to the limited duration of the little light which remained, he rode at a sharp trot along the uneven way toward Dublin. He had not proceeded far at this rate when he overtook a gentleman on horseback, who was listlessly walking his steed in the same direction, and who, on seeing a cavalier thus wending his way on the same route, either with a view to secure good company upon the road, or for some other less obvious purpose, spurred on also, and took his place by the side of our young friend. O'Connor looked upon his uninvited companion with a jealous eye, for his night adventure of a few months since was forcibly recalled to his memory by the circumstances of his present situation. The person who rode by his side was, as well as he could descry, a tall, lank man, with a hooked nose, heavy brows, and sallow complexion, having something grim and ascetic in the character of his face. After turning slightly twice or thrice towards O'Connor, as if doubtful whether to address him, the stranger at length accosted the young man.

"A fair evening this, sir," said he, "and just cool enough to make a brisk ride pleasant."

O'Connor assented drily, and without waiting for a renewal of the conversation, spurred his horse into a canter, with the intention of leaving his new companion behind. That personage was not, however, so easily to be shaken off; he, in turn, put his horse to precisely the same pace, and remarked composedly,—

"I see, sir, you wish to make the most of the light we've left us; dark riding, they say, is dangerous riding hereabout. I suppose you ride for the city?"

O'Connor made no answer.

"I presume you make Dublin your halting-place?" repeated the man.

"You are at liberty, sir," replied O'Connor, somewhat sharply, "to presume what you please; I have good reasons, however, for not caring to bandy words with strangers. Where I rest for the night cannot concern anybody but myself."

"No offence, sir—no offence meant," replied the man, in the same even tone, "and I hope none taken."

A silence of some minutes ensued, during which O'Connor suddenly slackened his horse's pace to a walk. The stranger made a corresponding alteration in that of his.

"Your pace, sir, is mine," observed the stranger. "We may as well breathe our beasts a little."

Another pause followed, which was at length broken by the stranger's observing,—

"A lucky chance, in truth. A comrade is an important acquisition in such a ride as ours promises to be."

"I already have one of my own choosing," replied O'Connor drily; "I ride attended."

"And so do I," continued the other, "and doubtless our trusty squires are just as happy in the rencounter as are their masters."

A considerable silence ensued, which at length was broken by the stranger.

"Your reserve, sir," said he, "as well as the hour at which you travel, leads me to conjecture that we are both bound on the same errand. Am I understood?"

"You must speak more plainly if you would be so," replied O'Connor.

"Well, then," resumed he, "I half believe that we shall meet to-night—where it is no sin to speak loyalty."

"Still, sir, you leave me in the dark as to your meaning," replied O'Connor.

"At a certain well of sweet water," said the man with deliberate significance—"is it not so—eh—am I right?"

"No, sir," replied O'Connor, "your sagacity is at fault; or else, it may be, your wit is too subtle, or mine too dull; for, if your conjectures be correct, I cannot comprehend your meaning—nor indeed is it very important that I should."

"Well, sir," replied he, "I am seldom wrong when I hazard a guess of this kind; but no matter—if we meet we shall be better friends, I promise you."

They had now reached the little town of Chapelizod, and darkness had closed in. At the door of a hovel, from which streamed a strong red light, the stranger drew his bridle, and called for a cup of water. A ragged urchin brought it forth.

"Pax Domini vobiscum," said the stranger, restoring the vessel, and looking upward steadfastly for a minute, as if in mental prayer, he raised his hat, and in doing so exhibited the monkish tonsure upon his head; and as he sate there motionless upon his horse, with his sable cloak wrapped in ample folds about him, and the strong red light from the hovel door falling upon his thin and well-marked features, bringing into strong relief the prominences of his form and attire, and shining full upon the drooping head of the tired steed which he bestrode—this equestrian figure might have furnished no unworthy study for the pencil of Schalken.

In a few minutes they were again riding side by side along the street of the straggling little town.

"I perceive, sir," said O'Connor, "that you are a clergyman. Unless this dim light deceives me, I saw the tonsure when you raised your hat just now."

"Your eyes deceived you not—I am one of a religious order," replied the man, "and perchance not on that account a more acceptable companion to you."

"Indeed you wrong me, reverend sir," said O'Connor. "I owe you an apology for receiving your advances as I have done; but experience has taught me caution; and until I know something of those whom I encounter on the highway, I hold with them as little communication as I can well avoid. So far from being the less acceptable a companion to me by reason of your sacred office, believe me, you need no better recommendation. I am myself an humble child of the true Church; and her ministers have never claimed respect from me in vain."

The priest looked searchingly at the young man; but the light afforded but an imperfect scrutiny.

"You say, sir," rejoined he after a pause, "that you acknowledge our father of Rome—that you are one of those who eschew heresy, and cling constantly to the old true faith—that you are free from the mortal taint of Protestant infidelity."

"That do I with my whole heart," rejoined O'Connor.

"Are you, moreover, one of those who still look with a holy confidence to the return of better days? When the present order of things, this usurped government and abused authority, shall pass away like a dark dream, and fly before the glory of returning truth. Do you look for the restoration of the royal heritage to its rightful owner, and of these afflicted countries to the bosom of mother Church?"

"Happy were I to see these things accomplished," rejoined O'Connor; "but I hold their achievement, except by the intervention of Almighty Providence, impossible. Methinks we have in Ireland neither the spirit nor the power to do it. The people are heartbroken; and so far from coming to the field in this quarrel, they dare not even speak of it above their breath."

"Young man, you speak as one without understanding. You know not this people of Ireland of whom you speak. Believe me, sir, the spirit to right these things is deep and strong in the bosoms of the people. What though they do not cry aloud in agony for vengeance, are they therefore content, and at their heart's ease?

"'Quamvis tacet Hermogenes, cantor tamen atque,
Optimus est modulator.'

"Their silence is not dumbness—you shall hear them speak plainly yet."

"Well, it may be so," rejoined O'Connor; "but be the people ever so willing, another difficulty arises—where are the men to lead them on?—who are they?"

The priest again looked quickly and suspiciously at the speaker; but the gloom prevented his discerning the features of his companion. He became silent—perhaps half-repenting his momentary candour, and rode slowly forward by O'Connor's side, until they had reached the extremity of the town. The priest then abruptly said,—

"I find, sir, I have been wrong in my conjecture. Our paths at this point diverge, I believe. You pursue your way by the river's side, and I take mine to the left. Do not follow me. If you be what you represent yourself, my command will be sufficient to prevent your doing so; if otherwise, I ride armed, and can enforce what I conceive necessary to my safety. Farewell."

And so saying, the priest turned his horse's head in the direction which he had intimated, rode up the steep ascent which loomed over the narrow level by the river's side; and his dark form quickly disappeared beyond the brow of the dusky hill. O'Connor's eyes instinctively followed the retreating figure of his companion, until it was lost in the profound darkness; and then looking back for any dim intimation of the presence of his trusty follower, he beheld nothing but the dark void. He listened; but no sound of horse's hoofs betokened pursuit. He shouted—he called upon his squire by name; but all in vain; and at length, after straining his voice to its utmost pitch for six or ten minutes without eliciting any other reply than the prolonged barking of half the village curs in Chapelizod, he turned away, and pursued his course alone, consoling himself with the reflection that his attendant was at least as well acquainted with the way as was he himself, and that he could not fail to reach the "Cock and Anchor" whenever he pleased to exert himself for the purpose.

## CHAPTER XLII.

### THE SQUIRES.

O'Connor had scarcely been joined by the priest, when Larry Toole, who jogged quietly on, pipe in mouth, behind his master, was accosted by his reverence's servant, a stout, clean-limbed fellow, arrayed in blue frieze, who rode a large, ill-made horse, and bumped listlessly along at that easy swinging jog at which our southern farmers are wont to ride. The fellow had a shrewd eye, and a pleasant countenance withal to look upon, and might be in years some five or six and thirty.

"God save you, neighbour," said he.

"God save you kindly," rejoined Mr. Toole graciously.

"A plisint evenin' for a quiet bit iv a smoke," rejoined the stranger.

"None better," rejoined Larry, scanning the stranger's proportions, to see whether, in his own phrase, "he liked his cut." The scrutiny evidently resulted favourably, for Larry removed his pipe, and handing it to his new acquaintance, observed courteously, "Maybe you'd take a draw, neighbour."

"I thank you kindly," said the stranger, as he transferred the utensil from Larry's mouth to his own. "It's turning cowld, I think. I wish to the Lord we had a dhrop iv something to warm us," observed he, speaking out of the unoccupied corner of his mouth.

"We'll be in Chapelizod, plase God," said Larry Toole, "in half an hour, an' if ould Tim Delany isn't gone undher the daisies, maybe we won't have a taste iv his best."

"Are you follyin' that gintleman?" inquired the stranger, with his pipe indicating O'Connor, "that gintleman that the masther is talking to?"

"I am so," rejoined Larry promptly, "an' a good gintleman he is; an' that's your masther there. What sort is he?"

"Oh, good enough, as masthers goes—no way surprisin' one way or th' other."

"Where are you goin' to?" pursued Larry.

"I never axed, bedad," rejoined the man, "only to folly on, wherever he goes—an' divil a hair I care where that is. What way are you two goin'?"

"To Dublin, to be sure," rejoined Larry. "I wisht we wor there now. What the divil makes him ride so unaiqual—sometimes cantherin', and other times mostly walkin'—it's mighty nansinsical, so it is."

"By gorra, I don't know, anless fancy alone," rejoined the stranger.

"Here's your pipe," continued he, after some pause, "an' I thank you kindly, misther—misther—how's this they call you?"

"Misther Larry Toole is the name I was christened by," rejoined the gentleman so interrogated.

"An' a rale illegant name it is," replied the stranger. "The Tooles is a royal family, an' may the Lord restore them to their rights."

"Amen, bedad," rejoined Larry devoutly.

"My name's Ned Mollowney," continued he, anticipating Larry's interrogatory, "from the town of Ballydun, the plisintest spot in the beautiful county iv Tipperary. There isn't it's aquil out for fine men and purty girls." Larry sighed.

The conversation then took that romantic turn which best suited the melancholy chivalry of Larry's mind, after which the current of their mutual discoursing, by the attraction of irresistible association, led them, as they approached the little village, once more into suggestive commentaries upon the bitter cold, and sundry pleasant speculations respecting the creature comforts which awaited them under Tim Delany's genial roof-tree.

"The holy saints be praised," said Ned Mollowney, "we're in the village at last. The tellin' iv stories is the dhryest work that ever a boy tuck in hand. My mouth is like a cindher all as one."

"Tim Delany's is the second house beyant that wind in the street," said Larry, pointing down the road as they advanced. "We'll jist get down for a minute or two, an' have somethin' warrum by the fire; we'll overtake the gintlemen asy enough."

"I'm agreeable, Mr. Toole," said the accommodating Ned Mollowney. "Let the gintlemen take care iv themselves. They're come to an age when they ought to know what they're about."

"This is it," said Larry, checking his horse before a low thatched house, from whose doorway the cheerful light was gleaming upon the bushes opposite.

The two worthies dismounted, and entered the humble place of entertainment. Tim Delany's company was singularly fascinating, and his liquor was, if possible, more so—besides, the evening was chill, and his hearth blazed with a fire, the very sight of which made the blood circulate freely, and the finger-tops grow warm. Larry Toole was prepossessed in favour of Ned Mollowney, and Ned Mollowney had fallen in love with Larry Toole, so that it is hardly to be wondered at that the two gentlemen yielded to the combined seduction of their situation, and seated themselves snugly by the fire, each with his due allowance of stimulating liquor, and with a very vague and uncertain kind of belief in the likelihood of their following their masters respectively until they had made themselves particularly comfortable. It was not until after nearly two hours of blissful communion with his delectable companion, that Larry Toole suddenly bethought him of the fact that he had allowed his master, at the lowest calculation, time enough to have ridden to and from the "Cock and Anchor" at least half a dozen times. He, therefore, hurriedly bade good-night, with many a fond vow of eternal friendship for the two companions of his princely revelry, mounted his horse with some little difficulty, and becoming every moment more and more confused, and less and less perpendicular, found himself at length—with an indistinct remembrance of having had several hundred falls upon every possible part of his body, and upon every possible geological substance, from soft alluvial mud up to plain lime-stone, during the course of his progress—within the brick precincts of the city. The horse, with an instinctive contempt for Mr. Toole's judgment, wholly disregarded that gentleman's vehement appeals to the bridle, and quietly pursued his well-known way to the hostelry of the "Cock and Anchor."

Our honest friend had hardly dismounted, which he did with one eye closed, and a hiccough, and a happy smile which mournfully contrasted with his filthy and battered condition, when he at once became absolutely insensible, from which condition he did not recover till next morning, when he found himself partially in bed, quite undressed, with the exception of his breeches, boots, and spurs, which he had forgotten to remove, and which latter, along with his feet, he had deposited upon the pillow, allowing his head to slope gently downward towards the foot of the bed.

As soon as Mr. Toole had ascertained where he was, and begun to recollect how he came there, he removed his legs from the pillow, and softly slid upon the floor. His first solicitude was for his clothes, the spattered and villainous condition of which appalled him; his next was to endeavour to remember whether or not his master had witnessed his weakness. Absorbed in this severe effort of memory, he sat upon the bedside, gazing upon the floor, and scratching his head, when the door opened, and his friend the groom entered the chamber.

"I say, old gentleman, you've been having a little bit of a spree," observed he, gazing pleasantly upon the disconsolate figure of the little man, who sat in his shirt and jack-boots, staring at him with a woe-begone and bewildered air. "Why, you had a bushel of mud about your body when you came in, and no hat at all. Well, you had a pleasant night of it—there's no denying that."

"No hat;" said Larry desolately. "It isn't possible I dropped my hat off my head unknownest. Bloody wars, my hat! is it gone in airnest?"

"Yes, young gentleman, you came here bareheaded. The hat is gone, and that's a fact," replied the groom.

"I thought my coat was bad enough; but—oh! blur-anagers, my hat!" ejaculated Larry with abandonment. "Bad luck go with the liquor—tare-an-ouns, my hat!"

"There's a shoe off the horse," observed the groom; "and the seat is gone out of your breeches as clean as if it never was in it. Well, but you had a pleasant evening of it—you had."

"An' my breeches desthroyed—ruined beyant cure! See, Tom Berry, take a blundherbuz, will you, and put me out of pain at wonst. My breeches! Oh, divil go with the liquor! Holy Moses, is it possible?—my breeches!"

In an agony of contrition and desperate remorse, Larry Toole clasped his hands over his eyes and remained for some minutes silent; at length he said—

"An' what did the masther say? Don't be keeping me in pain—out with it at wonst."

"What master?" inquired the groom.

"What masther?" echoed Mr. Toole—"why Mr. O'Connor, to be sure."

"I'm sure I can't say," replied the man; "I have not seen him this month."

"Wasn't he here before me last night?" inquired the little man.

"No, nor after neither," replied his visitor.

"Do you mane to tell me that he's not in the house at all?" interrogated Mr. Toole.

"Yes," replied he, "Mr. O'Connor is not in the house; the horse did not cross the yard this month. Will that do you?"

"Be the hoky," said Larry, "that's exthramely quare. But are you raly sure and quite sartin?"

"Yes, I tell you yes," replied he.

"Well, well," said Mr. Toole, "but that puts me to the divil's rounds to undherstand it—not come at all. What in the world's gone with him—not come—where else could he go to? Begorra, the whole iv the occurrences iv last night is a blaggard mysthery. What the divil's gone with him—where is he at all?—why couldn't he wait a bit for me an' I'd iv tuck the best care iv him? but gintlemen is always anruly. What the divil's keepin' him? I wouldn't be surprised if he made a baste iv himself in some public-house last night. A man ought never to take a dhrop more than jist what makes him plisant—bad luck to it. Lend me a breeches, an' I'll pray for you all the rest of my days. I must go out at wonst an' look for him; maybe he's at Mr. Audley's lodgings—ay, sure enough, it's there he is. Bad luck to the liquor. Why the divil did I let him go alone? Oh! sweet bad luck to it," he continued in fierce anguish, as he held up the muddy wreck of his favourite coat before his aching eyes—"my elegant coat—bad luck to it again—an' my beautiful hat—once more bad luck to it; an' my breeches—oh! it's fairly past bearin'—my elegant breeches! Bad luck to it for a threacherous drop—an' the masther lost, and no one knows what's done with him. Up with that poker, I tell you, and blow my brains out at once; there's nothing before me in this life but the divil's own delight—finish me, I tell you, and let me rest in the shade. I'll never hould up my head again, there's no use in purtendin'. Oh! bad luck to the dhrink!"

In this distracted frame of mind did Larry continue for nearly an hour, after which, with the aid of some contributions from the wardrobe of honest Tom Berry, he clothed himself, and went forth in quest of his master.

CHAPTER XLIII.

THE WILD WOOD—THE OLD MANSION-HOUSE OF FINISKEA—SECRETS, AND A SURPRISE.

O'Connor pursued his way towards the city, following the broken horse-track, which then traversed the low grounds which lie upon the left bank of the Liffey. The Phoenix Park, or, as it was then called, the Royal Park, was at the time of which we write a much wilder place than it now is. There were no trim plantations nor stately clumps of tufted trees, no signs of care or culture. Broad patches of shaggy thorn spread with little interruption over the grounds, and regular roads were then unknown. The darkness became momentarily deeper and more deep as O'Connor pursued his solitary way; and the difficulty of proceeding grew every instant greater, for the heavy rains had interrupted his path with deep sloughs and pools, which became at length so frequent, and so difficult of passage, that he was fain to turn from the ordinary track, and seek an easier path along the high grounds which overhang the river. The close screen of the wild gnarled thorns which covered the upper level on which he now moved, still further deepened the darkness; and he became at length so entirely involved in the pitchy gloom, that he dismounted, and taking his horse by the head, led him forward through the tangled brake, and under the knotted branches of the old hoary thorns, stumbling among the briers and the crooked roots, and every moment encountering the sudden obstruction, either of some stooping branch, or the trunk of one of the old trees; so that altogether his progress was as tedious and unpleasant as it well could be. His annoyance became the greater as he proceeded; for he was so often compelled to turn aside, and change his course, to avoid these interruptions, that in the utter darkness he began to grow entirely uncertain whether or not he was moving in the right direction. The more he paused, and the oftener he reflected, the more entirely puzzled and bewildered did he become. Glad indeed would he have been that he had followed the track upon which he had at first entered, and run the hazard of all the sloughs and pools which crossed it; but he was now embarked in another route; and even had he desired it, so perplexed was he, that he could not have effected his retreat. Fully alive to the ridiculousness, as well as the annoyance of his situation, he slowly and painfully stumbled forward, conscious that if only he could move for half an hour or thereabout consistently in the same direction, he must disengage himself in some quarter or another from the entanglement in which he was involved. In vain he looked round him; nothing but entire darkness encountered him. In vain he listened for any sound which might intimate the neighbourhood of any living thing. Nothing but the hushed soughing of the evening breeze through the old boughs was audible; and he was forced to continue his route in the same troublesome uncertainty.

At length he saw, or thought he saw, a red light gleaming through the trees. It disappeared—it came again. He stopped, uncertain whether it was one of those fitful marsh-fires which but mock the perplexity of benighted travellers; but no—this light shone clearly, and with a steady beam, through the branches; and towards it he directed his steps, losing it now, and again recovering it, till at length, after a longer probation than he had at first expected, he gained a clear space of ground, intersected only by a few broken hedges and ditches, but free from the close wood which had so entirely darkened his advance. In this position he was enabled to discern that the light which had guided him streamed from the window of an old shattered house, partially surrounded by a dilapidated wall, having a few ruinous outhouses attached to it. In this building he beheld the old mansion-house of Finiskea, which then occupied the ground on which at present stands the powder-magazine, and which, by a slight alteration in sound, though without any analogy in meaning, has given its name to the Phoenix Park. The light streamed through the diamond panes of a narrow casement; and still leading his horse, O'Connor made his way over the broken fences towards the old house. As he approached, he perceived several figures moving to and fro in the chamber from which the light issued, and detected, or thought he did so, among them the remarkable form of the priest who had lately been his companion upon the road. As he advanced, someone inside drew a curtain across the window, though, as O'Connor conjectured, wholly unaware of his approach, and thus precluded any further reconnoitering on his part.

"At all events," thought he, "they can spare me some one to put me upon my way. They can hardly complain if I intrude upon such an errand."

With this reflection, he led his horse round the corner of the building to the door, which was sheltered by a small porch roofed with tiles. By the faint light, which in the open space made objects partially discernible, he perceived two men, as it appeared to him, fast asleep—half sitting and half lying on the low step of the door. He had just come near enough to accost them, when, somewhat to his surprise, he was seized from behind in a powerful grip, and his arms pinioned to his sides. A single antagonist he would easily have shaken off; but a reinforcement was at hand.

"Up, boys—be stirring—open the door," cried the hoarse voice of the person who held O'Connor.

The two figures started to their feet; their strength, combined with the efforts of his first assailant, effectually mastered O'Connor, and one of them shoved the door open.

"Pretty watch you keep," said he, as the party hurried their prisoner, wholly without the power of resistance, into the house.

Three or four powerful, large-limbed fellows, well armed, were seated in the hall, and arose on his entrance. O'Connor saw that resistance against such odds were idle, and resolved patiently to submit to the issue, whatever it might be.

"Gentlemen that's caught peeping is sometimes made to see more than they have a mind to," observed one of O'Connor's conductors.

Another removed his sword, and having satisfied himself that he had not any other weapon upon his person, observed,—

"You may let his elbows loose; but jist keep him tight by the collar."

"Let the gentlemen know there's a bird limed," observed the first speaker; and one of the others passed from the narrow hall to execute the mission.

After some little delay, O'Connor, who awaited the result with more of curiosity and impatience than of alarm, was conducted by two of the armed men who had secured him through a large passage terminating in a chamber, which they also traversed, and by a second door at its far extremity found entrance into a rude but spacious apartment, floored with tiles, and with a low ceiling of dark plank, supported by ponderous beams. A large wood fire burned in the hearth, beside which some half dozen men were congregated; several others were seated by a massive table, on which were writing materials, with which two or three of them were busily employed; a number of open letters were also strewn upon it, and here and there a brace of horse-pistols or a carbine showed that the party felt neither very secure, nor very much disposed to surrender without a struggle, should their worst anticipations be realized, in any attempt to surprise them.

Most of those who were present bore, in their disordered dress and mud-soiled boots, the evidence of recent travel. They were lighted chiefly by the broad, uncertain gleam of the blazing wood fire, in which the misty flame of two or three wretched candles which burned upon the table shone pale and dim as the last stars of night in the red dawn of an autumnal sun. In this strong and ruddy light the groups of figures, variously attired, some seated by the table, and others standing with their ample cloaks still folded around them, acquired by the contrast of broad light and shade a character of picturesqueness which had in it something wild and imposing. This singular tableau occupied the further end of the room, which was one of considerable length, and as the prisoner was led forward to the bar of the tribunal, those who composed it eyed him sternly and fixedly.

"Bind his hands fast," said a lean and dark-featured man, with a singularly forbidding aspect and a deep, stern voice, who sat at the head of the table with a pile of papers beside him. Spite of O'Connor's struggles, the order was speedily executed, and with such good-will that the blood almost started from his nails.

"Now, sir," continued the same speaker, "who are you, and what may your errand be?"

"Before I answer your questions you must satisfy me that you have authority to ask them," replied O'Connor. "Who, I pray, are you, who dare to seize the person, and to bind the limbs of a free man? I shall know this ere one of your questions shall have a reply."

"I have seen you, young sir, before—scarce an hour since," observed one of those who stood by the hearth. "Look at me, and say do you remember my features?"

"I do," replied O'Connor, who had no difficulty in recognizing those of the priest who had parted from him so abruptly on that evening—"of course I recollect your face; we rode side by side from Leixlip to-day."

"You recollect my caution too—you cannot have forgotten that," continued the priest, menacingly. "You know how peremptorily I warned you against following me, yet you have dogged me here; on your own head be the consequences—the fool shall perish in his folly."

"I have not dogged you here, sir," replied O'Connor; "I seek my way to Dublin. The river banks are so soft that a horse had better swim than seek to keep them; I therefore took the upper ground, and after losing myself among the woods, at length saw a light, reached it, and here I am."

The priest heard the statement with a sinister smile.

"A truce to these inventions, sir," said he. "It is indeed possible that you speak the truth, but it is in the highest degree probable that you lie; it is, in a word, plain—satisfactorily plain, that you followed me hither, as I suspected you might have done; you have dogged me, sir, and you have seen all that you sought to behold; you have seen my place of destination and my company. I care not with what motive you have acted—that is between yourself and your Maker. If you are a spy, which I shrewdly suspect, Providence has defeated your treason, and punished the traitor; if mere curiosity impelled you, you will remember that ill-directed curiosity was the sin which brought death upon mankind, and cease to wonder that its fruits may be bitter to yourself. What say you, young man?"

"I have told you plainly how I happened to reach this place," replied O'Connor; "I have told you once—I will repeat the statement no more; and once again I ask, on what authority you question me, and dare thus to bind my hands and keep me here against my will?"

"Authority sufficient to satisfy our own consciences," rejoined the priest. "The responsibility rests not upon you; enough it is for you to know that we have the power to detain you, and that we exercise that power, as we most probably shall another, still less conducive to your comfort."

"You have the power to make me captive, I admit," rejoined O'Connor—"you have the power to murder me, as you threaten, but though power to keep or kill is all the justification a robber or a bravo needs, methinks such an argument should hardly satisfy a consecrated minister of Christ."

The expression with which the priest regarded the young man grew blacker and more truculent at this rebuke, and after a silence of a few seconds he replied,—

"We are doubly authorized in what we do—ay, trebly warranted, young traitor. God Almighty has given us the instinct of self-defence, which in a righteous cause it is laudable to consult and indulge; the Church, too, tells us in these times to deal strictly with the malignant persecutors of God's truth; and lastly, we have a royal warranty—the authority of the rightful king of these realms, investing us with powers to deal summarily with rebels and traitors. Let this satisfy you."

"I honour the king," rejoined O'Connor, "as truly as any man here, seeing that my father lost all in the service of his illustrious sire, but I need some more satisfactory assurance of his delegated authority than the bare assertion of a violent man, of whom I know absolutely nothing, and until you show me some instrument empowering you to act thus, I will not acknowledge your competency to subject me to an examination, and still resolutely protest against your detaining me here."

"You refuse, then, to answer our questions?" said the hard-featured little person who sat at the far end of the table.

"Until you show authority to put them, I peremptorily do refuse to answer them," replied the young man.

The little person looked expressively at the priest, who appeared to hold a high influence among the party. He answered the look by saying,—

"His blood be upon his own head."

"Nay, not so fast, holy father; let us debate upon this matter for a few minutes, ere we execute sentence," said a singularly noble-looking man who stood beside the priest. "Remove the prisoner," he added, with a voice of command, "and keep him strictly guarded."

"Well, be it so," said he, reluctantly.

The little man who sat at the head of the table made a gesture to those who guarded O'Connor, and the order thus given and sanctioned was at once carried into execution.


CHAPTER XLIV.

THE DOOM.

The young man was conveyed from the chamber by his two athletic conductors, the door closed upon the deliberations of the stern tribunal who were just about to debate upon the question of his life or death, and he was led round the corner of a lobby, a few steps from the chamber where his judges sat; a stout door in the wall was pushed open and he himself thrust through it into a cold, empty apartment, in perfect darkness, and the door shut and barred behind him.

Here, in solitude and darkness, the horrors of his situation rushed upon him with tremendous and overwhelming reality. His life was in the hands of fierce and relentless men, by whom, he had little doubt, he was already judged and condemned; bound and helpless, he must await, without the power of hastening or of deferring his fate by a single minute, the cold-blooded deliberations of the conclave who sat within. Unable even to hear the progress of the debate on whose result his life was suspended, a faint and dizzy sickness came upon him, and the cold dew burst from every pore; ghastly, shapeless images of horror hurried with sightless speed across his mind, and his brain throbbed with the fearful excitement of madness. With a desperate effort he roused his energies; but what could human ingenuity, even sharpened by the presence of urgent and terrific danger, suggest or devise? His hands were firmly bound behind his back; in vain he tugged with all his strength, in the fruitless hope of disengaging the cords which crushed them together. He groaned in downright agony as, strength and hope exhausted, he gave up the desperate attempt; nothing then could be done; there remained for him no hope—no chance. In this horrible condition he walked with slow steps to and fro in the dark chamber, in vain endeavouring to compose his terrible agitation.

"Were my hands but free," thought he, "I should let the villains know that against any odds a resolute man may sell his life dearly. But it is in vain to struggle; they have bound me here but too securely."

Thus saying, he leaned himself against the partition, to await, passively, the event which he knew could not be far distant. The surface against which he leaned was not that of the wall—it yielded slightly to his pressure—it was a door. With his knee and shoulder he easily forced it open, and entered another chamber, at the far-side of which he distinctly saw a stream of light, which, passing through a chink, fell upon the opposite wall, and, at the same time, he clearly heard the muffled sound of voices in debate. He made his way to the aperture through which the light found entrance, and as he did so, the sound of the voices fell more and more distinctly upon his ear. A small square, of about two feet each way, was cut in the wall, affording an orifice through which, probably, the closet in which he stood was imperfectly lighted in the daytime. A plank shutter was closed over this, and barred upon the outside, through the imperfect joints of which the light had found its way, and O'Connor now scanned the contents of the outer chamber. It was that in which the assembly, in whose presence he had, but a few minutes before, been standing, were congregated. A low, broad-shouldered man, whose dress was that of mourning, and who wore his own hair, which descended in meagre ringlets of black upon either side, leaving the bald summit of his head exposed, and who added to the singularity of his appearance not a little by a long, thick beard, which covered his chin and upper lip—this man, who sat nearly opposite to the opening through which O'Connor looked, was speaking and addressing himself to some person who stood, as it appeared, divided by little more than the thickness of the wall from the party whose life he was debating.

"And against all this," continued the speaker, "what weighs the life of one man—one life, at best useless to the country, and useless to the king—at best, I say? What came we here for? No light matter to take in hand, sirs; to be pursued with no small risk; each comes hither, cinctus gladio, in the cause of the king. That cause with our own lives we are bound to maintain; and why not, if need be, at the cost of the lives of others? No good can come of sparing this fellow—at the best, no advantage to the cause: and, on the other hand, should he prove a traitor, a spy, or even an idle babbler, the heaviest damage may befall us. Tush, tush, gentlemen, it is ill straining at gnats in such times. We are here a court-martial, or no court at all. If I find that such dangerous vacillation as this carries it in your councils, I shall, for one, henceforward hang my sword over the mantel-piece, and obey the new laws. What! one life against such a risk—one execution, to save the cause and secure us all. To us, who have served in the king's wars, and hanged rebels by the round dozen—even on suspicion of being so—such indecision seems incredible. There ought not to be two words about the matter. Put him to death."

Having thus acquitted himself, this somewhat unattractive personage applied himself, with much industry and absorption, to the task of chopping, shredding, rolling up, and otherwise preparing a piece of tobacco for the bowl of his pipe.

"I confess," said someone whom O'Connor could not see, "that in pleading what may be said on behalf of this young man, I have no ground to go upon beyond a mere instinctive belief in the poor fellow's honesty, and in the truth of his story."

"Pardon me, sir," replied one in whose voice O'Connor thought he recognized that of the priest, "if I say, that to act upon such fanciful impressions, as if they were grounded upon evidence, were, in nine cases out of every ten, the most transcendent and mischievous folly. I repeat my own conviction, upon something like satisfactory evidence, that he is not honest. I talked with the fellow this evening—perhaps a little too freely—but in that conference, if he lied not, I learned that he belonged to that most dangerous class—the worst with whom we have to contend—the lukewarm, professing, passive Catholics—the very stuff of which the worst kind of spies and informers are made. He, no doubt, guessed, from what I said—for, to be plain with you, I spoke too freely by a great deal, in the belief, I know not how assumed, that he was one of ourselves—he guessed, I say, something of the nature of my mission, and tracked me hither—at all events, by some strange coincidence, hither he came. It is for you to weigh the question of probabilities."

"It matters not, in my mind, why or how he came hither," observed the ill-favoured gentleman, who sate at the head of the table; "he is here, and he hath seen our meeting, and could identify many of us. This is too large a confidence to repose in a stranger, and I for one do not like it, and therefore I say let him be killed without any more parley or debate."

The old man paused, and a silence followed. With an agonized attention, O'Connor listened for one word or movement of dissent; it came not.

"All agreed?" said the bearded hero, preparing to light his tobacco pipe at the candle. "Well, so I expected."

The little man who had spoken before him knocked sharply with the butt of a pistol upon the table, and O'Connor heard the door of the room open. The same person beckoned with his hand, and one of the stalwart men who had assisted in securing him, advanced to the foot of the board.

"Let a grave be digged in the orchard," said he, "and when it is ready, bring the prisoner out and despatch him, Let it be all done and the grave closed in half an hour."

The man made a rude obeisance, and left the room in silence.

Bound as he was, O'Connor traced the four walls of the room, in the vague hope that he might discover some other outlet from the chamber than that which he had just entered. But in vain; nothing encountered him but the hard, cold wall; and even had it been otherwise, thus helplessly manacled, what would it have availed him? He passed into the room into which he had been first thrust by the two guards, and in a state little short of frenzy, he cast himself upon the floor.

"Oh God!" said he, "it is terrible to see death thus creeping toward me, and not to have the power to help myself. I am doomed—my life already devoted, and before another hour I shall lie under the clay, a corpse. Is there nothing to be done—no hope, no chance? Oh, God! nothing!"

As he lay in this strong agony, he heard, or thought he heard, the clank of the spade upon the stony soil without. The work was begun—the grave was opened. Madly he strained at the cords—he tugged with more than human might—but all in vain. Still with horrible monotony he heard the clank of the iron mattock tinkling and clanking in the gravelly soil. Oh! that he could have stopped his ears to exclude the maddening sound. The pulses smote upon his brain like floods of fire. With closed eyes, and teeth set, and hands desperately clenched, he drew himself together, in the awful spasms of uncontrollable horror. Suddenly this fearful paroxysm departed, and a kind of awful calm supervened. It was no dull insensibility to his real situation, but a certain collectedness and calm self-possession, which enabled him to behold the grim adversary of human kind, even arrayed in all the terrors of his nearest approach, with a steady eye.

"After all, when all's done, what have I to lose? Life had no more joys for me—happy I could never more have been. Why should the miserable dread death, and cling to life like cowards? What is it? A brief struggle—the agony of a few minutes—the instinctive yearnings of our nature after life; and this over, comes rest—eternal quiet."

He then endeavoured, in prayer, earnestly to commend his spirit to its Maker. While thus employed he heard steps upon the hard tiles of the passage. His heart swelled as though it would burst. He rightly guessed their mission. The bolt was slowly drawn; the dusky light of a lantern streamed into the room, and revealed upon the threshold the forms of three tall men.

"Lift him up—rise him, boys," said he who carried the lantern.

"You must come with us," said one of the two who advanced to O'Connor.

Resistance was fruitless, and he offered none. A cold, sick, overwhelming horror unstrung his joints and dimmed his sight. He suffered them to lead him passively from the room.

As O'Connor approached the outer door through which he was to pass to certain and speedy death, it were not easy to describe or analyze his sensations; every object he beheld in the brief glance he cast around him as he passed along the hall appeared invested with a strangely sharp and vivid intensity of distinctness, and had in its aspect something indefinably spectral and ghastly—like things beheld under the terrific spell of a waking nightmare. His tremendous situation seemed to him something unreal, incredible; he walked in an appalling dream; in vain he strove to fix his thoughts myriads and myriads of scenes and incidents, never remembered since childhood's days, now with strange distinctness and wild rapidity whirled through his brain. The hall-door stood half open, and the fellow who led the way had almost reached it, when it was on a sudden thrown wide, and a figure, muffled in a cloak, confronted the funeral procession.

The foremost man raised the ponderous weapon which he carried, and held it poised in the air, ready to shiver the head of the intruder should he venture to advance—the two guards who held O'Connor halted at the same time.

"How's this, Cormack!" said the stranger. "Do you lift your weapon against the life of a friend?—rub your eyes and waken—how is it you cannot know me?—you've been drinking, sirrah."

At the sound of the speaker's voice the man at once lowered his hatchet and withdrew, a little sulkily, like a rebuked mastiff.

"What means all this?" continued he in the cloak, looking searchingly at the party in the rear; "whom have we got here?—where made you this prisoner? So, so—this must be looked to. How were you about to deal with him, fellow?" he added, addressing himself to him whom he had first encountered.

"According to orders, captain," replied the man, doggedly.

"And how may that have been?" interrogated the gentleman in the cloak.

"End him," replied he, sulkily.

"Has he been before the council in the great parlour?" inquired the stranger.

"Yes, captain—long enough, too," replied the fellow.

"And they have ordered this execution?" added the newly arrived.

"Yes, sir—who else? Come on, boys—bring him out, will you? Time is running short," he added, addressing his comrades, and himself approaching the door.

"Re-conduct the prisoner to the council-board," said the stranger, in a tone of command.

Without a moment's hesitation they obeyed the order; and O'Connor, followed by the muffled figure of the stranger, for the second time entered the apartment where his relentless judges sate.

The new-comer strode up the room to the table at which the self-styled council were seated.

"God save you, gentlemen," said he, "and prosper the good work ye have taken in hand;" and thus speaking, he removed and cast upon the table his hat and cloak, thereby revealing the square-built form and harsh features of O'Hanlon.

O'Connor no sooner recognized the traits of his mysterious acquaintance, than he felt a hope which thrilled with a strange agony of his heart—a hope—almost a conviction—that he should escape; and unaccountable though it may appear, in this hope he felt more unmanned and agitated than he had done but a few moments before, in the apparent certainty of immediate and inevitable destruction.

The salutation of O'Hanlon was warmly, almost enthusiastically, returned, and after this interchange of friendly greeting, and a few brief questions and answers touching comparatively indifferent matters, he glanced toward O'Connor, and said,—

"I've so far presumed upon my favour with you, gentlemen, as to stay your orders in respect of that young gentleman, whom, it would appear, you have judged worthy of death. Death is a matter whose importance I've never very much insisted upon—that you know—at least, several among you, gentlemen, well know it, for you have seen me deal it somewhat unsparingly when the cause required it; but I profess I do not care in cool blood to take life upon insufficient reason. Life is lightly taken; but once gone, who can restore it? Therefore, I think it very meet that patient consideration should be had of all cases, when such deliberation is possible and convenient, before proceeding to the last irrevocable extremity. Pray you inform me upon what charges does this youth stand convicted, that his life should be forfeit?"

"It is briefly told," replied the priest. "On my way hither I encountered him; we rode and conversed together; and conjecturing that he travelled on the same errand as myself, I talked to him more freely than in all discretion I ought to have done. I discovered my mistake, and at Chapelizod I turned and left him, telling him with threats not to follow me; yet scarcely had I been here ten minutes, when this gentleman is found lurking near the house—and about to enter it. He is seized, bound, brought in here, and witnesses our assembly and proceedings. Under these suspicious circumstances, and with the knowledge of our meeting and its objects, were it wise to let him go? Surely not so—but the veriest madness."

"Young man," said O'Hanlon, turning to O'Connor, "what say you to this?"

"No more than what I already told these gentlemen—simply, that taking the upper level to avoid the sloughs by the river side, I became in the darkness entangled in the dense woods which cover these grounds, and at length, after groping my way through the trees as best I might, arrived by the merest chance at this place, and without the slightest knowledge, or even suspicion, either that I was following the course taken by that gentleman, or intruding myself upon any secret councils. I have no more to say—this is the simple truth."

"Well, gentlemen," said O'Hanlon, "you hear the prisoner's defence. What think you?"

"We have decided already, and he has now produced nothing new in his favour. I see no reason why we should alter our decision," replied the priest.

"You would, then, put him to death?" inquired he.

"Assuredly," replied the priest, calmly.

"But this shall not be, gentlemen; he shall not die. You shall slay me first," replied O'Hanlon. "I know this youth; and every word he has spoken I believe. He is the son of one who risked his life a hundred times, and lost all for the sake of the king and his country—one who, throughout the desperate and fruitless struggles of Irish loyalty, was in the field my constant comrade, and a braver and a better one none ever need desire. The son of such a man shall not perish by our hands; and for the risk of his talking elsewhere of this night's adventure, I will be his surety, with my life, that he mentions it to no one, and nowhere."

A silence of some seconds followed this unexpected declaration.

"Be it so, then," said the priest; "for my part, I offer no resistance."

"So say I," added the person who sat with the papers by him at the extremity of the board. "On you, however, Captain O'Hanlon, rest the whole responsibility of this act."

"On me alone. Were there the possibility of treason in that youth, I would myself perish ere I should move a hand to save him," replied O'Hanlon. "I gladly take upon myself the whole accountability, and all the consequences of the act."

"Your life and liberty are yours, sir," said the priest, addressing O'Connor; "see that you abuse neither to our prejudice. Unbind and let the prisoner go."

"Stay," said O'Hanlon. "Mr. O'Connor, I have one request to make."

"It is granted ere it is made. What can I return you in exchange for my life?" replied O'Connor.

"I wish to speak with you to-night," continued O'Hanlon, "on matters which concern you nearly. You will remain here—you can have a chamber. Farewell for the present. Conduct Mr. O'Connor to my apartment," he added, addressing the attendants, who were employed in loosening the strained cords which bound his hands; and with this direction, O'Hanlon mingled with the group at the hearth, and began to converse with them in a low voice.

O'Connor followed his guide through a narrow, damp-stained corridor, with tiled flooring, and up a broad staircase, with heavy oaken balustrades, and steps whose planks seemed worn by the tread of centuries; and then along another passage, more cheerless still than the first—several of the narrow windows, by which in the daytime it was lighted, had now lost every vestige of glass, and even of the wooden framework in which it had been fixed, and gave free admission to the fitful night-wind, as well as to the straggling boughs of ivy which mantled the old walls and clustered shelteringly about the ruined casements. Screening the candle which he carried behind the flap of his coat, to prevent its being extinguished by the gusts which somewhat rudely swept the narrow passage, the man led O'Connor to a chamber, which they both entered. It was not quite so cheerless as the desolate condition of the approach to it might have warranted one in expecting; a wood-fire, which had been recently replenished, blazed and crackled briskly upon the hearth, and shed an uncertain but cheerful glow through the recesses of the chamber. It was a spacious apartment, hung with stamped leather, in many places stained and rotted by the damp, and here and there hanging in rags from the wall, and exposing the bare, mildewed plaster beneath. The furniture was scanty, and in keeping with the place—old, dark, and crazy; and a wretched bed, with very spare covering, was, as it seemed, temporarily strewn upon the floor, near the hearth. The man placed the candle upon a small table, black with age, and patched and crutched up like a battered pensioner, and flinging some more wood upon the fire, turned and left the room in silence.

Alone, his first employment was to review again and again the strange events of that night; his next was to conjecture the nature of O'Hanlon's promised communication. Baffled in these latter speculations, he applied himself to examine the old chamber in which he sat, and to endeavour to trace the half-obliterated pattern of the tattered hangings. These occupations, along with sundry speculations just as idle, touching the original of a grim old portrait, faded and torn, which hung over the fireplace, filled up the tedious hours which preceded his expected interview with his preserver.

At length the weary interval elapsed, and the anxiously expected moment arrived. The door opened, and O'Hanlon entered. He approached the young man, who advanced to meet him, and extending his hand, grasped that of O'Connor with a warm and friendly pressure.


CHAPTER XLVI.

THE DOUBLE CONFERENCE—OLD PAPERS.

"When last I saw you," said O'Hanlon, seating himself before the hearth, and motioning O'Connor to take a chair also, "I told you that you ought to tame your rash young blood, and gave you thereupon an old soldier's best advice. It seems, however, that you are wayward and headlong still. Young soldiers look for danger—old ones are content to meet it when it comes, knowing well that it will come often enough, uninvited and unsought; nevertheless, we will pass by this night's adventure, and turn to other matters. First, however, it were meet and necessary that you should have somewhat to refresh you; you must needs be weary and exhausted."

"If you can give me some wine, it will be very welcome. I care not for anything more to-night," replied O'Connor.

"That can I," replied he, "and will myself do you reason." He arose, and after a few minutes' absence entered with two flasks, whose dust and cobwebs bespoke their antiquity, and filled two large, long-stemmed glasses with the generous liquor.

"Young man," said O'Hanlon, "from the moment I saw you in the inner room yonder, I know not how or wherefore my heart clave to you; and now knowing you for the son of my true friend, I feel for you the stronger love. I will tell you now how matters stand with us. I will hide nothing from you. I am old enough to have learned the last lesson of experience—the folly of too much suspicion. I will not distrust the son of Richard O'Connor. I need hardly tell you that those men whom you saw below stairs are no friends of the ruling powers, but devoted entirely to the service and the fortunes of the rightful heir of the throne of England and of Ireland, met here together not without great peril."

"I had conjectured as much from what I myself witnessed," rejoined O'Connor.

"Well, then, I tell you this—the cause is not a hopeless one; the exiled king has warm, zealous, and powerful friends where their existence is least suspected," continued O'Hanlon. "In the Parliament of England he has a strong and untiring party undetected—some of them, too, must soon wield the enormous powers of government, and have already gotten entire possession of the ear of the Queen; and so soon as events invite, and the time is ripe for action, a mighty and a sudden constitutional movement will be made in favour of the prince—a movement entirely constitutional and in the Parliament. This will, whether successful or not, raise the intolerant party here into fierce resistance—the resistance of the firelock and the sword; all the usurpers, the perjurers, and the plunderers who now possess the wealth and dignities of this spoiled and oppressed country, will arise in terror to defend their booty, and unless met and encountered, and defeated by the party of the young king in this island, will embolden the malignant rebels of the sister country to imitate their example, and so overawe the Parliament, and frustrate their beneficent intentions. To us, therefore, has fallen the humbler but important task of organizing here, in the heart of this country, and in entire secrecy, a power sufficient for the occasion. Fain would I have thee along with us in so great and good a work, but will not urge you now; think upon it, however—it is not so mad a scheme as you may have thought, but such a one as looked on calmly, with the cold eye of reason, seems practicable—ay, sure of success. Ponder the matter, then; give me no answer now—I will take none—but think well upon it, and after a week, and not sooner, when you have decided, tell me whether you will be one of us or not. Meanwhile, I have other matters to tell you of, in which perhaps your young heart will take a nearer interest."

He paused, and having replenished their glasses, and thrown a fresh supply of wood upon the fire, he continued,—

"Are you acquainted with a family named Ashwoode?"

"Yes," replied O'Connor, quickly, "I have known them long."

O'Hanlon looked searchingly at the young man, and then continued,—

"Yes," said he, "I see it is even so—your face betrays it—you loved the young lady, Mary Ashwoode—deny it not—I am your friend, and seek not idly or without purpose thus to question you. What thought you of Henry Ashwoode, now Sir Henry Ashwoode?"

"He was latterly much—entirely my friend," replied O'Connor.

"He so professed himself?" asked O'Hanlon.

"Ay," replied O'Connor, somewhat surprised at the tone in which the question was put, "he did so profess himself, and repeatedly."

"He is a villain—he has betrayed you," said the elder man, sternly.

"How—what—a villain! Henry Ashwoode deceive me?" said O'Connor, turning pale as death.

"Yes—unless I've been strangely practised on—he has villainously deceived alike you and his own sister—pretending friendship, he has sowed distrust between you."

"But have you evidence of what you say?" cried O'Connor. "Gracious God—what have I done!"

"I have evidence, and you shall hear and judge of it yourself," replied O'Hanlon; "you cannot hear it to-night, however, nor I produce it—you need some rest, and so in truth do I—make use of that poor bed—a tired brain and weary body need no luxurious couch—I shall see you in the morning betimes—till then farewell."

The young man would fain have detained O'Hanlon, and spoken with him, but in vain.

"We have talked enough for this night," said the elder man—"I have it not in my power now to satisfy you—I shall, however, in the morning—I have taken measures for the purpose—good-night."

So saying, O'Hanlon left the chamber, and closed the door upon his young friend, now less than ever disposed to slumber.

He threw himself upon the pallet, the victim of a thousand harassing and exciting thoughts—sleep was effectually banished; and at length, tired of the fruitless attitude of repose which he courted in vain, he arose and resumed his seat by the hearth, in anxious and weary expectation of the morning.

At length the red light of the dawn broke over the smoky city, and with a dusky glow the foggy sun emerged from the horizon of chimney-tops, and threw his crimson mantle of ruddy light over the hoary thorn-wood and the shattered mansion, beneath whose roof had passed the scenes we have just described. Never did the sick wretch, who in sleepless anguish has tossed and fretted through the tedious watches of the night, welcome the return of day with more cordial greeting than did O'Connor upon this dusky morn. The time which was to satisfy his doubts could not now be far distant, and every sound which smote upon his ear seemed to announce the approach of him who was to dispel them all.

Weary, haggard, and nervous after the fatigues and agitation of the previous day—unrefreshed by the slumbers he so much required, his irritation and excitement were perhaps even greater than under other circumstances they would have been. The torments of suspense were at length, however, ended—he did hear steps approach the chamber—the steps evidently of more than one person—the door opened, and O'Hanlon, followed by Signor Parucci, entered the room.

"I believe, young gentleman, you have seen this person before?" said O'Hanlon, addressing O'Connor, while he glanced at the Italian.

O'Connor assented.

"Ah! yees," said the Neapolitan, with a winning smile; "he has see me vary often. Signor O'Connor—he know me vary well. I am so happy to see him again—vary—oh! vary."

"Let Mr. O'Connor know briefly and distinctly what you have already told me," said O'Hanlon.

"About the letters?" asked the Italian.

"Yes, be brief," replied O'Hanlon.

"Ah! did he not guess?" rejoined the Neapolitan; "per crilla! the deception succeed, then—vary coning faylow was old Sir Richard—bote not half so coning as his son, Sir Henry. He never suspect—Mr. O'Connor never doubt, bote took all the letters and read them just so as Sir Henry said he would. Malora! what great meesfortune."

"Parucci, speak plainly to the point; I cannot endure this. Say at once what has he done—how have I been deceived?" cried O'Connor.

"You remember when the old gentleman—Mr. Audley, I think he is call—saw Sir Richard—immediately after that some letters passed between you and Mees Mary Ashwoode."

"I do remember it—proceed," replied O'Connor.

"Mees Mary's letters to you were cold and unkind, and make you think she did not love you any more," added Parucci.

"Well, well—say on—say on—for God's sake, man—say on," cried O'Connor, vehemently.

"Those letters you got were not written by her," continued the Italian, coolly; "they were all wat you call forged   written by another person, and planned by Sir Henry and Sir Reechard; and the same way on the other side—the letters you wrote to her were all stopped, and read by the same two gentlemen, and other letters written in stead, and she is breaking her heart, because she thinks you 'av betrayed her, and given her up—rotta di collo! they 'av make nice work!"

"Prove this to me, prove it," said O'Connor, wildly, while his eye burned with the kindling fire of fury.

"I weel prove it," rejoined Parucci, but with an agitated voice and a troubled face; "bote, corpo di Plato, you weel keel me if I tell—promise—swear—by your honour—you weel not horte me—you weel not toche me—swear, Signor, and I weel tell."

"Miserable caitiff—speak, and quickly—you are safe—I swear it," rejoined he.

"Well, then," resumed the Italian, with restored calmness, "I will prove it so that you cannot doubt any more—it was I that wrote the letters for them—I, myself—and beside, here is the bundle with all of them written out for me to copy—most of them by Sir Henry—you know his hand-writing—you weel see the character—corbezzoli! he is a great rogue—and you will find all the real letters from you and Mees Mary that were stopped—I have them here."

He here disengaged from the deep pocket of his coat, a red leathern case stamped with golden flowers, and opening it presented it to the young man.

With shifting colour and eyes almost blinded with agitation, O'Connor read and re-read these documents.

"Where is Ashwoode?" at length he cried; "bring me to him—gracious God, what a monster I must have appeared—will she—can she ever forgive me?"

Disregarding in entire contempt the mean agent of Ashwoode's villainy, and thinking only of the high-born principal, O'Connor, pale as death, but with perfect deliberateness, arose and took the sword which the attendant who conducted him to the room had laid by the wall, and replacing it at his side, said sternly,—

"Bring me to Sir Henry Ashwoode—where is he? I must speak with him."

"I cannot breeng you to him now," replied Parucci, in internal ecstasies, "for I cannot say where he is; bote I know vary well where he weel be to-day after dinner time, in the evening, and I weel breeng you; bote I hope very moche you are not intending any mischiefs; if I thought so, I would be vary sorry—oh! vary."

"Well, be it so, if it may not be sooner," said O'Connor, gloomily, "this evening at all events he shall account with me."

"Meanwhile," said O'Hanlon, "you may as well remain here; and when the time arrives which this Italian fellow names, we can start. I will accompany you, for in such cases the arm of a friend can do you no harm and may secure you fair play. Hear me, you Italian scoundrel, remain here until we are ready to depart with you, and that shall be whenever you think it time to seek Sir Henry Ashwoode; you shall have enough to eat and drink meanwhile; depart, and relieve us of your company."

Signor Parucci smiled sweetly from ear to ear, shrugged, and bowed, and then glided lightly from the room, exulting in the pleasant conviction that he had commenced operations against his ungrateful patron, by involving him in a scrape which must inevitably result in somewhat unpleasant exposures, and which had beside reduced the question of Sir Henry's life or death to an even chance.

CHAPTER XLVII.

"THE JOLLY BOWLERS"—THE DOUBLE FRAY AND THE FLIGHT.

At the time of which we write, there lay at the southern extremity of the city of Dublin, a bowling-green of fashionable resort, well known as "Cullen's Green." For greater privacy it was enclosed by a brick wall of considerable height, which again was surrounded by stately rows of lofty and ancient elms. A few humble dwellings were clustered about it; and through one of them, a low, tiled public-house, lay the entrance into this place of pastime. Thitherward O'Connor and O'Hanlon, having left their horses at the "Cock and Anchor," were led by the wily Italian.

"The players you say, will not stop till dusk," said O'Connor; "we can go in, and I shall wait until the party have broken up, to speak to Ashwoode; in the interval we can mix with the spectators, and so escape remark."

They were now approaching the little tavern embowered in tufted trees, and as they advanced, they perceived a number of hack carriages and led horses congregated upon the road about its entrance.

"Sir Henry is within; that iron-grey is his horse; sangue dun dua, there is no mistake," observed the Neapolitan.

The little party entered the humble tavern, but here they were encountered by a new difficulty.

"You can't get in to-night, gentlemen—sorry to disappint, gentlemen; but the green's engaged," said mine host, with an air of mysterious importance; "a private party, engaged two days since for fear of a disappint."

"Are they so strictly private, that they would not suffer two gentlemen to be spectators of their play?" inquired O'Hanlon.

"My orders is not to let anyone in, good, bad, or indifferent, while they are playing the match; that's my orders," replied the man; "sorry to disappint, but can't break my word with the gentlemen, you know."

"Is there any other entrance into the bowling-green?" inquired O'Connor, "except through that door."

"Divil a one, sir, where would it be?—divil a one, gentlemen," replied mine host, "no other way in or out."

"We will rest ourselves here for a time, then," said O'Connor.

Accordingly the party seated themselves in the low-roofed chamber through which the bowlers on quitting the ground must necessarily pass; and calling for some liquor to prevent suspicion, moodily awaited the appearance of the young baronet and his companions. Many a stern, impatient glance of expectation did O'Connor direct to the old door which alone separated him from the traitor and hypocrite who had with such monstrous fraud practised upon his unsuspecting confidence. At length he heard gay laughter and the tread of many feet approaching; the proprietor of "The Jolly Bowlers" opened the door, and several merry groups passed them by and took their departure, but O'Connor's eye in vain sought among them the form of young Ashwoode.

"I see the grey horse still at the door; I know it as well as I know my own hand," said the Italian; "as sure as I am leeving man, Sir Henry is there still."

After an interval so considerable that O'Connor almost despaired of the appearance of Ashwoode, voices were again audible, and steps approaching the door-way at a slow pace; the time between the first approach of those sounds, and the actual appearance of those who caused them, appeared to the overwrought anxiety of O'Connor all but interminable. At length, however, two figures entered from the bowling-green—the one was that of a spare but dignified-looking man, somewhat advanced in years, but carrying in his countenance a singular expression of jollity and good humour—the other was that of Sir Henry Ashwoode.

"God be thanked," said O'Hanlon, grasping the hilt of his sword, "here comes the perjured villain Wharton."

O'Connor had another object, however, and beheld no one existing thing but only the now hated form of his false friend; both he and O'Hanlon started to their feet as the two figures entered the small and darksome room. O'Connor threw himself directly in their path and said,—

"Sir Henry Ashwoode, a word with you."

The appeal was startling and unexpected, and there was in the voice and attitude of him who uttered it, something of deep, intense, constrained passion and resolution, which made the two companions involuntarily and suddenly check their advance. One moment sufficed for Sir Henry to recognize O'Connor, and another convinced him that his quondam friend had discovered his treachery, and was there to unmask, perhaps to punish him. His presence of mind, however, seldom, if ever, forsook him in such scenes as this—he instantly resolved upon the tone in which to meet his injured antagonist.

"Pray, sir," said he, with stern hauteur, "upon what ground do you presume to throw yourself thus menacingly in my way? Move aside and let me pass, or your rashness shall cost you dearly."

"Ashwoode—Sir Henry—you well know there is one consideration which would unstring my arm if lifted against your life—you presume upon the forbearance which this respect commands," said O'Connor. "Promise but this—that you will undeceive your sister, whom you have practised upon as cruelly as you have on me, and I will call you to no further account, and inflict no further humiliation."

"Very good, sir, very magnanimous, and exceedingly tragic," rejoined Ashwoode, scornfully. "Turn aside, sirrah, and leave my path open, or by the — you shall rue it."

"I will not leave the spot on which I stand but with my life, except on the conditions I have named," replied O'Connor.

"Once more, before I strike you, leave the way," cried Ashwoode, whose constitutional pugnacity began to be thoroughly aroused. "Turn aside, sirrah! How dare you confront gentlemen—insolent beggar, how dare you!"

Yielding to the furious impulse of the moment, Sir Henry Ashwoode drew his sword, and with the naked blade struck his antagonist twice with no sparing hand. The passions which O'Connor had, with all his energy, hitherto striven to master, would now brook restraint no longer; at this last extremity of insult the blood sprang from his heart in fiery currents and tingled through every vein; every feeling but the one deadly sense of outraged pride, of repeated wrong, followed and consummated by one degrading and intolerable outrage, vanished from his mind. With the speed of light his sword was drawn and presented at Ashwoode's breast. Each threw himself into the cautious attitude of deadly vigilance, and quick as lightning the bright blades crossed and clashed in the mortal rivalry of cunning fence. Each party was possessed of consummate skill in the use of the fatal weapon which he wielded, and several times in the course of the fierce debate, so evenly were they matched, the two, as by voluntary accommodation, paused in the conflict to take breath.

With faces pale as death with rage, and a consciousness of the deadly issue in which alone the struggle could end, and with eyes that glared like those of savage beasts at bay, each eyed the other. Thus alternately they paused and renewed the combat, and for long, with doubtful fortune. In the position of the antagonists there was, however, an inequality, and, as it turned out, a decisive one—the door through which Ashwoode and his companion had entered, and to which his back was turned, lay open, and the light which it admitted fell full in O'Connor's eyes. This, as all who have handled the foil can tell, is a disadvantage quite sufficient to determine even a less nicely balanced contest than that of which we write. After several pauses in the combat, and as many desperate renewals of it, Ashwoode, in one quick lunge, passed his blade through his opponent's sword-arm. Though the blood flowed plenteously, neither party seemed inclined to abate his deadly efforts. O'Connor's arm began to grow stiff and weak, and the energy and quickness of his action impaired; the consequences of this were soon exhibited. Ashwoode lunged twice or thrice rapidly, and one of these passes, being imperfectly parried, took effect in his opponent's breast. O'Connor staggered backward, and his hand and eye faltered for a moment; but he quickly recovered, and again advanced and again with the same result. Faint, dizzy, and half blind, but with resolution and rage, enhanced by defeat, he staggered forward again, wild and powerless, and was received once more upon the point of his adversary's sword. He reeled back, stood for a moment, his sword dropped upon the ground, and he shook his empty hand in fruitless menace at his triumphant antagonist, and then rolled headlong upon the pavement, insensible, and weltering in gore—the combat was over.

Ashwoode and O'Connor had hardly crossed their weapons when O'Hanlon sprang forward and sternly accosted Lord Wharton, for it was no other, who accompanied Ashwoode.

"My lord, you need not interfere," said he, observing a movement on Lord Wharton's part as if he would have separated the combatants. "This is a question which all your diplomacy will not arrange—they will fight it to the end. If you give them not fair play while I secure the door, I will send my sword through your excellency's body."

So saying, O'Hanlon drew his weapon, and keeping occasional watch upon Wharton—who, however, did not exhibit any further disposition to interfere—he strode to the outer door, which opened upon the public road, and to prevent interruption from that quarter, drew the bar and secured it effectually.

"Now, my lord," said he, returning and resuming his position, "I have secured this fortunate meeting against intrusion. What think you, while our friends are thus engaged, were we, for warmth and exercise sake, likewise to cross our blades? Will your lordship condescend to gratify a simple gentleman so far?"

"Out upon you, fellow; know you who I am?" said Wharton, with sturdy good-humour.

"I know thee well, Lord Wharton—a wily, selfish, double-dealing politician; a profligate in morals; an infidel in religion; and a traitor in politics. I know thee—who doth not?"

"Landlord," said Wharton, turning toward that personage, who, with amazement, irresolution, and terror in his face, inspected these violent proceedings, "landlord, I say, call in a lackey or two; I'll bring this ruffian to reason quickly. Have you gotten a pump in the neighbourhood? Landlord, I say, bestir thyself, or, by —, I'll spur thee with my sword-point."

"Stir not, if you would keep your life," said O'Hanlon, in a tone which the half-stupefied host of "The Jolly Bowlers" dared not disobey. "If you would not suffer death upon the spot where you stand, do not attempt to move one step, nor to speak one word. My lord," he continued, "I am right glad of this rencounter. I would have freely given half what I possess in the world to have secured it. Believe me, I will not leave it unimproved. My lord, in plain terms, for ten thousand reasons I desire your death, and will not leave this place till I have striven to effect it. Draw your sword, if you be a man; draw your sword, unless cowardice has come to crown your vices."

O'Hanlon drew his sword, and allowing Wharton hardly time sufficient to throw himself into an attitude of defence, he attacked him with deadly resolution. It was well for the viceroy that he was an expert swordsman, otherwise his career would undoubtedly have been abruptly terminated upon the floor of "The Jolly Bowlers." As it was, he received a thrust right through the shoulder, and staggering back, stumbled and fell upon the uneven pavement which studded the floor. This occurred almost at the same moment with O'Connor's fall, and believing that he had mortally hurt his noble antagonist, O'Hanlon, without stopping to look about him hastily lifted his fallen and senseless companion from the pavement and bore him in his arms through the outer door, which the landlord had at length found resolution enough to unbar. Fortunately a hackney coach stood there waiting for a chance job from some of the aristocratic bowlers within, and in this vehicle he hurriedly deposited his inanimate burden, and desiring the coachman to drive for his life into the city, sprang into the conveyance himself. Irishmen are proverbially ready at all times to aid an escape from the fangs of justice, and without pausing to ask a question, the coachman, to whom the sight of blood and of the naked sword, which O'Hanlon still carried, was warrant sufficient, mounted the box with incredible speed, pressed his hat firmly down upon his brows, shook the reins, and lashed his horses till they smoked again; and thus, at a gallop, O'Hanlon and his bleeding companion thundered onward toward the city. Ashwoode did not interfere to stay the fugitives, for he was not sorry to be relieved of the embarrassment which he foresaw in having the body of his victim left, as it were, in his charge. He therefore gladly witnessed its removal, and addressed himself to Lord Wharton, who was rising with some difficulty from his prostrate position.

"Are you hurt, my lord?" inquired Ashwoode, kneeling by his side and assisting him to rise.

"Hush! nothing—a mere scratch. Above all things, make no row about it. By —, I would not for worlds that anything were heard of it. Fortunately, this accident is a trivial one—the blood flows rather fast, though. Let's get into a coach, if, indeed, the scoundrels have not run away with the last of them."

They found one, however, at the door, and getting in with all convenient dispatch, desired the man to drive slowly toward the castle.

CHAPTER XLVIII.

THE STAINED RUFFLES.

We must now return for a brief space to Morley Court. The apartment which lay beneath what had been Sir Richard Ashwoode's bed-chamber, and in which Mary and her gay cousin, Emily Copland, had been wont to sit and work, and read and sing together, had grown to be considered, by long-established usage, the rightful and exclusive property of the ladies of the family, and had been surrendered up to their private occupation and absolute control. Around it stood full many a quaint cabinet of dark old wood, shining like polished jet, little bookcases, and tall old screens, and music stands, and drawing tables. These, along with a spinet and a guitar, and countless other quaint and pretty sundries indicating the habitual presence of feminine refinement and taste, abundantly furnished the chamber. In the window stood some choice and fragrant flowers, and the light fell softly upon the carpet through the clustering bowers of creeping plants which mantled the outer wall, in sombre rivalry of the full damask curtains, whose draperies hung around the deep receding casements.

Here sat Mary Ashwoode, as the evening, whose tragic events we have in our last chapter described, began to close over the old manor of Morley Court. Her embroidery had been thrown aside, and lay upon the table, and a book, which she had been reading, was open before her; but her eyes now looked pensively through the window upon the fair, sad landscape, clothed in the warm and melancholy tints of evening. Her graceful arm leaned upon the table, and her small, white hand supported her head and mingled in the waving tresses of her dark hair.

"At what hour did my brother promise to return?" said she, addressing herself to her maid, who was listlessly arranging some books in the little book-case.

"Well, I declare and purtest, I can't rightly remember," rejoined the maid, cocking her head on one side reflectively, and tapping her eyebrow to assist her recollection. "I don't think, my lady, he named any hour precisely; but at any rate, you may be sure he'll not be long away now."

"I thought he said seven o'clock," continued Mary; "would he were come! I feel very solitary to-day; and this evening we might pass happily together, for that strange man will not return to-night—he said so—my brother told me so."

"I believe Mr. Blarden changed his mind, my lady," said the maid; "for I know he gave orders before he went for a fire in his room to-night."

Even as she spoke she heard Sir Henry's step upon the stairs, and her brother entered the room.

"Harry, Harry, I am so glad to see you," said she, running lightly to him and throwing her arms around his neck. "Come, come, sit you down beside me; we shall be happy together at least for this evening. Come, Harry, come."

So saying she led him, passive and gloomy, to the fireside, and drew a chair beside that into which he had thrown himself.

"Dear brother, the time seemed so very tedious to-day while you were away," said she. "I thought it would never pass. Why are you so silent and thoughtful, brother? has anything happened to vex you?"

"Nothing," said he, glancing at her with a strange expression—"nothing to vex me—no, nothing—perhaps the contrary."

"Dear brother, have you heard good news? Come and tell me," said she; "though I fear from the sadness of your face you do but flatter me. Have you, Harry—have you heard or seen anything that gave you comfort?"

"No, not comfort; I know not what I say. Have you any wine here?" said Ashwoode, hurriedly; "I am tired and thirsty."

"No, not here," answered she, somewhat surprised at the oddity of the question, as well as by the abruptness and abstraction of his manner.

"Carey," said he, "run down—bring wine quickly; I'm exhausted—quite wearied. I have played more at bowls this afternoon than I've done for years," he added, addressing his sister as the maid departed on her errand.

"You do look very pale, brother," said she, "and your dress is all disordered; and, gracious God!—see all the ruffles of this hand are steeped in blood—brother, brother, for God's sake—are you hurt?"

"Hurt—I—?" said he hastily, and endeavouring to smile! "no, indeed—I hurt! far be it from me—this blood is none of mine; one of our party scratched his hand, and I bound his handkerchief round the wound, and in so doing contracted these tragic spots that startle you so. No, no, believe me, when I am hurt I will make no secret of it. Carey, pour some wine into that glass—fill it—fill it, child—there," and he drank it off—"fill it again—so two or three more, and I shall be quite myself again. How snug this room of yours is, Mary."

"Yes, brother, I am very fond of it; it is a pleasant old room, and one that has often seen me happier than I shall be again," said she, with a sigh; "but do you feel better? has the wine refreshed you? You still look pale," she added, with fears not yet half quieted.

"Yes, Mary, I am refreshed," he said, with a sudden and reckless burst of strange merriment that shocked her; "I could play the match through again—I could leap, and laugh and sing;" and then he added quickly in an altered voice—"has Blarden returned?"

"No," said she; "I thought you said he would remain in town to-night."

"I said wrong if I said so at all," replied Ashwoode; "and if he did intend to stay in town he has changed his plans—he will be here this evening; I thought I should have found him here on my return; I expect him every moment."

"When, dear brother, is this visit of his to end?" asked the girl imploringly.

"Not for weeks—for months, I hope," replied Ashwoode drily and quickly; "why do you inquire, pray?"

"Simply because I wish it were ended, brother," answered she sadly; "but if it vexes you I will ask no more."

"It does vex me, then," said Ashwoode, sternly; "it does, and you know it"—he accompanied these words with a look even more savage than the tone in which he had uttered them, and a silence of some minutes followed.

Ashwoode desired nothing so much as to speak with his sister intelligibly upon the subject of Blarden's designs, and of his own entire approval of them; but, somehow, often as he had resolved upon it, he had never yet approached the topic, even in imagination, in his sister's presence, without feeling himself unnerved and abashed. He now strove to fret himself into a rage, in the instinctive hope that under the influence of this stimulus he might find nerve to broach the subject in plain terms; he strode quickly to and fro across the floor, casting from time to time many an angry glance at the poor girl, and seeking by every mechanical agency to work himself into a passion.

"And so it is come to this at last," said he, vehemently, "that I may not invite my friends to my own house; or that if I dare to do so, they shall necessarily be exposed to the constant contempt and rudeness of those who ought to be their entertainers; all their advances towards acquaintance met with a hoity-toity, repulsive impertinence, and themselves treated with a marked and insulting avoidance, shunned as though they had the plague. I tell you now plainly, once for all, I will be master in my own house; you shall treat my guests with attention and respect; you must do so; I command you; you shall find that I am master here."

"No doubt of it, by —," ejaculated Nicholas Blarden, himself entering the room at the termination of Ashwoode's stormy harangue; "but where the devil is the good of roaring that way? your sister is not deaf, I suppose? Mistress Mary, your most obedient——"

Mary did not wait for further conference; but rising with a proud mien and a burning cheek, she left the room and went quickly to her own chamber, where she threw herself into a chair, covered her eyes with her hands, and burst into an agony of weeping.

"Well, but she is a fine wench," cried Nicholas Blarden, as soon as she had disappeared. "The tantarums become her better than good humour;" so saying, he half filled Ashwoode's glass with wine, and rinsed it into the fireplace; then coolly filled a bumper and quaffed it off, and then another and another.

"Sit down here and listen to me," said he to Ashwoode, in that insolent, domineering tone which he so loved to employ in accosting him, "sit down here, I say, young man, and listen to me while I give you a bit of my mind."

Ashwoode, who knew too well the consequences of even murmuring under the tyranny of his task-master, in silence did as he was commanded.

"I tell you what it is," said Blarden, "I don't like the way this affair is going on; the girl avoids me; I don't know her, by —, a curse better to-day than I did the first day I came into the house; this won't do, you know; it will never do; you had better strike out some expeditious plan, or it's very possible I may tire of the whole concern and cut it back, do you mind; you had better sharpen your wits, my fine fellow."

"The fault is your own," said Ashwoode gloomily; "if you desire expedition, you can command it, by yourself speaking to her; you have not as yet even hinted at your intentions, nor by any one act made her acquainted with your designs; let her see that you like her; let her understand you; you have never done so yet."

"She's infernally proud," said Blarden, "just as proud as yourself: but we know a knack, don't we, for bringing pride to its senses? Eh? Nothing, I believe, Sir Henry, like fear in such cases; don't you think so? I've known it succeed sometimes to a miracle—fear of one kind or another is the only way we have of working men or women. Mind I tell you she must be frightened, and well frightened too, or she'll run rusty. I have a knack with me—a kind of gift—of frightening people when I have a fancy; and if you're in earnest, as I guess you pretty well are, between us we'll tame her."

"It were not advisable to proceed at once to extremities," said Ashwoode, who, spite of his constitutional selfishness, felt some odd sensations, and not of the pleasantest kind, while they thus conversed. "You must begin by showing your wishes in your manner; be attentive to her; and, in short, let her unequivocally see the nature of your intentions; tell her that you want to marry her; and when she refuses, then it is time enough to commence those—those—other operations at which you hint."

"Well, d——n me, but there is some sense in what you say," observed Blarden, filling his glass again. "Umph! perhaps I've been rather backward; I believe I have; she's coy, shy, and a proud little baggage withal—I like her the better for it—and requires a lot of wooing before she's won; well, I'll make myself clear on to-morrow. I'm blessed if she sha'n't understand me beyond the possibility of question or doubt; and if she won't listen to reason, then we'll see whether there isn't a way to break her spirit if she was as proud as the Queen." With these words Blarden arose and drained the flask of wine, then observed authoritatively,—

"Get the cards and follow me to the parlour. I want something to amuse me; be quick, d'ye hear?"

And so saying he took his departure, followed by Sir Henry Ashwoode, whose condition was now more thoroughly abject and degraded than that of a purchased slave.


CHAPTER XLIX.

OLD SONGS—THE UNWELCOME LISTENER—THE BARONET'S PLEDGE.

Next day Mary Ashwoode sat alone in the same room in which she had been so unpleasantly intruded upon on the evening before. The unkindness of her brother had caused her many a bitter tear during the past night, and although still entirely in the dark as to Blarden's designs, there was yet something in his manner during the brief moment of their yesterday evening's rencontre which alarmed her, and suggested, in a few hurried and fevered dreams which troubled her broken slumbers of the night past, his dreaded image in a hundred wild and fantastic adventures.

She sat, as we have already said, alone in the self-same room, and as mechanically she pursued her work, her thoughts were far away, and wherever they turned still were they clouded with anxiety and sorrow. Wearied at length with the monotony of an occupation which availed not even momentarily to draw her attention from the griefs which weighed upon her, she threw her work aside, and taking the guitar which in gayer hours had often yielded its light music to her touch, and trying to forget the consciousness of her changed and lonely existence in the happier recollections which returned in these once familiar sounds, she played and sang the simple melodies which had been her favourites long ago; but while thus her hands strayed over the chords of the instrument, and the low and silvery cadences of her sweet voice recalled many a touching remembrance of the past, she was startled and recalled at once from her momentary forgetfulness of the present by a voice close behind her which exclaimed,—

"Capital—never a better—encore, encore;" and on looking hurriedly round, her glance at once encountered and recognized the form and features of Nicholas Blarden. "Go on, go on, do," said that gentleman in his most engaging way, and with an amorous grin; "do—go on, can't you—by —, I'm half sorry I said a word."

"I—I would rather not," stammered she, rising and colouring; "I have played and sung enough—too much already."

"No, no, not at all," continued Blarden, warming as he proceeded; "hang me, no such thing, you were just going on strong when I came in—come, come, I won't let you stop."

Her heart swelled with indignation at the coarse, familiar insolence of his manner; but she made no other answer than that conveyed by laying down the instrument, and turning from it and him.

"Well, rot me, but this is too bad," continued he, playfully; "come, take it up again—come, you must tip us another stave, young lady—do—curse me if I heard half your songs, you're a perfect nightingale."

So saying he took up the guitar, and followed her with it towards the fireplace.

"Come, you won't refuse, eh?—I'm in earnest," he continued; "upon my soul and oath I want to hear more of it."

"I have already told you, sir," said Mary Ashwoode, "that I do not wish to play or sing any more at present. I am sure you are not aware, Mr. Blarden, that this is my private apartment; no one visits me here uninvited, and at present I wish to be alone."

Thus speaking, she resumed her seat and her work, and sat in perfect silence, her heaving breast and glowing cheeks alone betraying the strength of her emotions.

"Ho, ho! rot me, but she's sulky," cried Blarden, with a horse-laugh, while he flung the guitar carelessly upon the table; "sure you wouldn't turn me out—that would be very hard usage, and no mistake. Eh! Miss Mary?"

Mary continued to ply her silks in silence, and Blarden threw himself into a chair opposite to her.

"I like to rise you—hang me, if I don't," said Blarden, exultingly—"you are always a snug-looking bit of goods, but when your blood's up, you're a downright beauty—rot me, but you are—why the devil don't you talk to me—eh?" he added, more roughly than he had yet spoken.

Mary Ashwoode began now to feel seriously alarmed at the man's manner, and as her eyes encountered his gloating gaze, her colour came and went in quick succession.

"Confoundedly pretty, sure enough, and well you know it, too," continued he—"curse me, but you are a fine wench—and I'll tell you what's more—I'm more than half in love with you at this minute, may the devil have me but I am."

Thus speaking, he drew his chair nearer hers.

"Mr. Blarden—sir—I insist on your leaving me," said Mary, now thoroughly frightened.

"And I insist on not leaving you," replied Blarden, with an insolent chuckle—"so it's a fair trial of strength between us, eh?—ho, ho, what are you afraid of?—stick up to your fight—do then—I like you all the better for your spirit—confound me but I do."

He advanced his chair still nearer to that on which she was seated.

"Well, but you do look pretty, by Jove," he exclaimed. "I like you, and I am determined to make you like me—I am—you shall like me."

He arose, and approached her with a half amorous, half menacing air.

Pale as death, Mary Ashwoode arose also, and moved with hurried, trembling steps towards the door. He made a movement as if to intercept her exit, but checked the impulse, and contented himself with observing with a scowl of spite and disappointment, as she passed from the room,—

"Pride will have a fall, my fine lady—you'll be tame enough yet for all your tantarums, by Jove."

Breathless with haste and agitation, Mary reached the study, where she knew her brother was now generally to be found. He was there engaged in the miserable labour of looking through accounts and letters, in arranging the complicated records of his own ruin.

"Brother," said she, running to his side with the earnestness of deep agitation, "brother, listen to me."

He raised his eyes, and at a glance easily divined the cause of her excitement.

"Well," said he, "speak on—I hear."

"Brother," she resumed, "that man—that Mr. Blarden, came uninvited into my study; he was at first very coarse and free in his manner—very disagreeable and impudent—he refused to leave me when I requested him to do so, and every moment became more and more insolent—his manner and language terrified me. Brother, dear brother, you must not expose me to another such scene as that which has just passed."

Ashwoode paused for a good while, with the pen still in his fingers, and his eyes fixed abstractedly upon his sister's pale face. At length he said,—

"Do you wish me to make this a quarrel with Blarden? Was there enough to warrant a—a duel?"

He well knew, however, that he was safe in putting the question, and in anticipating her answer, he calculated rightly the strength of his sister's affection for him.

"Oh! no, no, brother—no!" she cried, with imploring terror; "dear brother, you are everything to me now. No, no; promise that you will not!"

"Well, well, I do," said Ashwoode; "but how would you have me act?"

"Do not ask this man to prolong his visit," replied she; "or if he must, at least let me go elsewhere while he remains here."

"You have but one female relative in Ireland with a house to receive you," rejoined Ashwoode, "and that is Lady Stukely; and I have reason to think she would not like to have you as a guest just now."

"Dear Harry—dear brother, think of some place," said she, with earnest entreaty. "I now feel secure nowhere; that rude man, the very sight of whom affrights me, will not forbear to intrude upon my privacy; alone—in my own little room—anywhere in this house—I am equally liable to his intrusions and his rudeness. Dear brother, take pity on me—think of some place."

"Curse that beast Blarden!" muttered Sir Henry Ashwoode, between his teeth. "Will nothing ever teach the ruffian one particle of tact or common sense? What good end could he possibly propose to himself by terrifying the girl?"

Ashwoode bit his lips and frowned, while he thought the matter over. At length he said,—

"I shall speak to Blarden immediately. I begin to think that the man is not fit company for civilized people. I think we must get rid of him at whatever temporary inconvenience, without actual rudeness. Without anything approaching to a quarrel, I can shorten his visit. He shall leave this either to-night or before seven o'clock to-morrow morning."

"And you promise there shall be no quarrel—no violence?" urged she.

"Yes, Mary, I do promise," rejoined Ashwoode.

"Dear, dear brother, you have set my heart at rest," cried she. "Yes, you are my own dear brother—my protector!" And with all the warmth and enthusiasm of unsuspecting love, she threw her arms around his neck and kissed her betrayer.

Mary had scarcely left the room in which Sir Henry Ashwoode was seated, when he perceived Blarden sauntering among the trees by the window, with his usual swagger; the young man put on his hat and walked quickly forth to join him; as soon as he had come up with him, Blarden turned, and anticipating him, said,—

"Well, I have spoken out, and I think she understands me too; at any rate, if she don't, it's no fault of mine."

"I wish you had managed it better," said Ashwoode; "there is a way of doing these things. You have frightened the foolish girl half out of her wits."

"Have I, though?" exclaimed Blarden, with a triumphant grin. "She's just the girl we want—easily cowed. I'm glad to hear it. We'll manage her—we'll bring her into training before a week—hang me, but we will."

"You began a little too soon, though," urged Ashwoode; "you ought to have tried gentle means first."

"Devil the morsel of good in them," rejoined Blarden. "I see well enough how the wind sits—she don't like me; and I haven't time to waste in wooing. Once we're buckled, she'll be fond enough of me;

matrimony 'll turn out smooth enough—I'll take devilish good care of that; but the courtship will be the devil's tough business. We must begin the taming system off-hand; there's no use in shilly shally."

"I tell you," rejoined Ashwoode, "you have been too precipitate—I speak, of course, merely in relation to the policy and expediency of the thing. I don't mean to pretend that constraint may not become necessary hereafter; but just now, and before our plans are well considered, and our arrangements made, I think it was injudicious to frighten her so. She was talking of leaving the house and going to Lady Stukely's, or, in short, anywhere rather than remain here."

"Threaten to run away, did she?" cried Blarden, with a whistle of surprise which passed off into a chuckle.

"Yes, in plain terms, she said so," rejoined Ashwoode.

"Then just turn the key upon her at once," replied Blarden—"lock her up—let her measure her rambles by the four walls of her room! Hang me, if I can see the difficulty."

Ashwoode remained silent, and they walked side by side for a time without exchanging a word.

"Well, I believe I'm right," cried Blarden, at length; "I think our game is plain enough, eh? Don't let her budge an inch. Do you act turnkey, and I'll pay her a visit once a day for fear she'd forget me—I'll be her father confessor, eh?—ho, ho!—and between us I think we'll manage to bring her to before long."

"We must take care before we proceed to this extremity that all our agents are trustworthy," said Ashwoode. "There is no immediate danger of her attempting an escape, for I told her that you were leaving this either to-night or to-morrow morning, and she's now just as sure as if we had her under lock and key."

"Well, what do you advise? Can't you speak out? What's all the delay to lead to?" said Blarden.

"Merely that we shall have time to adjust our schemes," replied Ashwoode; "there is more to be done than perhaps you think of. We must cut off all possibility of correspondence with friends out of doors, and we must guard against suspicion among the servants; they are all fond of her, and there is no knowing what mischief might be done even by the most contemptible agents. Some little preparation before we employ coercion is absolutely indispensable."

"Well, then, you'd have me keep out of the way," said Blarden. "But mind you, I won't leave this; I like to have my own eye upon my own business."

"There is no reason why you should leave it," rejoined Ashwoode. "The weather is now cold and broken, so that Mary will seldom leave the house; and when she remains in it, she is almost always in the little drawing-room with her work, and books, and music; with the slightest precaution you can effectually avoid her for a few days."

"Well, then, agreed—done and done—a fair go on both sides," replied Blarden, "but it must not be too long; knock out some scheme that will wind matters up within a fortnight at furthest; be lively, or she shall lead apes, and you swing as sure as there's six sides to a die."

## CHAPTER L

Larry Toole, having visited in vain all his master's usual haunts, returned in the evening of that day on which we last beheld him, to the "Cock and Anchor," in a state of extreme depression and desolateness.

"By the holy man," said Larry, in reply to the inquiries of the groom, who encountered him at the yard gate, "he's gone as clane as a whistle. It's dacent thratement, so it is—gone, and laves me behind to rummage the town for him, and divil a sign of him, good or bad. I'm fairly burstin' with emotions. Why did he make off with himself? Why the devil did he desart me? There's no apology for sich minewvers, nor no excuse in the wide world, anless, indeed, he happened to be dhrounded or dhrunk. I'm fairly dry with the frettin'. Come in with me, and we'll have a sorrowful pot iv strong ale together by the kitchen fire; for, bedad, I want something badly."

Accordingly the two worthies entered the great old kitchen, and by the genial blaze of its cheering hearth, they discussed at length the probabilities of recovering Larry's lost master.

"Usedn't he to take a run out now and again to Morley Court?" inquired the groom; "you told me so."

"By the hokey," exclaimed Larry, with sudden alacrity, "there is some sinse in what you say—bedad, there is. I don't know how in the world I didn't think iv going out there to-day. But no matter, I'll do it to-morrow."

And in accordance with this resolution, upon the next day, early in the forenoon, Mr. Toole pursued his route toward the old manor-house. As he approached the domain, however, he slackened his pace, and, with extreme hesitation and caution, began to loiter toward the mansion, screening his approach as much as possible among the thick brushwood which skirted the rich old timber that clothed the slopes and hollows of the manor in irregular and stately masses. Sheltered in his post of observation, Larry lounged about until he beheld Sir Henry emerge from the hall door and join Nicholas Blarden in the tête-à-tête which we have in our last chapter described. Our romantic friend no sooner beheld this occurrence, than he felt all his uneasiness at once dispelled. He marched rapidly to the hall door, which remained open, and forthwith entered the house. He had hardly reached the interior of the hall, when he was encountered by no less a person than the fair object of his soul's idolatry, the beauteous Mistress Betsy Carey.

"La, Mr. Laurence," cried she, with an affected start, "you're always turning up like a ghost, when you're least expected."

"By the powers of Moll Kelly!" rejoined Larry, with fervour, "it's more and more beautiful, the Lord be merciful to us, you're growin' every day you live. What the divil will you come to at last?"

"Well, Mr. Toole," rejoined she, relaxing into a gracious smile, "but you do talk more nonsense than any ten beside. I wonder at you, so I do, Mr. Toole. Why don't you have a discreeterer way of conversation and discourse?"

"Och! murdher!—heigho! beautiful Betsy," sighed Larry, rapturously.

"Did you walk, Mr. Toole?" inquired the maiden.

"I did so," rejoined Larry.

"Young master's just gone out," continued the maid.

"So I seen, jewel," replied Mr. Toole.

"An' you may as well come into the parlour, an' have some drink and victuals," added she, with an encouraging smile.

"Is there no fear of his coming in on me?" inquired Larry, cautiously.

"Tilly vally, man, who are you afraid of?" exclaimed the handmaiden, cheerily. "Come, Mr. Toole, you used not to be so easily frightened."

"I'll never be afraid to folly your lead, most beautiful and bewildhering iv famales," ejaculated Mr. Toole, gallantly. "So here goes; folly on, and I'll attind you behind."

Accordingly, they both entered the great parlour, where the table bore abundant relics of a plenteous meal, and Mistress Betsy Carey, with her own fair hands, placed a chair for him at the table, and heaping a plate with cold beef and bread, laid it before her grateful swain, along with a foaming tankard of humming ale. The maid was gracious, and the beef delicious; his ears drank in her accents, and his throat her ale, and his heart and mouth were equally full. Thus, in a condition as nearly as human happiness can approach to unalloyed felicity, realizing the substantial bliss of Mahomet's paradise, Mr. Toole ogled and ate, and glanced and guzzled in soft rapture, until the force of nature could no further go on, and laying down his knife and fork, he took one long last draught of ale, measuring, it is supposed, about three half-pints, and then, with an easy negligence, wiping the froth from his mouth with the cuff of his coat, he addressed himself to the fair dame once more,—

"They may say what they like, by the hokey! all the world over; but divil bellows me, if ever I seen sich another beautiful, fascinating, flusthrating famale, since I was the size iv that musthard pot—may the divil bile me if I did," ejaculated Mr. Toole, rapturously throwing himself into the chair with something between a sigh and a grunt, and ready to burst with love and repletion.

The fair maiden endeavoured to look contemptuous; but she smiled in spite of herself.

"Well, well, Mr. Toole," she exclaimed, "I see there is no use in talking; a fool's a fool to the end of his days, and some people's past cure. But tell me, how's Mr. O'Connor?"

"Bedad, it's time for me to think iv it," exclaimed Larry, briskly. "Do you know what brought me here?"

"How should I know?" responded she, with a careless toss of her head, and a very conscious look.

"Well," replied Mr. Toole, "I'll tell you at once. I lost the masther as clane as a new shilling, an' I'm fairly braking my heart lookin' for him; an' here I come, trying would I get the chance iv hearing some soart iv a sketch iv him."

"Is that all?" inquired the damsel, drily.

"All!" ejaculated Larry; "begorra. I think it's enough, an' something to spare. All! why, I tell you the masther's lost, an' anless I get some news of him here, it's twenty to one the two of us 'ill never meet in this disappinting world again. All! I think that something."

"An' pray, what should I know about Mr. O'Connor?" inquired the girl, tartly.

"Did you see him, or hear of him, or was he out here at all?" asked he.

"No, he wasn't. What would bring him?" replied she.

"Then he is gone in airnest," exclaimed Larry, passionately; "he's gone entirely! I half guessed it from the first minute. By jabers, my bitther curse attind that bloody little public. He's lost, an' tin to one he's in glory, for he was always unfortunate. Och! divil fly away with the liquor."

"Well, to be sure," ejaculated the lady's maid, with contemptuous severity, "but it is surprising what fools some people is. Don't you think your master can go anywhere for a day or two, but he must bring you along with him, or ask your leave and licence to go where he pleases forsooth? Marry, come up, it's enough to make a pig laugh only to listen to you."

Just at this moment, and when Larry was meditating his reply, steps were heard in the hall, and voices in debate. They were those of Nicholas Blarden and of Sir Henry Ashwoode. Larry instantly recognized the latter, and his companion both of them.

"They're coming this way," gasped Larry, with agonized alarm. "Tare an' ouns, evangelical girl, we're done for. Put me somewhere quick, or begorra it's all over with us."

"What's to be done, merciful Moses? Where can you go?" ejaculated the terrified girl, surveying the room with frantic haste. "The press. Oh! thank God, the press. Come along, quick, quick, Mr. Toole, for gracious goodness sake."

So saying, she rushed headlong at a kind of cupboard or press, whose doors opened in the panelling of the wall, and fumbling with frightful agitation among her keys, she succeeded at length in unlocking it, and throwing open its door, exhibited a small orifice of about four feet and a half by three in the wall.

"Now, Mr. Toole, into it, as you vally your precious life—quick, quick, for the love of heaven," ejaculated the maiden.

Larry was firmly persuaded that the feat was a downright physical impossibility; yet with a devotion and desperation which love and terror combined alone could inspire, he mounted a chair, and, supported by all the muscular strength of his soul's idol, scrambled into the aperture. A projecting shelf about half way up threw his figure so much out of equilibrium, that the task of keeping him in his place was no light one. By main strength, however, the girl succeeded in closing the door and locking her visitor fairly in, and before her master entered the chamber, Mr. Toole became a close prisoner, and the key which confined him was safely deposited in the charming Betsy's pocket.

Blarden roared lustily to the servants, and with sundry impressive imprecations, commanded them to remove every vestige of the breakfast of which the prisoner had just clandestinely partaken. Meanwhile he continued to walk up and down the room, whistling a lively ditty, and here and there, at particularly sprightly parts, drumming with his foot in time upon the floor.

"Well, that job's done at last," said he. "The room's clean and quiet, and we can't do better than take a twist at the cards. So let's have a pack, and play your best, d'ye mind."

This was addressed to Ashwoode, who, of course, acquiesced.

"Oh, bloody wars, I'm in for it," murmured Larry, "they'll be playin' here to no end, and I smothering fast, as it is; I'll never come out iv this pisition with my life."

Few situations could indeed be conceived physically more uncomfortable. A shelf projecting about midway pressed him forward, exerting anything but a soothing influence upon the backbone, so that his whole weight rested against the door of his narrow prison, and was chiefly sustained by his breast-bone and chin. In this very constrained attitude, and afraid to relieve his fatigue by moving even in the very slightest degree, lest some accidental noise should excite suspicion and betray his presence, the ill-starred squire remained; his discomforts still further enhanced by the pouring of some pickles, which had been overturned upon an upper shelf, in cool streams of vinegar down his back.

"I could not have betther luck," murmured he. "I never discoorsed a famale yet, but I paid through the nose for it. Didn't I get enough iv romance, bad luck to it, an' isn't it a plisint pisition I'm in at last—locked up in an ould cupboard in the wall, an' fairly swimming in vinegar. Oh, the women, the women. I'd rather than every stitch of cloth on my back, I walked out clever an' clane to meet the young masther, and not let myself be boxed up this way, almost dying with the cramps and the snuffication. Oh, them women, them women!"

Thus mourned our helpless friend in inarticulate murmurings. Meanwhile young Ashwoode opened two or three drawers in search of a pack of cards.

"There are several, I know, in that locker," said Ashwoode. "I laid some of them there myself."

"This one?" inquired Blarden, making the interrogatory by a sharp application of the head of his cane to the very panel against which Larry's chin was resting. The shock, the pain, and the exaggerated loudness of the application caused the inmate of the press, in spite of himself, to ejaculate,—

"Oh, holy Pether!"

"Did you hear anything queer?" inquired Blarden, with some consternation. "Anyone calling out?"

"No," said Ashwoode.

"Well, see what the nerves is," cried Blarden, "by —, I'd have bet ten to one I heard a voice in the wall the minute I hit that locker door—this — weather don't agree with me."

This sentence he wound up by administering a second knock where he had given the first; and Larry, with set teeth and a grin, which in a horse-collar would have won whole pyramids of gingerbread, nevertheless bore it this time with the silent stoicism of a tortured Indian.

"The nerves is a — quare piece of business," observed Mr. Blarden—a philosophical remark in which Larry heartily concurred—"but get the cards, will you—what the — is all the delay about?"

In obedience to Ashwoode's summons, Mistress Betsy Carey entered the room.

"Carey," said he, "open that press and take out two or three packs of cards."

"I can't open the locker," replied she, readily, "for the young mistress put the key astray, sir—I'll run and look for it, if you please, sir."

"God bless you," murmured Larry, with fervent gratitude.

"Hand me that bunch of keys from under your apron," said Blarden, "ten to one we'll find some one among them that'll open it."

"There's no use in trying, sir," replied the girl, very much alarmed, "it's a pitiklar soart of a lock, and has a pitiklar key—you'll ruinate it, sir, if you go for to think to open it with a key that don't fit it, so you will—I'll run and look for it if you please, sir."

"Give me that bunch of keys, young woman; give them, I tell you," exclaimed Blarden.

Thus constrained, she reluctantly gave the keys, and among them the identical one to whose kind offices Mr. O'Toole owed his present dignified privacy.

"Come in here, Chancey," said Mr. Blarden, addressing that gentleman, who happened at that moment to be crossing the hall—"take these keys here and try if any of them will pick that lock."

Chancey accordingly took the keys, and mounting languidly upon a chair, began his operations.

It were not easy to describe Mr. Toole's emotions as these proceedings were going forward—some of the keys would not go in at all—others went in with great difficulty, and came out with as much—some entered easily, but refused to turn, and during the whole of these various attempts upon his "dungeon keep," his mental agonies grew momentarily more and more intense, so much so that he was repeatedly prompted to precipitate the dénouement, by shouting his confession from within. His heart failed him, however, and his resolution grew momentarily feebler and more feeble—he would have given worlds at that moment that he could have shrunk into the pickle-pot, whose contents were then streaming down his back—gladly would he have compounded for escape at the price of being metamorphosed for ever into a gherkin. His prayers were, however, unanswered, and he felt his inevitable fate momentarily approaching.

"This one will do it—I declare to God I have it at last," drawled Chancey, looking lazily at a key which he held in his hand; and then applying it, it found its way freely into the key-hole.

"Bravo, Gordy, by —," cried Blarden, "I never knew you fail yet—you're as cute as a pet fox, you are."

Mr. Blarden had hardly finished this flattering eulogium, when Chancey turned the key in the lock: with astonishing violence the doors burst open, and Larry Toole, Mr. Chancey, and the chair on which he was mounted, descended with the force of a thunderbolt on the floor. In sheer terror, Chancey clutched the interesting stranger by the throat, and Larry, in self-defence, bit the lawyer's thumb, which had by a trifling inaccuracy entered his mouth, and at the same time, with both his hands, dragged his nose in a lateral direction until it had attained an extraordinary length and breadth. In equal terror and torment the two combatants rolled breathless along the floor; the charming Betsy Carey screamed murder, robbery, and fire—while Ashwoode and Blarden both started to their feet in the extremest amazement.

"How the devil did you get into that press?" exclaimed Ashwoode, as soon as the rival athletes had been separated and placed upon their feet, addressing Larry Toole.

"Oh! the robbing villain," ejaculated Mistress Betsy Carey—"don't suffer nor allow him to speak—bring him to the pump, gentlemen—oh! the lying villain—kick him out, Mr. Chancey—thump him, Sir Henry—don't spare him, Mr. Blarden—turn him out, gentlemen all—he's quite aperiently a robber—oh! blessed hour, but it's I that ought to be thankful—what in the world wide would I do if he came powdering down on me, the overbearing savage!"

"Och! murder—the cruelty iv women!" ejaculated Larry, reproachfully—"oh! murdher, beautiful Betsy."

"Don't be talking to me, you sneaking, skulking villain," cried Mistress Carey, vehemently, "you must have stole the key, so you must, and locked yourself up, you frightful baste. For goodness gracious sake, gentlemen, don't keep him talking here—he's dangerous—the Turk."

"Oh! the villainy iv women!" repeated Larry, with deep pathos.

A brief cross-examination of Mistress Carey and of Larry Toole sufficed to convict the fair maiden of her share in concealing the prisoner.

"Now, Mr. Toole," said Ashwoode, addressing that personage, "you have been once before turned out of this house for misconduct—I tell you, that if you do not make good use of your time, and run as fast as your best exertions will enable you, you shall have abundant reason to repent it, for in five minutes more I will set the dogs after you; and if ever I find you here again, I will have you ducked in the horse-pond for a full hour—depart, sirrah—away—run."

Larry did not require any more urgent remonstrances to induce him to expedite his retreat—he made a contrite bow to Sir Henry—cast a look of melancholy reproach at the beautiful Betsy, who, with a heightened colour, was withdrawing from the scene, and then with sudden nimbleness, effected his retreat.

"The fellow," said Ashwoode, "is a servant of that O'Connor, whom I mentioned to you. I do not think we shall ever have the pleasure of his company again. I am glad the thing has happened, for it proves that we cannot trust Carey."

"That it does," echoed Blarden, with an oath.

"Well, then, she shall take her departure hence before a week," rejoined Ashwoode. "We shall see about her successor without loss of time. So much for Mistress Carey."

## CHAPTER LI

## FLORA GUY.

"Why, I thought you had done for that fellow, that O'Connor," exclaimed Blarden, after he had carefully closed the door. "I thought you had pinked him through and through like a riddle—isn't he dead—didn't you settle him?"

"So I thought myself, but some troublesome people have the art of living through what might have killed a hundred," rejoined Ashwoode; "and I do not at all like this servant of his privately coming here, to hold conference with my sister's maid—it looks suspicious; if it be, however, as I suspect, I have effectually countermined them."

"Well, then," replied Blarden, with an oath, "at all events we must set to work now in earnest."

"The first thing to be done is to find a substitute for the girl whom I am about to dismiss," said Ashwoode, "we must select carefully, one whom we can rely upon—do you choose her?"

"Why, I'm no great judge of such cattle," rejoined Blarden. "But here's Chancey that understands them. I stake this ring to a sixpence he has one in his eye this very minute that'll fit our purpose to a hair—what do you say, Gordy, boy—can you hit on the kind of wench we want—eh, you old sly boots?"

Chancey sat sleepily before the fire, and a languid, lazy smile expanded his sallow sensual face as he gazed at the bars of the grate.

"Are you tongue-tied, or what?" exclaimed Blarden; "speak out—can you find us such a one as we want? she must be a regular knowing devil, and no mistake—as sly as yourself—a dead hand at a scheming game like this—a deep one."

"Well, maybe I do," drawled Chancey, "I think I know a girl that would do, but maybe you'd think her too bad."

"She can't be too bad for the work we want her for—what the devil do you mean by BAD?" exclaimed Blarden.

"Well," continued Chancey, disregarding the last interrogatory, "she's Flora Guy, she attends in the 'Old Saint Columbkil,' a very arch little girl—I think she'll do to a nicety."

"Use your own judgment, I leave it all to you," said Blarden, "only get one at once, do you mind, you know the sort we want."

"I suppose she can't come any sooner than to-morrow, she must have notice," said Chancey, "but I'll go in there to-day if you like, and talk to her about it; I'll have her out with you here to-morrow to a certainty, an' I declare to God she's a very smart little girl."

"Do so," said Ashwoode, "and the sooner the better."

Chancey arose, stuffed his hands into his breeches pockets according to his wont, and with a long yawn lounged out of the room.

"Do you keep out of the way after this evening," continued Sir Henry, addressing himself to Blarden; "I will tell her that you are to leave us this night, and that your visit ends; this will keep her quiet until all is ready, and then she must be tractable."

"Do you run and find her, then," said Blarden, "and tell her that I'm off for town this evening—tell her at once—and mind, bring me word what she says—off with you, doctor—ho, ho, ho!—mind, bring me word what she says—do you hear?"

With this pleasant charge ringing in his ears, Sir Henry Ashwoode departed upon his honourable mission.

Chancey strolled listlessly into town, and after an easy ramble, at length found himself safe and sound once more beneath the roof of the 'Old Saint Columbkil.' He walked through the dingy deserted benches and tables of the old tavern, and seating himself near the hearth, called a greasy waiter who was dozing in a corner.

"Tim, I'm rayther dry to-day, Timothy," said Mr. Chancey, addressing the functionary, who shambled up to him more than half asleep; "what will you recommend, Timothy—what do you think of a pot of light ale?"

"Pint or quart?" inquired Tim shortly.

"Well, we'll say a pint to begin with, Timothy," said Chancey, meekly; "and do you see, Timothy, if Miss Flora Guy is on the tap; I wish she would bring it to me herself—do you mind, Timothy?"

Tim nodded and departed, and in a few minutes a brisk step was heard, and a neat, good-humoured looking wench approached Mr. Chancey, and planted a pint pot of ale before him.

"Well, my little girl," said Chancey, with the quiet dignity of a patron, "would you like to get a fine situation in a baronet's family, my dear; to be own maid to a baronet's sister, where they eat off of silver every day in the week, and have more money than you or I could count in a twelve-month?"

"Where's the good of liking it, Mr. Chancey?" replied the girl, laughing; "it's time enough to be thinking of it when I get the offer."

"Well, you have the offer this minute, my little girl," rejoined Chancey; "I have an elegant place for you—upon my conscience I have—up at Morley Court, with Sir Henry Ashwoode; he's a baronet, dear, and you're to be own maid to Miss Mary Ashwoode."

"It can't be the truth you're telling me," said the girl, in unfeigned amazement.

"I declare to G—d, and upon my soul, it is the plain truth," drawled Chancey; "Sir Henry Ashwoode, the baronet, asked me to recommend a tidy, sprightly little girl, to be own maid to his elegant, fine sister, and I recommended you—I declare to G—d but I did, and I come in to-day from the baronet's house to hire you, so I did."

"Well, an' is it in airnest you are?" said the girl.

"What I'm telling you is the rale truth," rejoined Chancey: "I declare to G—d upon my soul and conscience, and I wouldn't swear that in a lie, if you like to take the place you can get it."

"Well, well, after that—why, my fortune's made," cried the girl, in ecstasies.

"It is so, indeed, my little girl," rejoined Chancey; "your fortune's made, sure enough."

"An' my dream's out, too; for I was dreaming of nothing but washing, and that's a sure sign of a change, all the live-long night," cried she, "washing linen, and such lots of it, all heaped up; well, I'm a sharp dreamer—ain't I, though?"

"You will take it, then?" inquired Chancey.

"Will I—maybe I won't," rejoined she.

"Well, come out to-morrow," said Chancey.

"I can't to-morrow," replied she; "for all the table-cloth is to be done, an' I would not like to disappoint the master after being with him so long."

"Well, can you next day?"

"I can," replied she; "tell me where it is."

"Do you know Tony Bligh's public—the old 'Bleeding Horse?'" inquired he.

"I do—right well," she rejoined with alacrity.

"They'll direct you there," said Chancey; "ask for the manor of Morley Court; it's a great old brick house, you can see it a mile away, and whole acres of wood round it—it's a wonderful fine place, so it is; remember it's Sir Henry himself you're to see when you go there; an' do you mind what I'm saying to you, if I hear that you were talking and prating about the place here to the chaps that's idling about, or to old Pottles, or the sluts of maids, or, in short, to anyone at all, good or bad, you'll be sure to lose the situation; so mind my advice, like a good little girl, and don't be talking to any of them about where you're going; for it wouldn't look respectable for a baronet to be hiring his servants out of a tavern—do you mind me, dear."

"Oh, never fear me, Mr. Chancey," she rejoined; "I'll not say a word to a living soul; but I hope there's no fear the place will be taken before me, by not going to-morrow."

"Oh! dear me! no fear at all, I'll keep it open for you; now be a good girl, and remember, don't disappoint."

So saying he drained his pot of ale to the last drop, and took his departure in the pleasing conviction that he had secured the services of a fitting instrument to carry out the infernal schemes of his employers.

CHAPTER LII.

OF MARY ASHWOODE'S WALK TO THE LONESOME WELL—AND OF WHAT SHE SAW THERE—AND SHOWING HOW SCHEMES OF PERIL BEGAN TO CLOSE AROUND HER.

On the following evening, Mary Ashwoode, in the happy conviction that Nicholas Blarden was far away, and for ever removed from her neighbourhood, walked forth at the fall of the evening unattended, to ramble among the sequestered, but now almost leafless woods, which richly ornamented the old place. Through sloping woodlands, among the stately trees and wild straggling brushwood, now densely crowded together, and again opening in broad vistas and showing the level sward, and then again enclosing her amid the gnarled and hoary trunks and fantastic boughs, all touched with the mellow golden hue of the rich lingering light of evening, she wandered on, now treading the smooth sod among the branching roots, now stepping from mossy stone to stone across the wayward brook—now pausing on a gentle eminence to admire the glowing sky and the thin haze of evening, mellowing all the distant shadowy outlines of the landscape; and by all she saw at every step beguiled into forgetfulness of the distance to which she had wandered.

She now approached what had been once a favourite spot with her. In a gentle slope, and almost enclosed by wooded banks, was a small clear well, an ancient lichen-covered arch enclosed it; and all around in untended wildness grew the rugged thorn and dwarf oak, crowding around it with a friendly pressure, and embowering its dark clear waters with their ivy-clothed limbs; close by it stood a tall and graceful ash, and among its roots was placed a little rustic bench where, in happier times, Mary had often sat and read through the pleasant summer hours; and now, alas! there was the little seat and there the gnarled roots and the hoary stems of the wild trees, and the graceful ivy clusters, and the time-worn mossy arch that vaulted the clear waters bubbling so joyously beneath; how could she look on these old familiar friends, and not feel what all who with changed hearts and altered fortunes revisit the scenes of happier times are doomed to feel?

For a moment she paused and stood lost in vain and bitter regrets by the old well-side. Her reverie was, however, soon and suddenly interrupted by the sound of something moving among the brittle brushwood close by; she looked quickly in the direction of the noise, and though the light had now almost entirely failed, she yet discovered, too clearly to be mistaken, the head and shoulders of Nicholas Blarden, as he pushed his way among the bushes toward the very spot where she stood. With an involuntary cry of terror she turned, and running at her utmost speed, retraced her steps toward the old mansion; not daring even to look behind her, she pursued her way among the deepening shadows of the old trees with the swiftness of terror; and, as she ran, her fears were momentarily enhanced by the sound of heavy foot-falls in pursuit, accompanied by the loud short breathing of one exerting his utmost speed. On—on she flew with dizzy haste; the distance seemed interminable, and her exhaustion was such that she felt momentarily tempted to forego the hopeless effort, and surrender herself to the mercy of her pursuer. At length she approached the old house—the sounds behind her abated; she thought she heard hoarse volleys of muttered imprecations, but not hazarding even a look behind, she still held on her way, and at length, almost wild with fear, entered the hall and threw herself sobbing into her brother's arms.

"Oh God! brother; he's here; am I safe?" and she burst into hysterical sobs.

As soon as she was a little calmed, he asked her,—

"What has alarmed you, Mary; what have you seen to agitate you so?"

"Oh! brother; have you deceived me; is that fearful man still an inmate of the house?" she said.

"No; I tell you no," replied Ashwoode, "he's gone; his visit ended with yesterday evening; he's fifty miles away by this time; tut—tut—folly, child; you must not be so fanciful."

"Well, brother, he has deceived you," she rejoined, with the earnestness of terror; "he is not gone; he is about this place; so surely as you stand there, I saw him; and, O God! he pursued me, and had my strength faltered for a moment, or my foot slipped, I should have been in his power;" she leaned down her head and clasped her hands across her eyes, as if to exclude some image of horror.

"This is mere raving, child," said Ashwoode, "the veriest folly; I tell you the man is gone; you heard, if anything at all, a dog or a hare springing through the leaves, and your imagination supplied the rest. I tell you, once for all, that Blarden is threescore good miles away."

"Brother, as surely as I see you, I saw him this night," she replied. "I could not be mistaken; I saw him, and for several seconds before I could move, such was the palsy of terror that struck me. I saw him, and watched him advancing towards me—gracious heaven! for while I could reckon ten; and then, as I fled, he still pursued; he was so near that I actually heard his panting, as well as the tread of his feet;—brother—brother—there was no mistake; there could be none in this."

"Well, be it so, since you will have it," replied Ashwoode, trying to laugh it off; "you have seen his fetch—I think they call it so. I'll not dispute the matter with you; but this I will aver, that his corporeal presence is removed some fifty miles from hence at this moment; take some tea and get you to bed, child; you have got a fit of the vapours; you'll laugh at your own foolish fancies to-morrow morning."

That night Sir Henry Ashwoode, Nicholas Blarden, and their worthy confederate, Gordon Chancey, were closeted together in earnest and secret consultation in the parlour.

"Why did you act so rashly—what could have possessed you to follow the girl?" asked Ashwoode, "you have managed one way or another so thoroughly to frighten the girl, to make her so fear and avoid you, that I entirely despair, by fair means, of ever inducing her to listen to your proposals."

"Well, that does not take me altogether by surprise," said Blarden, "for I have been suspecting so much this many a day; we must then go to work in right earnest at once."

"What measures shall we take?" said Ashwoode.

"What measures!" echoed Blarden; "well, confound me if I know what to begin with, there's such a lot of them, and all good—what do you say, Gordy?"

"You ought to ask her to marry you off-hand," said Chancey, demurely, but promptly; "and if she refuses, let her be locked up, and treat her as if she was mad—do you mind; and I'll go to Patrick's-close, and bring out old Shycock, the clergyman; and the minute she strikes, you can be coupled; she'll give in very soon, you'll find; little Ebenezer will do whatever we bid him, and swear whatever we like; we'll all swear that you and she are man and wife already; and when she denies it, threaten her with the mad-house; and then we'll see if she won't come round; and you must first send away the old servants—every mother's skin of them—and get new ones instead; and that's my advice."

"It's not bad, either," said Blarden, knitting his brows twice or thrice, and setting his teeth. "I like that notion of threatening her with Bedlam; it's a devilish good idea; and I'll give long odds it will work wonders; what do you say, Ashwoode?"

"Choose your own measures," replied the baronet. "I'm incapable of advising you."

"Well, then, Gordy, that's the go," said Blarden; "bring out his reverence whenever I tip you the signal; and he shall have board and lodging until the job's done; he'll make a tip-top domestic chaplain; I suppose we'll have family prayers while he stays—eh?—ho, ho!—devilish good idea, that; and Chancey'll act clerk—eh? won't you, Gordy?" and, tickled beyond measure at the facetious suggestion, Mr. Blarden laughed long and lustily.

"I suppose I may as well keep close until our private chaplain arrives, and the new waiting-maid," said Blarden; "and as soon as all is ready, I'll blaze out in style, and I'll tell you what, Ashwoode, a precious good thought strikes me; turn about you know is fair play; and as I'm fifty miles away to-day, it occurs to me it would be a deuced good plan to have you fifty miles away to-morrow—eh?—we could manage matters better if you were supposed out of the way, and that she knew I had the whole command of the house, and everything in it; she'd be a cursed deal more frightened; what do you think?"

"Yes, I entirely agree with you," said Ashwoode, eagerly catching at a scheme which would relieve him of all prominent participation in the infamous proceedings—an exemption which, spite of his utter selfishness, he gladly snatched at. "I will do so. I will leave the house in reality."

"No—no; my tight chap, not so fast," rejoined Blarden, with a savage chuckle. "I'd rather have my eye on you, if you please; just write her a letter, dated from Dublin, and say you're obliged to go anywhere you please for a month or so; she'll not find you out, for we'll not let her out of her room; and now I think everything is settled to a turn, and we may as well get under the blankets at once, and be stirring betimes in the morning."


CHAPTER LIII.

THE DOUBLE FAREWELL.

Next day Mistress Betsy Carey bustled into her young mistress's chamber looking very red and excited.

"Well, ma'am," said she, dropping a short indignant courtesy, "I'm come to bid you good-bye, ma'am."

"How—what can you mean, Carey?" said Mary Ashwoode.

"I hope them as comes after me," continued the handmaiden, vehemently, "will strive to please you in all pints and manners as well as them that's going."

"Going!" echoed Mary; "why, this can't be—there must be some great mistake here."

"No mistake at all, ma'am, of any sort or description; the master has just paid up my wages, and gave me my discharge," rejoined the maid. "Oh, the ingratitude of some people to their servants is past bearing, so it is."

And so saying, Mistress Carey burst into a passion of tears.

"There is some mistake in all this, my poor Carey," said the young lady; "I will speak to my brother about it immediately; don't cry so."

"Oh! my lady, it ain't for myself I'm crying; the blessed saints in heaven knows it ain't," cried the beautiful Betsy, glancing devotionally upward through her tears; "not at all and by no means, ma'am, it's all for other people, so it is, my lady; oh! ma'am, you don't know the badness and the villainy of people, my lady."

"Don't cry so, Carey," replied Mary Ashwoode, "but tell me frankly what fault you have committed—let me know why my brother has discharged you."

"Just because he thinks I'm too fond of you, my lady, and too honest for what's going on," cried she, drying her eyes in her apron with angry vehemence, and speaking with extraordinary sharpness and volubility; "because I saw Mr. O'Connor's man yesterday—and found out that the young gentleman's letters used to be stopped by the old master, God rest him, and Sir Henry, and all kinds of false letters written to him and to you by themselves, to breed mischief between you. I never knew the reason before, why in the world it was the master used to make me leave every letter that went between you, for a day or more in his keeping. Heaven be his bed; I was too innocent for them, my lady; we were both of us too simple; oh dear! oh dear! it's a quare world, my lady. And that wasn't all—but who do you think I meets to-day skulking about the house in company with the young master, but Mr. Blarden, that we all thought, glory be to God, was I don't know how far off out of the place; and so, my lady, because them things has come to my knowledge, and because they knowed in their hearts, so they did, that I'd rayther be crucified than hide as much as the black of my nail from you, my lady, they put me away, thinking to keep you in the dark. Oh! but it's a dangerous, bad world, so it is—to put me out of the way of tellin' you whatever I knowed; and all I'm hoping for is, that them that's coming in my room won't help the mischief, and try to blind you to what's going on;" hereupon she again burst into a flood of tears.

"Good God," said Mary Ashwoode, in the low tones of horror, and with a face as pale as marble, "is that dreadful man here—have you seen him?"

"Yes, my lady, seen and talked with him, my lady, not ten minutes since," replied the maid, "and he gave me a guinea, and told me not to let on that I seen him—he did—but he little knew who he was speaking to—oh! ma'am, but it's a terrible shocking bad world, so it is."

Mary Ashwoode leaned her head upon her hand in fearful agitation. This ruffian, who had menaced and insulted and pursued her, a single glance at whose guilty and frightful aspect was enough to warn and terrify, was in league and close alliance with her own brother to entrap and deceive her—Heaven only could know with what horrible intent.

"Carey, Carey," said the pale and affrighted lady, "for God's sake send my brother—bring him here—I must see Sir Henry, your master—quickly, Carey—for God's sake quickly."

The young lady again leaned her head upon her hand and became silent; so the lady's maid dried her eyes, and left the room to execute her mission.

The apartment in which Mary Ashwoode was now seated, was a small dressing-room or boudoir, which communicated with her bed-chamber, and itself opened upon a large wainscotted lobby, surrounded with doors, and hung with portraits, too dingy and faded to have a place in the lower rooms. She had thus an opportunity of hearing any step which ascended the stairs, and waited, in breathless expectation, for the sounds of her brother's approach. As the interval was prolonged her impatience increased, and again and again she was tempted to go down stairs and seek him herself; but the dread of encountering Blarden, and the terror in which she held him, kept her trembling in her room. At length she heard two persons approach, and her heart swelled almost to bursting, as, with excited anticipation, she listened to their advance.

"Here's the room for you at last," said the voice of an old female servant, who forthwith turned and departed.

"I thank you kindly, ma'am," said the second voice, also that of a female, and the sentence was immediately followed by a low, timid knock at the chamber door.

"Come in," said Mary Ashwoode, relieved by the consciousness that her first fears had been delusive—and a good-looking wench, with rosy cheeks, and a clear, good-humoured eye, timidly and hesitatingly entered the room, and dropped a bashful courtesy.

"Who are you, my good girl, and what do you want with me?" inquired Mary, gently.

"I'm the new maid, please your ladyship, that Sir Henry Ashwoode hired, if it pleases you, ma'am, instead of the young woman that's just gone away," replied she, her eyes staring wider and wider, and her cheeks flushing redder and redder every moment, while she made another courtesy more energetic than the first.

"And what is your name, my good girl?" inquired Mary.

"Flora Guy, may it please your ladyship," replied the newcomer, with another courtesy.

"Well, Flora," said her new mistress, "have you ever been in service before?"

"No, ma'am, if you please," replied she, "unless in the old Saint Columbkil."

"The old Saint Columbkil," rejoined Mary. "What is that, my good girl?"

The ignorance implied in this question was so incredibly absurd, that spite of all her fears and all her modesty, the girl smiled, and looked down upon the floor, and then coloured to the eyes at her own presumption.

"It's the great wine-tavern and eating-house, ma'am, in Ship Street, if you please," rejoined she.

"And who hired you?" inquired Mary, in undisguised surprise.

"It was Mr. Chancey, ma'am—the lawyer gentleman, please your ladyship," answered she.

"Mr. Chancey!—I never heard of him before," said the young lady, more and more astonished. "Have you seen Sir Henry—my brother?"

"Oh! yes, my lady, if you please—I saw him and the other gentleman just before I came upstairs, ma'am," replied the maid.

"What other gentleman?" inquired Mary, faintly.

"I think Sir Henry was the young gentleman in the frock suit of sky-blue and silver, ma'am—a nice young gentleman, ma'am—and there was another gentleman, my lady, with him; he had a plum-coloured suit with gold lace; he spoke very loud, and cursed a great deal; a large gentleman, my lady, with a very red face, and one of his teeth out. I seen him once in the tap-room. I remembered him the minute I set eyes on him, but I can't think of his name. He came in, my lady, with that young lord—I forget his name, too—that was ruined with play and dicing, my lady; and they had a quart of mulled sack—it was I that brought it to them—and I remembered the red-faced gentleman very well, for he was turning round over his shoulder, and putting out his tongue, making fun of the young lord—because he was tipsy—and winking to his own friends."

"What did my brother—Sir Henry—your master—what did he say to you just now?" inquired Mary, faintly, and scarcely conscious what she said.

"He gave me a bit of a note to your ladyship," said the girl, fumbling in the profundity of her pocket for it, "just as soon as he put the other girl—her that's gone, my lady—into the chaise—here it is, ma'am, if you please."

Mary took the letter, opened it hurriedly, and with eyes unsteady with agitation, read as follows:—

"MY DEAR MARY,—I am compelled to fly as fast as horseflesh can carry me, to escape arrest and the entire loss of whatever little chance remains of averting ruin. I don't see you before leaving this—my doing so were alike painful to us both—perhaps I shall be here again by the end of a month—at all events, you shall hear of me some time before I arrive. I have had to discharge Carey for very ill-conduct I have not time to write fully now. I have hired in her stead the bearer, Flora Guy, a very respectable, good girl. I shall have made at least two miles away in my flight before you read this. Perhaps you had better keep within your own room, for Mr. Blarden will shortly be here to look after matters in my absence. I have hardly a moment to scratch this line.

"Always your attached brother,

"HENRY ASHWOODE."

Her eye had hardly glanced through this production when she ran wildly toward the door; but, checking herself before she reached it, she turned to the girl, and with an earnestness of agony which thrilled to her very heart, she cried,—

"Is he gone? tell me, as you hope for mercy, is he—is he gone?"

"Who, who is it, my lady?" inquired the girl, a good deal startled.

"My brother—my brother: is he gone?" cried she more wildly still.

"I seen him riding away very fast on a grey horse, my lady," said the maid, "not five minutes before I came up stairs."

"Then it's too late. God be merciful to me! I am lost, I have none to guard me; I have none to help me—don't—don't leave me; for God's sake don't leave the room for one instant——"

There was an imploring earnestness of entreaty in the young lady's accents and manner, and a degree of excited terror in her dilated eyes and pale face, which absolutely affrighted the attendant.

"No, my lady," said she, "I won't leave you, I won't indeed, my lady."

"Oh! my poor girl," said Mary, "you little know the griefs and fears of her you've come to serve. I fear me you have changed your lot, however hard before, much for the worst in coming here; never yet did creature need a friend so much as I; and never was one so friendless before," and thus speaking, poor Mary Ashwoode leaned forward and wept so bitterly that the girl was almost constrained to weep too for very pity.

"Don't take it to heart so much, my lady; don't cry. I'll do my best, my lady, to serve you well; indeed I will, my lady, and true and faithful," said the poor damsel, approaching timidly but kindly to her young mistress's side. "I'll not leave you, my lady; no one shall harm you nor hurt a hair of your head; I'll stay with you night and day as long as you're pleased to keep me, my lady, and don't cry; sure you won't, my lady?"

So the poor girl in her own simple way strove to comfort and encourage her desolate mistress.

It is a wonderful and a beautiful thing how surely, spite of every difference of rank and kind and forms of language, the words of kindness and of sympathy—be they the rudest ever spoken, if only they flow warm from the heart of a fellow-mortal—will gladden, comfort, and cheer the sorrow-stricken spirit. Mary felt comforted and assured.

"Do you be but true to me; stay by my side in this season of my sorest trouble; and may God reward you as richly as I would my poor means could," said Mary, with the same intense earnestness of entreaty. "There is kindness and truth in your face. I am sure you will not deceive me."

"Deceive you, my lady! God forbid," said the poor maid, earnestly; "I'd die before I'd deceive you; only tell me how to serve you, my lady, and it will be a hard thing that I won't do for you."

"There is no need to conceal from you what, if you do not already know, you soon must," said Mary, speaking in a low tone, as if fearful of being overheard; "that red-faced man you spoke of, that talked so loud and swore so much, that man I fear—fear him more than ever yet I dreaded any living thing—more than I thought I could fear anything earthly—him, this Mr. Blarden, we must avoid."

"Blarden—Mr. Blarden," said the maid, while a new light dawned upon her mind. "I could not think of his name—Nicholas Blarden—Tommy, that is one of the waiters in the 'Columbkil,' my lady, used to call him 'red ruin.' I know it all now, my lady; it's he that owns the great gaming house near High Street, my lady; and another in Smock Alley; I heard Mr. Pottles say he could buy and sell half Dublin, he's mighty rich, but everyone says he's a very bad man: I couldn't think of his name, and I remember everything about him now; it's all found out. Oh! dear—dear; then it's all a lie; just what I thought, every bit from beginning to end—nothing else but a lie. Oh, the villain!"

"What lie do you speak of?" asked Mary; "tell me."

"Oh, the villain!" repeated the girl. "I wish to God, my lady, you were safe out of this house——"

"What is it?" urged Mary, with fearful eagerness; "what lie did you speak of? what makes you now think my danger greater?"

"Oh! my lady, the lies, the horrible lies he told me to-day, when Sir Henry and himself were hiring me," replied she. "Oh! my lady, I'm sure you are not safe here——"

"For God's sake tell me plainly, what did they say?" repeated Mary.

"Oh, ma'am, what do you think he told me? As sure as you're sitting there, he told me he was a mad-doctor," replied she; "and he said, my lady, how that you were not in your right mind, and that he had the care of you; and, oh, my God, my lady, he told me never to be frightened if I heard you crying out and screaming when he was alone with you, for that all mad people was the same way——"

"And was Sir Henry present when he told you this?" said Mary, scarce articulately.

"He was, my lady," replied she, "and I thought he turned pale when the red-faced man said that; but he did not speak, only kept biting his lips and saying nothing."

"Then, indeed, my case is hopeless," said Mary, faintly, while all expression, save that of vacant terror, faded from her face; "give me some counsel—advise me, for God's sake, in this terrible hour. What shall I do?"

"Ah, my lady, I wish to the blessed saints I could," rejoined the girl; "haven't you some friends in Dublin; couldn't I go for them?"

"No—no," said she, hastily, "you must not leave me; but, thank God, you have advised me well. I have one friend, and indeed only one, in Dublin, whom I may rely upon, my uncle, Major O'Leary; I will write to him."

She sat down, and with cold trembling hands traced the hurried lines which implored his succour; she then rang the bell. After some delay it was answered by a strange servant; and, after a few brief inquiries, to her unutterable horror she learned that all who remained of the old faithful servants of the family had been dismissed, and persons whose faces she had never seen before, hired in their stead.

These were prompt and decisive measures, and ominously portended some sinister catastrophe; the whole establishment reduced to a few strangers, and—as she had too much reason to fear—tools and creatures of the wretch Blarden. Having ascertained these facts, Mary Ashwoode, without giving the letter to the man, dismissed him with some trivial direction, and turning to her maid, said,—

"You see how it is; I am beset by enemies; may God protect and save me; what shall I do? my mind—my senses, will forsake me. Merciful heaven! what will become of me?"

"Shall I take it myself, my lady?" inquired the maid.

Mary raised herself eagerly, but with sudden dejection, said,—

"No—no; it cannot be; you must not leave me. I could not bear to be alone here; besides, they must not think you are my friend; no, no, it cannot be."

"Well, my lady," said the maid decisively, "we'll leave the house to-night; they'll not be on their guard against that, and once beyond the walls, you're safe."

"It is, I believe, the only chance of safety left me," replied Mary, distractedly; "and, as such, it shall be tried."


CHAPTER LIV.

THE TWO CHANCES—THE BRIBED COURIER.

"I don't half like the girl you've picked up," said Nicholas Blarden, addressing his favourite parasite, Chancey; "she don't look half sharp enough for our work; she hasn't the cut of a town lass about her; she's too like a milk-maid, too simple, too soft. I've confounded misgivings she's no schemer."

"Well, well—dear me, but you're very suspicious," said Chancey. "I'd like to know did ever anything honest come out of the 'Old Saint Columbkill!' there wasn't a sharper little wench in the place than herself, and I'll tell you that's a big word—no, no; there's not an inch of the fool about her."

"Well, she can't do us much mischief anyway," said Blarden; "the three others are as true as steel—the devil's own chickens; and mind you don't let the door-keys out of your pocket. Honour's all very fine, and ought not to be doubted; but there's nothing to my mind like a stiff bit of a rusty lock."

Chancey smiled sleepily, and slapped the broad skirt of his coat twice or thrice, producing therefrom the ringing clank which betoken the presence of the keys in question.

"So then we're all caged, by Jove," continued Blarden, rapturously; "and very different sorts of game we are too: did you ever see the show-box where the cats and the rats and the little birds are all boxed up together, higgledy-piggledy, in the same wire cage. I can't but think of it; it's so devilish like."

"Well, well—dear me; I declare to God but you're a terrible funny chap," said Chancey, enjoying a quiet chuckle; "but some way or another," he continued, significantly, "I'm thinking the cat will have a claw at the little bird yet."

"Well, maybe it will;" rejoined Blarden, "you never knew one yet that was not fond of a tit-bit when he could have it. Eh?"

Thus playfully they conversed, seasoning their pleasantries with sack and claret, and whatever else the cellars of Morley Court afforded, until evening closed, and the darkness of night succeeded.

Mary Ashwoode and her maid sat prepared for the execution of their adventurous project; they had early left the outer room in which we saw them last, and retired into her bedchamber to avoid suspicion; as the night advanced they extinguished the lights, lest their gleaming through the windows should betray the lateness of their vigil, and alarm the fears of their persecutors. Thus, in silence and darkness, not daring to speak, and almost afraid to breathe, they waited hour after hour until long past midnight. The well-known sounds of riotous swearing and horse-laughter, and the heavy trampling of feet, as the half-drunken revellers staggered to their beds, now reached their ears in noises faint and muffled by the distance. At length all was again quiet, and nearly a whole hour of silence passed away ere they ventured to move, almost to breathe.

"Now, Flora, open the outer door softly," whispered Mary, "and listen for any, the faintest sound; take off your shoes, and for your life move noiselessly."

"Never fear, my lady," responded the girl in a tone as low; and slipping off her shoes from her feet, she pressed her hand upon the young lady's wrist, to intimate silence, and glided into the little boudoir. With sickening anxiety the young lady heard her cross the small chamber, now and then stumbling against some pieces of furniture and cautiously groping her way; at length the door-handle turned, and then followed a silence. After an interval of a few seconds the girl returned.

"Well, Flora," whispered Mary, eagerly, as she approached, "is all still?"

"Oh! blessed hour! my lady, the door's locked on the outside," replied the maid.

"It can't be," said Mary Ashwoode, while her very heart sank within her. "Oh! Flora, Flora—girl, don't say that."

"It is indeed, my lady—as sure as I'm a living soul, it is so," replied she fearfully; "and it was wide open when I came up. Oh! blessed hour! my lady, what are we to do?"

"I will try; I will see; perhaps you are mistaken. God grant you may be," said the young lady, making her way to the door which opened on to the lobby. She reached it—turned the handle—pressed it with all her feeble strength, but in vain; it was indeed securely locked upon the outside; her project of escape was baffled at the very outset, and with a heart-sickening sense of terror and dismay—such as she had never felt before—she returned with her attendant to her chamber.

A night, sleepless, except for a few brief and fevered slumbers, crowded with terrors, passed heavily away, and the morning found Mary Ashwoode, pale, nervous, and feverish. She resolved, at whatever hazard, to endeavour to induce one of the new servants to convey her letter to Major O'Leary. The detection of this attempt could at worst result in nothing worse than to precipitate whatever mischief Blarden and his confederates had plotted, and which would if not so speedily, at all events as surely overtake her, were no such attempt made.

"Flora," said she, "I am resolved to try this chance, I fear me it is but a poor one; you, however, my poor girl, must not be compromised should it fail; you must not be exposed by your faithfulness to the vengeance of these villains; do you go into the next room, and I will try what may be done."

So saying, she rang the bell, and in a few minutes it was answered by the same man who had obeyed her summons on the day before. The man, although arrayed in livery, had by no means the dapper air of a professed footman, and possessed rather a villainous countenance than otherwise; he stood at the door with one hand fumbling at the handle, while he asked with an air half gruff and half awkward what she wanted. She sat in silence for a minute like the enchanter whose spells have been for the first time answered by the appearance of the familiar; too much agitated and affrighted to utter her mandate; with a violent effort she mastered her trepidation, and with an appearance of self-possession and carelessness which she was far from feeling, she said,—

"Can you, my good man, find a trusty messenger to carry a letter for me to a friend in Dublin?"

The man remained silent for some seconds, twisted his mouth into several strange contortions, and looked very hard indeed at her. At length he said, closing the door at the same time, and speaking in a low key,—

"Well, I don't say but I might find one, but there's a great many things would make it very costly; maybe you could not afford to pay him?"

"I could—I would—see here," and she took a diamond ring from her finger; "this is a diamond; it is of value—convey but this letter safely and it is yours."

The man took the ring from the table where she laid it, and examined it curiously.

"It's a pretty ring—it is," said he, removing it a little from his eye, and turning it in different directions so as to make it flash and sparkle in the light, "it is a pretty ring, rayther small for my fingers, though—it's a real diamond?"

"It is indeed, valuable—worth forty pounds at least," she replied.

"Well, then, here goes, it's worth a bit of a risk," and so saying he deposited it carefully in a corner of his waistcoat pocket, "give me the letter now, ma'am."

She handed him the letter, and he thrust it into the deepest abyss of his breeches pocket.

"Deliver that letter but safely," said she, "and what I have given you shall be but the earnest of what's to come, it is important—urgent—execute but the mission truly, and I will not spare rewards."

The man gave two short nods of huge significance, accompanied with a slight grunt.

"I say again, let me but have assurance that the message has been done," repeated she, "and you shall have abundant reason to rejoice, above all things dispatch—and—and—secrecy."

The man winked very hard with one eye, and at the same time with his crooked finger drew his nose so much on one side, that he seemed intent on removing that feature into exile somewhere about the region of his ear; and having performed this elegant and expressive pantomime for several seconds, he stooped forward, and in an emphatic whisper said,—

"Ne-ver fear."

He then opened the door and abruptly made his exit, leaving poor Mary Ashwoode full of agitating hopes.


## CHAPTER LV.

### THE FEARFUL VISITANT.

Two or three days had passed, during which Mary had ascertained the fact that every door affording egress from the house was kept constantly locked, and that the new servants, as well as Blarden and his companions, were perpetually on the alert, and traversing the lower apartments, so that even had the door of the mansion laid open it would have been impossible to attempt an escape without encountering some one of those whose chief object was to keep her in close confinement, perhaps the very man from whose presence her inmost soul shrank in terror—she felt, therefore, that she was as effectually and as helplessly a prisoner as if she lay in the dungeons of a gaol.

Often again had she endeavoured to see the man to whom she had confided her letter to Major O'Leary, but in vain; her summons was invariably answered by the others, and fearing to excite suspicion, she, of course, did not inquire for him, and so, after a time, desisted from her endeavours.

Her window commanded a partial view of the old shaded avenue, and hour after hour would she sit at her casement, watching in vain for the longed-for appearance of her uncle, and listening, as fruitlessly, for the clang of his horse's hoofs upon the stony court.

"Oh! Flora, will he ever come?" she would exclaim, with a voice of anguish, "will he ever—ever come to deliver me from this horrible thraldom? I watch in vain, from the light of early dawn till darkness comes—I watch in vain, for the welcome sight of my friend—in vain—in vain I listen for the sound of his approach—heaven pity me, where shall I turn for hope—all—all have forsaken me—all that ever I loved have fallen from me, and left me desolate in this extremity—has he, too, my last friend, forsaken me—will they leave me here to misery—oh, that I might lay me down where head and heart are troubled no more, and be at rest in the cold grave. He'll never come—no—no—no—never."

Then she would wring her hands, still gazing from the casement, and hopelessly sob and weep.

She knew not why it was that Nicholas Blarden had suffered her, for a day or two, to be exempt from the dreaded intrusions of his hated presence. But this afforded her little comfort; she knew not how soon—at what moment—the monster might choose to present himself before her under circumstances of horror so dreadful as those of her present friendless and forsaken abandonment to his mercy—and when these imminent fears were for an instant hushed, a thousand agonizing thoughts, arising from the partial revelations of her late servant, Carey, occupied her mind. That the correspondence between her and O'Connor had been falsified—she dreaded, yet she hoped it might be true—she feared, yet prayed it might be so—and while the thought that others had wrought their estrangement, and that the coolness of indifference had not touched the heart of him she so fondly loved visited her mind, a thousand bright, but momentary hopes, fluttered her poor heart, and, for an instant, her dangers and her fears were all forgotten.

The day had passed, and its broad, clear light had given place to the red, dusky glow of sunset, when Mary Ashwoode heard the measured tread of several persons approaching her room. With an instinctive consciousness of her peril, she started to her feet, while every tinge of colour fled entirely from her cheeks.

"Flora—stay by me—oh, God, they are coming!" she said, and the words had hardly escaped her lips, when the door of the boudoir, in which she stood, was pushed open, and Nicholas Blarden, followed by Gordon Chancey, entered the room. There was in the countenance of Blarden none of his usual affectation of good humour; on the contrary, it wore a scowl of undisguised and formidable menace, the effect of which was enhanced by the baleful significance of the malignant glance which he fixed upon her, and as he stood there biting his lips in ominous silence, and gazing with savage, gloating eyes, upon the affrighted girl, it were not easy to imagine an apparition more intimidating and hideous. Even Chancey seemed a little uneasy in the anticipation of what was coming, and the sallow face of the barrister looked more than usually sallow, and his glittering eyes more glossy than ever.

"Go out of the room, you—do you mind," said Blarden, grimly, addressing Flora Guy, who had placed herself a little in advance of her young mistress, and who stood mute and thunderstruck, looking upon the two intruders—"are you palsied, or what—quit the room when I command you, you brimstone fool;" and he clutched her by the shoulder, and thrust her headlong out of the chamber, flinging the door to, with a crash that made the walls ring again.

"Listen to me and mind me, and weigh my words, or you'll rue it," said he, with a tremendous oath, addressing himself to the speechless and terrified lady. "I have a bit of information to give you, and then a bit of advice after it; you must know it's my intention we shall be married; mind me, married to-morrow evening; I know you don't like it; but I do, and that's enough for my purpose; and whenever I make my mind up to a thing, there is not that power in earth, or heaven, or hell, to turn me from it. I was always considered a tough sort of a chap when I was in earnest about anything; and I can tell you I'm mighty well in earnest here; and now you may as well know how completely I have you under my thumb; there is not a servant in the house that does not belong to me; there is not a door in the house but the key of it is in my keeping; there is not a word spoken in the house but I hear it, nor a thing done that I don't know of it, and here's your letter for you," he shouted, and flung her letter to Major O'Leary open before her on the table. "How dare you tamper with my servant's honesty? how dare you?" thundered he, with a stamp upon the floor which made the ornaments on the cabinet dance and jingle; "but mind how you try it again—beware; mind how you offer to bribe them again; I give you fair warning; you're my property now—to do what I like with, just as much as my horse or my dog; and if you won't obey me, why I'll find a way to make you; to-morrow evening I'll have a parson here, and we'll be buckled; make no rout about it, and it will be better for you, for whatever you do or say, if I had to get you into a strait-waistcoat and clap a plaister over your mouth to keep you quiet, married we shall be; husband and wife, and plenty of witnesses to vouch for it; do you understand me, and no mistake; and if you're foolish enough to make a row about it, I'll tell you what I'll do in such a case," and he fixed his eyes with a still more horrible expression upon her. "I have a particular friend, do you mind—a very obliging, particular old friend that's a mad-doctor; do you hear me; not a very lucky one to be sure, for he has made devilish few cures; a mad-doctor, do you mind?—and I'll have him to reside here and superintend your treatment; do you hear me? don't stand gaping there like an idiot; do you hear me?"

Blarden during this address had advanced into the room and stood by the little table, leaning his knuckles upon it, and stooping forward and advancing his menacing and hideous face, so as to diminish still further the intervening distance, when, all on a sudden, like a startled bird, she darted across the room, and ere they had time to interpose, had opened the door, and was half-way across the lobby; she passed Flora Guy, who was sobbing at the door with her apron to her eyes, and at the head of the stairs beheld Sir Henry Ashwoode, no less confounded at the rencounter than was she herself.

"My brother! my brother!" she shrieked, and threw herself fainting into his arms.

Spite of all that was base in his character, the young man was so shocked and confounded that he turned pale as death, and speech and recollection for a moment forsook him.

Almost at the same instant Chancey and Blarden were at his side.

"What the devil ails you?" said Blarden, furiously, addressing Ashwoode, "what do you stand there hugging her for, you white-faced idiot?"

Ashwoode's lips moved; but he could not speak, and the senseless burden still lay in his arms.

"Let her go, will you, you damned oaf? take hold of the girl, Chancey, and you, you idiot, come here and lend a hand; carry her into her room, and mind, sweet lips, keep the key in your pocket; and if you want help tatter the bells; get down, will you, you moon-struck fool?" he continued, addressing Ashwoode; "what do you stand there for, with your whitewashed face?"

Ashwoode, scarcely knowing what he did, staggered down the stairs and made his way to the parlour, where he sat gasping, with his face buried in his hands. Meanwhile, with many a meek expression of pity, the lawyer assisted Flora Guy in bearing the inanimate body of her mistress into the chamber, where, in happy unconsciousness, she lay under the tender care of her humble friend and servant. Blarden and Chancey having accomplished the object of their mission, departed to the lower regions to enjoy whatever good cheer Morley Court afforded.

CHAPTER LVI.

EBENEZER SHYCOCK.

In pursuance of the arrangements which Mr. Blarden had, on the evening before, announced to his intended victim, Gordon Chancey was despatched early the next morning to engage the services of a clergyman for the occasion. He knew pretty well how to choose his man, and for the most part, when a plot was to be executed, in theatrical phrase, cast the parts well. He proceeded leisurely to the city, and sauntering through the streets, found himself at length in Saint Patrick's Close; beneath the shadow of the old Cathedral he turned down a narrow and deserted lane and stopped before a dingy, miserable little shop, over whose doorway hung a panel with the dusky and faded similitude of two great keys crossed, now scarcely discernible through the ancient dust and soot. The shop itself was a chaotic depository of old locks, holdfasts, chisels, crowbars, and in short, of rusty iron in almost every conceivable shape. Chancey entered this dusky shop, and accosting a very grimed and rusty-looking little boy who was, with a file, industriously employed in converting a kitchen candlestick into a cannon, inquired,—

"I say, my good boy, does the Reverend Doctor Ebenezer Shycock stop here yet?"

"Aye, does he," said the youth, inspecting the visitor with a broad and leisurely stare, while he wiped his forehead with his shirt sleeve.

"Up the stairs, is it?" demanded Chancey.

"Aye, the garrets," replied the boy. "And mind the hole in the top lobby," he shouted after him, as he passed through the little door in the back of the shop and began to ascend the narrow stairs.

He did "mind the hole in the top lobby" (a very necessary caution, by the way, as he might otherwise have been easily engulfed therein and broken either his neck or his leg, after descending through the lath and plaster, upon the floor of the landing-place underneath); and having thus safely reached the garret door, he knocked thereupon with his knuckles.

"Come in," answered a female voice, not of the most musical quality, and Chancey accordingly entered. A dirty, sluttish woman was sitting by the window, knitting, and as it seemed, she was the only inmate of the room.

"Is the Reverend Ebenezer at home, my dear?" inquired the barrister.

"He is, and he isn't," rejoined the female, oracularly.

"How's that, my good girl?" inquired Chancey.

"He's in the house, but he's not good for much," answered she.

"Has he been throwing up the little finger, my dear?" said Chancey, "he used to be rayther partial to brandy."

"Brandy—brandy—who says brandy?" exclaimed a voice briskly from behind a sheet which hung upon a string so as to screen off one corner of the chamber.

"Ay, ay, that's the word that'll waken you," said the woman. "Here's a gentleman wants to speak with you."

"The devil there is!" exclaimed the clerical worthy, abruptly, while with a sudden chuck he dislodged the sheet which had veiled his presence, and disclosed, by so doing, the form of a stout, short, bull-necked man, with a mulberry-coloured face and twinkling grey eyes—one of them in deep mourning. He wore a greasy red night-cap and a very tattered and sad-coloured shirt, and was sitting upright in a miserable bed, the covering of which appeared to be a piece of ancient carpet. With one hand he scratched his head, while in the other he held the sheet which he had just pulled down.

"How are you, Parson Shycock?" said Chancey; "how do you find yourself this morning, doctor?"

"Tolerably well. But what is it you want with me? out with it, spooney. Any job in my line, eh?" inquired the clergyman.

"Yes, indeed, doctor," replied Chancey, "and a very good job; you're wanted to marry a gentleman and a lady privately, not a mile and a half out of town, this evening; you'll get five guineas for the job, and I think that's no trifle."

The parson mused, and scratched his head again.

"Well," said he, "you must do a little job for me first. You can't be ignorant that we members of the Church militant are often hard up; and whenever I'm in a fix I pop wig, breeches, and gown, and take to my bed; you'll find the three articles in this lane, corner house—sign, three golden balls; present this docket—where the devil is it? ay, here; all right—present this along with two guineas, paid in advance on account of job: bring me the articles, and I'll get up and go along with you in a brace of shakes. And stay; didn't I hear some one talking of brandy? or—or was I dreaming? You may as well get in a half-pint, for I'm never the thing till I have some little moderate refreshment; so, dearly beloved, mizzle at once."

"Dear me, dear me, doctor," said Chancey, "how can you think I'd go for to bring two guineas along with me?"

"If you haven't the rhino, this is no place for you, my fellow-sinner," rejoined the couple-beggar; "and if you have, off with you and deliver the togs out of pop. You wouldn't have a clergyman walk the streets without breeches, eh, dearly beloved cove?"

"Well, well, but you're a wonderful man," rejoined Chancey, with a faint smile. "I suppose, then, I must do it; so give me the docket, and I'll be here again as soon as I can."

"And do you mind me, you stray sheep, you, don't forget the lush," added the pastor. "I'm very desirous to wet my whistle; my mums, by the hokey, is as dry as a Dutch brick. Good-bye to you, and do you mind, be back here in the twinkling of a brace of bed-posts."

With this injunction, and bearing the crumpled document, which the reverend divine had given him, as his credentials with the pawnbroker, Mr. Chancey cautiously lounged down the crazy stairs.

"I say, my nutty Nancy," observed the parson, after a long yawn and a stretch, addressing the female who sat at the window, "that chap's made of money. I had a pint with him once in Clarke's public—round the corner there. His name's Chancey, and he does half the bills in town—a regular Jew chap."

So saying, the Reverend Ebenezer Shycock, LL.D., unceremoniously rolled himself out of bed and hobbled to a crazy deal box, in which were deposited such articles of attire as had not been transmitted to the obliging proprietor of the neighbouring three golden balls.

While the reverend divine was kneeling before this box, and, with a tenderness suited to their frail condition, removing the few scanty articles of his wardrobe and laying them reverently upon a crazy stool beside him, Mr. Chancey returned, bearing the liberated decorations of the doctor's person, as also a small black bottle.

"Oh, dear me, doctor," said Chancey, "but I'm glad to see you're stirring. Here's the things."

"And the—the lush, eh?" inquired the clergyman, peering inquisitively round Chancey's side to have a peep at the bottle.

"Yes, and the lush too," said the barrister.

"Well, give me the breeches," said the doctor, with alacrity, clutching those essential articles and proceeding to invest his limbs therein. "And, Nancy, a sup of water and a brace of cups."

A cracked mug and a battered pewter goblet made their appearance, and, along with the ruin of a teapot which contained the pure element, were deposited on a chair—for tables were singularly scarce in the reverend doctor's establishment.

"Now, my beloved fellow-sinner, mix like a Trojan!" exclaimed the divine; "and take care, take care, pogey aqua, don't drown it with water; chise it, chise it, man, that'll do."

With these words he grasped the vessel, nodded to Chancey, and directing his two grey eyes with a greedy squint upon the liquor as it approached his lips, he quaffed it at a single draught.

Without waiting for an invitation, which Chancey thought his clerical acquaintance might possibly forget, the barrister mingled some of the same beverage for his own private use, and quietly gulped it down; seeing which, and dreading Mr. Chancey's powers, which he remembered to have already seen tested at "Clarke's public," the learned divine abstractedly inverted the brandy bottle into his pewter goblet, and shedding upon it an almost imperceptible dew from the dilapidated teapot, he terminated the symposium and proceeded to finish his toilet.

This was quickly done, and Mr. Gordon Chancey and the Reverend Ebenezer Shycock—two illustrious and singularly well-matched ornaments of their respective professions—proceeded arm in arm, both redolent of grog, to the nearest coach stand, where they forthwith supplied themselves with a vehicle; and while Mr. Chancey pretty fully instructed his reverend companion in the precise nature of the service required of him, and, as far as was necessary, communicated the circumstances of the whole case, they traversed the interval which separated Dublin city from the manor of Morley Court.

CHAPTER LVII.

THE CHAPLAIN'S ARRIVAL AT MORLEY COURT—THE KEY—AND THE BOOZE IN THE BOUDOIR.

The hall door was opened to the summons of the two gentlemen by no less a personage than Nicholas Blarden himself, who, having carefully locked it again, handed the key to his accomplice, Gordon Chancey.

"Here, take it, Gordy, boy," exclaimed he, "I make you porter for the term of the honeymoon. Keep the gates well, old boy, and never let the keys out of your pocket unless I tell you. And so," continued he, treating the Reverend Ebenezer Shycock to a stare which took in his whole person, "you have caught the doctor and landed him fairly. Doctor—what's your name? no matter—it's a delightful turn-up for a sinner like me to have the heavenly consolation of your pious company. Follow me in here; I dare say your reverence would not object to a short interview with the brandy flask, or something of the kind—even saints must wet their whistles now and again."

So saying, Blarden led the way into the parlour.

"Here, guzzle away, old gentleman, there's plenty of the stuff here," said Blarden, "only beware how you make a beast of yourself. You mustn't tie up your red rag, do you mind? We'll want you to stand and read; and if you just keep senses enough for that, you may do whatever you like with the rest."

The clergyman nodded, and with a single sweep of his grey eyes, took in the contents of the whole table. His shaking hand quickly grasped the neck of the brandy flask, and he filled out and quaffed a comforting bumper.

"Now, take it easy, do, or, by Jove, you'll not keep till evening," said Blarden. "Chancey, have an eye on the parson, for his mind's so intent on heaven that he may possibly forget where he is and what he's doing. After dinner, Ashwoode and I have to go into town—some matters that must be wound up before the evening's entertainment begins—we'll be out, however, at eight o'clock or so. And mind this," he continued, gripping the barrister's shoulder in his hand with an energizing pressure, and speaking into his ear to secure attention, "you know that little room upstairs wherein we had the bit of chat with my lady love—the—the boudoir, I think they call it—now, mind me well—when the dusk comes on, do you and his reverence there take your pipes and your brandy, or whatever else you're amusing yourselves with at the time, and sit in that same room together, so that not a mouse can cross the floor unknown to you. Don't forget this, for we can't be too sharp. Do you hear me, old Lucifer?"

"Never fear, never fear," rejoined Mr. Chancey. "The Reverend Ebenezer and I will spend the evening there—and, indeed, I declare to God, it's a very neat little room, so it is, for a quiet pipe and a pot of sack."

"Well, that's a point settled," rejoined Blarden. "And do you mind me, don't let that beastly old sot knock himself up before we come home. Do you hear me, old scarecrow," he continued, poking the reverend doctor somewhere about the region of the abdomen with the hilt of his sword, which he was adjusting at his side, and addressing himself to that gentleman, "if I find you drunk when I return this evening, I'll make it your last bout—I'll tap the brandy, old tickle pitcher, and stave the cask, and send you to seek your fortune in the other world. Mind my words—I'm not given to joking when I have real business on hand; and faith, you'll find me as ready to do as to promise."

So saying, he left the room.

"A rum cove, that, upon my little word," said the Reverend Ebenezer Shycock, filling out another bumper of his beloved cordial. "Take the bottle away at once; lock it up, my fellow-worm, lock it up, or I'll be at it again. Lock it up while I have this glass in my hand, or I must have another, and that might be—might, I say—possibly might—but d——n it, no, it can't—I will have one more." And so saying, with desperate resolution, he quaffed what he had already in his hand and filled out another.

Chancey did not wait till he had repeated his mandate, but quietly removed the seductive flask and placed it beyond the reach and the sight of his clerical friend, who, feeling himself a little pleasant, sat down before the hearth, and in a voice whose tone nearly resembled that of a raven labouring under an affection of the chest, he chaunted through his nose, with many significant winks and grimaces, a ditty at that time in high acceptance among the votaries of vice and license, and whose words were such as even the 'Old St. Columbkill' would hardly have tolerated. This performance over—which, by the way, Chancey relished in his own quiet way with intense enjoyment—the reverend gentleman, composed himself for a doze for several hours, from which he aroused himself to eat and to drink a little more.

Thus pleasantly the day wore on, until at length the sun descended in glory behind the far-off blue hills, and the pale twilight began to herald the approach of night.

That day Mary Ashwoode appeared to have lost all energy of thought and feeling; she lay pale and silent upon her bed, seeming scarcely conscious even of the presence of her faithful attendant. From the moment of her yesterday's interview with Blarden, and the meeting with her brother, she had been thus despairing and stupefied. Flora Guy sat in the window, sometimes watching the pale face of the wretched lady, and at others looking out upon the old woodlands and the great avenue, darkened among its double rows of huge old limes. As the day wore on she suddenly exclaimed,—

"Oh, my lady, here's a gentleman coming with Mr. Chancey up the avenue, I see them between the trees, and the coach driving away."

"Can it—can it be?" exclaimed Mary, starting wildly up in the bed—"is it he?"

"It's a little stout gentleman, with a red pimply face—they're talking under the window now, my lady; he has a band on, and a black gown across his arm—as sure as daylight, my lady—he is—blessed hour; he is a parson."

Mary Ashwoode did not speak, but the momentary flash of hope faded from her face, and was succeeded by a paleness so deadly that lips and cheeks looked bloodless as the marble lineaments of a statue; in dull and silent despair she sank again where she had lain before.

"Don't fear them, my lady," said the poor girl, placing herself by the bedside where, more like a corpse than a living being, her hapless mistress lay; "I will not leave you, and though they may threaten, they dare not hurt you—don't fear them, my lady."

The blanched cheeks and evident excitement of the honest maiden, however, too clearly belied her words of encouragement.

Twice or thrice the girl, in the course of the day, locking the door of her mistress's chamber, according to the orders of Nicholas Blarden and his confederates, but less in obedience to them than for the sake of her security, ran downstairs to learn whatever could be gathered from the servants of the intended movements of the conspirators; each time, as she descended the stairs, the parlour bell was rung, and a servant encountered her before she had well reached the hall; and Mr. Chancey, too, with his hands in his pockets, and his cunning eyes glittering suspiciously through their half-closed lids, would meet and question her before she passed: were ever sentinels more vigilant—was ever surveillance more jealous and complete?

During these excursions she picked up whatever was to be learned of the intentions of those in whose power her young mistress now helplessly and despairingly lay.

"Sir Henry Ashwoode and Mr. Blarden is gone to town together, my lady," said the maid, in a whisper, for she felt the vigilance of Chancey and his creatures might pursue her even to the chamber where she stood; "they'll not be out till about eight o'clock, my lady, at the soonest, maybe not till near nine or ten; at any rate it will be dark long before they come, and God knows what may turn up before then—don't lose heart, my lady—don't give up."

In vain, entirely in vain, however, were the words of hope and courage spoken; they fell cold and dead upon the palsied senses and stricken heart of despairing terror. Mary Ashwoode scarcely understood, and seemed not even to have heard them.

As the evening approached the poor girl made another exploring ramble, in the almost desperate speculation that she might possibly hit upon something which might suggest even a hint of some mode of escape. Having encountered Chancey and one of the serving men, as usual, and passed her examination, she crossed the large old hall, and without any definite pre-determination, entered Sir Henry's study, where he and Blarden had been sitting, and carelessly thrown upon the table a large key. For a moment she could scarcely believe her eyes, and her heart bounded high with hope as she grasped it quickly and rolled it in her apron—"Could it be the key of one of the doors through which alone liberty was to be regained?" With a deliberate step, which strangely belied her restless anxiety, she passed the door within which Chancey was sitting, and ascended to the young lady's chamber.

"My lady, is this it?" exclaimed she, almost breathless with excitement, and holding the key before the lady's face.

Mary Ashwoode with a momentary eagerness glanced at it.

"No, no," said she, faintly, "I know all the keys of the outer doors; it was I who brought them to my father every night; but this is none of them—no, no, no, no." There was a dulness and apathy upon the young lady, and a seeming insensibility to everything—to hope, to danger—to all, in short, which had intensely interested every faculty of mind and feeling but the day before—which frightened and dismayed her humble friend.

"Don't, my lady—don't give up—oh, sure you won't lose heart entirely; see if I won't think of something—never mind, if I don't think of some way or another yet."

The red discoloured tints of evening were now fading from the landscape, and rapidly giving place to the dim twilight—the harbinger of a night of dangers, terrors, and adventures; and as the poor maiden sat by the young lady's side, with a heart full of dark and ominous foreboding, she heard the door of the outer chamber—the little boudoir which we have often had occasion to mention—opened, and two persons entered it.

"They are here—they are come. Oh, God! they are here," exclaimed Mary Ashwoode, clasping her small hand in terror round the girl's wrist.

"The door's locked, my lady," said the girl, scarcely less terrified than her mistress; "they can't come in without letting us know first.' So saying, she ran to the door and peeped through the keyhole, to reconnoitre the party, and then stepping on tip-toe to the young lady, who, more dead than alive, was sitting by the bed-side, she said in a whisper,—

"Who do you think it is, ma'am? blessed hour! my lady, who should it be but that lawyer gentleman—that Mr. Chancey, and the old parson—they are settling themselves at the table."

Mr. Gordon Chancey and the Reverend Ebenezer Shycock were determined to make themselves comfortable in their new quarters. Accordingly they heaped wood and turf upon the expiring fire, and compelled the servant to ply the kitchen bellows, until the hearth crackled and roared again; then drawing the table to the fire-side—a pretty little work-table of poor Mary's—now covered with brandy-flasks, pieces of tobacco, pipes, and the other apparatus of their coarse debauch—the two worthies, illuminated by a pair of ponderous wax-candles, and by the blaze of a fire, and having drawn the curtains, sat themselves down and commenced their jolly vigils.

Chancey possessed the rare faculty of preserving his characteristic cunning throughout every phase and stage of intoxication short of absolute insensibility; on the present occasion, however, he was resolved not to put this convenient accomplishment to the test. The goodwill of Nicholas Blarden was too lucrative a possession to be lightly parted with, and he could not afford to hazard it by too free an indulgence upon the present important occasion; he therefore conducted his assaults upon the bottle with a very laudable abstemiousness. Not so, however, his clerical companion; he, too, had, in connection with his convivial frailties, a compensating gift of his own; he possessed, in an eminent degree, the power of recovering his intellects upon short notice from the influence of brandy, and of descending almost at a single bound from the loftiest altitude of drunken inspiration to the dull insipid level of ordinary sobriety; all he asked was fifteen minutes to bring himself to. He used to say with becoming pride—"If I could have done it in ten, I'd have been a bishop by this time; but dis aliter visum; I had not time one forenoon; being wapper-eyed, I was five minutes short of my allowance to get right, consequently officiated oddly—fell on my back on the way out, and couldn't get up; but what signifies it? I'm better off, as matters stand, ten to one; so here goes, my fellow-sinner, to it again; one brimmer more."

The reverend doctor, therefore, was much less cautious than his companion, and soon began to exhibit very unequivocal symptoms of a declension in his intellectual and physical energies, and a more than corresponding elevation in his hilarious spirits.

"I say," said Chancey, "my good man, you'd better stop; you have too much in as it is; they'll be here before half-an-hour, and if Mr. Blarden finds you this way, I declare to God I think he'll crack your neck down the staircase."

"Well, dearly beloved," said the clerical gentleman, "I believe you are right; I'll bring myself to. I am a little heavy-eyed or so; all I ask for is a towel and cold water." So saying, with many a screw of the lips, and many a hiccough, he made an effort to rise, but tumbled back—with an expression of the most heavenly benevolence—into his chair, knocking his head with an audible sound upon the back of it, and at the same time overturning one of the candles.

"Pull the bell, dearly beloved," said he, with a smile and a hiccough—"a basin of water and a towel."

"Devil broil you, for a drunken beast," said Chancey, seriously alarmed at the condition of the couple-beggar; "he'll never be fit for his work to-night."

"Fifteen minutes, neither more nor less," hiccoughed the divine, with the same celestial smile—"towel, basin of cold water, and fifteen minutes."

Chancey did procure the cold water and a napkin, which, being laid before the clergyman, he proceeded with much deliberation, while various expressions of stupendous solemnity and beaming benevolence flitted in beautiful alternations across his expressive countenance, to prepare them for use. He doffed his wig, and first bathing his head, face, and temples completely in the cool liquid, saturated the towel likewise therein, and wound it round his shorn head in the fashion of a Turkish turban; having accomplished which feat, he leaned back in his chair, closed his eyes, and became, to all intents and purposes, for the time being, stone dead.

Leaving his reverend companion undisturbed to the operation of his own hydropathic treatment, Gordon Chancey drew his seat near to the fire, and filling his pipe anew with tobacco, leaned back in the chair, crossed his legs, and more than half closing his eyes, prepared himself luxuriously for what he called "a raal elegant draw of particular pigtail."

CHAPTER LVIII.

THE SIGNAL.

Flora Guy peeped eagerly through the keyhole of her lady's chamber into the little apartment in which the two boon companions were seated. After reconnoitring for a very long time, she moved lightly to her mistress's side, and said, in a low but distinct tone,—

"Now, my lady, you must get up and rouse yourself—for God's sake, mistress dear, shake off the heaviness that's over you, and we have a chance left still."

"Are they not in the next room to us?" inquired Mary.

"Yes, my lady," replied the maid, "but the parson gentleman is drunk or asleep, and Mr. Chancey is there alone—and—and has the four keys beside him on the table; don't be frightened, my lady, do you stay quite quiet, and I'll go into the room."

Mary Ashwoode made no answer, but pressed the poor girl's hand in her cold fingers, and without moving, almost without breathing, awaited the result. Flora Guy, meanwhile, opened the door, and passed into the outer apartment, assuming, as she did so, an air of easy and careless indifference. Chancey turned as she entered the room, fanning the smoke of his tobacco pipe aside with his hand, and eying her with a jealous glance.

"Well, my little girl," said he, "and what makes you leave your young lady, my dear?"

"An' is a body never to get an instant minute to themselves?" rejoined she, with an indignant toss of her head; "why then, I tell you what it is, Mr. Chancey, I'm tired to death, so I am, sitting in that little room the whole blessed day, and not a word, good or bad, will the young lady say—she's gone stupid like."

"Is the door locked?" said Chancey, suspiciously, and at the same time rising and approaching the young lady's chamber.

As he did so, Flora Guy, availing herself instantly of this averted position, snatched up, without waiting to choose, one of the four great keys which lay upon the table, and replaced it dexterously with that which she had but a short time before shown to her mistress; in doing so, however, spite of all her caution, a slight clank was audible.

"Well, is it locked?" inquired the damsel, hoping by the loud tone in which she uttered the question to drown the suspicious sounds which threatened her schemes with instant detection.

"Yes, it is locked," rejoined Chancey, glancing quickly at the keys; "but what do you want there? move off from my place, will you?" and shambling to the table he hastily gathered the four keys in his grasp, and thrust them into his deep coat pocket.

"You're in a mighty quare humour, so you are, Mr. Chancey," said the girl, affecting a saucy tone, through which, had his ear been listening for the sound, he might have detected the quaver of extreme agitation, "you usedn't to be so cross by no means at the Columbkil, but mighty pleasant, so you used."

"Well, my little girl," said Chancey, whose suspicions were now effectually quieted, "I declare to God you're the first that ever said I was bad tempered, so you are—will you have something to drink?"

"What have you there, Mr. Chancey?" inquired she.

"This is brandy, my little girl, and this is sack, dear," rejoined Chancey, "both of them elegant; you must have whichever you like—which will you choose, dear?"

"Well, then, I'll have a little drop of the sack, mulled, I thank you, Mr. Chancey," replied she.

"There's nothing to mull it in here, my little girl," objected the barrister.

"Oh, but I'll get it in a minute though," replied she, "I'll run down for a saucepan."

"Well, dear, run away," replied he, "but don't be long, for Miss Ashwoode might want you, my little girl, and it wouldn't do if you were out of the way, you know."

Without waiting to hear the end of this charge, Flora Guy ran down the staircase, and speedily returned with the utensil required.

"Maybe I'd better go in for a minute first, and see if she wants me," suggested the girl.

"Very well, my dear," replied Chancey.

And accordingly, she turned the key in the chamber door, closed it again, and stood by the young lady's side; such was her agitation that for three or four seconds she could not speak.

"My lady," at length she said, "I have one of the keys—when I go in next I'll leave your room door unlocked, only closed just, and no more—the lobby door is ajar—I left it that way this very minute; and when you hear me saying 'the sack's upset!'—do you open your door, and cross the room as quick as light, and out on the lobby, and stop by the stairs, my lady, and I'll follow you as fast as I can. Here, my lady," continued the poor girl, bringing a small box from her mistress's toilet; "your rings, my lady—they'll be wanted—mind, your rings, my lady—there is the little case, keep it in your pocket; if we escape, my lady, they'll be wanted—mind, Mr. Chancey has ears like needle points. Keep up your heart, my lady, and in the name of God we'll try this chance."

"Into His hands I commit myself," said the young lady, with a tone and air of more firmness and energy than she had shown for days; "my heart is strengthened, my courage comes again—oh, thank God, I am equal to this dreadful hour."

Flora Guy made a gesture of silence, and then, opening the door briskly, and shutting it again with an ostentatious noise, and drawing the key from the lock, she crossed the room to where Chancey, who had watched her entrance, was sitting.

"Well, my dear," said he, "how is that delicate young lady in there?"

"Why, she's raythur bad, I'm afraid," rejoined the girl; "she's the whole day long in a sort of a heavy dulness like—she don't seem to mind anything."

"So much the better, my dear," said Chancey, "she'll be the less inclined to gad, or to be troublesome—come, mix the spices and the sugar, dear, and settle the liquor in the saucepan—you want some refreshment, so you do, for I declare to God, I never saw anyone so pale in all my life as you are this minute."

"I'll not be long so," said the girl, affecting a tone of briskness, and proceeding to mingle the ingredients in the little saucepan, "for I think if I was dead itself, let alone a little bit tired, a cup of mulled sack would cheer me up again."

So saying, she placed the little saucepan on the bar.

"Is the parson asleep?" inquired she.

"Indeed, my dear, I'm very much afraid it's tipsy he is," drawled Chancey, demurely, "take care of that clergyman, my dear, for indeed I'm afraid he has very loose conduct."

"Will I blacken his nose with a burned cork?" inquired she.

"Oh! no, my little girl," replied Chancey, with a tranquil chuckle, and turning his sleepy grey eyes upon the apoplectic visage of the stupefied drunkard who sat bolt upright before him; "no, no, we don't know the minute he may be wanted; he'll have to perform the ceremony very soon, my dear; and Mr. Blarden, if he took the fancy, would think nothing of braining half a dozen of us. I declare to God he wouldn't."

"Well, Mr. Chancey, will you mind the little saucepan for one minute," said she, "while I'm putting a bit of turf or a few sticks under it."

"Indeed I will," said he, turning his eyes lazily upon the utensil, but doing nothing more to secure it. Flora Guy accordingly took some wood, and, pretending to arrange the fire, overturned the wine; the loud hiss of the boiling liquid, and the sudden cloud of whirling steam and ashes, ascending toward the ceiling, and puffing into his face, half confounded the barrister, and at the same instant, Flora Guy, clapping her hands, and exclaimed with a shrill cry,—

"The sack's upset! the sack's upset! lend a hand, Mr. Chancey—Mr. Chancey, do you hear?" and, while thus conjured, the barrister, in obedience to her vociferous appeal, made some indistinct passes at the saucepan with the poker, which he had grasped at the first alarm; the damsel, without daring to look directly where every feeling would have riveted her eyes, beheld a dark form glide noiselessly behind Chancey, and pass from the room. For the moment, so intense was her agony of anxiety, she felt upon the very point of fainting; in an instant more, however, she had recovered all her energies, and was bold and quick-witted as ever; one glance in the direction of the lady's chamber showed her the door slowly swinging open; fortunately the barrister was at the moment too much occupied with the extraction of the remainder of the saucepan from the fire, to have yet perceived the treacherous accident, one glance at which would have sealed their ruin, and Flora Guy, running noiselessly to the door, remedied the perilous disclosure by shutting it softly and quickly; and then, with much clattering of the key, and a good deal of pushing beside, forcing it open again, she passed into the room and spoke a little in a low tone, as if to her mistress; and then, returning, she locked the door of the then untenanted chamber in real earnest, and, crossing to Chancey, said:—"I wonder at you, so I do, Mr. Chancey; you frightened the young mistress half out of her wits; and I'm all over dust and ashes; I must run down and wash every inch of my face and hands, so I must; and here, Mr. Chancey, will you keep the key of the bed-room till I come back? afraid I might drop it; and don't let it out of your hands."

"I will indeed, dear; but don't be long away," rejoined the barrister, extending his hand to receive the key of the now vacant chamber.

So Flora Guy boldly walked forth upon the lobby, and closing the chamber door behind her, found herself in the vast old gallery, hung round with grim and antique portraits, and lighted only by the fitful beams of a clouded moon shining doubtfully through the stained glass of a solitary window.

Mary Ashwoode awaited her approach, concealed in a small recess or niche in the wall, shrined like an image in the narrow enclosure of carved oak, not daring to stir, and with a heart throbbing as though it would burst.

"My lady, are you there?" whispered the maid, scarce audibly; great nervous excitement renders the sense morbidly acute, and Mary Ashwoode heard the sound distinctly, faint though it was, and at some distance from her; she stepped falteringly from her place of concealment, and took the hand of her conductress in a grasp cold as that of death itself, and side by side they proceeded down the broad staircase. They had descended about half-way when a loud and violent ringing from the bell of the chamber where Chancey was seated made their very hearts bound with terror; they stood fixed and breathless on the stair where the fearful peal had first reached their ears. Again the summons came louder still, and at the same moment the sounds of steps approached from below, and the gleam of a candle quickly followed; Mary Ashwoode felt her ears tingle and her head swim with terror; she was on the point of sinking upon the floor. In this dreadful extremity her presence of mind did not forsake Flora Guy: disengaging her hand from that of her terrified mistress, she tripped lightly down the stairs to meet the person who was approaching—a turn in the staircase confronted them, and she saw before her the serving man whose treachery had already defeated Mary Ashwoode's hopes of deliverance.

"What keeps you such a time answering the bell?" inquired she, saucily, "you needn't go up now, for I've got your message; bring up clean cups and a clean saucepan, for everything's destroyed with the dust and dirt Mr. Chancey's after kicking up; what did he do, do you think, but upsets the sack into the fire. Now be quick with the things, will you? the bell won't be easy one minute till they're done."

"Give me a kiss, sweet lips," exclaimed the man, setting down his candle, "and I'll not be a brace of shakes about the message; come, you must," he continued, playfully struggling with the affrighted girl.

"Well, do the message first, at any rate," said she, forcing herself, with some difficulty, from his grasp, as the bell rang a third time; "it will be a nice piece of business, so it will, if Mr. Chancey comes down and catches you here, pulling me about, so it will, you'll look well, won't you, when he's telling it to Mr. Blarden?—don't be a fool."

The reiterated application to the bell had more effect upon the serving man than all her oratory, and muttering a curse or two, he ran down, determined, vindictively, to bring up soiled cups, and a dirty saucepan. The man had hardly departed, when the maid exclaimed, in a hurried whisper, "Come—come—quick—quick, for your life!" and with scarcely the interval of three seconds, they found themselves in the hall.

"Here's the key, my lady; see which of the doors does it open," whispered she, exhibiting the key in the dusky and imperfect light.

"Here—here—this way," said Mary Ashwoode, moving with weak and stumbling steps through a tiled lobby which opened upon the great hall, and thence along a narrow passage upon which several doors opened. "Here, here," she exclaimed, "this door—this—I cannot open it—my strength is gone—this is it—for God's sake, quickly."

After two or three trials, Flora Guy succeeded in getting the key into the lock, and then exerting the whole strength of her two hands, with a hoarse jarring clang the bolt revolved, the door opened, and they stood upon the fresh and dewy sward, beneath the shadow of the old ivy-mantled walls. The girl locked the door upon the outside, fearful that its lying open should excite suspicion, and flung the key away into the thick weeds and brushwood.

"Now, my lady, the shortest way to the high road?" inquired Flora in a hurried whisper, and supporting, as well as she could, the tottering steps of her mistress, "how do you feel, my lady? Don't lose heart now, a few minutes more and you will be safe—courage—courage, my lady."

"I am better now, Flora," said Mary faintly, "much better—the cool air refreshes me." As she thus spoke, her strength returned, her step grew fleeter and firmer, and she led the way round the irregular ivy-clothed masses of the dark old building and through the stately trees that stood gathered round it. Over the unequal sward they ran with the light steps of fear, and under the darksome canopy of the vast and ancient linden-trees, gliding upon the smooth grass like two ghosts among the chequered shade and dusky light. On, on they sped, scarcely feeling the ground beneath their feet as they pursued their terrified flight; they had now gained the midway distance in the ancient avenue between the mansion and great gate, and still ran noiselessly and fleetly along, when the quick ear of Mary Ashwoode caught the distant sounds of pursuit.

"Flora—Flora—oh, God! we are followed," gasped the young lady.

"Stop an instant, my lady," rejoined the maid, "let us listen for a second."

They did pause, and distinctly, between them and the old mansion, they heard, among the dry leaves with which in places the ground was strewn, the tread of steps pursuing at headlong speed.

"It is—it is, I hear them," said Mary distractedly.

"Now, my lady, we must run—run for our lives; if we but reach the road before them, we may yet be saved; now, my lady, for God's sake don't falter—don't give up."

And while the sounds of pursuit grew momentarily louder and more loud, they still held their onward way with throbbing hearts, and eyes almost sightless with fatigue and terror.

CHAPTER LIX.

HASTE AND PERIL.

The rush of feet among the leaves grew every moment closer and closer upon them, and now they heard the breathing of their pursuer—the sounds came near—nearer—they approached—they reached them.

"Oh, God! they are up with us—they are upon us," said Mary, stumbling blindly onward, and at the same moment she felt something laid heavily upon her shoulder—she tottered—her strength forsook her, and she fell helplessly among the branching roots of the old trees.

"My lady—oh, my lady—thank God, it's only the dog," cried Flora Guy, clapping her hands in grateful ecstasies; and at the same time, Mary felt a cold nose thrust under her neck and her chin and cheeks licked by her old favourite, poor Rover. More dead than alive, she raised herself again to her feet, and before her sat the great old dog, his tail sweeping the rustling leaves in wide circles, and his good-humoured tongue lolling from among his ivory fangs. With many a frisk and bound the fine dog greeted his long-lost mistress, and seemed resolved to make himself one of the party.

"No, no, poor Rover," said Mary, hurriedly—"we have rambled our last together—home, Rover, home."

The old dog looked wonderingly in the face of his mistress.

"Home, Rover—home," repeated she, and the noble dog did credit to his good training by turning dejectedly, and proceeding at a slow, broken trot homeward, after stopping, however, and peeping round his shoulder, as though in the hope of some signal relentingly inviting his return.

Thus relieved of their immediate fears, the two fugitives, weak, exhausted, and breathless, reached the great gate, and found themselves at length upon the high road. Here they ventured to check their speed, and pursue their way at a pace which enabled them to recover breath and strength, but still fearfully listening for any sound indicative of pursuit.

The moon was high in the heavens, but the dark, drifting scud was sailing across her misty disc, and giving to her light the character of ceaseless and ever varying uncertainty. The road on which they walked was that which led to Dublin city, and from each side was embowered by tall old trees, and rudely fenced by unequal grassy banks. They had proceeded nearly half-a-mile without encountering any living being, when they heard, suddenly, a little way before them, the sharp clang of horses' hoofs upon the road, and shortly after, the moon shining forth for a moment, revealed distinctly the forms of two horsemen approaching at a slow trot.

"As sure as light, my lady, it's they," said Flora Guy, "I know Sir Henry's grey horse—don't stop, my lady—don't try to hide—just draw the hood over your head, and walk on steady with me, and they'll never mind us, but pass on."

With a throbbing heart, Mary obeyed her companion, and they walked side by side by the edge of the grassy bank and under the tall trees—the distance between them and the two mounted figures momentarily diminishing.

"I say he's as lame as a hop-jack," cried the well-known voice of Nicholas Blarden, as they approached—"hav'n't you an eye in your head, you mouth, you—look there—another false step, by Jove."

Just at this moment the girls, looking neither to the right nor left, and almost sinking with fear, were passing them by.

"Stop you, one of you, will you?" said Blarden, addressing them, and at the same time reining in his horse.

Flora Guy stopped, and making a slight curtsey, awaited his further pleasure, while Mary Ashwoode, with faltering steps and almost dead with terror, walked slowly on.

"Have you light enough to see a stone in a horse's hoof, my dimber hen?—have you, I say?"

"Yes, sir," faltered the girl, with another curtsey, and not venturing to raise her voice, for fear of detection.

"Well, look into them all in turn, will you?" continued Blarden, "while I walk the beast a bit. Do you see anything? is there a stone there?—is there?"

"No, sir," said she again, with a curtsey.

"No, sir," echoed he—"but I say 'yes, sir,' and I'll take my oath of it. D——n it, it can't be a strain. Get down, Ashwoode, I say, and look to it yourself; these blasted women are fit for nothing but darning old stockings—get down, I say, Ashwoode."

Without awaiting for any more formal dismissal, Flora Guy walked quickly on, and speedily overtook her companion, and side by side they continued to go at the same moderate pace, until a sudden turn in the road interposing trees and bushes between them and the two horsemen, they renewed their flight at the swiftest pace which their exhausted strength could sustain; and need had they to exert their utmost speed, for greater dangers than they had yet escaped were still to follow.

Meanwhile Nicholas Blarden and Sir Henry Ashwoode mended their pace, and proceeded at a brisk trot toward the manor of Morley Court. Both rode on more than commonly silent, and whenever Blarden spoke, it was with something more than his usual savage moroseness. No doubt their rapid approach to the scene where their hellish cruelty and oppression were to be completed, did not serve either to exhilarate their spirits or to soothe the asperities of Blarden's ruffian temper. Now and then, indeed, he did indulge in a few flashes of savage exulting glee at his anticipated triumph over the hereditary pride of Sir Henry, against whom, with all a coward's rancour, he still cherished a "lodged hate," and in mortifying and insulting whom his kestrel heart delighted and rioted with joy. As they approached the ancient avenue, as if by mutual consent, they both drew bridle and reduced their pace to a walk.

"You shall be present and give her away—do you mind?" said Blarden, abruptly breaking silence.

"There's no need for that—surely there is none?" said Ashwoode.

"Need or no need, it's my humour," replied Blarden.

"I've suffered enough already in this matter," replied Sir Henry, bitterly; "there's no use in heaping gratuitous annoyances and degradation upon me."

"Ho, ho, running rusty," exclaimed Blarden, with the harsh laugh of coarse insult—"running rusty, eh? I thought you were broken in by this time—paces learned and mouth made, eh?—take care, take care."

"I say," repeated Ashwoode, impetuously, "you can have no object in compelling my presence, except to torment me."

"Well, suppose I allow that—what then, eh?—ho, ho!" retorted Blarden.

Sir Henry did not reply, but a strange fancy crossed his mind.

"I say," resumed Blarden, "I'll have no argument about it; I choose it, and what I choose must be done—that's enough."

The road was silent and deserted; no sound, save the ringing of their own horses' hoofs upon the stones, disturbed the stillness of the air; dark, ragged clouds obscured the waning moon, and the shadows were deepened further by the stooping branches of the tall trees which guarded the road on either side. Ashwoode's hand rested upon the pommel of his holster pistol, and by his side moved the wretch whose cunning and ferocity had dogged and destroyed him—with startling vividness the suggestion came. His eyes rested upon the dusky form of his companion, all calculations of consequences faded away from his remembrance, and yielding to the dark, dreadful influence which was upon him, he clutched the weapon with a deadly gripe.

"What are you staring at me for?—am I a stone wall, eh?" exclaimed Blarden, who instinctively perceived something odd in Ashwoode's air and attitude, spite of the obscurity in which they rode.

The spell was broken. Ashwoode felt as if awaking from a dream, and looked fearfully round, almost expecting to behold the visible presence of the principle of mischief by his side, so powerful and vivid had been the satanic impulse of the moment before.

They turned into the great avenue through which so lately the fugitives had fearfully sped.

"We're at home now," cried Blarden; "come, be brisk, will you?" And so saying, he struck Ashwoode's horse a heavy blow with his whip. The spirited animal reared and bolted, and finally started at a gallop down the broad avenue towards the mansion, and at the same pace Nicholas Blarden also thundered to the hall door.

## CHAPTER LX.

### THE UNTREASURED CHAMBER.

Their obstreperous summons at the door was speedily answered, and the two cavaliers stood in the hall.

"Well, all's right, I suppose?" inquired Blarden, tossing his gloves and hat upon the table.

"Yes, sir," replied the servant, "all but the lady's maid; Mr. Chancey's been calling for her these five minutes and more, and we can't find her."

"How's this—all the doors locked?" inquired Blarden vehemently.

"Ay, sir, every one of them," replied the man.

"Who has the keys?" asked Blarden.

"Mr. Chancey, sir," replied the servant.

"Did he allow them out of his keeping—did he?" urged Blarden.

"No, sir—not a moment—for he was saying this very minute," answered the domestic, "he had them in his pocket, and the key of Miss Mary's room along with them; he took it from Flora Guy, the maid, scarce a quarter of an hour ago."

"Then all is right," said Blarden, while the momentary blackness of suspicion passed from his face, "the girl's in some hole or corner of this lumbering old barrack, but here comes Chancey himself, what's all the fuss about—who's in the upper room—the—the boudoir, eh?" he continued, addressing the barrister, who was sneaking downstairs with a candle in his hand, and looking unusually sallow.

"The Reverend Ebenezer and one of the lads—they're sitting there," answered Chancey, "but we can't find that little girl, Flora Guy, anywhere."

"Have you the keys?" asked Blarden.

"Ay, dear me, to be sure I have, except the one that I gave to little Bat there, to let you in this minute. I have the three other keys; dear me—dear me—what could ail me?" And so saying, Chancey slapped the skirt of his coat slightly so as to make them jingle in his pocket.

"The windows are all fast and safe as the wall itself—screwed down," observed Blarden, "let's see the keys—show them here."

Chancey accordingly drew them from his pocket, and laid them on the table.

"There's the three of them," observed he, calmly.

"Have you no more?" inquired Blarden, looking rather aghast.

"No, indeed, the devil a one," replied Chancey, thrusting his arm to the elbow in his coat pocket.

"D—n me, but I think this is the key of the cellar," ejaculated Blarden, in a tone which energized even the apathetic lawyer, "come here, Ashwoode, what key's this?"

"It is the cellar key," said Ashwoode, in a faltering voice and turning very pale.

"Try your pockets for another, and find it, or —." The aposiopesis was alarming, and Blarden's direction was obeyed instantaneously.

"I declare to God," said Chancey, much alarmed, "I have but the three, and that in the door makes four."

"You damned oaf," said Blarden, between his set teeth, "if you have botched this business, I'll let you know for what. Ashwoode, which of the keys is missing?"

After a moment's hesitation, Ashwoode led the way through the passage which Mary and her companion had so lately traversed.

"That's the door," said he, pointing to that through which the escape had been effected.

"And what's this?" cried Blarden, shouldering past Sir Henry, and raising something from the ground, just by the door-post, "a handkerchief, and marked, too—it's the young lady's own—give me the key of the lady's chamber," continued he, in a low changed voice, which had, in the ears of the barrister, something more unpleasant still than his loudest and harshest tones—"give me the key, and follow me."

He clutched it, and followed by the terror-stricken barrister, and by Sir Henry Ashwoode, he retraced his steps, and scaled the stairs with hurried and lengthy strides. Without stopping to glance at the form of the still slumbering drunkard, or to question the servant who sat opposite, on the chair recently occupied by Chancey, he strode directly to the door of Mary Ashwoode's sleeping apartment, opened it, and stood in an untenanted chamber.

For a moment he paused, aghast and motionless; he ran to the bed—still warm with the recent pressure of his intended victim—the room was, indeed, deserted. He turned round, absolutely black and speechless with rage. As he advanced, the wretched barrister—the tool of his worst schemes—cowered back in terror. Without speaking one word, Blarden clutched him by the throat, and hurled him with his whole power backward. With tremendous force he descended with his head upon the bar of the grate, and thence to the hearthstone; there, breathless, powerless, and to all outward seeming a livid corpse, lay the devil's cast-off servant, the red blood trickling fast from ears, nose, and mouth. Not waiting to see whether Chancey was alive or dead, Mr. Blarden seized the brandy flask and dashed it in the face of the stupid drunkard—who, disturbed by the fearful hubbub, was just beginning to open his eyes—and leaving that reverend personage drenched in blood and brandy, to take care of his boon companion as best he might, Blarden strode down the stairs, followed by Ashwoode and the servants.

"Get horses—horses all," shouted he, "to the stables—by Jove, it was they we met on the road—the two girls—quick to the stables—whoever catches them shall have his hat full of crowns."

Led by Blarden, they all hurried to the stables, where they found the horses unsaddled.

"On with the saddles—for your life be quick," cried Blarden, "four horses—fresh ones."

While uttering his furious mandates, with many a blasphemous imprecation, he aided the preparations himself, and with hands that trembled with eagerness and rage, he drew the girths, and buckled the bridles, and in almost less than a minute, the four horses were led out upon the broken pavement of the stable-yard.

"Mind, boys," cried Blarden, "they are two mad-women—escaped mad-women—ride for your lives. Ashwoode, do you take the right, and I'll take the left when we come on the road—do you follow me, Tony—and Dick, do you go with Sir Henry—and, now, devil take the hindmost." With these words he plunged the spurs into his horse's flanks, and with the speed of a thunder blast, they all rode helter-skelter, in pursuit of their human prey.

CHAPTER LXI.

THE CART AND THE STRAW.

While this was passing, the two girls continued their flight toward Dublin city. They had not long passed Ashwoode and Nicholas Blarden, when Mary's strength entirely failed, and she was forced first to moderate her pace to a walk, and finally to stop altogether and seat herself upon the bank which sloped abruptly down to the road.

"Flora," said she, faintly, "I am quite exhausted—my strength is entirely gone; I must perforce rest myself and take breath here for a few minutes, and then, with God's help, I shall again have power to proceed."

"Do so, my lady," said Flora, taking her stand beside her mistress, "and I'll watch and listen here by you. Hish! don't I hear the sound of a car on the road before us?"

So, indeed, it seemed, and at no great distance too. The road, however, just where they had placed themselves, made a sweep which concealed the vehicle, whatever it might be, effectually from their sight. The girl clambered to the top of the bank, and thence commanding a view of that part of the highway which beneath was hidden from sight, she beheld, two or three hundred yards in advance of them, a horse and cart, the driver of which was seated upon the shaft, slowly wending along in the direction of the city.

"My lady," said she, descending from her post of observation, "if you have strength to run on for only a few perches more of the road, we'll be up with a car, and get a lift into town without any more trouble; try it, my lady."

Accordingly they again set forth, and after a few minutes' further exertion, they came up with the vehicle and accosted the driver, a countryman, with a short pipe in his mouth, who, with folded arms, sat listlessly upon the shaft.

"Honest man, God bless you, and give us a bit of a lift," said Flora Guy; "we've come a long way and very fast, and we are fairly tired to death."

The countryman drew the halter which he held, and uttering an unspellable sound, addressed to his horse, succeeded in bringing him and the vehicle to a standstill.

"Never say it twiste," said he; "get up, and welcome. Wait a bit, till I give the straw a turn for yees; not for it; step on the wheel; don't be in dread, he won't move."

So saying, he assisted Mary Ashwoode into the rude vehicle, and not without wondering curiosity, for the hand which she extended to him was white and slender, and glittered in the moonlight with jewelled rings. Flora Guy followed; but before the cart was again in motion, they distinctly heard the far-off clatter of galloping hoofs upon the road. Their fears too truly accounted for these sounds.

"Merciful God! we are pursued," said Mary Ashwoode; and then turning to the driver, she continued, with an agony of imploring terror—"as you look for pity at the dreadful hour when all shall need it, do not betray us. If it be as I suspect, we are pursued—pursued with an evil—a dreadful purpose. I had rather die a thousand deaths than fall into the hands of those who are approaching."

"Never fear," interrupted the man; "lie down flat both of you in the cart and I'll hide you—never fear."

They obeyed his directions, and he spread over their prostrate bodies a covering of straw; not quite so thick, however, as their fears would have desired; and thus screened, they awaited the approach of those whom they rightly conjectured to be in hot pursuit of them. The man resumed his seat upon the shaft, and once more the cart was in motion.

Meanwhile, the sharp and rapid clang of the hoofs approached, and before the horsemen had reached them, the voice of Nicholas Blarden was shouting—

"Holloa—holloa, honest fellow—saw you two young women on the road?"

There was scarcely time allowed for an answer, when the thundering clang of the iron hoofs resounded beside the conveyance in which the fugitives were lying, and the horsemen both, with a sudden and violent exertion, brought their beasts to a halt, and so abruptly, that although thrown back upon their haunches, the horses slid on for several yards upon the hard road, by the mere impetus of their former speed, knocking showers of fire flakes from the stones.

"I say," repeated Blarden, "did two girls pass you on the road—did you see them?"

"Divil a sign of a girl I see," replied the man, carelessly; and to their infinite relief, the two fugitives heard their pursuer, with a muttered curse, plunge forward upon his way. This relief, however, was but momentary, for checking his horse again, Blarden returned.

"I say, my good chap, I passed you before to-night, not ten minutes since, on my way out of town, not half-a-mile from this spot—the girls were running this way, and if they're between this and the gate—they must have passed you."

"Devil a girl I seen this— Oh, begorra! you're right, sure enough," said the driver, "what the devil was I thinkin' about—two girls—one of them tall and slim, with rings on her fingers—and the other a short, active bit of a colleen?"

"Ay—ay—ay," cried Blarden.

"Sure enough they did overtake me," said the man, "shortly after I passed two gentlemen—I suppose you are one of them—and the little one axed me the direction of Harold's-cross—and when I showed it to them, bedad they both made no more bones about it, but across the ditch with them, an' away over the fields—they're half-way there by this time—it was jist down there by the broken bridge—they were quare-looking girls."

"It would be damned odd if they were not—they're both mad," replied Blarden; "thank you for your hint."

And so saying, as he turned his horse's head in the direction indicated, he chucked a crown piece into the cart. As the conveyance proceeded, they heard the driver soliloquizing with evident satisfaction—

"Bedad, they'll have a plisint serenade through the fields, the two of them," observed he, standing upon the shafts, and watching the progress of the two horsemen—"there they go, begorra—over the ditch with them. Oh, by the hokey, the sarvint boy's down—the heart's blood iv a toss—an' oh, bloody wars! see the skelp iv the whip the big chap gives him—there they go again down the slope—now for it—over the gripe with them—well done, bedad, and into the green lane—devil take the bushes, I can't see another sight iv them. Young women," he continued, again assuming his sitting position, and replacing his pipe in the corner of his mouth—"all's safe now—they're clean out of sight—you may get up, miss."

Accordingly, Mary Ashwoode and Flora Guy raised themselves.

"Here," said the latter, extending her hand toward the driver, "here's the silver he threw to you."

"I wisht I could airn as much every day as aisily," said the man, securing his prize; "that chap has raal villiany in his face; he looks so like ould Nick, I'm half afeard to take his money; the crass of Christ about us, I never seen such a face."

"You're an honest boy at any rate," said Flora Guy, "you brought us safe through the danger."

"An' why wouldn't I—what else 'id I do?" rejoined the countryman; "it wasn't for to sell you I was goin'."

"You have earned my gratitude for ever," said Mary Ashwoode; "my thanks, my prayers; you have saved me; your generosity, and humanity, and pity, have delivered me from the deadliest peril that ever yet overtook living creature. God bless you for it."

She removed a ring from her finger, and added—"Take this; nay, do not refuse so poor an acknowledgment for services inestimable."

"No, miss, no," rejoined the countryman, warmly, "I'll not take it; I'll not have it; do you think I could do anything else but what I did, and you putting yourself into my hands the way you did, and trusting to me, and laving yourselves in my power intirely? I'm not a Turk, nor an unnatural Jew; may the devil have me, body and soul, the hour I take money, or money's worth, for doin' the like."

Seeing the man thus resolved, she forbore to irritate him by further pressing the jewel on his acceptance, and he, probably to put an end to the controversy, began to shake and chuck the rope halter with extraordinary vehemence, and at the same time with the heel of his brogue, to stimulate the lagging jade, accompanying the application with a sustained hissing; the combined effect of all which was to cause the animal to break into a kind of hobbling canter; and so they rumbled and clattered over the stony road, until at length their charioteer checked the progress of his vehicle before the hospitable door-way of "The Bleeding Horse"—the little inn to which, in the commencement of these records, we have already introduced the reader.

"Hould that, if you plase," said he, placing the end of the halter in Flora Guy's hand, "an' don't let him loose, or he'll be makin' for the grass and have you upset in the ditch. I'll not be a minute in here; and maybe the young lady and yourself 'id take a drop of something; the evenin's mighty chill entirely."

They both, of course, declined the hospitable proposal, and their conductor, leaving them on the cart, entered the little hostelry; outside the door were two or three cars and horses, whose owners were boozing within; and feeling some return of confidence in the consciousness that they were in the neighbourhood of persons who could, and probably would, protect them, should occasion arise, Mary Ashwoode, with her light mantle drawn around her, and the hood over her head, sat along with her faithful companion, awaiting his return, under the embowering shadow of the old trees.

"Flora, I am sorely perplexed; I know not whither to go when we have reached the city," said Mary, addressing her companion in a low tone. "I have but one female relative residing in Dublin, and she would believe, and think, and do, just as my brother might wish to make her. Oh, woeful hour! that it should ever come to this—that I should fear to trust another because she is my own brother's friend."

She had hardly ceased to speak when a small man, with his cocked hat set somewhat rakishly on one side, stepped forth from the little inn door; he had just lighted his pipe, and was inhaling its smoke with anxious attention lest the spark which he cherished should expire before the ignition of the weed became sufficiently general; his walk was therefore slow and interrupted; the top of his finger tenderly moved the kindling tobacco, and his two eyes squinted with intense absorption at the bowl of the pipe; by the time he had reached the back of the cart in which Mary Ashwoode and her attendant were seated, his labours were crowned by complete success, as was attested by the dense volumes of smoke which at regular intervals he puffed forth. He carried a cutting-whip under his arm, and was directing his steps toward a horse which, with its bridle thrown over a gate-post, was patiently awaiting his return. As he passed the rude vehicle in which the two fugitives were couched, he happened to pause for a moment, and Mary thought she recognized the figure before her as that of an old acquaintance.

"Is that Larry—Larry Toole?" inquired she.

"It's myself, sure enough," rejoined that identical personage; "an' who are you—a woman, to be sure, who else 'id be axin' for me?"

"Larry, don't you know me?" said she.

"Divil a taste," replied he. "I only see you're a female av coorse, why wouldn't you, for, by the piper that played before Moses, I'm never out of one romance till I'm into another."

"Larry," said she, lowering her voice, "it is Miss Ashwoode who speaks to you."

"Don't be funnin' me, can't you?" rejoined Larry, rather pettishly. "I've got enough iv the thricks iv women latterly; an' too much. I'm a raal marthyr to famale mineuvers; there's a bump on my head as big as a goose's egg, glory be to God! an' my bones is fairly aching with what I've gone through by raison iv confidin' myself to the mercy of women. Oh thunder——"

"I tell you, Larry," repeated Mary, "I am, indeed, Miss Ashwoode."

"No, but who are you, in earnest?" urged Larry Toole; "can't you put me out iv pain at wonst; upon my sowl I don't know you from Moses this blessed minute."

"Well, Larry, although you cannot recognize my voice," said she, turning back her hood so as to reveal her pale features in the moonlight, "you have not forgotten my face."

"Oh, blessed hour! Miss Mary," exclaimed Larry, in unfeigned amazement, while he hurriedly thrust his pipe into his pocket, and respectfully doffed his hat.

"Hush, hush," said Mary, with a gesture of caution. "Put on your hat, too; I wish to escape observation; put it on, Larry; it is my wish."

Larry reluctantly complied.

"Can you tell me where in town my uncle O'Leary is to be found?" inquired she, eagerly.

"Bedad, Miss Mary, he isn't in town at all," replied the man; "they say he married a widdy lady about ten days ago; at any rate he's gone out of town more than a week; I didn't hear where."

"I know not whither to turn for help or counsel, Flora," said she, despairingly, "my best friend is gone."

"Well," said Larry—who, though entirely ignorant of the exact nature of the young lady's fears, had yet quite sufficient shrewdness to perceive that she was, indeed, involved in some emergency of extraordinary difficulty and peril—"well, miss, maybe if you'd take a fool's advice for once, it might turn out best," said Larry. "There's an ould gentleman that knows all about your family; he was out at the manor, and had a long discourse, himself and Sir Richard—God rest him—a short time before the ould masther died; the gentleman's name is Audley; and, though he never seen you but once, he wishes you well, and 'id go a long way to sarve you; an' above all, he's a raal rock iv sinse. I'm not bad myself, but, begorra, I'm nothin' but a fool beside him; now do you, Miss Mary, and the young girl that's along with you, jist come in here; you can have a snug little room to yourselves, and I'll go into town and have the ould gentleman out with you before you know what you're about, or where you are; he'll ax no more than the wind iv the word to bring him here in a brace iv shakes; and my name's not Larry if he don't give you suparior advice."

A slight thing determines a mind perplexed and desponding; and Mary Ashwoode, feeling that whatever objection might well be started against the plan proposed by Larry Toole, yet felt that, were it rejected, she had none better to follow in its stead; anything rather than run the risk of being placed again in her brother's keeping; there was no time for deliberation, and therefore she at once adopted the suggestion. Larry, accordingly, conducted them into the little inn, and consigned them to the care of a haggard, slovenly girl, who, upon a hint from that gentleman, conducted them to a little chamber, up a flight of stairs, looking out upon the back yard, where, with a candle and a scanty fire, she left the two anxious fugitives; and, as she descended, they heard the clank of the iron shoes, as Larry spurred his horse into a hard gallop, speeding like the wind upon his mission.

The receding sounds of his rapid progress had, however, hardly ceased to be heard, when the fears and anxieties which had been for a moment forgotten, returned with heavier pressure upon the poor girl's heart, and she every moment expected to hear the dreaded voices of her pursuers in the passage beneath, or to see their faces entering at the door. Thus restlessly and fearfully she awaited the return of her courier.

CHAPTER LXII.

THE COUNCIL—SHOWING WHAT ADVICE MR. AUDLEY GAVE, AND HOW IT WAS TAKEN.

Larry Toole was true to his word. Without turning from the direct course, or pausing on his way for one moment, he accomplished the service which he had volunteered, and in an incredibly short time returned to the little inn, bringing Mr. Audley with him in a coach.

With an air of importance and mystery, suitable to the occasion, the little gentleman, followed by his attendant, proceeded to the chamber where Miss Ashwoode and her maid were awaiting his arrival. Mary arose as he entered the room, and Larry, from behind, ejaculated, in a tone of pompous exultation, "Here he is, Miss Mary—Mr. Audley himself, an' no mistake."

"Tut, tut, Larry," exclaimed the little gentleman, turning impatiently toward that personage, whose obstreperous announcement had disarranged his plans of approach; "hold your tongue, Larry, I say—ahem!"

"Mr. Audley," said Mary, "I hope you will pardon—"

"Not one word of the kind—excuse the interruption—not a word," exclaimed the little gentleman, gallantly waving his hand—"only too much honour—too proud, Miss Ashwoode, I have long known something of your family, and, strange as it may appear, have felt a peculiar interest in you—although I had not the honour of your acquaintance—for the sake of—of other parties. I have ever entertained a warm regard for your welfare, and although circumstances are much, very much changed, I cannot forget relations that once subsisted—ahem!" This was said diplomatically, and he blew his nose with a short decisive twang. "I understand, my poor young lady," he continued, relapsing into the cordial manner that was natural to him, "that you are at this moment in circumstances of difficulty, perhaps of danger, and that you have been disappointed in this emergency by the absence of your relative, Major O'Leary, with whose acquaintance, by-the-bye, I am honoured, and a more worthy, warm-hearted—but no matter—in his absence, then, I venture to tender my poor services—pray, if it be not too bold a request, tell me fully and fairly, the nature of your embarrassment; and if zeal, activity, and the friendliest dispositions can avail to extricate you, you may command them all—pray, then, let me know what I can do to serve you." So saying, the old gentleman took the pale and lovely lady's hand, with a mixture of tenderness and respect which encouraged and assured her.

Larry having withdrawn, she told the little gentleman all that she could communicate, without disclosing her brother's implication in the conspiracy. Even this reserve, the old gentleman's warm and kindly manner, and the good-natured simplicity, apparent in all he said and did, effectually removed, and the whole case, in all its bearings, and with all its circumstances, was plainly put before him. During the narrative, the little gentleman was repeatedly so transported with ire as to slap his thigh, sniff violently, and mutter incoherent ejaculations between his teeth; and when it was ended, was so far overcome by his feelings, that he did not trust himself to address the young lady, until he had a little vented his indignation by marching and countermarching, at quick time, up and down the room, blowing his nose with desperate abandonment, and muttering sundry startling interjections. At length he grew composed, and addressing Mary Ashwoode, observed,—

"You are quite right, my dear young lady—quite right, indeed, in resolving against putting yourself into the hands of anybody under Sir Henry's influence—perfectly right and wise. Have you no relatives in this country, none capable of protecting you, and willing to do so?"

"I have, indeed, one relative," rejoined she, but—"

"Who is it?" interrupted Audley.

"An uncle," replied Mary.

"His name, my dear—his name?" inquired the old gentleman, impatiently.

"His name is French—Oliver French," replied she, "but—"

"Never mind," interrupted Audley again, "where does he live?"

"He lives in an old place called Ardgillagh," rejoined she, "on the borders of the county of Limerick."

"Is it easily found out?—near the high road from Dublin?—near any town?—easily got at?" inquired he, with extra-ordinary volubility.

"I've heard my brother say," rejoined she, "that it is not far from the high road from Dublin; he was there himself. I believe the place is well known by the peasantry for many miles round; but——"

"Very good, very good, my dear," interposed Mr. Audley again. "Has he a family—a wife?"

"No," rejoined Mary; "he is unmarried, and an old man."

"Pooh, pooh! why the devil hasn't he a wife? but no matter, you'll be all the welcomer. That's our ground—all the safer that it's a little out of the way," exclaimed the old man. "We'll steal a march—they'll never suspect us; we'll start at once."

"But I fear," said Mary, dejectedly, "that he will not receive me. There has long been an estrangement between our family and him; with my father he had a deadly quarrel while I was yet an infant. He vowed that neither my father nor any child of his should ever cross his threshold. I've been told he bitterly resented what he believed to have been my father's harsh treatment of my mother. I was too young, however, to know on which side the right of the quarrel was; but I fear there is little hope of his doing as you expect, for some six or seven years since my brother was sent down, in the hope of a reconciliation, and in vain. He returned, reporting that my uncle Oliver had met all his advances with scorn. No, no, I fear—I greatly fear he will not receive me."

"Never believe it—never think so," rejoined old Audley, warmly; "if he were man enough to resent your mother's wrongs, think you his heart will have no room for yours? Think you his nature's changed, that he cannot pity the distressed, and hate tyranny any longer? Never believe me, if he won't hug you to his heart the minute he sees you. I like the old chap; he was right to be angry—it was his duty to be in a confounded passion; he ought to have been kicked if he hadn't done just as he did—I'd swear he was right. Never trust me, if he'll not take your part with his whole heart, and make you his pet for as long as you please to stay with him. Deuce take him, I like the old fellow."

"You would advise me, then, to apply to him for protection?" asked Mary Ashwoode, "and I suppose to go down there immediately."

"Most unquestionably so," replied Mr. Audley, with a short nod of decision—"most unquestionably —start to-night; we shall go as far as the town of Naas; I will accompany you. I consider you my ward until your natural protectors take you under their affectionate charge, and guard you from grief and danger as they ought. My good girl," he continued, addressing Flora Guy, "you must come along with your mistress; I've a coach at the door. We shall go directly into town, and my landlady shall take you both under her care until I have procured two chaises, the one for myself, and the other for your mistress and you. You will find Mrs. Pickley, my landlady, a very kind, excellent person, and ready to assist you in making your preparations for the journey."

The old gentleman then led his young and beautiful charge, with a mixture of gallantry and pity, by the hand down the little inn stairs, and in a very brief time Mary Ashwoode and her faithful attendant found themselves under the hospitable protection of Mrs. Pickley's roof-tree.

## CHAPTER LXIII

Never was little gentleman in such a fuss as Mr. Audley—never were so many orders issued and countermanded and given again—never were Larry Toole's energies so severely tried and his intellects so distracted—impossible tasks and contradictory orders so "huddled on his back," that he well nigh went mad under the burthen; at length, however, matters were arranged, two coaches with post-horses were brought to the door, Mary Ashwoode and her attendant were deposited in one, along with such extempore appliances for wardrobe and toilet as Mrs. Pickley, in a hurried excursion, was enabled to collect from the neighbouring shops and pack up for the journey, and Mr. Audley stood ready to take his place in the other.

"Larry," said he, before ascending, "here are ten guineas, which will keep you in bread and cheese until you hear from me again; don't on any account leave the 'Cock and Anchor,' your master's horse and luggage are there, and, no doubt, whenever he returns to Dublin, which I am very certain must soon occur, he will go directly thither; so be you sure to meet him there, should he happen during my absence to arrive; and mark me, be very careful of this letter, give it him the moment you see him, which, please God, will be very soon indeed; keep it in some safe place—don't carry it in your breeches pocket, you blockhead, you'll grind it to powder, booby! indeed, now that I think on't, you had better give it at once in charge to the innkeeper of the 'Cock and Anchor;' don't forget, on your life I charge you, and now good-night."

"Good-night, and good luck, your honour, and may God speed you!" ejaculated Larry, as the vehicles rumbled away. The charioteers had received their directions, and Mary Ashwoode and her trusty companion, confused and bewildered by the rapidity with which events had succeeded one another during the day, and stunned by the magnitude of the dangers which they had so narrowly escaped, found themselves, scarcely crediting the evidence of their senses, rapidly traversing the interval which separated Dublin city from the little town of Naas.

It is not our intention to weary our readers with a detailed account of the occurrences of the journey, nor to present them with a catalogue of all the mishaps and delays to which Irish posting in those days, and indeed much later, was liable; it is enough to state that upon the evening of the fourth day the two carriages clattered into the wretched little village which occupied the road on which opened the avenue leading up to the great house of Ardgillagh. The village, though obviously the abode of little comfort or cheerfulness, was not on that account the less picturesque; the road wound irregularly where it stood, and was carried by an old narrow bridge across a wayward mountain stream which wheeled and foamed in many a sportive eddy within its devious banks. Close by, the little mill was couched among the sheltering trees, which, extending in irregular and scattered groups through the village, and mingling with the stunted bushes and briars of the hedges, were nearly met from the other side of the narrow street by the broad branching limbs of the giant trees which skirted the wild wooded domain of Ardgillagh. Thus occupying a sweeping curve of the road, and embowered among the shadowy arches of the noble timber, the little village had at first sight an air of tranquillity, seclusion, and comfort, which made the traveller pause to contemplate its simple attractions and to admire how it could be that a few wretched hovels with crazy walls and thatch overgrown with weeds, thus irregularly huddled together beneath the rude shelter of the wood, could make a picture so pleasing to the eye and so soothing to the heart. The vehicles were drawn up by their drivers before the door of a small thatched building which, however, stood a whole head and shoulders higher than the surrounding hovels, exhibiting a second storey with three narrow windows in front, and over its doorway, from which a large pig, under the stimulus of a broomstick, was majestically issuing, a sign-board, the admiration of connoisseurs for miles round, presenting a half-length portrait of the illustrious Brian Borhome, and admitted to be a startling likeness. Before this mansion—the only one in the place which pretended to the character of a house of public entertainment—the post-boys drew bridle, and brought the vehicles to a halt. Mr. Audley was upon the road in an instant, and with fussy gallantry assisting Mary Ashwoode to descend. Their sudden arrival had astounded the whole household—consternation and curiosity filled the little establishment. The proprietor, who sat beneath the capacious chimney, started to his feet, swallowing, in his surprise, a whole potato, which he was just deliberately commencing, and by a miracle escaped choking. The landlady dropped a pot, which she was scrubbing, upon the back of a venerable personage who was in a stooping posture, lighting his pipe, and inadvertently wiped her face in the pot clout; everybody did something wrong, and nobody anything right; the dog was kicked and the cat scalded, and in short, never was known in the little village of Ardgillagh, within the memory of man, except when Ginckle marched his troops through the town, such a universal hubbub as that which welcomed the two chaises and their contents to the door of Pat Moroney's hospitable mansion.

Mrs. Moroney, with more lampblack upon her comely features than she was at that moment precisely aware of, hastened to the door, which she occupied as completely and exclusively as the corpulent specimen of Irish royalty over her head did his proper sign-board; all the time gazing with an admiring grin upon Mr. Audley and the lady whom he assisted to descend; and at exceedingly short and irregular intervals, executing sundry slight ducks, intended to testify her exuberant satisfaction and respect, while all around and about her were thrust the wondering visages of the less important inmates of the establishment; many were the murmured criticisms, and many the ejaculations of admiration and surprise, which accompanied every movement of the party under observation.

"Oh! but she's a fine young lady, God bless her!" said one.

"But isn't she mighty pale, though, entirely?" observed another.

"That's her father—the little stout gentleman; see how he houlds her hand for fear she'd thrip comin' out. Oh! but he's a nate man!" remarked a third.

"An' her hand as white as milk; an' look at her fine rings," said a fourth.

"She's a rale lady; see the grand look of her, and the stately step, God bless her!" said a fifth.

"See, see; here's another comin' out; that's her sisther," remarked another.

"Hould your tongues, will yees?" ejaculated the landlady, jogging her elbow at random into somebody's mouth.

"An' see the little one taking the box in her hand," observed one.

"Look at the tall lady, how she smiles at her, God bless her! she's a rale good lady," remarked another.

"An' now she's linkin' with him, and here they come, by gorra," exclaimed a third.

"Back with yees, an' lave the way," exclaimed Mrs. Moroney; "don't you see the quality comin'?"

Accordingly, with a palpitating heart, the worthy mistress of King Brian Borhome prepared to receive her aristocratic guests. With due state and ceremony she conducted them into the narrow chamber which, except the kitchen, was the only public apartment in the establishment. After due attention to his fair charge, Mr. Audley inquired of the hostess,—

"Pray, my good worthy woman, are we not now within a mile or less of the entrance into the domain of Ardgillagh?"

"The gate's not two perches down the road, your honour," replied she; "is it to the great house you want to go, sir?"

"Yes, my good woman; certainly," replied he.

"Come here, Shawneen, come, asthore!" cried she, through the half-open door. "I'll send the little gossoon with you, your honour; he'll show you the way, and keep the dogs off, for they all knows him up at the great house. Here, Shawneen; this gintleman wants to be showed the way up to the great house; and don't let the dogs near him; do you mind? He hasn't much English," said she, turning to her guest, by way of apology, and then conveying her directions anew in the mother tongue.

Under the guidance of this ragged little urchin, Mr. Audley accordingly set forth upon his adventurous excursion.

Mrs. Moroney brought in bread, milk, eggs, and in short, the best cheer which her limited resources could supply; and, although Mary Ashwoode was far too anxious about the result of Mr. Audley's visit to do more than taste the tempting bowl of new milk which was courteously placed before her, Flora Guy, with right good will and hearty appetite, did ample justice to the viands which the hostess provided.

After some idle talk between herself and Flora Guy, Mrs. Moroney observed in reply to an interrogatory from the girl,—

"Twenty or thirty years ago there wasn't such a fox-hunter in the country as Mr. French; but he's this many a year ailing, and winter after winter, it's worse and worse always he's getting, until at last he never stirs out at all; and for the most part he keeps his bed."

"Is anyone living with him?" inquired Flora.

"No, none of his family," answered she; "no one at all, you may say; there's no one does anything in his place, an' very seldom anyone sees him except Mistress Martha and Black M'Guinness; them two has him all to themselves; and, indeed, there's quare stories goin' about them."

CHAPTER LXIV.

MISTRESS MARTHA AND BLACK M'GUINNESS.

Mr. Audley, preceded by his little ragged guide, walked thoughtfully on his way to visit the old gentleman, of whose oddities and strange and wayward temper the keeper of the place where they had last obtained a relay of horses had given a marvellous and perhaps somewhat exaggerated account. Now that he had reached the spot, and that the moment approached which was to be the crisis of the adventure, he began to feel far less confident of success than he had been while the issue of his project was comparatively remote.

They passed down the irregular street of the village, and beneath the trees which arched overhead like the vast and airy aisles of some huge Gothic pile, and after a short walk of some two or three hundred yards, during which they furnished matter of interesting speculation to half the village idlers, they reached a rude gate of great dimensions, but which had obviously seen better days. There was no lodge or gate-house, and Mr. Audley followed the little conductor over a stile, which occupied the side of one of the great ivy-mantled stone piers; crossing this, he found himself in the demesne. A broken and irregular avenue or bridle track—for in most places it was little more—led onward over hill and through hollow, along the undulations of the soft green sward, and under the fantastic boughs of gnarled thorns and oaks and sylvan birches, which in thick groups, wild and graceful as nature had placed them, clothed the varied slopes. The rude approach which they followed led them a wayward course over every variety of ground—now flat and boggy, again up hill, and over the grey surface of lichen-covered rocks—again down into deep fern-clothed hollows, and then across the shallow, brawling stream, without bridge or appliance of any kind, but simply through its waters, forced, as best they might, to pick their steps upon the moss-grown stones that peeped above the clear devious current. Thus they passed along through this wild and extensive demesne, varied by a thousand inequalities of ground and by the irregular grouping of the woods, which owed their picturesque arrangement to the untutored fancies of nature herself, whose dominion had there never known the intrusions of the axe, or the spade, or the pruning-hook, but exulted in the unshackled indulgence of all her wildest revelry. After a walk of more than half-an-hour's duration, through a long vista among the trees, the grey gable of the old mansion of Ardgillagh, with its small windows and high and massive chimney stacks, presented itself.

There was a depressing air of neglect and desertion about the old place, which even the unimaginative temperament of Mr. Audley was obliged to acknowledge. Rank weeds and grass had forced their way through the pavement of the courtyard, and crowded in patches of vegetation even to the very door of the house. The same was observable, in no less a degree, in the great stable-yard, the gate of which, unhinged, lay wide open, exhibiting a range of out-houses and stables, which would have afforded lodging for horse and man to a whole regiment of dragoons. Two men, one of them in livery, were loitering through the courtyard, apparently not very well knowing what to do with themselves; and as the visitors approached, a whole squadron of dogs, the little ones bouncing in front with shrill alarm, and the more formidable, at a majestic canter and with deep-mouthed note of menace, bringing up the rear, came snarling, barking, and growling, towards the intruders at startling speed.

"Piper, Piper, Toby, Fan, Motheradauna, Boxer, Boxer, Toby!" screamed the little guide, advancing a few yards before Mr. Audley, who, in considerable uneasiness, grasped his walking cane with no small energy. The interposition of the urchin was successful, the dogs recognized their young friend, the angry clangour was hushed and their pace abated, and when they reached Mr. Audley and his guide, in compliment to the latter they suffered the little gentleman to pass on, with no further question than a few suspicious sniffs, as they applied their noses to the calves of that gentleman's legs. As they continued to approach, the men in the court, now alarmed by the vociferous challenge of the dogs, eyed the little gentleman inquisitively, for a visitor at Ardgillagh was a thing that had not been heard of for years. As Mr. Audley's intention became more determinate, and his design appeared more unequivocally to apply for admission, the servant, who watched his progress, ran by some hidden passage in the stable-yard into the mansion and was ready to gratify his curiosity legitimately, by taking his post in the hall in readiness to answer Mr. Audley's summons, and to hold parley with him at the door.

"Is Mr. French at home?" inquired Mr. Audley.

"Ay, sir, he is at home," rejoined the man, deliberately, to allow himself time fully to scrutinize the visitor's outward man.

"Can I see him, pray?" asked the little gentleman.

"Why, raly, sir, I can't exactly say," observed the man, scratching his head. "He's upstairs in his own chamber—indeed, for that matter, he's seldom out of it. If you'll walk into the room there, sir, I'll inquire."

Accordingly, Mr. Audley entered the apartment indicated and sat himself down in the deep recess of the window to take breath. He well knew the kind of person with whom he had to deal, previously to encountering Oliver French in person. He had heard quite enough of Mistress Martha and of Black M'Guinness already, to put him upon his guard, and fill him with just suspicions as to their character and designs; he therefore availed himself of the little interval to arrange his plans of operation in his own mind. He had not waited long, when the door opened, and a tall, elderly woman, with a bunch of keys at her side, and arrayed in a rich satin dress, walked demurely into the room. There was something unpleasant and deceitful in the expression of the half-closed eyes and thin lips of this lady which inspired Mr. Audley with instinctive dislike of her—an impression which was rather heightened than otherwise by the obvious profusion with which her sunken and sallow cheeks were tinged with rouge. This demure and painted lady made a courtesy on seeing Mr. Audley, and in a low and subdued tone which well accorded with her meek exterior, inquired,—

"You were asking for Mr. Oliver French, sir?"

"Yes, madam," replied Mr. Audley, returning the salute with a bow as formal; "I wish much to see him, if he could afford me half an hour's chat."

"Mr. French is very ill—very—very poorly, indeed," said Mistress Martha, closing her eyes, and shaking her head. "He dislikes talking to strangers. Are you a relative, pray, sir?"

"Not I, madam—not at all, madam," rejoined Mr. Audley.

A silence ensued, during which he looked out for a minute at the view commanded by the window; and as he did so, he observed with the corner of his eyes that the lady was studying him with a severe and searching scrutiny. She was the first to break the silence.

"I suppose it's about business you want to see him?" inquired she, still looking at him with the same sharp glance.

"Just so," rejoined Mr. Audley; "it is indeed upon business."

"He dislikes transacting business or speaking of it himself," said she. "He always employs his own man, Mr. M'Guinness. I'll call Mr. M'Guinness, that you may communicate the matter to him."

"You must excuse me," said Mr. Audley. "My instructions are to give my message to Mr. Oliver French in person—though indeed there's no secret in the matter. The fact is, Madam, my mission is of a kind which ought to make me welcome. You understand me? I come here to announce a—a—an acquisition, in short a sudden and, I believe, a most unexpected acquisition. But perhaps I've said too much; the facts are for his own ear solely. Such are my instructions; and you know I have no choice. I've posted all the way from Dublin to execute the message; and between ourselves, should he suffer this occasion to escape him, he may never again have an opportunity of making such an addition to—but I must hold my tongue—I'm prating against orders. In a word, madam, I'm greatly mistaken, or it will prove the best news that has been told in this house since its master was christened."

He accompanied his announcement with a prodigious number of nods and winks of huge significance, and all designed to beget the belief that he carried in his pocket the copy of a will, or other instrument, conveying to the said Oliver French of Ardgillagh the gold mines of Peru, or some such trifle.

Mistress Martha paused, looked hard at him, then reflected again. At length she said, with the air of a woman who has made up her mind,—

"I dare to say, sir, it is possible for you to see Mr. French. He is a little better to-day. You'll promise not to fatigue him—but you must first see Mr. M'Guinness. He can tell better than I whether his master is sufficiently well to-day for an interview of the kind."

So saying, Mrs. Martha sailed, with saint-like dignity, from the room.

"She rules the roost, I believe," said Mr. Audley within himself. "If so, all's smooth from this forth. Here comes the gentleman, however—and, by the laws, a very suitable co-mate for that painted Jezebel."

As Mr. Audley concluded this criticism, a small man, with a greasy and dingy complexion, and in a rusty suit of black, made his appearance.

This individual was, if possible, more subdued, meek, and Christian-like than the lady who had just evacuated the room in his favour. His eyes were, if possible, habitually more nearly closed; his step was as soft and cat-like to the full; and, in a word, he was in air, manner, gait, and expression as like his accomplice as a man can well be to one of the other sex.

A short explanation having passed between this person and Mr. Audley, he retired for a few minutes to prepare his master for the visit, and then returning, conducted the little bachelor upstairs.

## CHAPTER LXV

THE CONFERENCE—SHOWING HOW OLIVER FRENCH BURST INTO A RAGE AND FLUNG HIS CAP ON THE FLOOR.

Mr. Audley followed Black M'Guinness as we have said up the stairs, and was, after an introductory knock at the door, ushered by him into Oliver French's bed-room. Its arrangements were somewhat singular—a dressing-table with all the appliances of the most elaborate cultivation of the graces, and a huge mirror upon it, stood directly opposite to the door; against the other wall, between the door and this table, was placed a massive sideboard covered with plate and wine flasks, cork-screws and cold meat, in the most admired disorder—two large presses were also visible, one of which lay open, exhibiting clothes, and papers, and other articles piled together in a highly original manner—two or three very beautiful pictures hung upon the walls. At the far end of the room stood the bed, and at one side of it a table covered with wines and viands, and at the other, a large iron-bound chest, with a heavy bunch of keys dangling from its lock—a little shelf, too, occupied the wall beside the invalid, abundantly stored with tall phials with parchment labels, and pill-boxes and gallipots innumerable. In the bed, surrounded by the drapery of the drawn curtains, lay, or rather sat, Oliver French himself, propped up by the pillows: he was a corpulent man, with a generous double chin; a good-natured grey eye twinkled under a bushy, grizzled eye-brow, and a countenance which bore unequivocally the lines of masculine beauty, although considerably disfigured by the traces of age, as well as of something very like intemperance and full living: he wore a silk night-gown and a shirt of snowy whiteness, with lace ruffles, and on his head was a crimson velvet cap.

Grotesque as were the arrangements of the room, there was, nevertheless, about its occupant an air of aristocratic superiority and ease which at once dispelled any tendency to ridicule.

"Mr. Audley, I presume," said the invalid.

Mr. Audley bowed.

"Pray, sir, take a chair. M'Guinness, place a chair for Mr. Audley, beside the table here. I am, as you see, sir," continued he, "a confirmed valetudinarian; I suffer abominably from gout, and have not been able to remove to my easy chair by the fire for more than a week. I understand that you have some matters of importance to communicate to me; but before doing so, let me request of you to take a little wine, you can have whatever you like best—there's some Madeira at your elbow there, which I can safely recommend, as I have just tasted it myself—o-oh! Damn—the gout—you'll excuse me, sir—a cursed twinge."

"Very sorry to see you suffering," responded Mr. Audley—"very, indeed, sir."

"It sha'n't, however, prevent my doing you reason, sir," replied he, with alacrity. "M'Guinness, two glasses. I drink, sir, to our better acquaintance. Now, M'Guinness, you may leave the room."

Accordingly Mr. M'Guinness withdrew, and the gentlemen were left tête-à-tête.

"And now, sir," continued Oliver French, "be so good as to open the subject of your visit."

Mr. Audley cleared his voice twice or thrice, in the hope of clearing his head at the same time, and then, with some force and embarrassment, observed,—

"I am necessarily obliged, Mr. French, to allude to matters which may possibly revive unpleasant recollections. I trust, indeed, my dear sir,—I'm sure that you will not suffer yourself to be distressed or unduly excited, when I tell you that I must recall to your memory a name which I believe does not sound gratefully to your ear—the name of Ashwoode."

"Curse them," was the energetic commentary of the invalid.

"Well, sir, I dare venture to say that you and I are not very much at variance in our estimate of the character of the Ashwoodes generally," said Mr. Audley. "You are aware, I presume, that Sir Richard has been some time dead."

"Ha! actually gone to hell?—no, sir, I was not aware of this. Pray, proceed, sir," responded Oliver French.

"I am aware, sir, that he treated his lady harshly," resumed Audley.

"Harshly, harshly, sir," cried the old man, with an energy that well nigh made his companion bounce from his seat—"why, sir, beginning with neglect and ending with blows—through every stage of savage insult and injury, his wretched wife, my sister—the most gentle, trusting, lovely creature that ever yet was born to misery, was dragged by that inhuman monster, her husband, Sir Richard Ashwoode; he broke her heart—he killed her, sir—killed her. She was my sister—my only sister; I was justly proud of her—loved her most dearly, and the inhuman villain broke her heart."

Through his clenched teeth he uttered a malediction, and with a vehemence of hatred which plainly showed that his feelings toward the family had undergone no favourable change.

"Well, sir," resumed Mr. Audley, after a considerable interval, "I cannot wonder at the strength of your feelings in this matter, more especially at this moment. I myself burn with indignation scarce one degree less intense than yours against the worthy son of that most execrable man, and upon grounds, too, very nearly similar."

He then proceeded to recount to his auditor, waxing warm as he went on, all the circumstances of Mary Ashwoode's sufferings, and every particular of the grievous persecution which she had endured at the hands of her brother, Sir Henry. Oliver French ground his teeth and clutched the bed-clothes as he listened, and when the narrative was ended, he whisked the velvet cap from his head, and flung it with all his force upon the floor.

"Oh, God Almighty! that I had but the use of my limbs," exclaimed he, with desperation—"I would give the whole world a lesson in the person of that despicable scoundrel. I would—but," he added bitterly, "I am powerless—I am a cripple."

"You are not powerless, sir, for purposes nobler than revenge," exclaimed Audley, with eagerness; "you may shelter and protect the helpless, friendless child of calamity, the story of whose wrongs has so justly fired you with indignation."

"Where is she—where?" cried Oliver French, eagerly—"I ought to have asked you long ago."

"She is not far away—she even now awaits your decision in the little village hard by," responded Mr. Audley.

"Poor child—poor child!" ejaculated Oliver, much agitated. "And did she—could she doubt my willingness to befriend her—good God—could she doubt it?—bring her—bring her here at once—I long to see her—poor bird—poor bird—the world's winter has closed over thee too soon. Alas! poor child—tell her—tell her, Mr. Audley, that I long to see her—that she is most welcome—that all which I command is heartily and entirely at her service. Plead my apology for not going myself to meet her—as God knows I would fain do; you see I am a poor cripple—a very worthless, helpless, good-for-nothing old man. Tell her all better than I can do it now. God bless you, sir—God bless you, for believing that such an ill-conditioned old fellow as I am had yet heart enough to feel rightly sometimes. I had rather die a thousand deaths than that you had not brought the poor outcast child to my roof. Tell her how glad—how very, very happy—how proud it makes me that she should come to her old uncle Oliver—tell her this. God bless you, sir!"

With a cordial pressure, he gripped Audley's hand, and the old gentleman, with a heart overflowing with exultation and delight, retraced his steps to the little village, absolutely bursting with impatience to communicate the triumphant result of his visit.

## CHAPTER LXVI.

### THE BED-CHAMBER.

Black M'Guinness and Mistress Martha had listened in vain to catch the purport of Mr. Audley's communication. Unfortunately for them, their master's chamber was guarded by a double door, and his companion had taken especial pains to close both of them before detailing the subject of his visit. They were, however a good deal astonished by Mr. French's insisting upon rising forthwith, and having himself clothed and shaved. This huge, good-natured lump of gout was, accordingly, arrayed in full suit—one of the handsomest which his wardrobe commanded—his velvet cap replaced by a flowing peruke—his gouty feet smothered in endless flannels, and himself deposited in his great easy chair by the fire, and his lower extremities propped up upon stools and pillows. These preparations, along with a complete re-arrangement of the furniture, and other contents of the room, effectually perplexed and somewhat alarmed his disinterested dependents.

Mr. Audley returned ere the preparations were well completed, and handed Mary Ashwoode and her attendant from the chaise. It needs not to say how the old bachelor of Ardgillagh received her—with, perhaps, the more warmth and tenderness that, as he protested, with tears in his eyes, she was so like her poor mother, that he felt as if old times had come again, and that she stood once more before him, clothed in the melancholy beauty of her early and ill-fated youth. It were idle to describe the overflowing kindness of the old man's greeting, and the depth of gratitude with which his affectionate and hearty welcome was accepted by the poor grieved girl. He would scarcely, for the whole evening, allow her to leave him for one moment; and every now and again renewed his pressing invitation to her and to Mr. Audley to take some more wine or some new delicacy; he himself enforcing his solicitations by eating and drinking in almost unbroken continuity during the whole time. All his habits were those of the most unlimited self-indulgence; and his chief, if not his sole recreation for years, had consisted in compounding, during the whole day long, those astounding gastronomic combinations, which embraced every possible variety of wine and liqueur, of vegetable, meat, and confection; so that the fact of his existing at all, under the extraordinary regimen which he had adopted, was a triumph of the genius of digestion over the demon of dyspepsia, such as this miserable world has seldom witnessed. Nevertheless, that he did exist, and that too, apparently, in robust though unwieldy health, with the exception of his one malady, his constitutional gout, was a fact which nobody could look upon and dispute. With an imperiousness which brooked no contradiction, he compelled Mr. Audley to eat and drink very greatly more than he could conveniently contain—browbeating the poor little gentleman into submission, and swearing, in the most impressive manner, that he had not eaten one ounce weight of food of any kind since his entrance into the house; although the unhappy little gentleman felt at that moment like a boa constrictor who has just bolted a buffalo, and pleaded in stifled accents for quarter; but it would not do. Oliver French, Esq., had not had his humour crossed, nor one of his fancies contradicted, for the last forty years, and he was not now to be thwarted or put down by a little "hop-o'-my-thumb," who, though ravenously hungry, pretended, through mere perverseness, to be bursting with repletion. Mr. Audley's labours were every now and again pleasingly relieved by such applications as these from his merciless entertainer.

"Now, my good friend—my worthy friend—will you think it too great a liberty, sir, if I ask you to move the pillow a leetle under this foot?"

"None in the world, sir—quite the contrary—I shall have the very greatest possible pleasure," would poor Mr. Audley reply, preparing for the task.

"You are very good, sir, very kind, sir. Just draw it quietly to the right—a little, a very little—you are very good, indeed, sir. Oh—oh, O—oh, you—you booby—you'll excuse me, sir—gently—there, there—gently, gently. O—oh, you damned handless idiot—pray pardon me, sir; that will do."

Such passages as these were of frequent occurrence; but though Mr. Audley was as choleric as most men at his time of life, yet the incongruous terms of abuse were so obviously the result of inveterate and almost unconscious habit, stimulated by the momentary twinges of acute pain, that he did not suffer this for an instant to disturb the serenity and goodwill with which he regarded his host, spite of all his oddities and self-indulgence.

In the course of the evening Oliver French ordered Mistress Martha to have beds prepared for the party, and that lady, with rather a vicious look, withdrew. She soon returned, and asked in her usual low, dulcet tone, whether the young lady could spare her maid to assist in arranging the room, and forthwith Flora Guy consigned herself to the guidance of the sinister-looking Abigail.

"This is a fine country, isn't it?" inquired Mistress Martha, softly, when they were quite alone.

"A very fine country, indeed, ma'am," rejoined Flora, who had heard enough to inspire her with a certain awe of her conductress, which inclined her as much as possible to assent to whatever proposition she might be inclined to advance, without herself hazarding much original matter.

"It's a pity you can't see it in the summer time; this is a very fine place indeed when all the leaves are on the trees," repeated Mistress Martha.

"Indeed, so I'd take it to be, ma'am," rejoined the maid.

"Just passing through this way—hurried like, you can't notice much about it though," remarked the elderly lady, carelessly.

"No, ma'am," replied Flora, becoming more reserved, as she detected in her companion a wish to draw from her all she knew of her mistress's plans.

"There are some views that are greatly admired in the neighbourhood—the glen and the falls of Glashangower. If she could stay a week she might see everything."

"Oh! indeed, it's a lovely place," observed Flora, evasively.

"That old gentleman, that Mr. Audley, your young mistress's father, or—or uncle, or whatever he is"—Mistress Martha here made a considerable pause, but Flora did not enlighten her, and she continued—"whatever he is to her, it's no matter, he seems a very good-humoured nice old gentleman —he's in a great hurry back to Dublin, where he came from, I suppose."

"Well, I really don't know," replied the girl.

"He looks very comfortable, and everything handsome and nice about him," observed Mistress Martha again. "I suppose he's well off—plenty of money—not in want at all."

"Indeed he seems all that," rejoined the maid.

"He's cousin, or something or another, to the master, Mr. French; didn't you tell me so?" asked the painted Abigail.

"No, ma'am; I didn't tell you; I don't know," replied she.

"This is a very damp old house, and full of rats; I wish I had known a week ago that beds would be wanting; but I suppose it was a sudden thing," said the housekeeper.

"Indeed, I suppose it just was, ma'am," responded the attendant.

"Are you going to stay here long?" asked the old lady, more briskly than she had yet spoken.

"Raly, ma'am, I don't know," replied Flora.

The old painted termagant shot a glance at her of no pleasant meaning; but for the present checked the impulse in which it had its birth, and repeated softly—"You don't know; why, you are a very innocent, simple little girl."

"Pray, ma'am, if it's not making too bold, which is the room, ma'am?" asked Flora.

"What's your young lady's name?" asked the matron, directly, and disregarding the question of the girl.

Flora Guy hesitated.

"Do you hear me—what's your young lady's name?" repeated the woman, softly, but deliberately.

"Her name, to be sure; her name is Miss Mary," replied she.

"Mary what?" asked Martha.

"Miss Mary Ashwoode," replied Flora, half afraid as she uttered it.

Spite of all her efforts, the woman's face exhibited disagreeable symptoms of emotion at this announcement; she bit her lips and dropped her eyelids lower than usual, to conceal the expression which gleamed to her eyes, while her colour shifted even through her rouge. At length, with a smile infinitely more unpleasant than any expression which her face had yet worn, she observed,—

"Ashwoode, Ashwoode. Oh! dear, to be sure; some of Sir Richard's family; well, I did not expect to see them darken these doors again. Dear me! who'd have thought of the Ashwoodes looking after him again? well, well, but they're a very forgiving family," and she uttered an ill-omened tittering.

"Which is the room, ma'am, if you please?" repeated Flora.

"That's the room," cried the stalwart dame, with astounding vehemence, and at the same time opening a door and exhibiting a large neglected bed-chamber, with its bed-clothes and other furniture lying about in entire disorder, and no vestige of a fire in the grate; "that's the room, miss, and make the best of it yourself, for you've nothing else to do."

In this very uncomfortable predicament Flora Guy applied herself energetically to reduce the room to something like order, and although it was very cold and not a little damp, she succeeded, nevertheless, in giving it an air of tolerable comfort by the time her young mistress was prepared to retire to it.

As soon as Mary Ashwoode had entered this chamber her maid proceeded to narrate the occurrences which had just taken place.

"Well, Flora," said she, smiling, "I hope the old lady will resume her good temper by to-morrow, for one night I can easily contrive to rest with such appliances as we have. I am more sorry, for your sake, my poor girl, than for mine, however, and wherever I lay me down, my rest will be, I fear me, very nearly alike."

"She's the darkest, ill-lookingest old woman, God bless us, that ever I set my two good-looking eyes upon, my lady," said Flora. "I'll put a table to the door; for, to tell God's truth, I'm half afeard of her. She has a nasty look in her, my lady—a bad look entirely."

Flora had hardly spoken when the door opened, and the subject of their conversation entered.

"Good evening to you, Miss Ashwoode," said she, advancing close to the young lady, and speaking in her usual low soft tone. "I hope you find everything to your liking. I suppose your own maid has settled everything according to your fancy. Of course, she knows best how to please you. I'm very delighted to see you here in Ardgillagh, as I was telling your innocent maid there—very glad, indeed; because, as I said, it shows how forgiving you are, after all the master has said and done, and the way he has always spit on every one of your family that ever came here looking after his money—though, indeed, I'm sure you're a great deal too good and too religious to care about money; and I'm sure and certain it's only for the sake of Christian charity, and out of a forgiving disposition, and to show that there isn't a bit of pride of any sort, or kind, or description in your carcase—that you're come here to make yourself at home in this house, that never belonged to you, and that never will, and to beg favours of the gentleman that hates, and despises, and insults everyone that carries your name—so that the very dogs in the streets would not lick their blood. I like that, Miss Ashwoode—I do like it," she continued, advancing a little nearer; "for it shows you don't care what bad people may say or think, provided you do your Christian duty. They may say you're come here to try and get the old gentleman's money; they may say that you're eaten up to the very backbone with meanness, and that you'd bear to be kicked and spit upon from one year's end to the other for the sake of a few pounds—they'll call you a sycophant and a schemer—but you don't mind that—and I admire you for it—they'll say, miss—for they don't scruple at anything—they'll say you lost your character and fortune in Dublin, and came down here in the hope of finding them again; but I tell you what it is," she continued, giving full vent to her fury, and raising her accents to a tone more resembling the scream of a screech-owl than the voice of a human being, "I know what you're at, and I'll blow your schemes, Miss Innocence. I'll make the house too hot to hold you. Do you think I mind the old bed-ridden cripple, or anyone else within its four walls? Hoo! I'd make no more of them or of you than that old glass there;" and so saying, she hurled the candlestick, with all her force, against the large mirror which depended from the wall, and dashed it to atoms.

"Hoo! hoo!" she screamed, "you think I am afraid to do what I threatened; but wait—wait, I say; and now good-night to you, Miss Ashwoode, for the first time, and pleasant dreams to you."

So saying, the fiendish hag, actually quivering with fury, quitted the room, drawing the door after her with a stunning crash, and leaving Mary Ashwoode and her servant breathless with astonishment and consternation.

CHAPTER LXVII.

THE EXPULSION.

While this scene was going on in Mary Ashwoode's chamber, our friend Oliver French, having wished Mr. Audley good-night, had summoned to his presence his confidential servant, Mr. M'Guinness. The corpulent invalid sat in his capacious chair by the fireside, with his muffled legs extended upon a pile of pillows, a table loaded with the materials of his protracted and omnigenous repast at his side. Black M'Guinness made his appearance, evidently a little intoxicated, and not a little excited. He proceeded in a serpentine course through the chamber, overturning, of malice prepense, everything in which he came in contact.

"What the devil ails you, sir?" ejaculated Mr. French—"what the plague do you mean? D—n you, M'Guinness, you're drunk, sir, or mad."

"Ay, to be sure," ejaculated M'Guinness, grimly. "Why not—oh, do—I've no objection; damn away, sir, pray, do."

"What do you mean by talking that way, you scoundrel?" exclaimed old French.

"Scoundrel!" repeated M'Guinness, overturning a small table, and all thereupon, with a crash upon the floor, and approaching the old gentleman, while his ugly face grew to a sickly, tallowy white with rage, "you go for to bring a whole lot of beggarly squatters into the house to make away with your substance, and to turn you against your faithful, tried, trusty, and dutiful servants," he continued, shaking his fist in his master's face. "You do, and to leave them, ten to one, in their old days unprovided for. Damn ingratitude!—to the devil with thankless, unnatural vermin! You call me scoundrel. Scoundrel was the word—by this cross it was."

While Oliver French, speechless with astonishment and rage, gazed upon the audacious menial, Mistress Martha herself entered the chamber.

"Yes, they are, you old dark-hearted hypocrite—they're settled here—fixed in the house—they are," screamed she; "but they sha'n't stay long; or, if they do, I'll not leave a whole bone in their skins. What did they ever do for you, you thankless wretch?"

"Ay, what did they ever do for you?" shouted M'Guinness.

"Do you think we're fools—do you? and idiots—do you? not to know what you're at, you ungrateful miscreant! Turn them out, bag and baggage—every mother's skin of them, or I'll show them the reason why, turn them out, I say."

"You infernal hag, I'd see you in hell or Bedlam first," shouted Oliver, transported with fury. "You have had your way too long, you accursed witch—you have."

"Never mind—oh!—you wretch," shrieked she—"never mind—wait a bit—and never fear, you old crippled sinner, I'll be revenged on you, you old devil's limb. Here's your watch for you," screamed she, snatching a massive, chased gold watch from her side, and hurling it at his head. It passed close by his ear, and struck the floor behind him, attesting the force with which it had been thrown, as well as the solidity of its workmanship, by a deep mark ploughed in the floor.

Oliver French grasped his crutch and raised it threateningly.

"You old wretch, I'll not let you strike the woman," cried M'Guinness, snatching the poker, and preparing to dash it at the old man's head. What might have been the issue of the strife it were hard to say, had not Mr. Audley at that moment entered the room.

"Heyday!" cried that gentleman, "I thought it had been robbers—what's all this?"

M'Guinness turned upon him, but observing that he carried a pistol in each hand, he contented himself with muttering a curse and lowering the poker which he held in his hand.

"Why, what the devil—your own servants—your own man and woman!" exclaimed Mr. Audley. "I beg your pardon, sir—pray excuse me, Mr. French; perhaps I ought not to have intruded upon you."

"Pray don't go, Mr. Audley—don't think of going," said Oliver, eagerly, observing that his visitor was drawing to the door. "These beasts will murder me if you leave me; I can't help myself—do stay."

"Pray, madam, you are the amiable and remarkably quiet gentlewoman with whom I was to-day honoured by an interview? God bless my body and soul, can it possibly be?" said Mr. Audley, addressing himself to the lady.

"You vile old swindling schemer," shrieked she, returning—"you skulking, mean dog—you brandy-faced old reprobate, you—hoo! wait, wait—wait awhile; I'll master you yet—just wait—never mind—hoo!" and with something like an Indian war-whoop she dashed out of the room.

"Get out of this apartment, you ruffian, you—M'Guinness, get out of the room," cried old French, addressing the fellow, who still stood grinning and growling there.

"No, I'll not till I do my business," retorted the man, doggedly; "I'll put you to bed first. I've a right to do my own business; I'll undress you and put you to bed first—bellows me, but I will."

"Mr. Audley, I beg pardon for troubling you," said Oliver, "but will you pull the bell if you please, like the very devil."

"Pull away till you are black in the face; I'll not stir," retorted M'Guinness.

Mr. Audley pulled the bell with a sustained vehemence which it put Mr. French into a perspiration even to witness.

"Pull away, old gentleman—you may pull till you burst—to the devil with you all. I'll not stir a peg till I choose it myself; I'll do my business what I was hired for; there's no treason in that. D—— me, if I stir a peg for you," repeated M'Guinness, doggedly.

Meanwhile, two half-dressed, scared-looking servants, alarmed by Mr. Audley's persevering appeals, showed themselves at the door.

"Thomas—Martin—come in here, you pair of boobies," exclaimed French, authoritatively; "Martin, do you keep an eye on that scoundrel, and Thomas, run you down and waken the post-boy and tell him to put his horses to, and do you assist him, sir, away!"

With unqualified amazement in their faces, the men proceeded to obey their orders.

"So, so," said Oliver, still out of breath with anger, "matters are come to a pleasant pass, I'm to be brained with my own poker—by my own servant—in my own house—very pleasant, because forsooth, I dare to do what I please with my own—highly agreeable, truly! Mr. Audley, may I trouble you to give me a glass of noyeau—let me recommend that to you, Mr. Audley, it has the true flavour—nay, nay—I'll hear of no excuse—I'm absolute in my own room at least—come, my dear sir—I implore—I insist—nay, I command; come—come—a bumper; very good health, sir; a pleasant pair of furies!—just give me the legs of that woodcock while we are waiting."

Accordingly Mr. Oliver French filled up the brief interval after his usual fashion, by adding slightly to the contents of his stomach, and in a little time the servant whom he had dispatched downward, returned with the post-boy in person.

"Are your horses under the coach, my good lad?" inquired old French.

"No, but they're to it, and that's better," responded the charioteer.

"You'll not have far to go—only to the little village at the end of the avenue," said Mr. French. "Mr. Audley, may I trouble you to fill a large glass of Creme de Portugal; thank you; now, my good lad, take that," continued he, delighted at an opportunity of indulging his passion for ministering to the stomach of a fellow mortal, "take it—take it—every drop—good—now Martin, do you and Thomas find that termagant—fury—Martha Montgomery, and conduct her to the coach—carry her down if necessary—put her into it, and one of you remain with her, to prevent her getting out again, and let the other return, and with my friend the post-boy, do a like good office by my honest comrade Mr. M'Guinness—mind you go along with them to the village, and let them be set down at Moroney's public-house; everything belonging to them shall be sent down to-morrow morning, and if you ever catch either of them about the place—duck them—whip them—set the dogs on them—that's all."

Shrieking as though body and soul were parting, Mrs. Martha was half-carried, half-dragged from the scene of her long-abused authority; screaming her threats, curses, and abuse in volleys, she was deposited safely in the vehicle, and guarded by the footman—who in secret rejoiced in common with all the rest of the household at the disgrace of the two insolent favourites—and was forced to sit therein until her companion in misfortune being placed at her side, they were both, under a like escort, safely deposited at the door of the little public-house, scarcely crediting the evidence of their senses for the reality of their situation.

Henceforward Ardgillagh was a tranquil place, and day after day old Oliver French grew to love the gentle creature, whom a chance wind had thus carried to his door, more and more fondly. There was an artlessness and a warmth of affection, and a kindliness about her, which all, from the master down to the humblest servant, felt and loved; a grace, and dignity, and a simple beauty in every look and action, which none could see and not admire. The strange old man, whose humour had never brooked contradiction, felt for her, he knew not why, a tenderness and respect such as he never before believed a mortal creature could inspire; her gentle wish was law to him; to see her sweet face was his greatest joy—to please her his first ambition; she grew to be, as it were, his idol.

It was her chief delight to ramble unattended through the fine old place. Often, with her faithful follower, Flora Guy, she would visit the humble dwellings of the poor, wherever grief or sickness was, and with gentle words of comfort and bounteous pity, cheer and relieve. But still, from week to week it became too mournfully plain that the sweet, sad face was growing paler and ever paler, and the graceful form more delicately slight. In the silent watches of the night often would Flora Guy hear her loved young mistress weep on for hours, as though her heart were breaking; yet from her lips there never fell at any time one word of murmuring, nor any save those of gentle kindness; and often would she sit by the casement and reverently read the pages of one old volume, and think and read again, while ever and anon the silent tears, gathering on the long, dark lashes, would fall one by one upon the leaf, and then would she rise with such a smile of heavenly comfort breaking through her tears, that peace, and hope, and glory seemed beaming in her pale angelic face.

Thus from day to day, in the old mansion of Ardgillagh, did she, whose beauty none, even the most stoical, had ever seen unmoved—whose artless graces and perfections all who had ever beheld her had thought unmatched, fade slowly and uncomplainingly, but with beauty if possible enhanced, before the eyes of those who loved her; yet they hoped on, and strongly hoped—why should they not? She was young—yes, very young, and why should the young die in the glad season of their early bloom?

Mr. Audley became a wondrous favourite with his eccentric entertainer, who would not hear of his fixing a time for his departure, but partly by entreaties, partly by bullying, managed to induce him to prolong his stay from week to week. These concessions were not, however, made without corresponding conditions imposed by the consenting party, among the foremost of which was the express stipulation that he should not be expected, nor by cajolery nor menaces induced or compelled, to eat or drink at all more than he himself felt prompted by the cravings of his natural appetite to do. The old gentlemen had much in common upon which to exercise their sympathies; they were both staunch Tories, both admirable judges of claret, and no less both extraordinary proficients in the delectable pastimes of backgammon and draughts, whereat, when other resources failed, they played with uncommon industry and perseverance, and sometimes indulged in slight ebullitions of acrimonious feeling, scarcely exhibited, however, before they were atoned for by fervent apologies and vehement vows of good behaviour for the future.

Leaving this little party to the quiet seclusion of Ardgillagh, it becomes now our duty to return for a time to very different scenes and other personages.

CHAPTER LXVIII.

THE FRAY.

It now becomes our duty to return for a short time to Sir Henry Ashwoode and Nicholas Blarden, whom we left in hot pursuit of the trembling fugitives. The night was consumed in vain but restless search, and yet no satisfactory clue to the direction of their flight had been discovered; no evidence, not even a hint, by which to guide their pursuit. Jaded by his fruitless exertions, frantic with rage and disappointment, Nicholas Blarden at peep of light rode up to the hall door of Morley Court.

"No news since?" cried he, fixing his bloodshot eyes upon the man who took his horse's bridle, "no news since?"

"No, sir," cried the fellow, shaking his head, "not a word."

"Is Sir Henry within?" inquired Blarden, throwing himself from the saddle.

"No, sir," replied the man.

"Not returned yet, eh?" asked Nicholas.

"Yes, sir, he did return, and he left again about ten minutes ago," responded the groom.

"And left no message for me, eh?" rejoined Blarden.

"There's a note, sir, on a scrap of paper, on the table in the hall, I forgot to mention," replied the man—"he wrote it in a hurry, with a pencil, sir."

Blarden strode into the hall, and easily discovered the document—a hurried scrawl, scarcely legible; it ran as follows:—

"Nothing yet—no trace—I half suspect they're lurking in the neighbourhood of the house. I must return to town—there are two places which I forgot to try. Meet me, if you can—say in the old Saint Columbkil; it's a deserted place, in the morning about ten or eleven o'clock.

"HENRY ASHWOODE."

Blarden glanced quickly through this effusion.

"A precious piece of paper, that!" muttered he, tearing it across, "worthy of its author—a cursed greenhorn; consume him for a mouth, but no matter—no matter yet. Here, you rake-helly squad, some of you," shouted he, addressing himself at random to the servants, one of whom he heard approaching, "here, I say, get me some food and drink, and don't be long about it either, I can scarce stand." So saying, and satisfied that his directions would be promptly attended to, he shambled into one of the sitting-rooms, and flung himself at his full length upon a sofa; his disordered and bespattered dress and mud-stained boots contrasted agreeably with the rich crimson damask and gilded backs and arms of the couch on which he lay. As he applied himself voraciously to the solid fare and the wines with which he was speedily supplied, a thousand incoherent schemes, and none of them of the most amiable kind, busily engaged his thoughts. After many wandering speculations, he returned again to a subject which had more than once already presented itself. "And then for the brother, the fellow that laid his blows on me before a whole play-house full of people, the vile spawn of insolent beggary, that struck me till his arm was fairly tired with striking—I'm no fool to forget such things—the rascally forging ruffian—the mean, swaggering, lying bully—no matter—he must be served out in style, and so he shall. I'll not hang him though, I may turn him to account yet, some way or other—no, I'll not hang him, keep the halter in my hand—the best trump for the last card—hold the gallows over him, and make him lead a pleasant sort of life of it, one way or other. I'll not leave a spark of pride in his body I'll not thrash out of him. I'll make him meeker and sleeker and humbler than a spaniel; he shall, before the face of all the world, just bear what I give him, and do what I bid him, like a trained dog—sink me, but he shall."

Somewhat comforted by these ruminations, Nicholas Blarden arose from a substantial meal, and a reverie, which had occupied some hours; and without caring to remove from his person the traces of his toilsome exertions of the night past, nor otherwise to render himself one whit a less slovenly and neglected-looking figure than when he had that morning dismounted at the hall door, he called for a fresh horse, threw himself into the saddle, and spurred away for Dublin city.

He reached the doorway of the old Saint Columbkil, and, under the shadow of its ancient sign-board, dismounted. He entered the tavern, but Ashwoode was not there; and, in answer to his inquiries, Mr. Blarden was informed that Sir Henry Ashwoode had gone over to the "Cock and Anchor," to have his horse cared for, and that he was momentarily expected back.

Blarden consulted his huge gold watch. "It's eleven o'clock now, every minute of it, and he's not come—hoity toity rather, I should say, all things considered. I thought he was better up to his game by this time—but no matter—I'll give him a lesson just now."

As if for the express purpose of further irritating Mr. Blarden's already by no means angelic temper, several parties, composed of second-rate sporting characters, all laughing, swearing, joking, betting, whistling, and by every device, contriving together to produce as much clatter and uproar as it was possible to do, successively entered the place.

"Well, Nicky, boy, how does the world wag with you?" inquired a dapper little fellow, approaching Blarden with a kind of brisk, hopping gait, and coaxingly digging that gentleman's ribs with the butt of his silver-mounted whip.

"What the devil brings all these chaps here at this hour?" inquired Blarden.

"Soft is your horn, old boy," rejoined his acquaintance, in the same arch strain of pleasantry; "two regular good mains to be fought to-day—tough ones, I promise you—Fermanagh Dick against Long White—fifty birds each—splendid fowls, I'm told—great betting—it will come off in little more than an hour."

"I don't care if it never comes off," rejoined Blarden; "I'm waiting for a chap that ought to have been here half an hour ago. Rot him, I'm sick waiting."

"Well, come, I'll tell you how we'll pass the time. I'll toss you for guineas, as many tosses as you like," rejoined the small gentleman, accommodatingly. "What do you say—is it a go?"

"Sit down, then," replied Blarden; "sit down, can't you? and begin."

Accordingly the two friends proceeded to recreate themselves thus pleasantly. Mr. Blarden's luck was decidedly bad, and he had been already "physicked," as his companion playfully remarked, to the amount of some five-and-twenty guineas, and his temper had become in a corresponding degree affected, when he observed Sir Henry Ashwoode, jaded, haggard, and with dress disordered, approaching the place where he sat.

"Blarden, we had better leave this place," said Ashwoode, glancing round at the crowded benches; "there's too much noise here. What say you?"

"What do I say?" rejoined Blarden, in his very loudest and most insolent tone—"I say you have made an appointment and broke it, so stand there till it's my convenience to talk to you—that's all."

Ashwoode felt his blood tingling in his veins with fury as he observed the sneering significant faces of those who, attracted by the loud tones of Nicholas Blarden, watched the effect of his insolence upon its object. He heard conversations subside into whispers and titters among the low scoundrels who enjoyed his humiliation; yet he dared not answer Blarden as he would have given worlds at that moment to have done, and with the extremest difficulty restrained himself from rushing among the vile rabble who exulted in his degradation, and compelling them at least to respect and fear him. While he stood thus with compressed lips and a face pale as ashes with rage, irresolute what course to take, one of the coins for which Blarden played rolled along the table, and thence along the floor for some distance.

"Go, fetch that guinea—jump, will you?" cried Blarden, in the same boisterous and intentionally insolent tone. "What are you standing there for, like a stick? Pick it up, sir."

Ashwoode did not move, and an universal titter ran round the spectators, whose attention was now effectually enlisted.

"Do what I order you—do it this moment. Damn your audacity, you had better do it," said Blarden, dashing his clenched fist on the table so as to make the coin thereon jump and jingle.

Still Ashwoode remained resolutely fixed, trembling in every joint with very passion; prudence told him that he ought to leave the place instantly, but pride and obstinacy, or his evil angel, held him there.

The sneering whispers of the crowd, who now pressed more nearly round them in the hope of some amusement, became more and more loud and distinct, and the words, "white feather," "white liver," "muff," "cur," and other terms of a like import reached Ashwoode's ear. Furious at the contumacy of his wretched slave, and determined to overbear and humble him, Blarden exclaimed in a tone of ferocious menace,—

"Do as I bid you, you cursed, insolent upstart—pick up that coin, and give it to me—or by the laws, you'll shake for it."

Still Ashwoode moved not.

"Do as I bid you, you robbing swindler," shouted he, with an oath too appalling for our pages, and again rising, and stamping on the floor, "or I'll give you to the crows."

The titter which followed this menace was unexpectedly interrupted. The young man's aspect changed; the blood rushed in livid streams to his face; his dark eyes blazed with deadly fire; and, like the bursting of a storm, all the gathering rage and vengeance of weeks in one tremendous moment found vent. With a spring like that of a tiger, he rushed upon his persecutor, and before the astonished spectators could interfere, he had planted his clenched fists dozens of times, with furious strength, in Blarden's face. Utterly destitute of personal courage, the wretch, though incomparably a more powerful man than his light-limbed antagonist, shrank back, stunned and affrighted, under the shower of blows, and stumbled and fell over a wooden stool. With murderous resolution, Ashwoode instantly drew his sword, and another moment would have witnessed the last of Blarden's life, had not several persons thrown themselves between that person and his frantic assailant.

"Hold back," cried one. "The man's down—don't murder him."

"Down with him—he's mad!" cried another; "brain him with the stool."

"Hold his arm, some of you, or he'll murder the man!" shouted a third, "hold him, will you?"

Overpowered by numbers, with his face lacerated and his clothes torn, and his naked sword still in his hand, Ashwoode struggled and foamed, and actually howled, to reach his abhorred enemy—glaring like a baffled beast upon his prey.

"Send for constables, quick—quick, I say," shouted Blarden, with a frantic imprecation, his face all bleeding under his recent discipline.

"Let me go—let me go, I tell you, or by the father that made me, I'll send my sword through half-a-dozen of you," almost shrieked Ashwoode.

"Hold him—hold him fast—consume you, hold him back!" shouted Blarden; "he's a forger!—run for constables!"

Several did run in various directions for peace officers.

"Wring the sword from his hand, why don't you?" cried one; "cut it out of his hand with a knife!"

"Knock him down!—down with him! Hold on!"

Amid such exclamations, Ashwoode at length succeeded, by several desperate efforts, in extricating himself from those who held him; and without hat, and with clothes rent to fragments in the scuffle, and his face and hands all torn and bleeding, still carrying his naked sword in his hand, he rushed from the room, and, followed at a respectable distance by several of those who had witnessed the scuffle, and by his distracted appearance attracting the wondering gaze of those who traversed the streets, he ran recklessly onward to the "Cock and Anchor."

CHAPTER LXIX.

THE BOLTED WINDOW.

Followed at some distance by a wondering crowd, he entered the inn-yard, where, for the first time, he checked his flight, and returned his sword to the scabbard.

"Here, ostler, groom—quickly, here!" cried Ashwoode. "In the devil's name, where are you?"

The ostler presented himself, gazing in unfeigned astonishment at the distracted, pale, and bleeding figure before him.

"Where have you put my horse?" said Ashwoode.

"The boy's whisping him down in the back stable, your honour," replied he.

"Have him saddled and bridled in three seconds," said Ashwoode, striding before the man towards the place indicated. "I'll make it worth your while. My life—my life depends on it!"

"Never fear," said the fellow, quickening his pace, "may I never buckle a strap if I don't."

With these words, they entered the stable together, but the horse was not there.

"Confound them, they brought him to the dark stable, I suppose," said the groom, impatiently. "Come along, sir."

"'Sdeath! it will be too late! Quick!—quick, man!—in the fiend's name, be quick!" said Ashwoode, glaring fearfully towards the entrance to the inn-yard.

Their visit to the second stable was not more satisfactory.

"Where the devil's Sir Henry Ashwoode's horse?" inquired the groom, addressing a fellow who was seated on an oat-bin, drumming listlessly with his heels upon its sides, and smoking a pipe the while—"where's the horse?" repeated he.

The man first satisfied his curiosity by a leisurely view of Ashwoode's disordered dress and person, and then removed his pipe deliberately from his mouth, and spat upon the ground.

"Where's Sir Henry's horse?" he repeated. "Why, Jim took him out a quarter of an hour ago, walking down towards the Poddle there. I'm thinking he'll be back soon now."

"Saddle a horse—any horse—only let him be sure and fleet," cried Ashwoode, "and I'll pay you his price thrice over!"

"Well, it's a bargain," replied the groom, promptly; "I don't like to see a gentleman caught in a hobble, if I can help him out of it. Take my advice, though, and duck your head under the water in the trough there; your face is full of blood and dust, and couldn't but be noticed wherever you went."

While the groom was with marvellous celerity preparing the horse which he selected for the young man's service, Ashwoode, seeing the reasonableness of his advice, ran to the large trough full of water which stood before the pump in the inn-yard; but as he reached it, he perceived the entrance of some four or five persons into the little quadrangle whom, at a glance, he discovered to be constables.

"That's him—he's our bird! After him!—there he goes!" cried several voices.

Ashwoode sprang up the stairs of the gallery which, as in most old inns, overhung the yard. He ran along it, and rushed into the first passage which opened from it. This he traversed with his utmost speed, and reached a chamber door. It was fastened; but hurling himself against it with his whole weight, he burst it open, the hoarse voices of his pursuers, and their heavy tread, ringing in his ears. He ran directly to the casement; it looked out upon a narrow by-lane. He strove to open it, that he might leap down upon the pavement, but it resisted his efforts; and, driven to bay, and hearing the steps at the very door of the chamber, he turned about and drew his sword.

"Come, no sparring," cried the foremost, a huge fellow in a great coat, and with a bludgeon in his hand; "give in quietly; you're regularly caged."

As the fellow advanced, Ashwoode met him with a thrust of his sword. The constable partly threw it up with his hand, but it entered the fleshy part of his arm, and came out near his shoulder blade.

"Murder! murder!—help! help!" shouted the man, staggering back, while two or three more of his companions thrust themselves in at the door.

Ashwoode had hardly disengaged his sword, when a tremendous blow upon the knuckles with a bludgeon dashed it from his grasp, and almost at the same instant, he received a second blow upon the head, which felled him to the ground, insensible, and weltering in blood, the execrations and uproar of his assailants still ringing in his ears.

"Lift him on the bed. Pull off his cravat. By the hoky, he's done for. Devil a kick in him. Open his vest. Are you hurted, Crotty? Get some water and spirits, some of yees, an' a towel. Begorra, we just nicked him. He's an active chap. See, he's opening his mouth and his eyes. Hould him, Teague, for he's the devil's bird. Never mind it, Crotty. Devil a fear of you. Tear open the shirt. Bedad, it was close shaving. Give him a drop iv the brandy. Never a fear of you, old bulldog."

These and such broken sentences from fifty voices filled the little chamber where Ashwoode lay in dull and ghastly insensibility after his recent deadly struggle, while some stuped the wounds of the combatants with spirits and water, and others applied the same medicaments to their own interiors, and all talked loud and fast together, as men are apt to do after scenes of excitement.

We need not follow Ashwoode through the dreadful preliminaries which terminated in his trial. In vain did he implore an interview with Nicholas Blarden, his relentless prosecutor. It were needless to enter into the evidence for the prosecution, and that for the defence, together with the points made arguments, and advanced by the opposing counsel; it is enough to know that the case was conducted with much ability on both sides, and that the jury, having deliberated for more than an hour, at length found the verdict which we shall just now state. A baronet in the dock was too novel an exhibition to fail in drawing a full attendance, and the consequence was, that never was known such a crowd of human beings in a compass so small as that which packed the court-house upon this memorable occasion.

Throughout the whole proceedings, Sir Henry Ashwoode, though deadly pale, conducted himself with singular coolness and self-possession, frequently suggesting questions to his counsel, and watching the proceedings apparently with a mind as disengaged from every agitating consciousness of personal danger as that of any of the indifferent but curious bystanders who looked on. He was handsomely dressed, and in his degraded and awful situation preserved, nevertheless, in his outward mien and attire, the dignity of his rank and former pretensions. As is invariably the case in Ireland, popular sympathy moved strongly in favour of the prisoner, a feeling of interest which the grace, beauty, and evident youth of the accused, as well as his high rank—for the Irish have ever been an aristocratic race—served much to enhance; and when the case closed, and the jury retired after an adverse charge from the learned judge, to consider their verdict, perhaps Ashwoode himself would have seemed, to the careless observer, the least interested in the result of all who were assembled in that densely crowded place, to hear the final adjudication of the law. Those, however, who watched him more narrowly could observe, in this dreadful interval, that he raised his handkerchief often to his face, keeping it almost constantly at his mouth to conceal the nervous twitching of the muscles which he could not control. The eyes of the eager multitude wandered from the prisoner to the jury-box, and thence to the impassive parchment countenance of the old ermined effigy who presided at the harrowing scene, and not one ventured to speak above his breath. At length, a sound was heard at the door of the jury-box—the jury was returning. A buzz ran through the court, and then the prolonged "hish," enjoining silence, while one by one the jurors entered and resumed their places in the box. The verdict was—Guilty.

In reply to the usual interrogatory from the officer of the court, Sir Henry Ashwoode spoke, and though many there were moved, even to sobs and tears, yet his manner had recovered its grace and collectedness, and his voice was unbroken and musical as when it was wont to charm all hearers in the gay saloons of fashion, and splendour, and heedless folly, in other times—when he, blasted and ruined as he stood there, was the admired and courted favourite of the great and gay.

"My lord," said he, "I have nothing to urge which, in the strict requirements of the law, avails to abate the solemn sentence which you are about to pronounce—for my life I care not—something is, however, due to my character and the name I bear—a name, my lord, never, never except on this day, never clouded by the shadow of dishonour—a name which will yet, after I am dead and gone, be surely and entirely vindicated; vindicated, my lord, in the entire dispersion of the foul imputations and fatal contrivances under which my fame is darkened and my life is taken. Far am I from impeaching the verdict that I have just heard. I will not arraign the jurymen, nor lay to their charge that I am this day wrongfully condemned, but to the charge of those who, on that witness table, have sworn my life away—perjurers procured for money, whose exposure I leave to time, and whose punishment to God. Knowing that although my body shall ignominiously perish, and though my fame be tarnished for an hour, yet shall truth and years, with irresistible power, bring my innocence to light—rescue my character and restore the name I bear. He who stands in the shadow of death, as I do, has little to fear in human censure, and little to gather from the applause of men. My life is forfeited, and I must soon go into the presence of my Creator, to receive my everlasting doom; and in presence of that almighty and terrible God before whom I must soon stand, and as I look for mercy when He shall judge me, I declare, that of this crime, of which I am pronounced guilty, I am altogether innocent. I am a victim of a conspiracy, the motives of which my defence hath truly showed you. I never committed the crime for which I am to suffer. I repeat that I am innocent, and in witness of the truth of what I say, I appeal to my Maker and my Judge, the Eternal and Almighty God."

Having thus spoken, Ashwoode received his sentence, and was forthwith removed to the condemned cell.

Ashwoode had many and influential friends, and it required but a small exercise of their good offices to procure a reprieve. He would not suffer himself to despond—no, nor for one moment to doubt his final escape from the fangs of justice. He was first reprieved for a fortnight, and before that term expired again for six weeks. In the course of the latter term, however, an event occurred which fearfully altered his chances of escape, and filled his mind with the justest and most dreadful apprehensions. This was the recall of Wharton from the viceroyalty of Ireland.

The new lord-lieutenant could not see, in the case of the young Whig baronet, the same extenuating circumstances which had wrought so effectually upon his predecessor, Wharton. The judge who had tried the case refused to recommend the prisoner to the mercy of the Crown; and the viceroy accordingly, in his turn, refused to entertain any application for the commutation or further suspension of his sentence; and now, for the first time, Sir Henry Ashwoode felt the tremendous reality of his situation. The term for which he was reprieved had nearly expired, and he felt that the hours which separated him from the deadly offices of the hangman were numbered. Still, in this dreadful consciousness, there mingled some faint and flickering ray of hope—by its uncertain mockery rendering the terrors of his situation but the more intolerable, and by the sleepless agonies of suspense, unnerving the resolution which he might have otherwise summoned to his aid.

CHAPTER LXX.

Desperately wounded, O'Connor lay between life and death for many weeks in the dim and secluded apartment whither O'Hanlon had borne him after his combat with Sir Henry Ashwoode. There, fearing lest his own encounter with Wharton, and its startling result, should mark them for pursuit and search, he placed O'Connor under the charge of trusty creatures of his own—for some time not daring to visit him except under cover of the night. This alarm, however, soon subsided; and consequently less precaution was adopted. O'Connor's wounds were, as we have said, most dangerous, and for fully two months he lay upon the fiery couch of fever, alternately raving in delirium, and locked in the dull stupor of entire apathy and exhaustion. Through this season of pain and peril he was sustained, however, by the energies of a young and vigorous constitution. The fever, at length, abated, and the unclouded light of reason returned; still, however, in body he was weak, so weak that, sorely against his will, he was perforce obliged to continue the occupant of his narrow bed, in the dingy and secluded lodgings in which he lay. Impatient to learn something of her who entirely filled his thoughts, and of the truth of whose love for him he now felt the revival of more than hope, he chafed and fretted in the narrow limits of his dark and gloomy chamber. Spite of all the remonstrances of the old crone who attended him, backed by the more awful fulminations of his apothecary, O'Connor would not submit any longer to the confinement of his bed; and, but for the firm and effectual resistance of O'Hanlon, would have succeeded, weak as he was, in making his escape from the house, and resuming his ordinary occupations and pursuits, as though his health had not suffered, nor his strength become impaired, so as to leave him scarcely the power of walking a hundred steps, without the extremest exhaustion and lassitude. To O'Hanlon's expostulations he was forced to yield, and even pledged his word to him not to attempt a removal from his hated lodgings, without his consent and approbation. In reply to a message to his friend Audley, he learned, much to his mortification, that that gentleman had left town, and as thus full of disquiet and anxiety, one day O'Connor was seated, pale and languid, in his usual place by the window, the door of his apartment opened, and O'Hanlon entered. He took the hand of the invalid and said,—

"I commend your patience, young man, you have been my parole prisoner for many days. When is this durance to end?"

"I'faith, I believe with my life," rejoined O'Connor, "I never knew before what weariness and vexation in perfection are—this dusky room is hateful to me, it grows narrower and narrower every day—and those old houses opposite—every pane of glass in their windows, and every brick in their walls I have learned by rote—I am tired to death. But, seriously, I have other and very different reasons for wishing to be at liberty again—reasons so urgent as to leave me no rest by night or day. I chafe and fret here like a caged bird. I have been too long shut up—my strength will never come again unless I am allowed to breathe the fresh air—you are all literally killing me with kindness."

"And yet," rejoined O'Hanlon, "I have never been thought an over-careful leech, and truth to say, had I suffered you to have your own way, you would not now have been a living man. I know, as well as any of them, how to tend a wound, and this I will say, that in all my practice it never yet has been my lot to meet with so ill-conditioned and cross-grained a patient as yourself. Why, nothing short of downright force has kept you in your room—your life is saved in spite of yourself."

"If you keep me here much longer," replied O'Connor, "it will prove but indifferent economy as regards my bodily health, for I shall undoubtedly cut my throat before another week."

"There shall be no need, my friend, to find such an escape," replied O'Hanlon, "for I now absolve you of your promise, hitherto so well observed; nay, more, I advise you to leave the house to-day. I think your strength sufficient, and the occasion, moreover, demands that you should visit an acquaintance immediately."

"Who is it?" inquired O'Connor, starting to his feet with alacrity, "thank God I am at length again my own master."

"When I this day entered the yard of the 'Cock and Anchor'," answered O'Hanlon, "the inn where you and I first encountered, I found a fellow inquiring after you most earnestly; he had a letter with which he was charged. It is from Sir Henry Ashwoode, who lies now in prison, and under sentence of death. You start, and no wonder—his old associates have convicted him of forgery."

"Gracious Heaven, is it possible?" exclaimed O'Connor.

"Nay, certain," continued O'Hanlon, "nor has he any longer a chance of escape. He has been twice reprieved—but his friend Wharton is recalled—his reprieve expires in three days' time, and then he will be inevitably executed."

"Good God, is this—can it be reality?" exclaimed O'Connor, trembling with the violence of his agitation, "give me the letter." He broke the seal, and read as follows:—

"EDMOND O'CONNOR,—I know I have wronged you sorely. I have destroyed your peace and endangered your life. You are more than avenged. I write this in the condemned cell of the gaol. If you can bring yourself to confer with me for a few minutes, come here. I stand on no ceremony, and time presses. Do not fail. If you be living I shall expect you.

"HENRY ASHWOODE."

O'Connor's preparations were speedily made, and leaning upon the arm of his elder friend, he, with slow and feeble steps, and a head giddy with his long confinement, and the agitating anticipation of the scene in which he was just about to be engaged, traversed the streets which separated his lodging from the old city gaol—a sombre, stern, and melancholy-looking building, surrounded by crowded and dilapidated houses, with decayed plaster and patched windows, and a certain desolate and sickly aspect, as though scared and blasted by the contagious proximity of that dark receptacle of crime and desperation which loomed above them. At the gate O'Hanlon parted from him, appointing to meet him again in the "Cock and Anchor," whither he repaired. After some questions, O'Connor was admitted. The clanging of bolts, and bars, and door-chains, smote heavily on his heart—he heard no other sounds but these and the echoing tread of their own feet, as they traversed the long, dark, stone-paved passages which led to the dungeon in which he whom he had last seen in the pride of fashion, and youth, and strength, was now a condemned felon, and within a few hours of a public and ignominious death. The turnkey paused at one of the narrow doors opening from the dusky corridor, and unclosing it, said,—

"A gentleman, sir, to see you."

"Request him to come in," replied a voice, which, though feebler than it used to be, O'Connor had no difficulty in recognizing. In compliance with this invitation, he with a throbbing heart entered the prison-room. It was dimly lighted by a single small window set high in the wall, and darkened by iron bars. A small deal table, with a few books carelessly laid upon it, occupied the centre of the cell, and two heavy stools were placed beside it, on one of which was seated a figure, with his back to the light, to conceal, with a desperate tenacity of pride, the ravages which the terrific mental fever of weeks had wrought in his once bold and handsome face. By the wall was stretched a wretched pallet; and upon the plaster were written and scratched, according to the various moods of the miserable and guilty tenants of the place, a hundred records, some of slang philosophy, some of desperate drunken defiance, and some again of terror, but all bearing reference to the dreadful scene to which this was but the ante-chamber and the passage. Many hieroglyphical emblems of unmistakable significance had also been traced upon the walls by the successive occupants of the place, such as coffins, gallows-trees, skulls and cross-bones; the most striking among which symbols was a large figure of death upon a horse, sketched with much spirit, by some moralizing convict, with a piece of burned stick, and to which some waggish successor had appropriately added, in red chalk, a gigantic pair of spurs. As soon as O'Connor entered, the turnkey closed the door, and he and Sir Henry Ashwoode were left alone. A silence of some minutes, which neither party dared to break, ensued.


CHAPTER LXXI.

THE FAREWELL.

O'Connor was the first to speak. In a low voice, which trembled with agitation, he said,—

"Sir Henry Ashwoode, I have come here in answer to a note which reached me but a few minutes since. You desired a conference with me; is there any commission with which you would wish to charge me?—if so, let me know it, and it shall be done."

"None, none, Mr. O'Connor, thank you," rejoined Ashwoode, recovering his characteristic self-possession, and continuing proudly, "if you add to your visit a patient audience of a few minutes, you will have conferred upon me the only favour I desire. Pray, sit down; it is rather a hard and a homely seat," he added, with a haggard, joyless smile—"but the only one this place supplies."

Another silence followed, during which Sir Henry Ashwoode restlessly shifted his attitude every moment, in evident and uncontrollable nervous excitement. At length he arose, and walked twice or thrice up and down the narrow chamber, exhibiting without any longer care for concealment his pale, wasted face in the full light which streamed in through the grated window, his sunken eyes and unshorn chin, and worn and attenuated figure.

"You hear that sound," said he, abruptly stopping short, and looking with the same strange smile upon O'Connor; "the clank upon the flags as I walk up and down—the jingle of the fetters—isn't it strange—isn't it odd—like a dream—eh?"

Another silence followed, which Ashwoode again abruptly interrupted.

"You know all this story?—of course you do—everybody does—how the wretches have trapped me—isn't it terrible—isn't it dreadful? Oh! you cannot know what it is to mope about this place alone, when it is growing dark, as I do every evening, and in the night time. If I had been another man, I'd have been raving mad by this time. I said alone—did I?" he continued, with increasing excitement; "oh! that it were!—oh! that it were! He comes there—there," he screamed, pointing to the foot of the bed, "with all those infernal cloths and fringes about his face, morning and evening. Ah, God! such a thing—half idiot, half fiend; and still the same, though I curse him till I'm hoarse, he won't leave it. Can't they wait—can't they wait? for-ever is a long day. As I'm a living man, he's with me every night—there—there is the body, gaping and nodding—there—there—there!"

As he shouted this with frantic and despairing horror, shaking his clenched hands toward the place of his dreaded nightly visitant, O'Connor felt a thrill of horror such as he had never known before, and hardly recovered from this painful feeling, when Sir Henry Ashwoode turned to the little table on which, among many things, a vessel of water was placed, and filling some out into a cracked cup, he added to it drops from a phial, and hastily swallowed the mixture.

"Laudanum is all the philosophy or religion I can boast; it's well to have even so much," said he, returning the bottle to his pocket. "It's a dead secret, though, that I have got any; this is a present from the doctor they allow me to see, and I'm on honour not—to poison myself—isn't it comical?—for fear he should get into a scrape; but I've another game to play—no fear of that—no, no."

Another silence followed, and Sir Henry Ashwoode said quickly,—

"What do the people say about it? Do they think I forged that accursed bond? Do they think me guilty?"

O'Connor declared his entire ignorance of public rumour, alleging his own illness, and consequent close confinement, as the cause of it.

"They sha'n't believe me guilty, no, they sha'n't. Look ye, sir, I have one good feeling left," he resumed, vehemently; "I will not let my name suffer. If the most resolute firmness to the very last, and the most solemn renunciation of the charges preferred against me, reiterated at the foot of the gallows, with the halter about my neck—if these can beget a belief of my innocence, my name shall be clear—my name shall not suffer; this last outrage I will avert; but oh, my God! is there no chance yet—must I—must I perish? Will no one save me—will no one help me? Oh, God! oh, God! is there no pity—no succour; must it come?"

Thus crying, he threw himself forward upon the table, while every joint and muscle quivered and heaved with fierce hysterical sobs which, more like a succession of short convulsive shrieks than actual weeping, betrayed his agony, while O'Connor looked on with a mixture of horror and pity, which all that was past could not suppress.

At length the paroxysm subsided. The wretched man filled out some more water, and mingling some drops of laudanum in it, he drank it off, and became comparatively composed.

"Not a word of this to any living being, I charge you," said he, clutching O'Connor's arm in his attenuated hand, and fixing his sunken fiery eyes upon his; "I would not have my folly known; I'm not always so weak as you have seen me. It must be, that's all—no help for it. It's rather a novel thing, though, to hang a baronet—ha! ha! You look scared—you think my wits are unsettled; but you're wrong. I don't sleep; I hav'n't for some time; and want of rest, you know, makes a man's manner odd; makes him excitable—nervous. I'm more myself now."

After a short pause, Sir Henry Ashwoode resumed,—

"When we had that affray together, in which would to God you had run me through the heart, you put a question to me about my sister—poor Mary; I will answer that now, and more than answer it. That girl loves you with her whole heart; loves you alone; never loved another. It matters not to tell how I and my father—the great and accursed first cause of all our misfortunes and miseries—effected your estrangement. The Italian miscreant told you truth. The girl is gone I know not whither, to seek an asylum from me—ay, from me. To save my life and honour. I would have constrained her to marry the wretch who has destroyed me. It was he—he who urged it, who cajoled me. I joined him, to save my life and honour! and now—oh! God, where are they?"

O'Connor rose, and said somewhat sternly,—

"May God pardon you, Sir Henry Ashwoode, for all you have done against the peace of that most noble and generous being, your sister. What I have suffered at your hands I heartily forgive."

"I ask forgiveness nowhere," rejoined Ashwoode, stoically; "what's done is done. It has been a wild and fitful life, and is now over. What forgiveness can you give me or she that's worth a thought?—folly, folly!"

"One word of earnest hope before I leave you; one word of solemn warning," said O'Connor; "the vanities of this world are fading fast and for ever from your view; you are going where the applause of men can reach you no more! I conjure you, then, for the sake of your eternal peace, if your sentence be a just one, do not insult your Creator by denying your guilt, and pass into His awful presence with a lie upon your lips."

Ashwoode paused for a moment, and then walked suddenly up to O'Connor, and almost in a whisper said,—

"Not a word of that, my course is chosen; not one word more. Observe, what has passed between us is private; now leave me." So saying, Ashwoode turned from him, and walked toward the narrow window of his cell.

"Farewell, Sir Henry Ashwoode, farewell for ever; and may God have mercy upon you," said O'Connor, passing out upon the dark and narrow corridor.

The turnkey closed the door with a heavy crash upon his prisoner, and locked it once more, and thus the two young men, who had so often and so variously encountered in the unequal path of life, were parted never again to meet in the wayward scenes of this chequered and changeful existence. Tired and agitated, O'Connor threw himself into the first coach he met, and was deposited safely in the "Cock and Anchor." It were vain to attempt to describe the ecstasies and transports of honest Larry Toole at the unexpected recovery of his long-lost master; we shall not attempt to do so. It is enough for our purpose to state that at the "Cock and Anchor" O'Connor received two letters from his old friend, Mr. Audley, and one conveying a pressing invitation from Oliver French of Ardgillagh, in compliance with which, early on the next morning, he mounted his horse, and set forth, followed by his trusty squire, upon the high road to Naas, resolved to task his strength to the uttermost, although he knew that even thus he must necessarily divide his journey into many more stages than his impatience would have allowed, had more rapid travelling in his weak condition been possible.

CHAPTER LXXII.

THE ROPE AND THE RIOT IN GALLOWS GREEN—AND THE WOODS OF ARDGILLAGH BY MOONLIGHT.

At length came that day, that dreadful day, whose evening Sir Henry Ashwoode was never to see. Noon was the time fixed for the fatal ceremonial; and long before that hour, the mob, in one dense mass of thousands, had thronged and choked the streets leading to the old gaol. Upon this awful day the wretched man acquired, by a strange revulsion, a kind of stoical composure, which sustained him throughout the dreadful preparations. With hands cold as clay, and a face white as ashes, and from which every vestige of animation had vanished, he proceeded, nevertheless, with a calm and collected demeanour to make all his predetermined arrangements for the fearful scene. With a minute elaborateness he finished his toilet, and dressed himself in a grave, but particularly handsome suit. Could this shrunken, torpid, ghastly spectre, in reality be the same creature who, a few months since, was the admiration and envy of half the beaux of Dublin?

There was little or none of the fitful excitability about him which had heretofore marked his demeanour during his confinement; on the contrary, a kind of stupor and apathy had supervened, partly occasioned by the laudanum which he had taken in unusually large quantities, and partly by the overwhelming horror of his situation. He seemed to observe and hear nothing. When the gaoler entered to remove his irons, shortly before the time of his removal had arrived, he seemed a little startled, and observing the physician who had attended him among those who stood at the door of his cell, he beckoned him toward him.

"Doctor, doctor," said he in a dusky voice, "how much laudanum may I safely take? I want my head clear to say a few words, to speak to the people. Don't give me too much; but let me, with that condition, have whatever I can safely swallow. You know—you understand me; don't oblige me to speak any more just now."

The physician felt his pulse, and looked in his face, and then mingled a little laudanum and water, which he applied to the young man's pale, dry lips. This dose was hardly swallowed, when one of the gaol officials entered, and stated that the ordinary was anxious to know whether the prisoner wished to pray or confer with him in private before his departure. The question had to be twice repeated ere it reached Sir Henry. He replied, however, quickly, and in a low tone,—

"No, no, not for the world. I can't bear it; don't disturb me—don't, don't."

It was now intimated to the prisoner that he must proceed. His arms were pinioned, and he was conducted along the passages leading to the entrance of the gaol, where he was received by the sheriff. For a moment, as he passed out into the broad light and the keen fresh air, he beheld the vast and eager mob pressing and heaving like a great dark sea around him, and the mounted escort of dragoons with drawn swords and gay uniforms; and without attaching any clear or definite meaning to the spectacle, he beheld the plumes of a hearse, and two or three fellows engaged in sliding the long black coffin into its place. These sights, and the strange, gaping faces of the crowd, and the sheriff's carriage, and the gay liveries, and the crowded fronts and roofs of the crazy old houses opposite, for one moment danced like the fragment of a dream across his vision, and in the next he sat in the old-fashioned coach which was to convey him to the place of execution.

"Only twenty-seven years, only twenty-seven years, only twenty-seven years," he muttered, vacantly and mechanically repeating the words which had reached his ear from those who were curiously reading the plate upon the coffin as he entered the coach—"only twenty-seven, twenty-seven."

The awful procession moved on to the place of its final destination; the enormous mob rushing along with it—crowding, jostling, swearing, laughing, whistling, quarrelling, and hustling, as they forced their way onward, and staring with coarse and eager curiosity whenever they could into the vehicle in which Ashwoode sat. All the sights—the haggard, smirched, and eager faces, the prancing horses of the troopers, the well-known shops and streets, and the crowded windows—all sailed by his eyes like some unintelligible and heart-sickening dream. The place of public execution for criminals was then, and continued to be for long after, a spot significantly denominated "Gallows Hill," situated in the neighbourhood of St. Stephen's Green, and not far from the line at present traversed by Baggot Street. There a permanent gallows was erected, and thither, at length, amid thousands of crowding spectators, the melancholy procession came, and proceeded to the centre of area, where the gallows stood, with the long new rope swinging in the wind, and the cart and the hangman, with the guard of soldiers, prepared for their reception. The vehicles drew up, and those who had to play a part in the dreadful scene descended. The guard took their place, preserving a narrow circle around the fatal spot, free from the pressure of the crowd. The carriages were driven a little away, and the coffin was placed close under the gallows, while Ashwoode, leaning upon the chaplain and upon one of the sheriffs, proceeded toward the cart, which made the rude platform on which he was to stand.

"Sir Henry Ashwoode," observes a contemporary authority, the Dublin Journal, "showed a great deal of calmness and dignity, insomuch that a great many of the mob, especially among the women, were weeping. His figure and features were handsome, and he was finely dressed. He prayed a short time with the ordinary, and then, with little assistance, mounted the hurdle, whence he spoke to the people, declaring his innocence with great solemnity. Then the hangman loosened his cravat, and opened his shirt at the neck, and Sir Henry turning to him, bid him, as it was understood, to take a ring from his finger, for a token of forgiveness, which he did, and then the man drew the cap over his eyes; but he made a sign, and the hangman lifted it up again, and Sir Henry, looking round at all the multitude, said again, three times, 'In the presence of God Almighty, I stand here innocent;' and then, a minute after, 'I forgive all my enemies, and I die innocent;' then he spoke a word to the hangman, and the cap being pulled down, and the rope quickly adjusted, the hurdle was moved away, and he swung off, the people with one consent crying out the while. He struggled for a long time, and very hard; and not for more than an hour was the body cut down, and laid in the coffin. He was buried in the night-time. His last dying words have begot among most people a great opinion of his innocence, though the lawyers still hold to it that he was guilty. It was said that Mr. Blarden, the prosecutor, was in a house in Stephen's Green, to see the hanging, and as soon as the mob heard it, they went and broke the windows, and, but for the soldiers, would have forced their way in, and done more violence."

Thus speaks the Dublin Journal, and the extract needs no addition from us.

Gladly do we leave this hateful scene, and turn from the dreadful fate of him whose follies and vices had wrought so much misery to others, and ended in such fearful ignominy and destruction to himself. We leave the smoky town, with all its fashion, vice, and villainy; its princely equipages; its prodigals; its paupers; its great men and its sycophants; its mountebanks and mendicants; its riches and its wretchedness. We leave that old city of strange compounds, where the sublime and the ridiculous, deep tragedies and most whimsical farces are ever mingling—where magnificence and squalor rub shoulders day by day, and beggars sit upon the steps of palaces. How much of what is wonderful, wild, and awful, has not thy secret history known! How much of the romance of human act and passion, vicissitude, joy and sorrow, grandeur and despair, has there not lived, and moved, and perished, age after age, under thy perennial curtain of solemn smoke!

Far, far behind, we leave the sickly smoky town—and over the far blue hills and wooded country—through rocky glens, and by sonorous streams, and over broad undulating plains, and through the quiet villages, with their humble thatched roofs from which curls up the light blue smoke among the sheltering bushes and tall hedge-rows—through ever-changing scenes of softest rural beauty, in day time and at even-tide, and by the wan, misty moonlight, we follow the two travellers who ride toward the old domain of Ardgillagh.

The fourth day's journey brought them to the little village which formed one of the boundaries of that old place. But, long ere they reached it, the sun had gone down behind the distant hills, under his dusky canopy of crimson clouds, and the pale moon had thrown its broad light and shadows over the misty landscape. Under the soft splendour of the moon, chequered by the moving shadows of the tall and ancient trees, they rode into the humble village—no sound arose to greet them but the desultory baying of the village dogs, and the soft sighing of the light breeze through the spreading boughs—and no signal of waking life was seen, except, few and far between, the red level beam of some still glowing turf fire, shining through the rude and narrow aperture that served the simple rustic instead of casement.

At one of these humble dwellings Larry Toole applied for information, and with ready courtesy the "man of the house," in person, walked with them to the entrance of the place, and shoved open one of the valves of the crazy old gate, and O'Connor rode slowly in, following, with his best caution, the directions of his guide. His honest squire, Larry, meanwhile, loitered a little behind, in conference with the courteous peasant, and with the laudable intention of procuring some trifling refection, which, however, he determined to swallow without dismounting, and with all convenient dispatch, bearing in mind a wholesome remembrance of the disasters which followed his convivial indulgence in the little town of Chapelizod. While Larry thus loitered, O'Connor followed the wild winding avenue which formed the only approach to the old mansion. This rude track led him a devious way over slopes, and through hollows, and by the broad grey rocks, white as sheeted phantoms in the moonlight, and the thick weeds and brushwood glittering with the heavy dew of night, and through the beautiful misty vistas of the ancient wild wood, now still and solemn as old cathedral aisles. Thus, under the serene and cloudless light of the sailing moon, he had reached the bank of the broad and shallow brook whose shadowy nooks and gleaming eddies were canopied under the gnarled and arching boughs of the hoary thorn and oak—and here tradition tells a marvellous tale.

It is narrated that when O'Connor reached this point, his jaded horse stopped short, refusing to cross the stream, and when urged by voice and spur, reared, snorted, and by every indication exhibited the extremest terror and an obstinate reluctance to pass the brook. The rider dismounted—took his steed by the head, patted and caressed him, and by every art endeavoured to induce him to traverse the little stream, but in vain; while thus fruitlessly employed, his attention was arrested by the sounds of a female voice, in low and singularly sweet and plaintive lamentation, and looking across the water, for the first time he beheld the object which so affrighted his steed. It was a female figure arrayed in a mantle of dusky red, the hood of which hung forward so as to hide the face and head: she was seated upon a broad grey rock by the brook's side, and her head leaned forward so as to rest upon her knees; her bare arm hung by her side, and the white fingers played listlessly in the clear waters of the brook, while with a wild and piteous chaunt, which grew louder and clearer as he gazed, she still sang on her strange mournful song. Spellbound and entranced, he knew not why, O'Connor gazed on in speechless and breathless awe, until at length the tall form arose and disappeared among the old trees, and the sounds melted away and were lost among the soft chiming of the brook, and heard no more. He dared not say whether it was reality or illusion, he felt like one suddenly recalled from a dream, and a certain awe, and horror, and dismay still hung upon him, for which he scarcely could account.

Without further resistance, the horse now crossed the brook; O'Connor remounted, and followed the shadowy track; but again he was destined to meet with interruption; the pathway which he followed, embowered among the branching trees and bushes, at one point wound beneath a low, ivy-mantled rock; he was turning this point, when his horse, snorting loudly, checked his pace with a recoil so sudden that he threw himself back upon his haunches, and remained, except for his violent trembling, fixed and motionless. O'Connor raised his eyes, and standing upon the rock which overhung the avenue, he beheld, for a moment, a tall female form clothed in an ample cloak of dusky red. The arms with the hands clasped, as if in the extremity of woe, firmly together, were extended above her head, the face white as the foam of the river, and the eyes preternaturally large and wild, were raised fixedly toward the broad bright moon; this phantom, for such it was, for a moment occupied his gaze, and in the next, with a scream so piercing and appalling that his very marrow seemed to freeze at the sound, she threw herself forward as though she would cast herself upon the horse and rider—and, was gone.

The horse started wildly off and galloped at headlong speed up the broken ascent, and for some time O'Connor had not collectedness to check his frantic course, or even to think; at length, however, he succeeded in calming the terrified animal—and, uttering a fervent prayer, he proceeded, without further adventure, till the tall gable of the old mansion in the spectral light of the moon among its thick embowering trees and rich ivy-mantles, with all its tall white chimney stacks and narrow windows with their thousand glittering panes, arose before his anxious gaze.


CHAPTER LXXIII.

THE LAST LOOK.

Time had flowed on smoothly in the quiet old place, with an even current unbroken and unmarred, except by one event. Sir Henry Ashwoode's danger was known to old French and Mr. Audley; but with anxious and effectual care they kept all knowledge of his peril and disgrace from poor Mary: this pang was spared her. The months that passed had wrought in her a change so great and so melancholy, that none could look upon her without sorrowful forebodings, without misgivings against which they vainly strove. Sore grief had done its worst: the light and graceful step grew languid and feeble—the young face wan and wasted—the beautiful eyes grew dim; and now in her sad and early decline, as in other times, when her smile was sunshine, and her very step light music, was still with her the same warm and gentle spirit; and even amid the waste and desolation of decay, still prevailed the ineffaceable lines of that matchless and touching beauty, which in other times had wrought such magic.

It was upon that day, the night of which saw O'Connor's long-deferred arrival at Ardgillagh, that Flora Guy, vainly striving to restrain her tears, knocked at Mr. Audley's chamber door. The old gentleman quickly answered the summons.

"Ah, sir," said the girl, "she's very bad, sir, if you wish to see her, come at once."

"I do, indeed, wish to see her, the dear child," said he, while the tears started to his eyes; "bring me to the room."

He followed the kind girl to the door, and she first went in, and in a low voice told her that Mr. Audley wished much to see her, and she, with her own sweet, sad smile, bade her bring him to her bedside.

Twice the old man essayed to enter, and twice he stayed to weep bitterly as a child. At length he commanded composure enough to enter, and stood by the bedside, and silently and reverently held the hand of her that was dying.

"My dear child! my darling!" said he, vainly striving to suppress his sobs, while the tears fell fast upon the thin small hand he held in his—"I have sought this interview, to tell you what I would fain have told you often before now but knew not how to speak of it, I want to speak to you of one who loved you, and loves you still, as mortal has seldom loved; of—of my good young friend O'Connor."

As he said this, he saw, or was it fancy, the faintest flush imaginable for one moment tinge her pale cheek. He had touched a chord to which the pulses of her heart, until they had ceased to beat, must tremble; and silently and slow the tears gathered upon her long dark lashes, and followed one another down her wan face, unheeded. Thus she listened while he related how truly O'Connor had loved her, and when the tale was ended she wept on long and silently.

"Flora," she said at length, "cut off a lock of my hair."

The girl did as she was desired, and in her thin and feeble hand her young mistress took it.

"Whenever you see him, sir," said she, "will you give him this, and say that I sent it for a token that to the last I loved him, and to help him to remember me when I am gone: this is my last message—and poor Flora, won't you take care of her?"

"Won't I, won't I!" sobbed the old man, vehemently. "While I have a shilling in the world she shall never know want—faithful creature"—and he grasped the honest girl's hand, and shook it, and sobbed and wept like a child.

He took the long dark ringlet, which he had promised to give to O'Connor; and seeing that his presence agitated her, he took a long last look at the young face he was never more to see in life, and kissing the small hand again and again, he turned and went out, crying bitterly.

Soon after this she grew much fainter, and twice or thrice she spoke as though her mind was busy with other scenes.

"Let us go down to the well side," she said, "the primroses and cowslips are always there the earliest;" and then she said again, "He's coming, Flora; he'll be here very soon, so come and dress my hair; he likes to see my hair dressed with flowers—wild flowers."

Shortly after this she sank into a soft and gentle sleep, and while she lay thus calmly, there came over her pale face a smile of such a pure and heavenly light, that angelic hope, and peace, and glory, shone in its beauty. The smile changed not; but she was dead! The sorrowful struggle was over—the weary bosom was at rest—the true and gentle heart was cold for ever—the brief but sorrowful trial was over—the desolate mourner was gone to the land where the pangs of grief, the tumults of passion, regrets, and cold neglect are felt no more.

Her favourite bird, with gay wings, flutters to the casement; the flowers she planted are sweet upon the evening air; and by their hearths the poor still talk of her and bless her; but the silvery voice that spoke, and the gentle hand that tended, and the beautiful smile that gave an angelic grace to the offices of charity, where are they?

The tapers are lighted in the silent chamber, and Flora Guy has laid early spring flowers on the still cold form that sleeps there in its serene sad beauty tranquilly and for ever; when in the court-yard are heard the tramp and clatter of a horse's hoofs—it is he—O'Connor,—he comes for her—the long lost—the dearly loved—the true-hearted—the found again.

'Twere vain to tell of frantic grief—words cannot tell, nor imagination conceive, the depth—the wildness—the desolation of that woe.


## CONCLUSION.

Some fifteen years ago there was still to be seen in the little ruined church which occupies a corner in what yet remains of the once magnificent domain of Ardgillagh, side by side among the tangled weeds, two gravestones; one recording the death of Mary Ashwoode, at the early age of twenty-two, in the year of grace 1710; the other, that of Edmond O'Connor, who fell at Denain, in the year of our Lord 1712. Thus they were, who in life were separated, laid side by side in death. It is a still and sequestered spot, and the little ruin clothed in rich ivy, and sheltered by the great old trees with its solemn and holy quiet, in such a resting-place as most mortals would fain repose in when their race is done.

For the rest our task is quickly done. Mr. Audley and Oliver French had so much gotten into one another's way of going on, that the former gentleman from week to week, and from month to month, continued to prolong his visit, until after a residence of eight years, he died at length in the mansion of Ardgillagh, at a very advanced age, and without more than two days' illness, having never experienced before, in all his life, one hour's sickness of any kind. Honest Oliver French outlived his boon companion by the space of two years, having just eaten an omelette and actually called for some woodcock-pie; he departed suddenly while the servant was raising the crust. Old Audley left Flora Guy well provided for at his death, but somehow or other considerably before that event Larry Toole succeeded in prevailing on the honest handmaiden to marry him, and although, questionless, there was some disparity in point of years, yet tradition says, and we believe it, that there never lived a fonder or a happier couple, and it is a genealogical fact, that half the Tooles who are now to be found in that quarter of the country, derive their descent from the very alliance in question.

Of Major O'Leary we have only to say that the rumour which hinted at his having united his fortunes with those of the house of Rumble, were but too well founded. He retired with his buxom bride to a small property, remote from the dissipation of the capital, and except in the matter of an occasional cock-fight, whenever it happened to be within reach, or a tough encounter with the squire, when a new pipe of claret was to be tasted, one or two occasional indiscretions, he became, as he himself declared, in all respects an ornament to society.

Lady Stukely, within a few months after the explosion with young Ashwoode, vented her indignation by actually marrying young Pigwiggynne. It was said, indeed, that they were not happy; of this, however, we cannot be sure; but it is undoubtedly certain that they used to beat, scratch, and pinch each other in private—whether in play merely, or with the serious intention of correcting one another's infirmities of temper, we know not. Several weeks before Lady Stukely's marriage, Emily Copland succeeded in her long-cherished schemes against the celibacy of poor Lord Aspenly. His lordship, however, lived on with a perseverance perfectly spiteful, and his lady, alas and alack-a-day, tired out, at length committed a faux pas—the trial is on record, and eventuated, it is sufficient to say, in a verdict for the plaintiff.

Of Chancey, we have only to say that his fate was as miserable as his life had been abject and guilty. When he arose after the tremendous fall which he had received at the hands of his employer, Nicholas Blarden, upon the memorable night which defeated all their schemes, for he did arise with life—intellect and remembrance were alike quenched—he was thenceforward a drivelling idiot. Though none cared to inquire into the cause and circumstances of his miserable privation, long was he well known and pointed out in the streets of Dublin, where he subsisted upon the scanty alms of superstitious charity, until at length, during the great frost in the year 1739, he was found dead one morning, in a corner under St. Audoen's Arch, stark and cold, cowering in his accustomed attitude.

Nicholas Blarden died upon his feather bed, and if every luxury which imagination can devise, or prodigal wealth procure, can avail to soothe the racking torments of the body, and the terrors of the appalled spirit, he died happy.

Of the other actors in this drama—with the exception of M'Quirk, who was publicly whipped for stealing four pounds of sausages from an eating house in Bride Street, and the Italian, who, we believe, was seen as groom-porter in Mr. Blarden's hell, for many years after—tradition is silent.


Joseph Sheridan Le Fanu – A Short Biography

Joseph Thomas Sheridan Le Fanu was born on August 28th, 1814, at 45 Lower Dominick Street, Dublin, into a literary family with Huguenot, Irish and English roots. Le Fanu was the middle child to an elder sister, Catherine, and a younger brother, William.

His grandmother, Alicia Sheridan Le Fanu, and his great-uncle Richard Brinsley Sheridan were playwrights. His mother was also writer, credited with a biography of Charles Orpen, the Irish physician, writer and clergyman who founded the Claremont Institution for the Deaf and Dumb at Glasnevin, Dublin.

Within a year of his birth the family moved to the Royal Hibernian Military School in the Phoenix Park, where his father, Thomas, a Church of Ireland clergyman, was appointed as chaplain. The Phoenix Park and the adjacent village and parish church of Chapelizod would later appear in many of Le Fanu's stories.

In 1826 the family moved again, this time to Abington, County Limerick, where Le Fanu's father took up his second rectorship.

The children were tutored but, according to his brother William, the tutor taught them little if anything and was finally dismissed in disgrace. Le Fanu was eager to learn and used his father's library to educate himself about the world. He was a creative child and by fifteen had taken to writing poetry and shared much of what he wrote with his mother and siblings. His father however was a strict Protestant churchman and raised his family in an almost Calvinist tradition, Le Fanu knew his work would not be welcomed nor appreciated by his father.

Although Thomas Le Fanu tried to live as though he were well-off, the family had many financial problems. To gain a better income Thomas took rectorships in the south of Ireland for the money, believing they would provide a decent living through their use of tithes. However, by 1830 the tithe system was becoming a source of tension. This episode in the region was known as the 'Tithe War' of 1831–36. In Thomas's parish there were approximately six thousand Catholics and only a few dozen members of the Church of Ireland. (In bad weather the Dean was forced to cancel Sunday services because so few parishioners would attend.) However, the government of the day compelled all farmers, including the majority Catholics, to pay tithes for the upkeep of the Protestant church. This religious injustice was both onerous and, of course, unpopular and its demise greatly welcomed. As disorder spread so the income fell dramatically and by 1832 had dried up entirely.

In 1832, the family moved back temporarily to Dublin, to Williamstown Avenue in a southern suburb, where Thomas had now gained a Government commission.

It was now that Trinity College, Dublin beckoned for the young Le Fanu in 1833 and with it the chance to study law. He was elected Auditor of the College Historical Society. Under the system used in Ireland at the time Le Fanu did not have to live in Dublin to attend lectures, but could study at home and take examinations at the university as and when necessary.

That same year Thomas had to borrow £100 from his cousin Captain Dobbins (who himself was to end up in a debtors' prison several years later) to visit his dying sister in Bath. She was also deeply in debt over her medical bills.

Le Fanu, although continuing to study, and by all accounts do well at his chosen subject, was now deeply involved in writing. So much so that whilst still at University he worked for the Dublin University magazine. In 1838 Le Fanu's first story The Ghost and the Bonesetter was published in the Dublin University Magazine (Interestingly he was later to become the proprietor and editor of the magazine in 1861).

Many of the numerous short stories he wrote at the time were to form the basis for his future novels, some of them appearing anonymously. Indeed throughout his career Le Fanu would constantly revise, cannabilise, embellish and re-publish his earlier works to use in his later efforts.

In 1838 the government had begun a system of paying rectors a fixed sum in order for them to carry out their duties. Alas this had come too late for Thomas who had little income save for some rent on a number of small properties he had inherited. When he died the estate was almost empty. Even his library was sold to pay off some of his debts.

By 1839 Le Fanu had graduated from Trinity College and had been called to the bar. However, Law for Le Fanu had been an education but it was not to be his career. He never practiced law but was now publishing many short stories and, by the following year, he acquired the first of several newspapers he would own and which would eventually include both the Dublin Evening Mail and the Warder.

Between 1838 and 1840 Le Fanu had written and published twelve stories which purported to be the literary remains of an 18th-century Catholic priest called Father Purcell. They were initially published in the Dublin University Magazine and forty years later were collected and published again as The Purcell Papers. Set mostly in Ireland they include classic stories of gothic horror, with grim, shadowed castles, as well as supernatural visitations from beyond the grave, together with madness and suicide. One of the themes running through them is a sad nostalgia for the dispossessed Catholic aristocracy of Ireland, whose ruined castles stand in mute salute and testament to this history.

An anonymous novella Spalatro: From the Notes of Fra Giacomo, published in the Dublin University Magazine in 1843, has only recently been seen and accepted as one of La Fanu's works. Spalatro has a typically Gothic Italian setting, with a bandit as hero, in the style of the very popular Ann Radcliffe. More disturbing, however, is the hero Spalatro's necrophiliac passion for an undead blood-drinking beauty, who seems to be a predecessor of Le Fanu's later female vampire Carmilla. Like Carmilla, this undead femme fatale is not portrayed in an entirely negative way and attempts, but fails, to save the hero Spalatro from the eternal damnation that seems to be his destiny.

Le Fanu had begun work on this story after the un-expected death of his elder sister Catherine in March 1841. She had been ailing for almost a decade but her death came as a great and over-whelming shock to him.

On 18 December 1844 Le Fanu married Susanna Bennett, the daughter of a leading Dublin barrister. The union would produce four children. After the marriage the couple travelled to his parents' home in Abington for the Christmas celebrations.

Le Fanu was now stretching his talents across the length of a novel. Sir Walter Scott was to influence The Cock and Anchor which was published in 1845.

The Le Fanu's had settled in on married life at a house in Warrington Place near the Grand Canal in Dublin. Their first child, Eleanor, was born in 1845, and then followed Emma in 1846, Thomas in 1847 and George in 1854.

By 1847, Le Fanu published his next novel; The Fortunes of Colonel Torlogh O'Brien. That same year he joined in support of John Mitchel and Thomas Francis Meagher in their campaign against the indifference of the government to the devastating Irish Famine. Others involved in the campaign included Samuel Ferguson and Isaac Butt, the latter had been a witness at the Le Fanu's wedding. Butt also wrote a forty-page analysis of the national disaster for the Dublin University Magazine in 1847. (It was this vigorous support that was to cost him the nomination as Tory MP for County Carlow in 1852).

In the 1850's Le Fanu and Susanna moved from Warrington Place to 18 Merrion Square, Dublin, where they would now live for the remainder of their lives.

His married life also became an increasing source of difficultly at this time. Susanna was prone to suffer from a range of neurotic symptoms. A crisis of faith had led her to attend religious services at the nearby

St. Stephen's Church and discuss religion with Le Fanu's brother, William. By this time Le Fanu had stopped attending church. Susanna also suffered from great anxiety after the deaths of several close relatives, including her father two years before. It is thought this also led to marital problems.

In April 1858 she suffered an "hysterical attack" and died the following day in circumstances that are still unclear. Susanna was buried in the Bennett family vault in Mount Jerome Cemetery beside her father and brothers. The anguish of Le Fanu's diaries suggests that he felt profound guilt as well as overwhelming loss.

From 1858 until the death of his mother in 1861 Le Fanu pretty much became a recluse. He turned to his cousin Lady Gifford for advice and encouragement, and she remained a close correspondent until her death at the end of the decade.

It was during this period that he produced some of his best work. Working only by the light of two candles he would write through the night and burnish his reputation as a major figure of 19th Century supernaturalism. His work challenged the then Gothic focus on the external source of horror and instead he wrote about it from the perspective of the inward psychological potential to strike fear in the hearts of men. He wrote to George Bentley his publisher that in his writing he sought "the equilibrium between natural and the super-natural."

As a successful editor and proprietor he now sought to leverage the growing market for his work. He would first serialise in the Dublin University Magazine, and then revise it for the English market. Both The House by the Churchyard and Wylder's Hand were published in this way.

Unfortunately, the reviews for the first of these two novels were decidedly lukewarm. Le Fanu therefore agreed to sign a contract with Richard Bentley, his London publisher, specifying that future novels be stories "of an English subject and of modern times", a step Bentley thought necessary for Le Fanu to satisfy the English audience. Le Fanu succeeded in this aim in 1864, with the publication of his classic Uncle Silas, which he set in Derbyshire.

A series of books now came forth: Wylder's Hand (1864), Guy Deverell (1865), The Tenants of Malory (1867), The Green Tea (1869), The Haunted Baronet (1870), Mr. Justice Harbottle (1872), The Room in the Dragon Volant (1872) and In a Glass Darkly. (1872).

Eventually though the lure of his childhood and the inspiration that evoked ensured that his last short stories would mean a return to using his beloved Irish folklore as an inspiration.

But his life was drawing to a close. Joseph Thomas Sheridan Le Fanu died in Merrion Square in his native Dublin on February 7th, 1873, at the age of 58.

He was buried in Mount Jerome Cemetery, Dublin, Ireland.

In M. R. James, Le Fanu had perhaps his greatest advocate, indeed were it not for him The Purcell Papers might never have been collected and published as a whole.

The author E. F. Benson stated that Le Fanu's stories "Green Tea", "The Familiar", and "Mr. Justice Harbottle" "are instinct with an awfulness which custom cannot stale, and this quality is due, as in The Turn of the Screw, to Le Fanu's admirably artistic methods in setting and narration" adding that "His best work is of the first rank, while as a 'flesh-creeper' he is unrivalled. No one else has so sure a touch in mixing the mysterious atmosphere in which horror darkly breeds".

Le Fanu's work also influenced many later writers. Most famously, Carmilla was to greatly influence Bram Stoker in the writing of Dracula. M. R. James' ghost fiction was also heavily influenced by Le Fanu's work.

As a writer Le Fanu found it remarkably easy to work across many genres but remains best known for his mystery and horror fiction. A meticulous craftsman he was adventurous in reworking plots and ideas from his earlier writing and use them again in later pieces. He was brilliant in his use of the understated tone and effect rather than shock horror. Intriguingly for the reader Le Fanu would leave out important details, keeping the work unexplained and mysterious. For him the supernatural is strongly implied but a natural explanation is also possible. The demonic monkey in "Green Tea" could be a delusion of the story's protagonist, who is the only person to see it; in "The Familiar", Captain Barton's death seems to be supernatural, but is not actually witnessed, and the ghostly owl may be a real bird. This technique of indirect horror influenced many later horror artists. Though other writers have since chosen less subtle techniques, Le Fanu's best tales, such as the vampire novella Carmilla, remain some of the most powerful in the genre.

Joseph Sheridan Le Fanu – A Concise Bibliography

Novels
Spalatro: From the Notes of Fra Giacomo (1843)
The Cock and Anchor (1845)
Torlogh O'Brien (1847)
The House by the Churchyard (1861)
Wylder's Hand (1863)
Uncle Silas (1864)
Guy Deverell (1865)
The Prelude (1865)
All in the Dark (1866)
The Tenants of Malory (1867)
Haunted Lives (1868)
A Lost Name (1868)
The Wyvern Mystery (1869)
Checkmate (1871)
The Rose and the Key (1871)
Carmilla (1872) (with Joseph Le Fanu)
Willing to Die (1873)
The Evil Guest (1895)

Collections
Ghost Stories and Tales of Mystery (1851)
In a Glass Darkly (1872)
The Purcell Papers (1880)

The Watcher and Other Weird Stories (1894)
A Chronicle of Golden Friars (1896)

Poetry
Scraps of Hibernian Ballads
The Poems of Joseph Sheridan Le Fanu (1896)

www.ingramcontent.com/pod-product-compliance
Lightning Source LLC
Chambersburg PA
CBHW052020020726
47501CB00004B/1156